PUDDING A

An anthology

PUDDING AND PIE

An anthology including
HIGHLAND FLING
CHRISTMAS PUDDING
PIGEON PIE

Nancy Mitford

An Arena Book
Published by Arrow Books Limited
62–65 Chandos Place, London WC2N 4NW

An imprint of Century Hutchinson Ltd

London   Melbourne   Sydney   Auckland
Johannesburg and agencies throughout
the world

Highland Fling first published by Thornton Butterworth 1931
New edition first published by Hamish Hamilton Ltd 1975
Hamlyn Paperbacks edition 1982
© The Duchess of Devonshire 1975

Christmas Pudding first published by Thornton Butterworth 1932
New edition first published by Hamish Hamilton Ltd 1975
Hamlyn Paperbacks edition 1983
© The Duchess of Devonshire 1975

Pigeon Pie first published by Hamish Hamilton Ltd 1940
New edition 1976
Hamlyn Paperbacks edition 1982
© The Duchess of Devonshire 1976

This edition © The Duchess of Devonshire 1975, 1976, 1986

Typeset in A.M. Baskerville by
WBC Print Ltd, Bristol
Printed and bound in Great Britain by
The Guernsey Press Co. Ltd., Guernsey, Channel Islands.
ISBN 0 09 950440 5

HIGHLAND FLING

To
HAMISH

1

Albert Gates came down from Oxford feeling that his life was behind him. The past alone was certain, the future strange and obscure in a way that it had never been until that very moment of stepping from the train at Paddington. All his movements until then had been mapped out unalterably in periods of term and holiday; there was never for him the question 'What next?'—never a moment's indecision as to how such a month or such a week would be spent. The death of his mother during his last year at Oxford, while it left him without any definite home ties, had made very little difference to the tenor of his life, which had continued as before to consist of terms and holidays.

But now he stood upon the station platform faced—not with a day or two of uncertain plans, but with all his future before him a complete blank. He felt it to be an extraordinary situation and enjoyed the feeling. 'I do not even know,' he thought, 'where I shall direct that taxicab.' This was an affectation, as he had no serious intention of telling the taxi to go anywhere else than the Ritz, as indeed a moment later he did.

On the way he pretended to himself that he was trying hard to concentrate on his future, but in fact he was, for the present, so much enjoying the sensation of being a sort of mental waif and stray, that he gave himself up entirely to that enjoyment. He knew that there would never be any danger for him of settling down to a life of idleness: the fear of being bored would soon drive him, as it had done so often in the past, to some sort of activity.

Meanwhile, the Ritz.

An hour later, he was sitting in that spiritual home of Oxonian youth, drinking a solitary cocktail and meditating on his own very considerable but diverse talents, when his best friend, Walter Monteath, came in through the swing doors with a girl called Sally Dalloch.

'Albert, darling!' cried Walter, seeing him at once, 'easily the nicest person we could have met at this moment.'

'How d'you do, Sally?' said Albert getting up. 'What's the matter, why are you so much out of breath?'

'Well, as a matter of fact it's rather exciting, and we came here to find somebody we could tell about it; we've been getting engaged in a taxi.'

'Is that why Walter's face is covered with red paint?'

'Oh, darling, look! Oh, the shame of it—large red mouths all over your face. Thank goodness it was Albert we met, that's all!' cried Sally, rubbing his face with her handkerchief. 'Here, lick that. There, it's mostly off now; only a nice healthy flush left. No, you can't kiss me in the Ritz, it's always so full of my bankrupt relations. Well, you see, Albert, why we're so pleased at finding you here, we had to tell somebody or burst. We told the taximan, really because he was getting rather tired of driving round and *round* and *round* Berkeley Square, poor sweet, and he was divine to us, and luckily, there were blinds—which so few taxis have these days, do they?—with little bobbles on them and he's coming to our wedding. But you're the first *proper* person.'

'Well,' said Albert, as soon as he could get a word in, 'I really do congratulate you—I think it's quite perfect. But I can't say that it comes as an overwhelming surprise to me.'

'Well, it did to me,' said Walter; 'I've never been so surprised about anything in my life. I'd no idea women—nice ones, you know—ever proposed to men, unless for some very good reason—like Queen Victoria.'

'But I had—an excellent reason,' said Sally, quite unabashed. 'I wanted to be married to you frightfully badly. I call that a good reason, don't you, Albert?'

'It's *a* reason,' said Albert, rather acidly. He disapproved of the engagement, although he had realized for some time that it was inevitable. 'And have you two young things got any money to support each other with?' he went on.

'No,' said Walter, 'that's really the trouble: we haven't; but we think that nowadays, when everyone's so poor, it doesn't matter particularly. And, anyway, it's cheaper to feed two than one, and it's always cheaper in the end to be happy because then one's never ill or cross or bored, and look at the money being bored runs away with alone, don't you agree? Sally thinks her family might stump up five hundred a year, and I've got about that, too; then we should be able to make something out of our wedding presents. Besides, why shouldn't I do some work? If you come to think of it, lots of people do. I might bring out a book of poems in handwriting with corrections like Ralph's. What are your plans, Albert?'

'My dear . . . vague. I have yet to decide whether I wish to be a great abstract painter, a great imaginative writer, or a great psycho-analyst. When I have quite made up my mind I shall go abroad. I find it impossible to work in this country; the weather, the people and the horses militate equally against any mental effort. Meanwhile I am waiting for some internal cataclysm to direct my energies into their proper channel, whatever it is. I try not to torture myself with doubts and questions. A sidecar for you, Walter—Sally? Three sidecars, please, waiter.'

'Dear Albert, you are almost too brilliant. I wish I could help you to decide.'

'No, Walter; it must come from within. What are you both doing this evening?'

'Oh, good! Now, he's going to ask us out, which is lovely, isn't it? Sally darling, because leaving Oxford this morning somehow ran away with all my cash. So I'll tell you what, Albert, you angel, we'll just hop over to Cartier's to get Sally a ring (so lucky the one shop in London where I've an account), and then we'll come back here to dinner at about nine. Is that all right? I feel like dining here tonight and I think we'll spend our honeymoon here too, darling, instead of trailing round rural England. We certainly can't afford the Continent; besides, it's always so uncomfortable abroad except in people's houses. Drink your sidecar, ducky, and come along.'

'Cartier will certainly be shut,' thought Albert, looking at their retreating figures; 'but I suppose they'll be able to kiss each other in the taxicab again.'

At half-past nine they reappeared as breathlessly as they had left, Sally wiping fresh marks of lipstick off Walter's face and displaying upon her left hand a large emerald ring. Albert, who had eaten nothing since one o'clock, was hungry and rather cross; he felt exhausted by so much vitality and secretly annoyed that Walter, whom he regarded as the most brilliant of his friends, should be about to ruin his career by entering upon the state of matrimony. He thought that he could already perceive the signs of a disintegrating intellect as they sat at dinner discussing where they should go afterwards. Every nightclub in London was suggested, only to be turned down with:

'Not there *again*—I couldn't bear it!'

By the time they had finished their coffee Sally said that it was too early yet to go on anywhere, and that she, personally, was tired out and wanted to go home. So, to Albert's relief, they departed once more, in a taxi.

The next morning Albert left for Paris. It had come to him during the night that he wished to be a great abstract painter.

2

Two years and two weeks later Albert Gates stood on a cross-Channel steamer, watching with some depression the cliffs of Dover, which looked more than ever, he thought, like Turner's picture of them. The day was calm but mildly wet, it having, of course, begun to rain on that corner of a foreign field which is forever England—the Calais railway station. Albert, having a susceptible stomach, was thankful for the calm while resentful of the rain, which seemed a little unnecessary in July. He stood alone and quite still, unlike the other passengers, most of whom were running to and fro collecting their various possessions, asking where they could change money and congratulating each other on the excellence of the crossing. Every mirror was besieged by women powdering their noses, an action which apparently never fails to put fresh courage and energy into females of the human species. A few scattered little groups of French people had already assumed the lonely and defiant aspect of foreigners in a strange land. Paris seemed a great distance away.

Albert remembered how once, as a child, returning from some holiday abroad, he had begun at this juncture to cry very bitterly. He remembered vividly the feelings of black rage which surged up in him when his mother, realizing in a dim way that those tears were not wholly to be accounted for by seasickness, tiredness, or even the near approach of another term at school, began to recite a dreary poem whose opening lines were:

> 'Breathes there a man with soul so dead
> Who never to himself hath said,
> "This is my own, my native land? . . ." '

She did not realize that there are people, and Albert among them, to whom their native land is less of a home than almost any other.

He thought of the journey from Calais to Paris. That, to him, was the real home-coming. Paris, the centre of art, literature and all culture! The two years that he had just spent there were the happiest of his whole life, and now the prospect of revisiting England, even for a short time, filled him with a sort of nervous misery. Before those two years Albert had never known real contentment. Eton and Oxford had meant for him a continual warfare against authority, which to one of his highly-strung temperament was enervating in the extreme.

He had certainly some consolation in the shape of several devoted friends; but, although he was not consciously aware of it, these very friendships made too great a demand upon his nervous energy.

What he needed at that stage of his development was regular, hard and congenial work, and this he had found in Paris.

So happy had he been there that it is doubtful whether he would ever have exchanged, even for a few days, the only place where he had known complete well-being for a city which had always seemed to him cold and unsympathetic, but for two circumstances. One was that Walter and Sally had written even more persuasively than usual to beg that he would stay with them in their London flat. He had not seen them since that evening when they dined with him at the Ritz, and Walter was the one person whom he had genuinely missed and found irreplaceable.

The other circumstance—the one that really decided him—was that he had recently shown his pictures to a London art dealer of his acquaintance, who had immediately offered to give him an exhibition the following autumn. As this was a man of some influence in the London world of art, owning the particularly pleasant Chelsea Galleries where the exhibition would be held, Albert felt that here was an opportunity not to be missed. He arranged therefore to bring

6

over his pictures immediately, intending to store them and look about for a studio where he himself could stay until the exhibition should be over, late in October. Paris was becoming hot and stuffy and he felt that a change of air would do him good. Also, he was really very much excited at the prospect of seeing Walter again.

Presently the ship approached the quay, and sailors began adjusting a gangway at the very spot where Albert stood. Inconsequently he remembered the landing of the Normans —how William the Conqueror, springing first from the boat, seized in his hands a sod of English soil. It would be hard to do that nowadays. Impossible even to be the first to land, he thought, as he was brushed from the gangway by a woman of determined features laden with hand luggage which she used as a weapon.

In the train he found himself sharing a carriage with two idiotic girls who were coming home from a term at some finishing school in Paris. They were rather obviously showing off on his account. After talking at some length of their clandestine affairs with two French officers, which appeared to consist solely in passing notes to them when visiting the Louvre on Thursday afternoons, but which they evidently regarded as the height of eroticism, they broached the subject of Art. It appeared that once a week they had spent two hours at some *atelier* drawing the death mask of Beethoven, the Venus of Milo and other better known casts in smudgy charcoal. These depressing efforts were now produced from a portfolio and pinned on to the opposite seat which was unoccupied. Albert learnt from their chatter that when a drawing was finished by a pupil at the *atelier*, 'Madame' would come round and add *'Quelques petits accents bien à leur place'*; in other words, the finishing touch. The pupil would then fix it and put it carefully away in a portfolio.

Presently one of the girls said:

'I think I must go on with my art, I might make quite a lot of money. You know, Julia once made two pounds by painting lampshades for her mother's dining-room, and I'm quite as good as she is.'

The other one remarked that she thought Art was marvellous.

They then began to play vulgar jazz tunes on a portable gramophone, a noise which Albert found more supportable than their chatter.

As the train drew near London he felt homesick and wretched. He longed to be back in his studio in Paris surrounded by his own pictures. It was a curious and rather squalid little abode, but he had been happy there and had grown attached to it. His neighbours had all been poor and friendly, and in spite of having seen practically none of his English friends and few French people of his own class for two years, he had not for a moment felt lonely.

Now he began to wish that he had never left it; the pouring rain outside the carriage and the young artists opposite him had plunged him into a state of the deepest gloom. The idea of seeing Walter again began to terrify him. Walter! How could one tell what changes a year of matrimony may not have wrought. Considering these things, Albert fell asleep in his corner.

When the train stopped at Victoria he got out drowsily, but was only half-awake until suddenly thrown into a most refreshing rage by the confiscation, from his registered luggage, of a copy of *Ulysses* which Walter had particularly asked him to procure.

'Sir!' he cried violently to the uninterested official, 'I am Albert Gates, an artist and seriously-minded person. I regard that work as literature of the highest order, not as pornography, and am bringing it to London for the enlightened perusal of my friend Monteath, one of your most notable, if unrecognized poets. Does this unutterable country, then, deny its citizens, not only the bodily comforts of decent food and cheap drink, but also the consolations of intellect?'

At this point, observing that his audience consisted of everybody on the platform except the one individual to whom he addressed himself, he followed his porter to a taxi and was soon on his way to Walter's flat in Fitzroy Square.

Driving up Grosvenor Place he was struck, as people so

8

often are when returning from an absence abroad, by the fundamental conservatism of London. Everything looked exactly the same as it had looked the very day that he left, two years before. The streets were wet and shiny, as they had been then; the rain fell in the same heart-rending drizzle, as though it had never for a moment stopped doing so, and never would again. The same Rolls-Royces contained hard-faced fashionable women in apparently the identical printed chiffon dresses and picture-hats of two years before, fashionable, but never *chic*.

He thought how typical it is of Englishwomen that they should always elect to dress in printed materials. A passion for fussy detail without any feeling for line or shape.

'And those picture-hats which have been worn year after year, ever since the time of Gainsborough and which inevitably destroy all smartness, they seem still to be blossoming upon all heads, in this repulsive town. If ever I marry, God send it may be a woman of taste.'

Albert disliked women, his views on the sex coinciding with those of Weininger—he regarded them as stupid and unprincipled; but certain ones that he had met in Paris made up for this by a sort of worldly wisdom which amused him, and a talent for clothes, food and *maquillage* which commanded his real and ungrudging admiration.

These and other reflections continued to occupy his mind, until, looking out of the window, he saw that the taxi had already arrived in Charlotte Street. He was now seized with the miserable feeling of nervousness which always assails certain people when they are about to arrive at a strange house, even though it should belong to a dear friend of whose welcome they are inwardly assured. He began to torture himself with doubts. Suppose Walter had not received the telegram announcing the day of his arrival, and they were spending a week-end in the country? Or, worse than that—for he could easily go to an hotel if it were necessary—suppose they had really not wanted him at all, or had put off some visit on his account, or—but at this moment the taxi stopped abruptly opposite a green front door which was

9

almost immediately opened by Walter. At the sight of his friend's welcoming face, Albert's doubts vanished completely.

'My dear!' cried Walter, 'my dear boy, my darling Albert. *How* we have been looking forward to this! Oh, how nice to see you again after all these years! Quickly! quickly—a cocktail. You must be dying for one. And here's Sally, who's been spending the whole day arranging flowers in your bedroom.'

'I do hope you won't die of discomfort here,' said Sally. 'Did Walter prepare you in the least bit for what you're going to suffer? There are no servants, my dear, except an idiot boy. You know, the sort that murders butlers in the evening papers, but he's quite sweet really, and as we haven't a butler we think it's fairly safe. Cocktail for you?'

The room into which Walter and Sally led the way was so lovely that Albert, who had half expected the usual green horror with sham 18th century flower pictures, was thrown into a state of almost exaggerated rapture. For a London drawing-room it was a particularly good shape, with large windows and cheerful outlook. The walls were covered with silver tissue a little tarnished; the curtains and chair covers were of white satin, which the grime of London was rapidly turning a lovely pearl colour; the floor and ceiling were painted a dull pink. Two huge vases of white wax flowers stood one each side of the fireplace; over the mantelpiece hung a Victorian mirror, framed in large white shells and red plush. Albert, as he walked about this exquisite room, praising and admiring, felt blissfully happy; the depression which had been gathering force ever since he left his studio that morning now left him for good.

He had always experienced in Walter's company a feeling of absolute ease and lack of strain. He now found, rather to his surprise, that the presence of Sally did nothing to impair their relationship; she gave him no sensation either of intruding or of being intruded upon. Walter and Sally together seemed almost like one person, and Albert realized at once how wrong he had been to oppose their union.

'How I should like,' he said, looking at her lovely face, 'to paint a portrait of Sally.'

'Well, why not? She'd love to sit for you, I know, and we've got a room with a perfectly good north light at the back of the house. Albert, *do*.'

'My dear, impossible. I can't work in London, you know. People think it an affectation, but I assure you that it is no such thing. I might even go so far as to say that I'm incapable of working in this country at all; a question, I suppose, of nerves.'

'How like Walter,' said Sally laughing. 'Poor angel, he's quite incapable of working in London, too. He gave up his last job after exactly three days.'

'Shut up, darling. You know quite well who it was that begged and implored me to leave, now don't you? Sally's father,' explained Walter, 'got me a job in a bank. I can't tell you what I suffered for three whole days. It was like a P. G. Wodehouse novel, only not funny at all, or perhaps I've no sense of humour. To begin with, I had to get up at eight every morning. One had much better be dead, you know. Then, my dear, the expense! I can't tell you what it cost me in taxis alone, not to mention the suit I had to buy—a most lugubrious black affair. There was no time to get back here for luncheon, and I couldn't go all day without seeing Sally, so we went to a restaurant which was recommended to us called "Simkins," too putting off. Sally was given some perfectly raw meat with blood instead of gravy, and naturally she nearly fainted, and she had to have brandy before I could get her out of the place. By then we were so upset that we felt we must go to the Ritz in order to be soothed, which meant more taxis. In the end we reckoned that those three days had cost me every penny of thirty pounds, so I gave it up. I can't afford that sort of thing, you know.'

'Poor father,' said Sally, 'he's very much worried about Walter. He has a sort of notion in his head that every man ought to have some regular work to do, preferably soldiering. He doesn't seem to understand about cultivating leisure at all, and he regards writing poetry as a most doubtful, if not immoral occupation.

'And he isn't as bad as your uncle Craigdalloch, who

11

actually said in my hearing of some young man, "Ah, yes, he failed for the Army, and was chucked out of the City, so they sent him to the Slade." Just think how pleased Tonks must have been to have him!'

Walter then asked Albert how long he intended to stay.

'Can you keep me till the end of next week?'

'My dear, don't be so childish. Now that we have at last persuaded you to come, you must stay quite a month if you won't be bored. I know London in August is very unfashionable, but it would cheer us up a lot to have you, and besides, think what a boon you would be to the gossip writers!'

'Yes, indeed,' said Sally, 'poor old Peter seems to be at the end of his tether already. His page the last few days has been full of nothing but scraps of general knowledge which one assimilates quite unconsciously. I call it cheating . . . I mean, when I want to read about wild ducks sitting on their eggs at the edge of a railway line I can buy a book of natural history; but I do like gossip to *be* gossip, don't you? This paragraph about the ducks was headed, "Observed by Jasper Spengal." Well, I was quite excited; you know what a talent Jasper has for observing things he's not meant to, and then it was only the beastly old duck after all. Well, I *mean* . . . If he's come down to that sort of thing already, it will be the habits of earthworms by August, I should think.'

'So you want me to stay and have my habits noted instead?' Albert felt all his resolution slipping away. After all, it was nice to see his old friends again. It occurred to him now that he had been very lonely in Paris.

'But you'll be leaving London yourselves?'

'Not until the end of August, anyhow, then we may go to the Lido for a little.'

Walter looked rather defiantly, like a naughty child, at Sally as he said this, and she pretended not to hear. She knew quite well, and had said so already more than once, that, terribly in debt as they were, this idea of going to the Lido was quite out of the question. Sally spent much of her life trying to put a brake on Walter's wild extravagances and they had more than once been on the verge of a quarrel over the Lido question.

The Monteaths led a precarious existence. They had married in the face of much opposition from both their families, especially Sally's, who looked upon Walter as a rather disreputable, if attractive, person and an undesirable son-in-law. However, as soon as they realized that Sally was quite determined to marry him whatever happened, they had softened to the extent of settling five hundred pounds a year on her. More they could not afford. Walter had about the same, which had been left him some years previously by an uncle; they struggled along as best they could on a joint income of one thousand a year. This they supplemented from time to time by writing articles for the weekly papers and by the very occasional sale of one of Walter's rather less obscure poems.

All might have been well except for his incurable extravagance. In many ways they were extremely economical. Unlike the type of young married couple who think it essential to have a house in the vicinity of Belgrave Square and a footman, they preferred to live in a tiny flat with no servants except an old woman and a boy, both of whom came in daily. Sally did most of the cooking and all the marketing herself and rather enjoyed it.

On the other hand, Walter seemed to have a talent for making money disappear. Whenever he was on the point of committing an extravagance of any kind he would excuse himself by explaining: 'Well, you see, darling, it's so much cheaper in the end.' It was his slogan. Sally soon learnt, to her surprise and dismay, that 'it's cheaper in the end' to go to the most expensive tailor, travel first class, stay at the best hotels, and to take taxis everywhere. When asked why it was cheaper, Walter would say airily: 'Oh, good for our credit, you know!' or 'So much better for one's clothes,' or, sulkily: 'Well, it is, that's all, everybody knows it is.'

He also insisted that Sally should be perfectly turned out, and would never hear of her economizing on her dresses. The result was that during one year of married life they had spent exactly double their income, and Sally had been obliged to sell nearly all her jewellery in order to pay even a few of the bills that were pouring in, so that the idea of going to the Lido, or indeed doing anything but stay quietly in London was, as she pointed out, quite ridiculous.

Walter, incapable always of seeing that lack of money would be a sufficient reason for giving up something that might amuse him, was inclined to be sulky about this; but Sally was not particularly worried. She generally had her own way in the end.

3

After dinner that evening, Walter said that Albert's first night in England must be celebrated otherwise than by going tamely to bed. Albert, remembering with an inward groan that Walter had always possessed an absolutely incurable taste for sitting up until daylight, submitted, tired though he was, with a good grace; and at half-past eleven they left the house in a taxi. Sally was looking particularly exquisite in a dress which quite obviously came from Patou.

Walter, explaining that it was too early as yet to go to a night-club, directed the taxicab to the Savoy, where they spent a fairly cheerful hour trying to make themselves heard through a din of jazz, and taking it in turns to dance with Sally.

After this, they went to a night-club called 'The Witch,' Walter explaining on the way that it had become more amusing since Captain Bruiser had taken it over.

'All the night-clubs now,' he told Albert, 'are run by ex-officers; in fact it is rather noticeable that the lower the night-club the higher is the field rank, as a rule, of its proprietor.'

Presently they arrived in a dark and smelly mews. Skirting two overflowing dustbins they opened a sort of stable-door, went down a good many stairs in pitch darkness and finally found themselves in a place exactly like a station waiting-room. Bare tables, each with its bouquet of dying flowers held together by wire, were ranged round the walls, the room was quite empty except for a young man playing tunes out of Cochran's revue on an upright piano. Albert was horrified to see that Walter paid three pounds for the privilege of merely passing through the door into this exhilarating spot.

A weary waiter asked what they would order. A little fruit drink? Apparently no wine of any sort could be forthcoming,

15

not even disguised in a ginger-beer bottle. They asked for some coffee but when it came it was too nasty to drink. This cost another pound. Depression began to settle upon the party, but they sat there for some time valiantly pretending to enjoy themselves.

'Let's go on soon,' said Walter, at the end of an hour, during which no other human being had entered the station waiting-room. They groped their way up the stairs and bumped into a body coming down, which proved to be that of Captain Bruiser. He asked them, in a cheerful, military voice, if they had had a good time. They replied that they had had of all times the best, and thanked him profusely for their delightful evening. He said he was sorry it had been so empty, and told them the names of all the celebrities who were there the night before.

After this, they sat for some while in a taxi, trying to decide where they should go next. The taximan was most helpful, vetoed 'The Electric Torch' on account of having as he said, 'taken some very ordinary gentlemen there earlier in the evening,' and finally suggested 'The Hay Wain.' 'Major Spratt is running it now, and I hear it is very much improved.'

To 'The Hay Wain' they went. Albert felt battered with fatigue and longed for his bed. This time they approached their destination by means of a fire-escape, and when they had successfully negotiated its filthy rungs, they found themselves in a long, low, rather beautiful attic. There were rushes on the floor, pewter and wild flowers (which being dead, slightly resembled bunches of hay) on the tables, and the seats were old-fashioned oak pews, narrow, upright, and desperately uncomfortable.

A waiter, dressed in a smock which only made him look more like a waiter than ever, handed them a menu written out in Gothic lettering. Ten or twelve other people were scattered about the room, none of them were in evening dress. They all looked dirty and bored.

'Is Rory Jones singing to-night?' asked Sally.

'Yes, madam; Mr Jones will be here in a few moments.'

16

An hour and a half later Rory Jones did appear, but he had just come from a private party, was tired, and not a little tipsy. After singing his best known and least amusing songs for a few minutes, he staggered away, to the unrestrained fury of Major Spratt, who could be heard expressing himself outside the door in terms of military abuse.

'Let's go on, soon.'

'On,' thought Albert wearily, 'never bed?'

The next place they visited, run by a certain Colonel Bumper, was called 'The Tally-Ho' and was an enormous basement room quite full of people, noise and tobacco smoke. It appeared that champagne was obtainable here, owing to the fact that the club had been raided by the police the week before and was shortly closing down for good.

Albert thought of Paris night-clubs with some regret. He felt that 'The Hay Wain' and 'The Witch' might be sufficiently depressing, but that 'The Tally-Ho' induced a positively suicidal mood—it had just that atmosphere of surface hilarity which is calculated to destroy pleasure.

'Let's go on soon,' said Walter, when they had drunk some very nasty champagne. Despite the cabman's warning, they now went to 'The Electric Torch' but found on arrival that the 'very ordinary people' had gone. Moreover the band had gone, the waiters had gone. Alone, amid piled up chairs and tables placed upside down on each other, stood the proprietor Captain Dumps. He was crying quite quietly into a large pocket handkerchief, and never saw them come or heard them creep silently away.

After this, to Albert's ill-concealed relief, they went home. It was half-past five and broad daylight poured in at his bedroom window. He calculated with his last waking thoughts that this ecstatic evening must have cost Walter, who had insisted on paying for everything, at least twenty pounds, and he felt vaguely sorry for Sally.

4

The following afternoon at about half-past three Sally and Walter got out of bed and roamed, rather miserably, in their pyjamas.

The daily woman had come and gone, and Albert's room proved, on inspection, to be empty. After a lengthy discussion as to whether they could bring themselves to eat anything and if so, what, they made two large cups of strong black coffee, which they drank standing and in silence. Sally then announced that she felt as if she were just recovering from a long and serious illness and began to open her morning letters. 'Bills, bills, and bills! Darling, why did we hire that Daimler to go down to Oxford? There must have been trains, if you come to think of it.'

'Yes, but—don't you remember?—we hadn't an A.B.C. We couldn't look them up. Give the bill to me.' He took it from her and began to burn holes in it with his cigarette, but Sally, engrossed in a letter, did not notice.

'Who's that from?'

'Aunt Madge. Listen to it:

'MY DEAREST SALLY,

'"You will no doubt have seen in the newspapers that your Uncle Craig has been appointed chairman of the mission to New South Rhodesia. . . ."'

'Of course I haven't! Does she imagine that I have nothing better to do than read the papers?'

'Go on,' said Walter.

'Where am I? Oh, yes!

'" . . . This was all very sudden and unexpected and has caused us inconvenience in a thousand ways, but the most unfortunate part of it is that we had arranged, as usual, several large shooting parties

18

at Dalloch Castle. I wrote and asked your father and mother if they would go up there and act as host and hostess, but Sylvia tells me that they have to pay their annual visit to Baden just then. It occurred to me that perhaps you and Walter are doing nothing during August and September, in which case, it would be a real kindness to us if you would stay at Dalloch and look after our guests. I know that this is a big thing to ask you to do and, of course, you must say no if you feel it would be too much for you. If you decide to go we will send you up in the car and you must invite some of your own friends. Dalloch will hold any amount of people.

"Yrs. affecly.,

"MADGE CRAIGDALLOCH.

"PS.—General Murgatroyd, a great friend of your Uncle Craig's, will be there to look after the keepers, etc."'

There was a long silence. Walter sat down rather heavily.

'Well?' said Sally.

'Well, what?'

'Shall we do it? Listen, my precious. I know it would be awful and I expect you'd simply hate it, poor sweet, and nothing to what I should, but still, facts must be faced. If we do this we shall save money for two solid months, and after that, if you like, we could probably afford to spend a little time in Paris, if we could let the flat. Albert might be able to tell us of some nice cheap hotel there.'

Walter became sulkier every minute.

'I won't stay at a cheap hotel in Paris. Paris to me means the Ritz. I'm very sorry—it's the way I'm made. Besides, it's well known to be cheaper in the end to stay at the Ritz, because otherwise one has to keep taking taxis there to see who's arrived. And I won't let the flat. It never pays to let houses, because of all the damage that is done by tenants.'

'Perhaps we could manage to have a week at the Ritz if we went to Scotland, funny creature,' she said, tickling the back of his neck.

Walter laughed and began kissing her hand, one finger at a time.

'What d'you think, then?'

'How d'you mean? What do I think?'

'Walter, you're being extremely tiresome, darling. You know quite well what I mean.'

'My precious angel, I've often noticed how clever you are at getting your own way, and if you've really made up your mind that we've got to have two months of potted hell in Scotland I suppose nothing can save us. But I should just like to say here and now, that I'm quite sure it would be cheaper in the end to go to the Lido. I know you wouldn't think so, but these economies always lead to trouble; I've seen it so often.'

'But, darling, we haven't even to pay our railway journey if we go in the car, and there can't be any expenses up there.'

'Well, mark my words. Anyhow, if we go, let's make Albert come too, and then we might get some fun out of it.'

'Yes, of course, and we could ask some other chums. Jane, perhaps. It won't be too bad really, you know. Sweet darling, not to make a fuss—are you sure you don't mind terribly? Shall I ring up Aunt Madge now?' She kissed the top of Walter's head and went over to the telephone.

'Hullo? Is Lady Craigdalloch there? . . . Mrs. Monteath. . . . Don't wander about, Walter, it puts me off. No, don't—that's my coffee . . . Hullo, Aunt Madge? Sally speaking. . . . Yes, we've just got it. . . . Well, we think we'd love to. . . . No, sweet of you. Can we come and see you sometime and talk it over? . . . yes, of course, you must be frightfully. When do you go? . . . Oh, goodness what a rush for you! . . . Yes, we could be there in about half an hour. . . . All right, we'll meet you there. . . . No, perfect for us. Goodbye!'

Sally hung up the receiver.

'Where d'you think we've got to meet them? You'd never guess, but it's so typical of them, really. The House of Lords! So come on, my angel, and dress, because I said we'd be there in half an hour.'

Sally and Walter were perched rather uncomfortably on a red leather fireguard in the Prince's Chamber of the House of Lords. The magnificent personage, of whom they had inquired whether they could see Lord Craigdalloch, presently returned from his quest for that nobleman. 'His lordship says he may be a little time, but I will inform her ladyship that you are here. Meanwhile, would you wait a few moments?' He walked rather pompously to the other end of the room where he stood motionless.

'Well, he doesn't seem to be informing her,' said Sally, 'unless by telepathy. Still, I'm quite happy here, aren't you? Of course, it just *is* one's spiritual home, that's all. *Why* didn't I marry a peer? I'd really forgotten what a divine place it is, such ages since I've been here.'

'Like church, isn't it? I keep expecting the organ to peal forth. It rather reminds me of our wedding in some ways.'

'More like a mausoleum, really. D'you see that very old man over there?'

'I see the seven oldest living creatures, if you mean one of them.'

'The one with the greenish face over by the statue of Queen Victoria.'

'My dear, I hadn't noticed him. But how awful! Can't we help in some way? Is he dying?'

'Oh, I expect sort of vaguely he is. This place mummifies people you know, without their having to die first, and they often go on creeping about like that for years. That's why they're called Die Hards. It is a most descriptive name for them, poor old sweets. Anyway, that particular one is a great friend of daddy's, and he disinherited his eldest son for marrying a Catholic.'

'Not really? It's rather heavenly to think such people do still exist. What happened to the son, though—was he quite broke?'

'Oh, no, not at all; the Catholic was immensely rich. So, to pay the old boy out, they took the grouse moor next to his in Scotland and started a stoat and weasel farm on it and quite soon all his grouse were eaten up by the weasels. Daddy says he never got over it—it nearly broke his heart.'

Walter looked round him for a few minutes in silence. 'I haven't seen anybody the least aristocratic-looking yet,' he

21

remarked presently, 'except, of course, the boy friend who is by way of informing your aunt that we are here. He's a lovely man, but all the others look exactly like very old and decrepit doctors. I can imagine any of them pulling out a thermometer and saying, "Well, well, and how are we to-day? Put out your tongue and say 'Ah.'" Now, there is rather a spry-looking one by the door. He might be a dentist or a *masseur*. What's the muttering about in the next room?'

'Someone making a speech. Uncle Craig, most likely, as they're all trooping out. They can put up with a lot here (they have to, poor angels!), but it's only the ones who can't walk that stay and listen to Uncle Craig, and you should see the expression on their faces when they realize what they're in for—pitiful, like trapped animals!

'I heard him speak once about the peeresses in their own right who want to sit in the House of Lords. It was quite unintelligible and no wonder. His only real reason for not wanting them is that he thinks they might have to use the peers' lavatory, and, of course, he couldn't *say* that. Another time he was speaking on the Prayer Book, but somehow he got all his notes mixed up so the last half of his speech was all about new sewers for Bixton. Nobody noticed, of course, and he was able to square the reporters afterwards. Such an old duck, you know, but not exactly cut out to be a legislator.'

'It has often occurred to me to wonder, if there were a revolution tomorrow, how the mob would know which were the nobles,' said Walter. 'Personally I've always been terrified that I should be left behind when all my friends were being hurried off in the tumbrils to the echoing cry of, *"A bas les aristos!"* Never mind, I shall have my turn next day when the intelligentsia is being wiped out.'

'On the contrary, my angel, you'll hang about hoping for weeks, until at last, after all your acquaintances have died gloriously in front of Buckingham Palace or the Albert Memorial, you'll be pitched into the Thames with the other *bourgeois*.'

'Of course, it just would be one's luck. Now who'd mind going to the scaffold between Lord Lonsdale and Mrs.

Meyrick! It would give one a social kick, you know. Think of the papers next day!

'"Among others I noticed on the scaffold yesterday Walter Monteath, the poet, was wearing his favourite green tie and chatting to Lord Lonsdale. He told me that his wife was busy at the moment but hopes to attend the executions to-day. Picture on back page."

'But as for all those old peers, they'll have to parade up and down Piccadilly in their coronets if they want to be taken in the smart tumbrils, and even then I expect people would think they were an advertisement for something.'

At this moment the magnificent personage strolled up to where Walter and Sally were sitting and said that Lord Craigdalloch was about to speak and if they would care to follow him he would conduct them to the Strangers' Gallery, which he then proceeded to do, leading them up and down several corridors and staircases until they came to a small door, through which he pushed them into inky blackness. They groped their way to seats into which they subsided thankfully. Far below them there emerged from the gloom a sort of choked muttering.

After a few moments their eyes became more or less accustomed to the darkness and they were able to distinguish various objects—the throne, the Peeresses' Gallery, occupied by the stately figure of Lady Craigdalloch, who blew kisses to them, and two or three large tables at which some men were writing. Finally, they recognised Lord Craigdalloch. He was standing near one of the tables, and the muttering seemed to proceed from his lips. Sally was sorry, though in no way surprised, to notice that his audience consisted solely of themselves, Aunt Madge, an old bearded man seated on one of the benches with a pair of crutches just out of his reach and another stretched at full length on a red divan.

The Monteaths feverishly endeavoured to catch a few words of what their uncle was saying, but without success. As they sat straining their ears, two Frenchmen were shown into the gallery and, feeling their way to a seat, began to converse in whispers. They seemed much intrigued by the man on the divan.

'Dites donc, ce lord sur le sofa, il est saou?'

'Je dirais plutôt malade.'

'Eh bien, moi j'crois qu'il est ivre.'

'Que c'est lugubre ici.'

'Oui, rudement rasant.'

Lord Craigdalloch now raised his voice slightly and the words, 'the noble lord behind me . . .' were heard.

'The noble lord behind him has evidently slipped away,' murmured Sally, observing the rows of empty benches.

The old man with the beard now began to scrabble feverishly for his crutches, and finally, after a prolonged and unsuccessful effort to reach them, took off his watch-chain and lassoed one of them with it. He then hooked the other one with the crutch part and drew it towards him. Having planted them firmly under his armpits he hopped away with incredible agility, not, however, before Lord Craigdalloch had just time to say, loudly and portentously, 'My noble friend opposite.'

The departure of the only conscious member of his audience seemed now to spur him to greater vocal efforts and whole sentences could be heard at a time.

'I am convinced, m'lords, that this danger is very real. It is a very real danger. What did Scipio Africanus say?' Here he began struggling with the notes he held in his hand, but was evidently unable to find what Scipio Africanus had said. The sleeper on the divan, subconsciously aware that something was expected of him, turned rather heavily and groaned out, ''Ear! 'ear!'

'M'lords, it has been said in another place,' continued the speaker in no way put out by this slight set-back, 'that it is a very real danger. The Dukeries, m'lords, with all due respect to the noble duke behind me, are *not* to be confounded with the Fisheries. As my noble friend has so aptly remarked, it is anomalous to pretend that they are analogous. . . .'

Another rather younger peer now came in, sat down opposite the divan and began to read some letters.

24

'Enfin, on vient au secours du pauvre vieux.'

'Mais non, il n'y fait même pas attention.'

'Mon Dieu! Eh bien, voilà. C'est le flegme Britannique. Que voulez-vous? Dites donc, si on partait? Ce n'est pas follement gai ici.'

'Est-ce qu'on ôse?'

'Allons. Filons vite. Courage, mon ami.'

The Frenchmen got up and left the gallery.

At last Lord Craigdalloch made his peroration, which was quite inaudible, and sat down. The man who was reading letters sprang to his feet as though fearful of interruption (a danger, however, which hardly seemed pressing as the house was empty except for the now prostrated Craigdalloch and their sleeping compeer on the sofa), and spoke rapidly and audibly:

'M'lords, I have been asked to reply to the noble lord and I wish at the outset to express the thanks of the Government to the noble lord for so readily agreeing last May to postpone his Question, in view of the position as it then stood. At that time there was some uncertainty. . . .'

Here Lady Craigdalloch leant over the rail of the Peeresses' Gallery and by a series of signals gave the Monteaths to understand that she was ready to go and would meet them outside.

When, after losing their way once or twice, they at last reached the Princes Chamber, they found her waiting there for them. A tall commanding woman with white hair and an Edwardian aspect, she had, in the days when big pale faces and Grecian features were admired to the exclusion of everything else, been considered a beauty. She had still considerable remains of looks and the unmistakable manner of one who has been courted in youth and flattered in middle-age.

'Dear Sally,' she said, embracing her niece rather voluminously, 'I knew you would like to hear your uncle's speech. It went off very well, didn't it? Always such an anxiety to the dear thing. How well you are looking, Sally. Where did you get so wonderfully sunburnt?'

'At Elizabeth Arden's, Aunt Madge.'

Lady Craigdalloch inwardly supposed that this must be one of Walter's Bright Young but Undesirable friends that she was always hearing so much about from Sally's mother. The creature probably has a villa in the South of France—so much the better, those sort of people are not wanted in England, where they merely annoy their elders and breed Socialism. In any case, she never understood this craving of the younger generation for a hideous brick-coloured complexion. If she had guessed for a moment that Sally stained hers every morning with stuff out of a bottle she would have thought her niece frankly mad.

'Craig will join us in a moment. He wishes us to begin tea without him.' She led the way down long, draughty, Gothic corridors to the tea-room, which, in contrast to other portions of the House, presented a scene of tempestuous gaiety. Several of the peers seated at the rather *intime* little tables were considerably under seventy, and one or two had relations and female friends with them whom they were entertaining with jokes and witticisms of the most abandoned description. Two bishops and some of their girl friends were fairly rollicking over a pot of tea, while the old man with crutches was being jocularly accused by the Lord Chancellor of having wiped his beard on the table-cloth, an allegation which he could hardly refute, having been caught by that dignitary in the very act. Altogether there was a spirit of goodwill and friendly banter which seemed more or less lacking elsewhere in the building.

While Walter and Sally were eating the fascinating mixed biscuits and strong tea which the nation, through the medium of Richard Coeur de Maison Lyons, provides at a slight profit for the sustenance of its administrators and their guests, Lady Craigdalloch explained in what their duties at Dalloch Castle would consist.

'You will find everything running very smoothly, I think. The servants have all been there for years and you'll have no trouble at all with them. You will, of course, give any orders for the comfort of the guests, such as, for instance, how many picnic luncheons will be required for the guns, and so on. Then, if you would meet the new arrivals in the hall and show them their rooms, that sort of thing makes people feel so much more at home than if they arrive and find no host or hostess.'

'When would you like us to go up there?' asked Sally.

'Let me think. The first guests, of course, arrive on the 10th. Could you go up about the 8th? You'll find General Murgatroyd. He's there now, dear thing, fishing.'

'Is it a big party for the 12th?'

'I think I can tell you exactly who will be there. Lord and Lady Prague—he is a great friend of your papa, Sally; very deaf, poor dear, but an extremely good shot. He married her *en secondes noces* some years ago. She was Florence Graiday. She will be a great help to you, I think, a wonderfully charming woman and so artistic. They will probably stay quite a month. They always do every year. Then a delightful young couple, the Chadlingtons. Brenda Chadlington is the daughter of a very old friend of mine. She is a most beautiful creature. The other two guns are Admiral Wenceslaus, a dear thing with only one eye; and Mr. Buggins, who is, of course, secretary of the Nelson Club, a very cultured man. His wife, poor woman, is shut up, has been quite mad for years.'

'Is General Murgatroyd married?' asked Sally rather nervously. She felt that all these women might prove to be very alarming.

'No, dear, he is not. That is to say, he *was* married but unfortunately, he was obliged to divorce his wife. None of us was surprised. She was a girl from the Baker Street Bazaar, you know. She got a hold over him somehow and made him marry her. But it all happened years ago—thirty years at least, I suppose. Here comes your Uncle Craig.'

Sally kissed her uncle, who seemed genuinely pleased to see her.

'We heard your speech, Uncle Craig,' she lied, 'from the Strangers' Gallery. It was most interesting.'

'Glad you think so, my dear. One has one's duty, you know; born into a certain position and so forth. It's no use pretending that one enjoys coming here, or that it will be very

27

pleasant going off to New South Rhodesia just when the moor has never been better. Still, as my poor father used to say, one's not only put here for enjoyment. All the same,' he added, brightening somewhat, 'Gillibrough tells me I may get the chance of shooting a lion or two and possibly some hartebeest in Rhodesia. Well, Walter, what d'you think of this place? Never been here before, eh? Finest legislative assembly in the world, you know, nothing to touch it anywhere. Made England what she is to-day—the House of Lords. The work that goes on here, you wouldn't believe it. There's no place like it for work, and all unpaid. And then the Socialists pretend we don't do our bit. I'll tell you one thing, Walter: the reform of the House of Lords will be the downfall of England.' He bristled at the idea, then continued more gently, 'So you two are going up to Dalloch to look after our guests for us, eh? Very kind of you, I think. Now, have you any friends of your own you'd like to ask for the shooting, eh?'

'We'd rather like to ask someone called Albert Gates, if we may, but he doesn't shoot, I'm afraid.'

'Doesn't shoot? And Walter doesn't shoot either? I can't think what all these young men are coming to. What does he do, then?'

'He studies painting, Uncle Craig.'

'An artist, is he? Well, well, how did you get to know him, then? As a matter of fact, now I come to think of it, I once knew an artist myself called Leighton—Lord Leighton. Not a bad fellow at all, really quite a decent sort of chap considering. If your friend paints he'll like being up at Dalloch: the views are really superb, wonderful colour effects, you know.'

'The old parts of the house are very paintable too,' said Lady Craigdalloch. 'Dear Mr. Buggins always does some charming water-colour sketches on non-shooting days.'

'See that youngish man who's just come in, Sally?' said her uncle suddenly.

Sally saw a man of unbelievable age creeping towards them, his limbs positively shaking with palsy.

'That's Prague, he's going to be at Dalloch with you. You'd

better meet him. Here, Prague! (He's very deaf so speak up, won't you?) *Prague, this is my niece, Mrs. Monteath. She's going to be at Dalloch.*

Lord Prague gave her a gouty hand and said in a quavering voice:

'You must be Johnnie's daughter, I suppose. Now, how is Johnnie?'

'Not very well,' screamed Sally. *'He's doing a cure at Baden.'*

'I'm very sorry to hear it. A young man like Johnnie should not be doing cures yet. Why, it's only yesterday he was my fag at Eton. Cure be damned! Little Johnnie. Yes, he was Captain of the Boats—only yesterday! Well, see you in Scotland, I hope. I must go now. They may divide on this. Coming, Craig?

Walter and Sally, on their return home, found Albert talking to Jane Dacre, Sally's greatest and, indeed, only woman friend.

'Jane, dear, how nice to see you! Did you know Albert before? Anyhow, I'm glad to see he gave you a cocktail.'

'No, we've never met before, and in point of fact, I gave him one. He didn't seem to know where the drinks are kept.'

'I have been telling Miss Dacre about our party last night,' said Albert. 'What have you two been doing this afternoon?'

'We have been visiting the greatest legislative assembly in the world, namely, the House of Lords, and one of the legislators took such a fancy to us that he has lent us a castle and a grouse moor in Scotland for two months. And this is a perfectly true fact, believe me or not as you like, but please both come and stay and bring your guns.'

Sally explained the circumstances.

'You must both come and help us with these Pragues and Murgatroyds and people. There's an admiral with one eye and a man with a lunatic wife, but he's not bringing her because she's in a loony bin. So do come, angels, won't you?'

Albert accepted without any hesitation.

'I have never been to Scotland,' he said, 'which, for an earnest student of the Victorian era, is a very serious

29

admission. I am happy to think that I shall soon see with my own eyes and in such charming company, that scenery of bens and braes which is so impregnated with the nineteenth century. It is also a unique chance, as I am told that no cultured people ever go there now, so much is it *démodé*.'

'I'd love to come, too,' said Jane, 'if I may let you know for certain in the morning. I shall have to ask the family—but I expect they'll be delighted. There is something so very respectable about Scotland.'

5

Jane Dacre sat in the restaurant car of the Scotch express about a month later. She had accepted Sally's invitation with great pleasure and her family's full consent, and was much looking forward to the visit, partly because she would thus avoid seeing her parents for a whole month, but chiefly because she was devoted to Walter and Sally, and rather in love with Albert.

Jane was a very ordinary sort of girl, but her character, as is so often the case with women, manifested itself by a series of contradictions and was understood by nobody. Thought by some to be exceptionally stupid, and by others brilliantly clever, she was in reality neither. She had certain talents which she was far too lazy to develop, and a sort of feminine astuteness that prevented her from saying silly things. Like many women she had taste without much intellect, her brain was like a mirror, reflecting the thoughts and ideas of her more intelligent friends and the books that she read. Although she was able to perceive originality in others, she was herself completely unoriginal. She had, however, a sense of humour, and except for a certain bitterness with which, for no apparent reason, she regarded her mother and father, the temperament of an angel.

Her attitude towards her parents was, indeed, very curious. She always spoke of them as though they were aged half-wits with criminal tendencies, whose one wish was to render her life miserable. Those of her friends who had met them never could account for this. They were charming, rather cultured people, obviously devoted to their only child, and Jane when she was actually with them seemed to return their devotion. That she was a great trial to them there could be no doubt. Men fell easily in love with her, and she was usually having an affair with some really unsuitable person. As she was most indiscreet she had acquired, among people of her parents' generation, a very bad reputation, which was hardly deserved. Up to the present she had not been married, having a sort of vague idea in her head that she wished to be the wife of a genius. In the same way that some girls will not marry for love alone but must have money too, only allowing themselves to fall in love with a millionaire, so Jane thought that she could never be happy except with a really clever man; she had little intellect of her own, and needed the constant stimulus of an intellectual companion.

She had intended to marry when and only when she had found the ideal person, but she was in no hurry. The idea rather bored her, and the example of her married friends (except for Walter and Sally) was, to say the least of it, unpromising.

Meanwhile, she fell in love right and left, and had many violent but short-lived love affairs, in the course of which she burnt her own fingers comparatively seldom.

The train was full of sportsmen, their wives and dogs, going North. The most depressing sight in the world, thought Jane, is a married couple travelling. The horror of it. Not only must they sleep, eat, walk, drive and go to the theatre together all their lives, but they cannot escape even in the train. It brings home to one what marriage really means more than anything else, except perhaps seeing a married couple at the bridge table. What is the terrifying chain which binds these wretched people together so inevitably? Love? Hardly, or they would look happier. Intellectual companionship? No, that certainly not; the misery on their faces is only exceeded by the boredom. Habit and convention, no doubt, aided by the natural slavishness of women. Probably they are too stupid to realize their own unhappiness. They all look terribly, terribly stupid.

As Jane glanced around, her attention was particularly attracted by one couple who seemed rather different from the rest, and yet in a way typical of them all.

The husband was an example of sporting Englishman to be

32

seen by the dozen on every race-course and with whom the Embassy is nightly packed. He was tall, rather burly, with a phenomenally small head, mouse-coloured hair and reddish moustache. Although possessing almost classical features he was as ugly an object as could be imagined.

His wife was more unusual looking. She was immensely long and thin, so that she appeared, as it were, out of drawing, like an object seen in a distorting mirror. Her face, terribly thin and haggard, was completely dominated by an enormously long thin nose which turned up slightly at the very end; her large dark eyes were set close together and looked short-sighted. Her mouth was simply a red line, showing up startlingly on her dead white skin with green shadows. Jane thought that she had never seen anyone look so much like an overbred horse. She even ate like one, appearing to sniff every mouthful cautiously before she allowed herself to nibble at it, as though she might at any moment shy away from the table. Her husband behaved to her just like a groom with a nervous mare. Jane felt that he must have had difficulty in accustoming her to being handled.

She was well-dressed in an English sort of way; her tweeds were perfectly cut, and everything she wore was obviously expensive. Beautiful rings gave the uncomfortable impression of being too big for her fingers, which were abnormally thin and nervous. Her pearls were real. She wore a regimental badge of diamonds and rubies on a thick crêpe de chine jumper. While lacking any real *chic*, she gave an impression of genuineness and worth so unusual as to be rather pleasant. The word 'bogus' could under no circumstances have applied to her.

Jane, who was clever with her own clothes, felt annoyed with the long thin woman who, she thought, might have made more of her appearance without in any way detracting from its originality.

'And is it necessary to look as bored as that?' Jane wondered. Of course, the husband was most uninspiring, but still she might look out of the window sometimes, or at her fellow-passengers instead of staring into space in that almost

33

loopy way. Perhaps she had a hidden life of her own into which she could retire at will, or possibly she was in fact as stupid as she looked. Jane hoped for her sake that this was so.

At last she turned to her husband and said something. Only her lips moved, the expression of her face was unchanged. He nodded. Presently he gave her a cigarette and she began to blow the smoke through her nostrils like a horse in the cold weather.

Jane paid her bill and wandered back to her third-class sleeper. When she reached it she stood for a few moments in the corridor looking out of the windows at sunny fields with immense shadows of trees and hedges lying across them. The setting sun made a yellow mist over everything.

'By the time I get back to England, autumn will have begun,' she thought vaguely. Her mind was full of Albert Gates.

Jane's love affairs generally consisted of three phases. During the first phase—which lasted over a length of time varying with the number of meetings, but not often exceeding two months—she was violently in love. When away from the object of her affections she would think of him constantly in a light which generally bore a very small relation to truth; when in his company she would force herself to be happy, although she was often disillusioned in little ways. The second phase was complicated, but rendered more exciting by the reciprocation of her feelings. This seldom lasted for very long, as the third phase, consisting of heartless, but determined backing out on the part of Jane, would almost immediately follow. The first and second phases were generally accompanied by shameful flirtation.

At the present moment Jane was undergoing the usual preliminary phase with regard to Albert. She had met him several times in London and thought him easily the most attractive person of her acquaintance. As she gazed out of the corridor window it occurred to her that here, most probably, was the genius for whom she had been searching for such a long time; her brain circled, as it were, round and round the subject, but she sought no conclusion and arrived at none.

34

Presently the long thin woman passed by on her way to the first-class sleepers, followed by her husband. In motion she looked more than ever like a horse.

Jane climbed into her sleeper and lay down. She was sharing the carriage with three other women, all, luckily, unknown to each other, so there was no conversation. They looked at her with some disapproval as, contrary to third-class convention, she undressed completely and put on a pair of pyjamas. She greased her face, brushed her hair and settled down for a horrible night of banging, jolting and waking up at countless stations. All the time she half thought, half dreamed of Albert, wondering if he would have arrived yet at Dalloch Castle, how long he intended to stay, and whether he was at all excited at the prospect of their meeting. Towards the morning she fell into a profound sleep.

When she woke up the train was passing through Highland scenery. Purple hills kept rising outside the carriage window and obscuring the sky. They were covered with little streams and sheep. Everything was very quiet, even the train seemed to make less noise than it had done the previous evening; the air had a peculiar quality of extreme clearness like cold water.

Jane felt, but quickly checked, a romantic tremor. She removed her gaze from the moors and began to dress. The other women were still asleep, looking like modern German pictures.

At Inverness, Jane had to change into a local train, which ambled for about an hour in rather an intimate sort of way over moors and through pine woods, stopping here and there at little toy stations. When she alighted at Dalloch Station she noticed the long thin woman of the previous night standing by the guard's van with her husband, and presumed that they must be going to the castle. Sure enough, when they had collected their luggage, which took some time because there was a great deal of it as well as two spaniels, they climbed into the motor-car where Jane was already installed and introduced themselves as the Chadlingtons. She gathered from labels on their hand luggage that they were Captain and Lady Brenda Chadlington, a name she seemed vaguely to know.

'Have you stayed at Dalloch before?' asked Lady Brenda as they drove out of the station yard.

'No; you see, I don't know the Craigdallochs. Sally Monteath asked me. Have you been here before?'

'Oh, yes! Every year since I can remember. Madge Craigdalloch is my mother's greatest friend and my god-mother. I can't imagine what it will be like without her and Craig, although I'm told the Monteaths are charming. What bad luck for poor Craig having to go off like that, wasn't it . . .?'

She rambled on in the bored, uninterested voice of one who has been taught to think any conversation is better than none. Her husband looked out of the window in silence.

Sally greeted them in the hall of Dalloch Castle on their arrival. She was looking lovelier than usual in a pair of pink satin pyjamas.

'Please excuse these clothes. I've just this moment woken up. We only got here last night after a most fiendish journey in the car. How tired you must all be. I've had hot-water bottles put in your beds and breakfast will be sent up at once. Shall we go upstairs?'

The Chadlingtons glanced at each other in a startled kind of way.

General Murgatroyd now appeared and was introduced to Jane. He evidently knew the Chadlingtons very well and offered to show them their rooms, while Sally, relieved to have got rid of them, carried off Jane to have breakfast with herself and Walter, who was still in bed.

'Let's fetch old Gates,' said Walter, 'and have a party in here.'

Sally turned on the gramophone while he went along the passage, soon to return with Albert, who looked sleepy but cheerful in a pair of orange pyjamas. Jane thought him more attractive even than in London.

Presently trays of delicious breakfast appeared and they all sat on the bed munching happily, except Albert who announced that he was unable to touch food in the morning and asked the slightly astonished housemaid for a glass of Maraschino.

Jane asked if he had also travelled up in the Craigdallochs' car.

'Indeed, yes,' he replied. 'What a journey, too; all through England's green unpleasant land, as Blake so truly calls it. My one happy moment was at Carlisle, where we spent a night. When I opened what I supposed to be a cupboard door in my room, I was greeted by inky blackness, through which was just visible a pile of sordid clothes and cries of: "Well, I'm damned!" and "What impertinence!" It was a conjugal bedroom!'

Jane laughed.

'I expect if you knew the truth it was no such thing.'

'Well, I thought of that myself, but came to the conclusion that people who were indulging in a little enjoyable sin would probably be in better tempers. They actually rang the bell and said very loudly to the maid so that I couldn't fail to hear: "The person next door *keeps* coming in. Will you please lock it on this side so that we can have some peace?" *Keeps coming in,* indeed, as though I wanted to know the details of their squalid *ménage*. However, I had my revenge. I cleaned my teeth very loudly every half-hour all through the night. It woke them up each time, too! I could hear them grumbling.'

'Has all the rest of the party arrived?' asked Jane.

'All except Lord and Lady Prague. The general, whom you saw downstairs, Admiral Wenceslaus and Mr. Buggins were all here last night,' said Walter. 'We had about half an hour's conversation with them before going to bed. Mr. Buggins seems rather nice and Sally has quite fallen for the admiral.'

'As I have for the general,' remarked Albert; 'but then I have always had a great *penchant* for soldiers. It fascinates me to think how brave they must be. Sometimes one sees them marching about in London, all looking so wonderfully brave. I admire that. Sailors, too, must be very courageous, but somehow one doesn't feel it in quite the same way. Perhaps the fact that they are clean-shaven makes them more akin to oneself. This particular admiral certainly fixed upon me an extremely fierce and penetrating eye; instinctively I thought here is the hero of many an ocean fight, a rare old sea-dog.'

'His eye,' said Walter, 'is glass. At least, one of them is. I don't want to disillusion you, Albert dear.'

'How fascinating!' cried Albert. 'I knew the moment I saw him that the admiral was not quite as we are. This accounts for it. How d'you think he lost it, Walter? I suppose it hardly could have been plucked out by pirates or the Inquisition? Do you think he is sensitive about it? Will he, for instance, mind if he sees me looking closely at him to discover which eye is which? I must find out how he lost it. I suppose it would be tactless to ask him right out? But the general may know. I don't despair. Or Mr. Buggins. I like Mr. Buggins. He appears to be a man of some culture. He saw my picture "Tape Measures" reproduced in the *Studio* and was kind enough to mention it appreciatively.

'Now, my dears, I am going to dress, as I can hardly wait to begin exploring this house, which promises, in my opinion, to be very rewarding to the intelligent student of the nineteenth century. What do you intend to put on, Walter? I fear I have no tweeds, so shall be obliged to wear some trousers and a jersey. Will that be suitable, do you think?'

He picked up his black taffeta wrap and left the room.

Meanwhile, General Murgatroyd escorted the Chadlingtons to the dining-room where they made a hearty breakfast of sausages, eggs, ham and strong tea. The general, who some two hours since had eaten enough for three, kept them company with a plate of brawn. They all spoke in monosyllables, their mouths full.

'Bad luck for poor old Craig.'

'Oh, rotten.'

'When did the Monteaths get here?'

'Last night—late.'

'Anybody else?'

'Stanislas is here and Buggins.'

'Anybody else?'

'Yes; namby-pamby chap called Gates—artist or something. Came with the Monteaths.'

'Who's to come?'

'Only Floss and Prague. Coming to-night.'

'Does Monteath shoot?'

'No, nor Gates. Just as well, from the look of them.'

'What's Mrs. Monteath like?'

'Oh, all right. Better than the others, I should say.'

'Pretty, isn't she?'

'Too much dolled up for me, otherwise quite handsome.'

'Finished your breakfast?'

'M'm!'

'Come and look at the river, then.'

'Wait a moment. We'll get our rods put up.'

'Not much use, too bright.'

'Oh, we might as well have a try, all the same.'

About two hours later, Jane, having bathed and changed out of her travelling clothes, wandered downstairs, where she came upon Albert, exquisitely dressed in bright blue trousers and a black sweater. He was roaming about, notebook in hand.

'My dear Jane,' he said, 'this house is unique. I am in ecstasies. Most of it seems scarcely to have been touched for the last fifty years. Nevertheless, we are only just in time. The hand of the modern decorator is already upon it. The drawing-room, alas! I find utterly ruined. Our absent hostess would appear to have that Heal *cum* Lenigen complex so prevalent among the British aristocracy. Happily, in this case, it has been muzzled, presumably by lack of funds, but its influence is creeping over the whole house. The oak, for instance, on these stairs and in the entrance hall has been pickled—a modern habit, which one cannot too heartily deplore—and much exquisite furniture has been banished to the servants' hall, some even to the attics. On the other hand, the boudoir, stone hall, billiard- and dining-rooms appear to be quite unspoilt. Come with me, my dear.'

Albert led the way to the dining-room, where the table was being laid for luncheon. It was a huge room with dark red brocade walls and a pale blue-and-yellow ceiling covered in real gold stars. At one end there arose an enormous Gothic mantelpiece of pitch-pine. Several Raeburns and two Winterhalters adorned the walls.

'Winterhalter,' murmured Albert, 'my favourite artist. I must call your attention to this clock, made of the very

40

cannon-ball which rolled to the feet of Ernest, 4th Earl of Craigdalloch during the battle of Inkerman. Shall we go and look at the outside of the castle? We have just time before lunch.'

They went into the garden and walked around the house, which was built in the Victorian feudal style, and rather resembled a large white cake with windows and battlements picked out in chocolate icing. Albert was thrown into raptures by its appearance.

When they returned to the front door they found Walter and the general standing on the steps.

'Ah! this house! this house!' cried Albert. 'I am enchanted by it. Good morning, General.'

'Good morning, Gates.'

'Walter, have you ever seen such a house? General, you agree, I hope, that it is truly exquisite?'

'Yes; I am attached to the place myself. Been here, man and boy, for the last fifty years or so. Best grouse moor in the country, you know, and as good fishing as you can find between here and the Dee, I swear it is.'

'It *is* lovely,' said Jane doubtfully. 'I wonder what we shall do all day though.'

'Do? Why, my dear young lady, by the time you've been out with the guns, or flogging the river all day, you'll be too tired to do anything except perhaps to have a set or two of lawn tennis. After dinner we can always listen to Craig's wireless. I've just asked the chauffeur to fix it up.'

'I personally shall be busy taking photographs,' said Albert. 'I am shortly bringing out a small brochure on the minor arts of the nineteenth century, and although I had already collected much material for it, there are in this house some objects so unique that I shall have to make a most careful revision of my little work. I also feel it is my duty to the nation to compile a catalogue of what I find here. You write, General?'

'I once wrote a series of articles for *Country Life* on stable bedding.'

'But how macabre! Then you, I and Walter, all three,

belong to the fellowship of the pen; but while you and I are in a way but tyros, I feeling frankly more at home with a paintbrush and you, most probably, with a fox's brush, Walter here is one of our latter day immortals.'

And he began to recite in a loud voice one of his friend's poems:

> *'Fallow upon the great black waste*
> *'And all esurient. But when*
> *'Your pale green tears are falling*
> *Falling   and*
> *Falling*
> *Upon the Wapentake, there was never*
> *So absolutely never*
> *Such disparity.'*

Walter blushed.

'*Please*, Albert.'

'My dear Walter, that is good. It is more than good—it has an enduring quality and I think will live. Do you not agree, general? You and I, Walter, will do a great deal of work here. I have found a room with a large green table in the centre very well lighted. It will be ideal for my purpose. Then I am hoping that Sally will perhaps give me a few sittings. Do you think that she might be persuaded?'

'My dear, she'd adore to. Sally very much believes in having herself reproduced in all mediums. Come on. There's the gong for lunch.'

By dinner-time that evening the whole party was assembled, Lord and Lady Prague having arrived in a motor-car soon after seven o'clock.

Sally had spent much time and thought over the arrangement of the table, feeling that it was her duty to try and make the first evening a success, and as she sat down she thought, with some satisfaction, that she had mixed up the party rather well. It soon became apparent, however, that the party was not mixing. Her own task, seated between Lord Prague and Captain Chadlington, might well have daunted a far more experienced conversationalist, the former being stone deaf and moreover thoroughly engrossed in the pleasures of the table, while the latter appeared to possess a vocabulary of exactly three words—'I say!' and 'No!'—which he used alternately. She fought a losing battle valiantly, remembering that the really important thing on these occasions is to avoid an oasis of silence. Walter declared afterwards that he distinctly heard her ask Lord Prague if he belonged to the London Group, and that, on receiving no answer, she then proceeded to recite *Lycidas* to him until the end of dinner.

Jane, whose partners were Admiral Wenceslaus and Mr. Buggins, courted disaster by embarking on a funny story Albert had told her about a lunatic woman with a glass eye. She only remembered in the middle that the admiral was one-eyed and that Mrs. Buggins languished in a lunatic asylum and had to change it quickly into a drunken man with one leg. The story lost much of its point and nobody laughed except Walter, who choked into his soup.

Albert sat next to Lady Prague, a spinsterish woman of about forty with a fat face, thin body and the remains of a depressingly insular type of good looks. Her fuzzy brown hair was arranged in a dusty bun showing ears which were evidently intended to be hidden, but which insisted on poking their way out. Her skin was yellow with mauve powder; except for this her face was quite free from any trace of *maquillage*, and the eyebrows grew at will. Her nails were cut short and unvarnished.

Albert was seized with spasms of hatred for her even before she spoke, which she did almost immediately in a loud unpleasing voice, saying:

'I didn't quite hear your name when we were introduced.'

Albert looked at her frolicking eyebrows with distaste and said very distinctly:

'Albert Memorial Gates.'

'Oh! What?'

'Albert Memorial Gates.'

'Yes. *Memorial*, did you say?'

'My name,' said Albert with some asperity, 'is Albert Memorial Gates. I took Memorial in addition to my

43

baptismal Albert at my confirmation out of admiration for the Albert Memorial, a very great work of art which may be seen in a London suburb called Kensington.'

'Oh,' said Lady Prague crossly, 'you might as well have called yourself Albert Hall.'

'I entirely disagree with you.'

Lady Prague looked helplessly at her other neighbour, Admiral Wenceslaus, but he was talking across Jane to Mr. Buggins and took no notice of her. She made the best of a bad job and turned again to Albert.

'Did I hear Mr. Buggins say that you are an artist?'

'*Artiste—peintre*—yes.'

'Oh, now do tell me, I'm so interested in art, what do you chiefly go in for?'

'Go in where?'

'I mean—water-colours or oils?'

'My principal medium is what you would call oils. Gouache, tempera and prepared dung are mediums I never neglect, while my bead, straw and button pictures have aroused a great deal of criticism not by any means all unfavourable.'

'It always seems to me a great pity to go in for oils unless you're really good. Now Prague's sister has a girl who draws quite nicely and she wanted to go on to Paris, but I said to her parents, "Why let her learn oils. There are too many oil paintings in the world already. Let her do water-colours. They take up much less room." Don't you agree?'

'I expect, in the case of your husband's niece, that you were perfectly right.'

'Now, do tell me, this is so interesting, what sort of things do you paint?'

'Chiefly abstract subjects.'

'Yes, I see, allegories and things like that. Art must be so fascinating, I always think. I have just been painted by Laszlo. By the way, did I see you at his exhibition? No? But I have seen you somewhere before, I know I have. It's a funny thing but I *never* forget a face—names, now I can't remember, but I never forget a face, do you?'

'So few people have faces,' said Albert, who was struggling to be polite. 'Everyone seems to have a name, but only one person in ten has a face. The old man sitting next to Sally, for instance, has no face at all.'

'That is my husband,' said Lady Prague, rather tartly.

'Then the fact must already have obtruded itself on your notice. But, take the general as an example. He hasn't got one either, in my opinion.'

'Oh, I see now what you mean,' she said brightly, 'that they are not paintable. But you surprise me. I have always been told that older people, especially men, were very paintable with all the wrinkles and lines—so much character. Now you went, I suppose, to the Dutch exhibition?'

'I did not. I wasn't in London last spring, as a matter of fact, but even if I had been I should have avoided Burlington House as sedulously then as I should later in the summer. I regard the Dutch school as one of the many sins against art which have been perpetrated through the ages.'

'You mean . . .' She looked at him incredulously. 'Don't you *like* Dutch pictures?'

'No, nor Dutch cheese, as a matter of fact!'

'I can't understand it. I simply worship them. There was a picture of an old woman by Rembrandt. I stood in front of it for quite a while one day and I *could have sworn* she breathed!'

Albert shuddered.

'Yes, eerie, wasn't it? I turned to my friend and said: "Laura, it's uncanny. I feel she might step out of the frame any moment." Laura Pastille (Mrs. Pastille, that's my friend's name) has copied nearly all the Dutch pictures in the National Gallery. For some she had to use a magnifying glass. She's very artistic. But I am amazed that you don't like them. I suppose you pretend to admire all these ugly things which are the fashion now. I expect you'll get over it in time. Epstein, for instance, and Augustus John—what d'you think about them?'

Albert contained himself with some difficulty and answered, breathing hard and red in the face, that he regarded Epstein as one of the great men of all time and would prefer

45

not to discuss him. (General Murgatroyd, overhearing this remark, turned to Walter and asked if that 'fella Gates' were an aesthete. Walter looked puzzled and said that he hoped so, he hoped they all were. The general snorted and continued telling Captain Chadlington about how he had once played a salmon for two hours.)

Lady Prague then said: 'Why do you live in Paris? Isn't England good enough for you?' She said this rather offensively. It was evident that Albert's feelings for her were heartily reciprocated.

'Well,' he replied, 'England is hardly a very good place for a serious artist, is it? One is not exactly encouraged to use one's brain over here, you know. When I arrived from Paris this last time they would not even leave me my own copy of *Ulysses*. Things have come to a pretty pass when it is impossible to get decent literature to read.'

'*In*decent literature, I suppose you mean.'

Albert felt completely out of his depth, but to his immense relief Admiral Wenceslaus now turned upon Lady Prague the conversational gambit of, 'And where did you come from to-day?' thus making it unnecessary for him to answer.

Mr. Buggins and Walter were getting on like a house on fire.

'Curious,' observed Mr. Buggins, 'for a house party of this size in Scotland to consist entirely of Sassenachs—seven men and not one kilt among them. I have the right, of course, to wear the Forbes tartan through my maternal grandmother, but I always think it looks bad with an English name, don't you agree?'

'Very bad,' said Walter. 'But you could wear it as a fancy dress, I suppose?'

'The kilt, my dear sir, is not a fancy dress.'

'My wife is Scottish; her father is Lord Craigdalloch's brother.'

'Yes, of course, Johnnie. Such an interesting family, the Dallochs; one of the oldest in Scotland.'

'Really?'

'Considering that you are allied to them by marriage it

surprises me that you should not be aware of that. Why, the cellars of this castle date from the tenth century. I suppose you know how it came to be built here?'

'I'm afraid I don't.'

'Well, the first Thane of Dalloch had no castle and one day when he was getting old he thought he would build himself a solid dwelling-place instead of the shieling or hut that had been his headquarters up to then. So he went to consult a wise woman who lived in a neighbouring shieling. He told her what was in his mind and asked where would be the best place for him to build his castle. She replied, "When you find a *bike*[1] in a *birk*,[2] *busk*[3] there the *bauk*."[4]

'The story goes that as he was walking away from the old woman's shieling he was stung by a wasp. He looked high and low for the *bike*, intending to destroy it, and presently found it in a *birk*. Instantly he recalled the witch's words. The next day he *busked* the *bauk* and soon a bonnie castle rose round the *birk*, which you can see to this very day in the cellars. To me, all these old legends are so fascinating.'

He then proceeded to tell Walter the whole history of the Dalloch family down to the present generation. Walter found it extremely dull and wondered how anyone could be bothered to remember such stuff, but he thought Mr. Buggins quite a nice old bore and tried to listen intelligently.

Albert was now struggling with Lady Brenda, who was far more difficult to get on with than Lady Prague. Being a duke's daughter she was always spoken of as having so much charm. The echo of this famous charm had even reached as far as Paris, and Albert was eagerly anticipating its influence upon himself.

He was doomed to immediate disappointment, finding that besides being an unusually stupid woman she had less sex appeal than the average cauliflower; and when, in the course of conversation, he learnt that her two children were called Wendy and Christopher Robin, his last hope of being charmed vanished for ever.

---

[1] Wasps' nest. [2] Birch tree. [3] Prepare. [4] Cross beam.

She told him that Lady Craigdalloch, her godmother, was improving the whole house, bit by bit.

'This year all the oak on the staircase has been pickled. Of course, it takes time as they are not well off, but Madge has such good taste. You should have seen the drawing-room before she redecorated it: a hideous white room with nothing but Victorian furniture, bead stools and those horrible little stiff sofas. It was my mother who suggested painting it green. Of course it is really lovely now.'

'You have known the house a long time?' he asked, stifling a groan.

'Oh, yes, since I was a child. We spent our honeymoon here.'

'I hope,' said Albert, 'in the lovely bed which Sally is occupying at present. I thought when I saw it how perfect for a honeymoon.'

Lady Brenda looked horrified. Luckily at this moment Sally got up and the women left the dining-room.

As soon as the door was shut upon them, Admiral Wenceslaus monopolized the conversation, holding forth on his favourite subject: Blockade. Walter and Albert, who had a hazy idea that a blockade was a sort of fence behind which the white men retired when pursued by Red Indians, now learnt that, on the contrary, it is a system of keeping supplies from the enemy in times of war. The admiral explained to them, and to the table at large, that it is permissible to ration neutrals to their pre-war imports in order to prevent the enemy country from importing goods through this channel.

'Why wasn't it done from the beginning?' he bawled, in a voice which Albert felt he must have acquired when addressing his men in stormy weather from the bridge, and rolling his eye round and round. 'Was there a traitor in the Government? That's what I should like to know.'

'Hear, hear!' said Lord Prague, doubtless from force of habit, as he was, in fact, unable to hear a word.

'We had them *there*.' The admiral screwed his thumb round and round on the table as though grinding up imaginary Germans. 'And all the time our poor fellows were being blown to atoms by British shells. . . .'

His speech, for it was virtually one, continued for about half an hour, and when it was finished they joined the ladies.

Albert felt disappointed. Other admirals he had met had provided excellent after-dinner company and he expected better things of the Silent Service than a lecture on Blockade.

7

After dinner the general marshalled them all into Lord Craigdalloch's study and turned on the wireless which was playing Grieg's suite from *Peer Gynt*. 'This is London calling.' (Crash! crash!) 'The Wireless Symphony Orchestra will now play "Solveig's Song." ' (Crash! crash! crash!)

Albert spoke to Jane in an undertone, but he was quickly checked by a look from Lady Prague who appeared to be in a state of aesthetic rapture.

When the Grieg came to an end it was announced that Miss Sackville-West would give readings from T. S. Eliot.

'Tripe!' said the general and turned it off. He then began to arrange about the next day's shooting.

'If any of the non-shooters would like to come out tomorrow,' he said, 'it will be a good opportunity as none of the drives are very far apart and it's all easy walking. Those who don't want to come all day can meet us for lunch.'

'Jane and I would love it if we shan't be in the way,' said Sally meekly.

The general, who had taken a fancy to her, smiled benignly:

'Do you good, my dear.'

'Great,' said Albert, 'as is my distaste for natural scenery, I feel it to be my duty, as a student of the nineteenth century, to gaze just once upon the glens and bens that so entranced Royal Victoria, both as the happy wife of that industrious and illustrious prince whose name I am so proud to bear, and as his lamenting relict. I should like to see the stag stand at bay upon its native crags, the eagle cast its great shadow over the cowering grouse; I should like dearly to find a caper-cailzie's nest. And I feel that I could choose no more suitable day on which to witness these glories of Victorian nature than the famous twelfth, when sportsmen all over the country set forth with dog and gun to see what they can catch.'

This speech was greeted by Captain Chadlington with a sort of admiring noise in his throat which can only be transcribed as 'Co-o-o-h.'

'Shall you come, Monteath?' asked the general, taking no notice of Albert.

'I think not, sir, thank you very much. I have rather a lot of work to do for the *Literary Times* and if everyone goes out it will be a good opportunity to get on with it.'

'Brenda and I will come, of course,' said Lady Prague briskly, 'so we shall be five extra beside the guns. Will you ring the bell, Mowbray?' The general did so. She added, with a disapproving look at Albert: 'Don't you shoot?'

'Excellently,' he replied in a threatening voice. 'With the water-pistol.'

'Perhaps you had no chance of learning when you were young; probably you have a good *natural* eye.'

The admiral looked annoyed and there was an awkward silence.

'Well, then,' said General Murgatroyd, 'that's all settled. Those who are coming out in the morning must be in the hall, suitably dressed, by ten. We shan't wait. I advise you to bring shooting-sticks.'

'What are they?' asked Albert, but his question was drowned by the overture from *William Tell* which suddenly burst upon the room.

The next day Jane came downstairs punctually at ten o'clock. Albert and Sally had apparently both found themselves unable to get up so early and had sent messages to say that they would join the guns for lunch. One of the footmen was just taking a glass of champagne to Albert's room. Jane wished that she had known this sooner; she had found it a great effort to wake up that morning herself, and was still very sleepy. She half contemplated going back to bed until luncheon time, but catching at that moment the eye of the admiral, and feeling by no means certain that it was

51

his glass one, she lacked the moral courage to do so.

In the hall scenes of horrible confusion were going forward; a perfect regiment of men tramped to and fro carrying things and bumping into each other. They all seemed furiously angry. Above the din could be heard the general's voice:

'What the——d'you think you're doing? Get out of that! Come here, blast you!'

Lady Prague, looking like a sort of boy scout, was struggling with a strap when she caught sight of Jane.

'My dear girl,' she said taking one end of it from between her teeth, 'you can't come out in that mackintosh. Whoever heard of black on the hill? Why, it's no good at all. That scarlet cap will have to go too, I'm afraid. It's easy to see you haven't been up here before. We must alter all this.' She dived into a cupboard, and after some rummaging produced a filthy old Burberry and forced Jane to put it on. Evidently made for some portly man it hung in great folds on Jane and came nearly to her ankles.

'I don't think I'll take a mackintosh at all,' she said, rather peevishly, 'and I hardly ever wear a hat in any case, so I'll leave that behind, too.'

'As you like, my dear, of course. I think you'll be perished with cold and it will probably rain; it looks to me quite threatening. Have your own way, but don't blame me if—Hullo! we seem to be off at last.'

Jane climbed rather miserably into a sort of 'bus and sat next to Lady Prague. She was disappointed that Albert had not come, having taken particular pains with her appearance that morning on his account.

The moor was about five miles away, and during the whole drive nobody spoke a word except General Murgatroyd, who continually admonished his dog, a broken-looking retriever of the name of Mons.

'Lie down, will you? No, get off that coat!' (Kick, kick, kick; howl, howl, howl.) 'Stop that noise, blast you!' (Kick, howl.)

Jane pitied the poor animal which seemed unable to do right in the eyes of its master.

When they arrived at their destination (a sort of sheep-track on the moor) they were met by two more guns who had come over from a neighbouring house to make up the numbers; and by a rabble of half-clothed and villainous-looking peasants armed for the most part with sticks. They reminded Jane of a film she had once seen called 'The Fourteenth of July.'

Their leader, an enormous man with red hair and wild eyes, came forward and addressed General Murgatroyd in a respectful but independent manner. When they had held a short parley he withdrew, and communicated the result of it to his followers, after which they all straggled away.

Jane supposed that they were the local unemployed, soliciting alms, and felt that the general must have treated them with some tact; once aroused, she thought, they might prove ugly customers.

Presently the whole party began to walk across the moor. Jane noticed that each of the men had an attendant who carried guns and a bag of cartridges. She wondered what their mission could be: perhaps to stand by and put the wounded birds out of their pain.

After an exhausting walk of about half an hour, during which Jane fell down several times (and the general said it would be easy walking, old humbug!), they arrived at a row of little roofless buildings, rather like native huts. The first one they came to was immediately, and silently, appropriated by Lord and Lady Prague, followed by their attendant.

Jane supposed that they were allocated in order of rank and wondered which would fall to her lot.

'Better come with me, Miss Dacre,' said General Murga-troyd. It was the first time he had spoken except to swear at his dog, which he did continually, breaking the monotony by thrashing the poor brute, whose shrieks could be heard for miles across the heather.

When they reached his hut (or butt) he shouted in a voice of thunder:

'Get in, will you, and lie down.'

Jane, though rather taken aback, was about to comply

when a kick from its master sent poor Mons flying into the butt, and she realized that the words had been addressed to that unfortunate and not to herself.

General Murgatroyd gave Jane his cartridge bag to sit on and paid no further attention to her. He and his attendant (the correct word for whom appeared to be *loader*) stood gazing over the top of the butt into space.

Seated on the floor, Jane could see nothing outside except a small piece of sky; she wondered why she had been made to leave her black mackintosh behind.

'I can neither see nor be seen. I expect it was that old woman's jealous spite. I don't believe she's a woman at all. She's just a very battered boy scout in disguise, and not much disguise, either.'

She began to suffer acutely from cold and cramp, and was filled with impotent rage. Eons of time passed over her. She pulled a stone out of the wall and scratched her name on another stone, then Albert's name, then a heart with an arrow through it (but she soon rubbed that off again). She knew the shape of the general's plus-fours and the pattern of his stockings by heart, and could have drawn an accurate picture of the inside of the butt blindfold, when suddenly there was an explosion in her ears so tremendous that for an instant she thought she must have been killed. It was followed by several more in quick succession, and a perfect fusillade began, up and down the line. This lasted for about twenty minutes, and Jane rather enjoyed it—'As good as an Edgar Wallace play.'

At last it died away again, and General Murgatroyd said, 'Well, the drive's over. You can get up now, if you like.' Jane endeavoured to stand, but her legs would hardly carry her. After rubbing them for a bit she was just able to stagger out of the butt. She saw all around her the same band of peasants that had met them when they left the 'bus earlier that morning. Most of them were carrying dead grouse and picking up others.

'How kind!' she thought. 'The general has taken pity on the poor creatures and given them permission to gather the birds for their evening meal. He must really be nicer than he looks.'

Thinking of the evening meal made Jane realize that she was extremely hungry. 'Luncheon time soon, I expect.' She glanced at her watch. Only eleven o'clock! It must have stopped. Still ticking, though. Perhaps the hands had got stuck. She asked Admiral Wenceslaus the time.

'Nearly eleven, by Jove! We shall have to show a leg if we're to get in two more drives before lunch.'

Jane could hardly restrain her tears on hearing this. She sat hopelessly on a rock, while the rest of the party wandered about the heather looking for dead grouse.

When one of them found a bird he would whistle up his dog and point to the little corpse saying, 'Seek hard,' and making peculiar noises in his throat. The dog would occasionally pick it up and give it into his master's hand, but more often would sniff away in another direction, in which case its master seized it by the scruff of the neck, rubbed its nose into the bird and gave it a good walloping.

Jane began to realize the full significance of the expression 'a dog's life.'

Lady Prague, who also strode about searching for grouse, presently came up to where Jane was sitting upon her rock, and asked why she didn't help.

'Because even if I did find a bird no bribe would induce me to touch it,' said Jane rather rudely, looking at Lady Prague's bloodstained hands.

In time the birds were all collected and hung upon the back of a small pony, and the party began to walk towards the butts from which the next drive was to take place. These were dimly visible on the side of the opposite mountain, and appeared to be a great distance away.

Jane walked by herself in a miserable silence, carefully watching her feet. In spite of this she fell down continually. The others were all talking and laughing over incidents of the drive. Jane admired them for keeping up their spirits in such circumstances. Their jokes were incomprehensible to her.

'I saw you take that bird of mine, old boy, but I wiped your eye twice, you know. Ha! Ha!'

'That dog o' yours has a good nose for other people's birds. Ha! Ha!'

'D'you remember poor old Monty at that very drive last year? All he shot was a beater and a bumble-bee.'

'Ah, yes! Poor Monty, poor Monty. Ha, ha, ha!'

The walk seemed endless. They came to a river which everyone seemed able to cross quite easily by jumping from stone to stone except Jane, who lost her balance in the middle and was obliged to wade. The water was ice-cold and came to her waist, but was not at first unpleasant, her feet were hot and sore, and both her ankles were swollen. Presently, however, the damp stockings began to rub her heels and every step became agony.

When they finally reached the butts Jane felt that she was in somewhat of a quandary. With whom ought she to sit this time? She hardly liked to inflict herself on General Murgatroyd again. Lord Prague and Captain Chadlington had their wives with them, and the admiral and Mr. Buggins were so very far ahead that she knew she would never have time to catch them up. She looked round rather helplessly, and saw standing near her one of the strangers who had come over for the day. As he was young and had a kind face, she ventured to ask if she might sit with him during the next drive. He seemed quite pleased and, making her a comfortable seat with his coat and cartridge bag, actually addressed her as if she were a human being. Jane felt really grateful; no one had so far spoken a word to her, except Lady Prague and General Murgatroyd, and they only from a too evident sense of duty.

The young man, whose name was Lord Alfred Sprott, asked if there was a cheery crowd at Dalloch Castle. Jane, more loyally than truthfully, said, 'Yes, a very cheery crowd.' She hoped that it was cheery where he was staying, too? He replied that it was top-hole, only a little stalking lodge, of course, but very cosy and jolly, quite a picnic. He told her some of the jolly jokes they had there. Jane, in her bemused condition, found him most entertaining; she laughed quite hysterically, and was sorry when the birds began to fly over them, putting an end to conversation.

In spite, however, of this spiritual sunshine Jane soon began to feel colder and more miserable even than before, and greatly looked forward to the next walk which might warm her up and dry her clothes.

This was not to be. While the birds were being picked up after that drive, she learnt, to her dismay, that the next one would take place from the same butts.

The wait between the two drives was interminable. Lord Alfred Sprott seemed to have come to the end of his witticisms and sat on his shooting-stick in a gloomy silence. Jane ventured one or two remarks, but they were not well received. She gathered that Lord Alfred had been shooting badly, and this had affected his spirits. She became more and more unhappy and shook all over with cold.

'I expect I shall be very ill after this,' she thought. 'I shall probably die, after lingering some weeks; then perhaps they will be sorry.' And tears of self-pity and boredom welled up in her eyes.

When the drive was over, they all began to walk towards the hut where luncheon was prepared. They were now obliged to keep in a straight line with each other, in order to put up game for the men, who carried their guns and let them off from time to time.

'Keep up please, Miss Dacre. Keep in line, please, or you'll be shot, you know.'

Jane thought that it seemed almost uncivilized to threaten an acquaintance that she must keep up or be shot, but she said nothing and struggled, fairly successfully, not to be left behind. As the result of this further misery one tiny bird was added to the bag.

8

Nothing in this world lasts for ever. The longest morning Jane could remember was at an end and the party had assembled in a little hut for luncheon. A good fire burnt in one corner and a smell of food and peat smoke created a friendly atmosphere. Jane felt happier, especially when she saw that Sally and Albert were seated on the floor in front of the fire.

Albert looked particularly alluring in an orange crêpe-de-chine shirt open at the neck, and a pair of orange-and-brown tartan trousers, tight to the knees and very baggy round the ankles. Under one arm he carried an old-fashioned telescope of black leather heavily mounted in brass, with which, he said, when asked why he had brought it, to view the quarry. He and Lord Alfred greeted each other with unconcealed disgust; they had been at Eton and Oxford together.

Luncheon was rather a silent meal. There was not nearly enough food to go round, and everyone was busy trying to take a little more than his or her share and then to eat it quickly for fear the others should notice. (The admiral choked rather badly from trying to save time by drinking with his mouth full. Lady Prague and General Murgatroyd thumped him on the back and made him look at the ceiling, after which he recovered.) Most of the baskets in which the food was packed seemed to contain a vast quantity of apples which nobody ate at all. Some very promising-looking packages were full of Petit-Beurre biscuits or dry bread, and the scarcity of food was rendered all the more tantalizing by the fact that what there was of it was quite excellent. The thermos flask which should have contained coffee proved to be empty.

Lady Prague and Lord Alfred carried on a desultory conversation about their mutual relations whose names appeared to be legion.

'I hear Buzzy has sold all his hunters.'

'Yes, I heard. An absolute tragedy, you know. But I'm afraid it's . . .'

'Yes, that's what my mother says. I don't know, though, really why it should be.'

'Well, my dear, every reason if you come to think of it. But what does Eileen say about all this—?'

'Haven't you heard?'

'No—what?'

'Eileen is staying down at Rose Dean.'

'No! Well, I must say I never, never would have thought it of her; though, mind you, I have always disliked Eileen. But really! Rose Dean—no that *is* a little too much. Then where is Looey? . . . (etc. etc.)' This was so interesting for everybody else.

When everything eatable had been consumed the general marshalled them all out of doors again. Admiral Wenceslaus was very indignant at this and said something to Jane about letting a cove finish his brandy in peace; but even he dared not mutiny and, muttering a few naval expressions, he followed the others out of the hut.

To Jane's great relief—for she was very tired and stiff—each of the women was now provided with a pony to ride. Albert walked between Jane's pony and Sally's. He looked round at the large crowd of people spread out over the moor, the ponies, dogs, and men with guns.

'We might be early settlers escaping from native tribes,' he observed. 'Led through unnatural hardships to civilization and safety by the iron will-power of one man, our beloved and sainted general. Alas, that within sight of help, his noble spirit should have flown. Poor, good old man, he will yet be enshrined in the heart of each one of us for ever.'

'Please don't laugh quite so loudly!' Lady Prague shouted to Jane and Sally, 'or all the birds will settle.'

'I wish,' said Albert, 'that I could spot an eagle or a stag with my telescope for the darling general to shoot at. He might take a fancy to me if I did. Our present lack of intimacy begins to weigh on my spirits.'

Albert searched the horizon with his telescope, but complained that, being unable to keep one eye shut, he saw nothing.

'If you ask me, I expect that's why the admiral rose from the ranks. Having only one eye, anyhow, he probably took prizes for viewing enemy craft quicker and more accurately than his shipmates. "A sail!—A sail! Ahoy!"' he cried, dancing a sort of hornpipe on the heather.

General Murgatroyd, who was beating his dog, stopped for a moment and asked Alfred Sprott if 'that fella thought the birds would be able to stand the sight of his orange shirt?' Lord Alfred grunted, he could hardly stand the sight of it himself.

'I ducked him once,' he said, 'in Mercury.'

'Good boy! Did you, then? Good for you, sir!'

'This scenery,' said Albert to Jane, 'is really most amusing. It is curious how often natural scenery belongs to one particular era. The Apennines, for instance, are purely Renaissance: Savernake was made for the age of chivalry: Chantilly and Fontainebleau for the seventeenth and eighteenth centuries: the Rhine for the Middle Ages, and so on. At other times these landscapes seem beautiful, but unreal. Scotland, as you will no doubt have noticed, was invented by the Almighty for the delectation of Victoria and Albert. Foreseeing their existence, He arranged really suitable surroundings for them, and these purple mountains and mauve streams will stand as a reminder of the Victorian age long after the Albert Memorial has turned to dust.'

'What,' asked Jane, 'would you call the landscape of today?'

Albert did not answer, but said faintly:

'Aren't we nearly there; I'm most dreadfully tired?'

Sally jumped off her pony.

'Do ride instead of me for a bit, Albert; I wanted a walk.'

General Murgatroyd could hardly contain himself when he saw Albert, his graceful figure swaying slightly from the hips, seated upon Sally's pony. He was tired himself, though nothing would have induced him to say so; if Prague could still walk so could he. Lord Prague, it may be noted, was to all intents and purposes dead, except on shooting days when he would come to life in the most astonishing manner, walking and shooting with the best. At other times he would sit in an arm-chair with his eyes shut and his hands folded, evidently keeping his strength for the next shoot. He hardly appeared able even to walk from his drawing-room to the dining-room and was always helped upstairs by his valet.

At about half a mile from their destination the horses were left behind and the party began to climb a fairly steep hill. When they reached the first butt Albert declared that he could go no farther and would stay where he was.

'That,' remarked Lord Alfred, who was passing it, 'is General Murgatroyd's butt.'

'Splendid!' And Albert, swinging himself on to the edge of it, sat there in a graceful position, his legs crossed, pretending to look through his telescope.

'Well, you'd better put on this mackintosh, Gates, that shirt would scare all the birds for miles.'

Lord Alfred went on his way feeling like the Good Samaritan.

Presently General Murgatroyd appeared with his loader. When he saw Albert he glared and muttered, but took no further notice of him and began to make his own arrangements for the drive.

'May I let off your gun, sir?' said Albert, pointing it straight into the general's face.

'Put that gun down this instant. My God! young man, I'm sure I don't know where you were brought up. When I was a kid I was sent to bed for a week because I pointed my toy pistol at the nurse.'

'I'm sorry,' said Albert, rather taken aback by his manner. 'I didn't know it was full.'

The general wiped his brow and looked round helplessly.

'You can sit on that stone,' he said, indicating one at the bottom of the butt.

'Oh, sir, please, must I sit there? I wanted to watch you. I shan't see anything from down here. Oh, please, may I stand up?'

Receiving no answer beyond a frigid stare, Albert, with a deep sigh, disposed himself upon the stone, sitting cross-legged like an idol. He then produced a slim volume from his pocket. 'I presume that you have read "The Testament of Beauty," sir?'

'Never heard of it.'

'Oh, sir, you must have heard of it. A very great poem by our Poet Laureate.'

'No, I haven't; I expect it's immoral stuff, anyway. Kipling ought to be the Poet Laureate, to my mind.'

'Alas! Philistine that I am, I must disagree with you. I cannot appreciate Sir Rudyard's writings as no doubt I should. "Lest we forget, lest *we* forget,"' he chanted. 'Have you a favourite poem, sir?'

The general remained silent, his eye on the horizon. As a matter of fact he *had* a favourite poem, but could not quite remember how it went—

> *'Under the wide and starry sky*
> *Dig my grave and let me lie.*
> *Home is the hunter home from the hill,*
> *And the hunter home from the hill.'*

Something more or less like that.

'You care for T. S. Eliot, sir? But no, of course, I heard you cut off the wireless last night when Mrs. Nicolson was about to read us some of his poems. How I wish I could be the one to convert you!' And he began to declaim in a loud and tragic voice:

> *'We are the stuffed men, the hollow men. . . .'*

'Oh, *will* you be quiet? Can't you see the birds are settling?'

'I can see nothing from down here except the very *séant* pattern of your exquisite tweeds. But no matter.'

Albert read for a time in silence.

The general was breathing hard. Presently he stiffened:

'Over you!—over you, sir!' he shouted.

Albert dropped his book in a puddle and leapt to his feet, knocking the general's arm by mistake. The gun went off with a roar and a large number of birds flew over their heads unscathed.

'You blasted idiot! Why can't you sit still where I told you? Of all the damned fools I ever met—'

'I regret that I cannot stay here to be insulted,' said Albert; and he strolled out of the butt.

'Come back, will you? Blast you! Can't you see the bloody drive is beginning?'

Albert paid no attention, but walked gracefully away over the heather, telescope in hand, towards the next butt. Its occupant luckily happened to be Mr. Buggins, who was rather amused by and inclined to tolerate Albert, so there were no further *contretemps*. Meanwhile, the general, infuriated beyond control, was seen to fall upon his loader and shake him violently.

When this eventful drive was over, Jane, Sally and Albert, finding themselves close to a road where the motor-cars were waiting, took the heaven-sent opportunity to go home. Jane on her arrival went straight to bed, where she remained the whole of the following day, entertaining riotous parties in her bedroom. Her ankles were so swollen that it was nearly a week before she could walk without the aid of a stick.

9

Jane was enjoying herself passionately. Curiously enough, she thought, she had not fallen in love with Albert at all, but simply regarded him as a most perfect companion. Always cheerful and amusing, he was at the same time seriously intellectual and had the capacity of throwing himself heart and soul into whatever he happened to be doing. He and Jane had spent much of their time collecting together all the Victorian odds-and-ends that they could find in the house. These they assembled in the billiard-room, where Albert was now busy photographing them for a brochure which he intended to produce entitled 'Recent Finds at Dalloch Castle,' and which was to form a supplement to his larger work, 'Household Art of the Nineteenth Century.'

Jane, who had up till then maintained a wholesome superiority with regard to everything Victorian, quickly smothered this feeling, and learnt from Albert really to admire the bead stools, lacquer boxes, wax flowers and albums of water-colour sketches which so fascinated him.

They practically lived in the billiard-room, hard at work the whole time, Albert making still-life compositions for his photographs, while Jane copied designs from chintzes and pieces of needlework in water-colours.

One day she was poking about in the attics trying to find more treasures for the catalogue when she noticed, poked away in a corner behind piles of furniture, a dusty glass dome. After a dangerous climb over rickety chests of drawers, derelict bedsteads and other rubbish, she managed to secure it and carry it to her bedroom, where she carefully removed the dome, which was opaque with dirt, expecting to discover some more wax fruit. Underneath it, however, she found to her amazement a representation in white wax of Jacob's

Ladder. It was quite perfect. Jacob, in a sort of night-gown and an enormous beard, lay upon a floor of green plush. His head rested on a large square stone, and from just behind this rose the ladder, delicately balanced against wax clouds which billowed out of the green plush. Two angels were rather laboriously climbing on it (whether up or down it would be hard to say), while three more angels, supported by wires which rose from behind the clouds, hovered round about, twitching and quivering delightfully whenever the stand was moved.

Jane washed and replaced the dome, and then carried this treasure down to the billiard-room in great triumph. When Albert saw it his joy and delight knew no bounds.

'It is easily our most important find and shall be the frontispiece of my book!' he cried. 'I have never seen anything half so lovely. It is a poem! How can I find out the name of the artist? I must endeavour to do so without delay. But how sad, my dear, to think that this jewel should belong to people who so evidently have no feeling for beauty! It ought, of course, to occupy a place of honour in a museum. Never mind, I shall photograph it from every angle and in all lights, so that the artistic public will be able to gain some slight idea of its exquisite form, and thus share, to a certain extent, in my own emotions.'

At that moment Lady Prague was seen to pass by the open door, and Albert, longing to share his enthusiasm with somebody, rather thoughtlessly dashed out, seized her by the arm, and said:

'Lady Prague, do come and see our wonderful new find. Something to cause the greatest sensation among all cultured persons—so amusing, so exquisite, so stimulating. . . .'

With the naïveté of a child showing off its new toy he led her up to the dome.

She stared at it for a moment, sniffed and said rather pityingly:

'What a lot of drip you do talk. Why, that's nothing more than a particularly unattractive form of dust-trap!'

She left the room.

All the excitement died out of Albert's face and was succeeded by an expression of the deepest disgust.

'Dust-trap!' he muttered between his teeth. 'You just wait until you see the booby-trap I'm going to make for you—you viviparous old vixen!'

Walter and Sally now came in and made up for Lady Prague's lack of appreciation by an enthusiasm almost as unbounded as Albert's. They walked round and round the dome, exclaiming:

'How beautiful!'—'How amusing!'—'That angel's so like Lord Prague, d'you see? And, of course, Jacob just *is* the admiral with a beard!'

> *'Green plush.*
> *Admiral Jacob lay beneath a dome*
> *Of crazy glass upon green plush.*
> *And in this "nautical" posture*
> *With angels rising from the Guinness foam*
> *The Admiral*
> *(Who was Jacob, too, out of the Bible)*
> *Fell, bucolically, asleep.'*

Even Lady Brenda was quite appreciative, saying that her children would simply love it.

'It reminds me so much of a lodging-house at Westgate where we used to go for our summer holidays when we were small. Every room in it had several domes of that sort.'

Albert breathlessly asked the address of this gold mine, but Lady Brenda had forgotten it and presently left them to go out fishing.

'What a disappointing woman that is,' said Jane when she had gone. 'I noticed her particularly in the train coming up here, and somehow thought she looked rather interesting. And then, when I heard her name, I was really excited to meet her. One's always being told how charming she is—so original and cultured. But she's a perfect fool, though I must say quite nice compared to old Prague.'

'She *is* cultured in the worst sort of way,' said Albert. 'But original! Oh, dear! I had a long conversation with her yesterday after tea so I know all about her originality. I'll tell you. She has, as I had supposed that she would, a green drawing-room with flower pictures which she picked up cheap (eighteenth century, so she says). She also has a stone-coloured dining-room with a sham stone floor. On the sideboard is a model of a ship. On the walls are old maps. The lights are shaded with maps. The firescreen is a map in needlework. The chairs are covered with *petit point* which she worked herself. Her bedroom is "very modern"; that is to say, it is painted silver and stippled all over. The ceiling is of Lalique glass as is the bed. The bathroom is painted to give the impression of a submarine forest. It has portholes instead of windows. I couldn't quite understand why.

'She reads few novels, but a great many "lives" and "memoirs." Her favourite novelists are Galsworthy, Masefield, David Garnett and Maurois, she "loves modern pictures, especially flower pictures," and admires some of John's portraits, but thinks Orpen the finest living artist. She has never been to the Tate Gallery, but always means to go.

'All this she told me herself, or rather I dug it out of her. I also gathered that she goes every year to the Ascot races in one of those picture-hats and a printed dress.'

'Four of them, you mean,' said Jane.

'Very likely. She goes quite often to the Embassy Night Club, but seldom stays up later than one or two o'clock. She has a great deal of committee work when in London, mostly connected with animals. Every year she goes for three weeks to Switzerland. Captain Chadlington prefers to stay at home and kill (foxes and birds), so she always goes with her great friend, Major Lagge, chaperoned by his sister and brother-in-law. Those sort of women, I have so often noticed, never take lovers, but they have some great friend with whom they go about literally like brother and sister. It is all most peculiar and unhealthy. I think, myself, that she is a creature so overbred that there is no sex or brain left, only nerves and the herd instinct. There are many like that in English society, a sufficiently uninteresting species. I find her, in a way, beautiful.'

'Oh, yes, she is certainly that,' said Jane, 'although personally, I can't admire her very much. She has such a maddening expression. And she's really very nice, too, you know. She's been sweet to Sally and me.'

'And her husband is good-looking. But what a dreary personality he has, most uncompanionable. I suppose he will in time become a sort of Murgatroyd, although I doubt whether he will ever acquire that *joie de vivre* which so characterizes the dear general.'

'Beastly old man!'

'Ah, no, Jane! I must admit to a very great *penchant* for the general. He is so delightfully uncompromising. Yesterday I heard him say that before the War the things he hated most were Roman Catholics and Negroes, but now, he said, banging on the table, now it's Germans. I wonder what he would do if he met a Roman Catholic Negro with a German father! Dare I dress up as one and see? I could black my face, wear a rosary and Prussian boots and come in crossing myself and singing "The Watch on the Rhine" to the tune of a Negro spiritual.'

Jane laughed.

'I'm afraid you must think me rather idiotic, my dear Jane. I have been in such spirits since I came up here. I can assure you that I am quite a different person in Paris—all hard work and no play, or very little. But, after all, it is the "hols." here, as we used to say, and talking of "hols.," do help me to think out a good practical joke for Lady Prague. How I hate that old woman! Do you think she and the general—Ah! General! What a delightful surprise! I imagined that you were busy stalking those grouse again.'

'No, Gates, we are not. Very few moors can be shot over more than four times a week, you know.'

'That *must* be a relief,' said Albert sympathetically.

The general looked with some disapproval at his *matelot* clothes—a pair of baggy blue trousers worn with a blue-and-white sweater and a scarlet belt, and said severely:

'If you will be so good as to clear that mess off the table, we were going to play billiards.'

'Oh, sir, this is dreadful! You could not possibly play on the floor, I suppose? No? Well, if you'll most kindly wait for one moment while I photograph this exquisite object which Jane has found, I shall be really grateful.'

Captain Chadlington and Admiral Wenceslaus now came in. The admiral was airing his favourite topic, Blockade.

'Oh, it was a terrible scandal. Thirty thousand tons of toffee found their way through Holland alone, my dear Chadlington, and this is a most conservative estimate, worked out by my friend Jinks (whose book on the subject I have lent to your wife). Many of the Germans taken prisoner at that time by our chaps had their pockets bulging British toffee. British toffee, my dear Chadlington!

'And then,' he added, with a catch in his voice, 'the glycerine!'

'Were their pockets bulging with that, too?' asked Captain Chadlington, who, as a prospective candidate for Parliament, was always ready to learn.

'Not their pockets. Dear me, no! Far, far worse than that—their shell-cases!'

'Oh, I say! That's disgraceful!'

'It is! Monstrous! But what I want to know is—who was the traitor? Read Page on the subject. He couldn't understand it—not a word. He couldn't make out what we were driving at. Why don't they blockade?—What on earth are you doing, Gates?'

Albert, balanced gracefully on a step-ladder, was taking a photograph of the Jacob's Ladder as seen from above.

'There,' he said, 'that's done. Now I will clear the table and you can play your little game.'

10

Jane and Albert did not stay to watch the billiards but strolled into the garden.

'I saw them playing yesterday evening,' said Albert. 'It is a curious but not a graceful game, and terribly monotonous. If it weren't such a beautiful day I should have advised you to watch them for a little, all the same: it is always interesting to see how others find their recreation. They play with ivory balls and long, tapering sticks.'

'Yes, I know,' said Jane. 'Look! there's Mr. Buggins sketching.'

'How delightful. We must go and talk to him.'

Mr. Buggins was sketching the old part of the house in water-colours; that is to say, he had drawn it with a pencil and was now busy colouring it in with small, rather dry brushes. It was careful work.

When he saw Albert approaching he was very much embarrassed, knowing quite well the attitude of the professional artist to the painstaking amateur; so, to cover his own confusion and to save Albert from feeling obliged to make a polite criticism of his work, he began to talk very fast about the house and its history.

'I love this part of the house, you know. That tower, and of course, the dungeons, were all that escaped the Great Fire in 1850. It is immensely old, probably eleventh century, and the walls are so thick that Lady Craigdalloch has been able to put two water-closets in the thickness alone.'

'How jolly for her!' said Albert, feeling that some remark was called for.

'Yes, very. Of course you know the history attaching to that tower?'

'No; do tell us, Mr. Buggins. I was thinking that there must be some legends connected with the castle.'

Jane and Albert sat down on the grass, and Mr. Buggins, clearing his throat, began his story.

'One of the Thanes of Dalloch,' he said, 'as they were then called, had a very beautiful daughter, the Lady Muscatel. Her apartment was in that tower, where she would sit all day spinning. At night, when the moon was full, she would often lean out of her window and gaze at it, and one night she was doing so when she heard from beneath her a faint noise of singing. Looking down, she beheld the handsome features of a young man of high degree, who told her that he had lost his way while out hunting.

'"Alas!" she said, "my father and brothers are from home, and I dare not open to you in their absence."

'He told her that he would not dream of trespassing on her hospitality and retired, fortified by a bottle of wine which she lowered to him in a basket.

'The next night he came again, and the next, and soon they were passionately in love with each other. But little did the unfortunate Muscatel realize that her lover was the only son of Thane McBane, head of a clan which her father was even then planning to exterminate. The warlike preparations for this raid which were going forward in the castle left the Lady Muscatel more and more to her own devices, so that one day she was able to leave her tower and go with Ronnie McBane to the nearest priest, who married them. Even so they dared not fly, but thought it better to wait until they should hear of a ship bound for France. Poor children! They knew full well that both their fathers would see them dead sooner than married (for Ronnie had by now divulged his fearful secret).

'At last Dalloch's preparations were completed and he and his men sallied forth, armed to the teeth, to wipe out the McBanes. The battle was a fearful one, but the conclusion was foregone. The unfortunate McBanes, taken unawares and overwhelmed by numbers, fought with the courage of desperation. One by one they fell, but each one that died accounted for three or four of the Dallochs. Ronnie McBane

71

was the last to succumb, and when he did so, bleeding from forty desperate wounds, it was with the knowledge that no fewer than thirty-two of his enemies, slain by his own hand, had preceded him. It was one of the bloodiest fights in the history of the clans.

'That evening the Lady Muscatel heard sounds of merry-making in the great hall, where her father and the wild clansmen were celebrating their victory with wine and song. She went down to see what was happening and the first thing that met her eyes was Ronnie's head, horribly mutilated, on a pike. The shock proved too much for her reason and she soon became insane, wandering about the house and crying for her lost love. When her child was born neither she nor it survived many days.

'They say that at the full moon she can still be heard, wailing, wailing; and some even declare that they have seen her wan form, carrying the head of her lover.

'But surely you have heard the *Lament of the Lady Muscatel?* No? It is a beautiful ballad. Personally, I think it one of the most beautiful that Scotland has produced, although it is comparatively little known. Let me see if I can remember it.' And clearing his throat, he recited the following ballad:

THE LAMENT OF THE LADY MUSCATEL

My lo'e he war winsome, my lo'e he war braw, [1]
Every nicht 'neath my windie he cam'.
He wad sing, oh, sae saft, till the nicht it waur o'er
I' the morn he was sadly gang ham'.

> *The pibroch i' the glen is bonny,*
> *But waley, waley, wheer's ma Ronnie?*

His e'en they were blew and his mou [2] *it war red,*
And his philabeg [3] *cam' to the knee;*
But noo ma puir Ronnie he's skaithless and deid,
Ah, wud that I a'so could dee.

> *The pibroch i' the glen is bonny,*
> *But waley, waley, wheer's ma Ronnie?*

[1] Brave.   [2] Mouth.   [3] Kilt.

I ganged ma gait sairly to yon branksome brae,
Wheer ma true lo'e war killed i' the ficht,
I sat on a creepy[4] and I greeted[5] the day,
And I sat greeting there till the nicht.

> *The pibroch i' the glen is bonny,*
> *But waley, waley, wheer's ma Ronnie?*

Ah, Ronnie, my true lo'e, ah, Ronnie, mine ane,
Shall I niver muir see ye ava?
I see your life's bluid poured out o'er yonder stane,
But your sperrit has flane far awa.

> *The pibroch i' the glen is bonny,*
> *But waley, waley, wheer's ma Ronnie?*

They gave me your heid, Ronnie, wropped oop i' sae,[6]
And I buried it 'neath yonder saugh;[7]
For ye've left me, my Ronnie, to gang a' agley
And I niver shall see ye nae muir.

> *The pibroch i' the glen is bonny,*
> *But waley, waley, wheer's ma Ronnie?*

Ma mither she mad' me ane parritch o' kail,
And she gave me ane snood for ma heid;
But a' I can do is to greet and to wail,
Ah, Mither, I wud I were deid.

> *The pibroch i' the glen is bonny,*
> *But waley, waley, wheer's ma Ronnie?*

But e'er the sun rise, Mither, muir o'er the brae,
And e'er ane muir morrow shall dawn;
My heid on its pillow sae saftly I'll lay,
But ma sperrit to him will ha' flawn.

> *The pirbroch i' the glen is bonny,*
> *But waley, waley, wheer's ma Ronnie?*

There was a short silence, broken by Albert, who said:
'How beautiful, and what a touching story! We must tell it

---

[4] Little stool.   [6] Silk.
[5] Cried, bewailed.   [7] Willow tree.

to Walter; he will be so much interested and might, I feel, write one of his charming poems round it. I think the ballad quite the finest I have ever heard.'

'I think so, too,' said Mr. Buggins, who had rarely known such an appreciative audience and was greatly enjoying himself. 'To the student of mediaeval Scottish history it is, of course, extremely illuminating, being so full of allusions to old customs, many of which survived until quite recently.'

'Were there many allusions of that sort?' asked Albert. 'They escaped me.'

'Yes, of course, because you are not conversant with the history of those times. But take, for instance, the line: "And his philabeg cam' to the knee." This is very significant when you know, as I do, that only three clans in all Scotland wore their philabeg to the knee—that is, covering the knee: the McBanes, the Duffs of Ogle and the McFeas. Their reasons for doing so open up many aspects of clan history. The McBanes wore it to the knee in memory of Thane Angus McBane, who, when hiding from the English soldiery in some bracken was given away by the shine of his knees; his subsequent brutal treatment and shameful death will, of course, be well known to you.'

'Of course,' murmured Albert, not wishing to appear too ignorant. 'This is all so fascinating,' he added. 'Why did the other two tribes wear it to the knee?'

'The Duffs of Ogle because they used a very curious type of long bow which could only be drawn kneeling. (You will often have heard the expression: "To Duff down," meaning "to kneel.") This gave great numbers of them a sort of housemaid's knee, so one of the Thanes gave an order that their philabegs must be made long enough for them to kneel on. The McFeas, of course, have always worn it very long on account of the old saw:

> *"Should McFea show the knee,*
> *The Devil's curse upon him be."*

Am I boring you?'

'On the contrary,' said Albert, 'I am very deeply

74

interested. I have so often wondered what the origin of "to Duff down" could be and now I know. Do tell us some more.'

'You may remember,' continued Mr. Buggins, 'that one verse of the Lady Muscatel's ballad begins:

'*"They gave me your heid, Ronnie, wropped oop i' sae."*

'This, of course, sounds rather peculiar—*sae*, you know, is *silk*—until you remember that only a man who had killed with his own hand in fair battle over forty warriors was entitled to have "his heid wropped oop i' sae" after his death. It was an honour that was very eagerly sought by all the clansmen and it must have consoled the Lady Muscatel in her great sorrow that she was able "to wrop her beloved's heid oop i' sae." There is a very curious legend connected with this custom.

'A young laird of Tomintoul died, they say of poison, in his bed, having only killed in his lifetime some thirty-nine warriors. His widow was distracted with grief and, although about to become a mother, she cut off his right hand, clasped it round a dirk and went herself into the thick of the fight. When she had slain one man with her husband's hand, she was able to go home and "wrop his heid oop i' sae." The Tomintouls to this day have as their family crest a severed hand with a dirk in memory of Brave Meg, as she was called. Those were strangely savage days, I often think.'

'Tell us some more,' said Jane.

'Let me see: what else can I remember? Oh, yes. The Lady Muscatel goes on to say: "I buried him 'neath yonder saugh." Up to comparatively recent times any man who had been killed by his father-in-law's clansmen was buried beneath a *saugh* (willow tree). There are some parts of Scotland where it would be impossible to find a saugh for miles that had not a grassy mound before it, telling a bloody tale. Tradition says that Ronnie's body was later exhumed and laid beside those of his wife and child in the chapel. "I sat on a creepy." A creepy was a wooden stool, often three-legged, on which women would sit to greet (or bewail) the loss of a loved one killed in the fight.'

'But was the fight always going on?' asked Albert.

'Very, very constantly. The wild clansmen were generally engaged in deadly feuds, which were often continued over many generations and were treated almost as a religion.'

'What,' asked Jane, 'is a "parritch o' kail"?'

'I am glad you mentioned that. *A parritch o' kail* is a curious and very intoxicating drink made of cabbage and oatmeal. Perhaps her mother hoped that the Lady Muscatel would drown her sorrows in it. Dear me!' he said, gathering up his painting materials, 'how I must have bored you.'

'My dear sir,' cried Albert, *'tout au contraire!* I'm entranced. But tell us one thing before you go. Have you ever seen the Lady Muscatel's ghost?'

'Alas! I have not; but Craigdalloch says that as a child he saw her constantly, sometimes looking out of the window' (he pointed to a little window in the tower)—'but more often walking in the great corridor which leads to her apartment. He has told me that she wears a grey wimple snood (you remember that she refers to a *snood* in the ballad), and carries in one hand a sort of parcel—the "heid," no doubt, "wropped oop i' sae." She is supposed to walk when the moon is full.'

The rasping voice of Lady Prague suddenly broke in upon them, causing Albert and Mr. Buggins to leap to their feet.

'Who is supposed to walk when the moon is full?'

Mr. Buggins told her the story rather shortly.

'Well,' she said, 'and I suppose you believe that sort of balderdash. Tosh—bosh and nonsense! Personally, I shall believe in ghosts when I have seen one, and not before. Surely you must have noticed by now that everyone knows somebody else who has seen a ghost, but they've never seen one themselves.'

'But Craig has seen the Lady Muscatel.'

'Craig! Silly old man, he'd see anything. I expect it was really a housemaid, if you ask me.'

She blew her nose and went towards the castle.

'Such a golden nature,' said Albert pensively. 'One would

76

hardly credit her with second sight, but still one never knows: the most unlikely people see ghosts—sometimes.'

That night Lady Prague took her bath, as she always did, before going to bed. She lay in the water for some time without washing very much; then dried herself briskly and put on a linen night-dress trimmed with crochet-lace, a pair of quilted slippers and a Chinese kimono with storks and fir-trees embroidered all over it. Thus attired, with her hair screwed in to a small lump on the top of her head, and a towel and a pair of combinations over one arm, she sallied forth into the great corridor. As she did so she noticed that the lights, by some mistake, had all been put out; but she was easily able to see her way because a curtain at the other end of the corridor was drawn back and a great shaft of moonlight fell through the window on to the carpet.

Lady Prague shuffled along until she had nearly reached her bedroom door, when suddenly she stood still, rooted to the ground with terror. A female form, immensely tall and unnatural-looking, had stepped into the shaft of moonlight. In its hand was a sort of round parcel which it held out towards the paralysed peeress; then, emitting a soft but terrifying wail, it vanished into the shadows. The sound of this wail seemed to unloosen Lady Prague's own tongue, and shriek upon piercing shriek resounded through the house.

Bedroom doors on every side now flew open and startled guests rushed out to the assistance of the fainting baroness. Albert, one of the first to be on the spot, quickly helped the poor lady to a chair, where she sat and rocked herself to and fro, moaning and sobbing in a distracted manner.

'What is the matter, Lady Prague?' said Albert sharply. 'Come, come now, you must try and pull yourself together: you are hysterical, you know. What is it? Are you ill?'

'Oh, oh! oh!' said Lady Prague in a sort of moaning sing-song. 'I saw her! I saw her! I saw her!'

'Whom did you see?'

'Oh! oh! oh! I saw her! . . . Lady Muscatel! She was over by that window. . . . Oh! oh! oh!'

'Fetch some water, Jane dear, will you?' said Albert. 'Now, Lady Prague, you are quite safe, you know, with us.'

'Let her talk about it,' said Mr. Buggins in an undertone, 'it will do her good. How I envy you, Lady Prague: it has been the dream of my life to see someone from another world and, of all people, Muscatel. How did she look?'

'Oh! oh! oh! . . . Dreadful! . . . All in grey, with a wimple snood. . . .'

'Nonsense!' said Albert, but nobody heard him.

'And she was holding a sort of parcel. . . . Oh! oh! oh!'

'The heid, no doubt, "wropped oop i' sae." *How* I do envy you! She didn't speak, I suppose?'

'Oh! oh! oh! . . . Yes, she did. She did: "Ronnie! Ronnie! mine ane Ronnie!"'

'Oh, you old liar!' said Albert, under his breath.

Jane, on her way back with a glass of water, nearly tripped up over something outside Albert's bedroom. It proved on investigation to be a large bath sponge wrapped up in a silk handkerchief. Suspicions that she had already entertained as to the true identity of the Lady Muscatel now crystallized into certainty. She put the sponge into Albert's bed; then, controlling her laughter, she rejoined the others and gave the water to Lady Prague, who drank it gratefully. She appeared to be partially restored and was describing her experience in some detail, looking searchingly at Albert as she did so.

'The worst part,' she said, 'of the whole thing was the creature's face, which I saw quite plainly in the moonlight. It was not so much mad as foolish and idiotic. Really, I assure you, the stupidest face I ever saw.'

'She has guessed,' thought Jane.

'Come, Lady Prague,' said Albert, 'not as bad as all that surely; not idiotic?'

'Perhaps *wanting*, more than idiotic, and hideous beyond belief.'

Later, when they were all returning to their rooms and peace had descended upon the house, Jane said to Albert:

'You know, my dear, she scored in the end.'

'I'm afraid,' he replied, 'that she did.'

11

'Suddenly, just in time, I realized that he was a filthy Hun, so of course I turned my back on him and refused to shake hands. I think he noticed; anyway, I hope so. I hope he felt his position.'

General Murgatroyd looked round triumphantly. It was the end of dinner. The women had left the dining-room, and the general who had been shooting that day with the son of an old friend who had taken a neighbouring moor, was telling his experiences.

'Quite right, Murgatroyd. That's the way to treat 'em—the swine! Now, if only we had blockaded them from the very first he wouldn't have been alive to-day, with any luck.'

The admiral swilled off his seventh glass of port.

'Never shake hands with niggers, Catholics or Germans if I can help it,' continued the general.

Walter, knowing that Albert was an ardent pacifist and foreseeing some trouble, tried to change the conversation by asking him how his work had progressed that day; but the latter, whose face was burning, took no notice of him. Leaning towards General Murgatroyd he said in a level voice:

'Is this the way you always behave when you meet an ex-enemy, even under the roof of a mutual friend?'

'Of course—the filthy swine!' shouted the general. 'And so would you, young man, if you'd been through the last war. I think it's the most shocking thing—the way some of you young people have quite forgotten what your elders suffered in those four years.'

'We haven't exactly forgotten it,' said Albert; 'but it was never anything to do with us. It was your war and I hope you enjoyed it, that's all,' he added, losing all control over himself. 'You made it, as you are trying, by disgusting rudeness to citizens of a great and friendly nation, to make another one, trying your very hardest, too, on your own admission. But let me tell you that even when you have succeeded, even when you have brought another war upon us, it won't be any good. None of my generation will go and fight. We don't care for wars, you see. We have other things to think about.'

'Albert, *please*!' said Walter, 'don't let's talk about this any more,' he begged; but no one paid any attention to him.

Great veins stood out on the general's forehead.

'Do you mean that you would sit still and do nothing to prevent your country being invaded, governed, by a lot of filthy foreigners?'

'Really, General, I cannot feel that it would necessarily harm the country. Many of us hope in time to see, under one government, the United States of Europe, which was Napoleon's dream. The Germans are a people of undoubted culture and known for their exceptional efficiency. I daresay we should be no worse off under their administration than we are at present. If it is on sentimental grounds that you object to it, remember that for over a hundred years of undoubted prosperity England was ruled over by German—even German-speaking sovereigns.'

The general tried to speak, but Albert continued ruthlessly:

'People of your class notoriously enjoy wars and fighting. This is only natural. You have been educated to that end. Your very recreations consist entirely in killing things, and it is clearly more exciting to kill men than rabbits or foxes. But in future you will do well to avoid stirring up the great civilized nations against each other. That's all.'

'Quite right,' said Lord Prague, who imagined from the few words that had penetrated to his consciousness and from Albert's impassioned manner that he was reviling all foreigners. 'That is the proper spirit, Mr. Gates. Down with the Huns! Down with the Frogs! Down with the Macaronis!

80

Down with Uncle Sam! England for the English!'

Exhausted by the effort of this oration he lay back once more in his chair and closed his eyes.

Nobody paid any attention to him, and there was a long silence, accentuated by heavy breathing and the sound of the admiral gulping down his thirteenth glass of port.

At last it was broken by Mr. Buggins.

'Gates is, of course, entitled to his own opinions. I can see his point of view although, naturally, it differs from my own. Being very young and very enthusiastic, he expresses himself violently and rashly and probably says a great deal more than he means. None the less, there is something to be said for his argument.

'All cultured persons are, to a certain extent, cosmopolitan. They feel at home among people of equal culture to whatever nationality they may happen to belong. I feel this very strongly myself. Italy is to me a second Fatherland; although I have no Italian blood I feel as much at home there as I do in England, having perhaps more congenial friends in Rome than I have anywhere else.

'Gates, who is an artist—may I remind you?—of recognized ability, would feel naturally more at his ease among other artists, whatever their nationality, than he would, say, in the company of English foxhunting squires.

'Artists, poets, musicians and writers are, of course, less affected by the governments under whose rule they may happen to find themselves than perhaps any other class. Therefore, it is hardly surprising if they do not greatly mind what form that government takes—'

'Then are loyalty and patriotism to count for nothing?' the general interrupted in a furious voice.

'Nothing at all!' said Lord Prague, who had opened his eyes again and appeared anxious to take part in the argument.

'Patriotism,' said Albert, 'is a virtue which I have never understood. That it should exist in any but the most primitive minds has always mystified me. I regard it as one step higher than the Chinese family worship, but it seems to me that at

81

our stage of civilization we should have got past all that sort of thing.

'I am very glad, certainly, to be English-speaking. That I regard as a very great advantage, both as a matter of convenience and also because there is no language so rich in literature. Otherwise, what is there to be proud of in this hideous island, where architecture generally vies with scenery to offend the eye and which has produced no truly great men, none to compare with, for instance, Napoleon?'

'I should have thought, my dear Gates, if I may say so, that with your strongly pacifist views you would look upon Napoleon as the most despicable of men,' said Mr. Buggins.

'No, indeed; Napoleon was the greatest of all pacifists. He fought only for peace, and would have achieved what I spoke of just now—the United States of Europe, except for the jealous and pettifogging policy of certain British statesmen.'

'That, I should say, is a matter of opinion, and I doubt whether you are right,' said Mr. Buggins. 'But at the same time, Gates, there is something I should like to say to you, which is, that I think you have no right to speak as you did of the men who fought in the War, sneering at them and hoping they enjoyed it, and so on. I know you did not really mean to say much, but remember that sort of thing does no good and only creates more bitterness between our two generations, as though enough did not exist already. I know that many of us seem to you narrow-minded, stupid and unproductive. But if you would look a little bit below the surface you might realize that there is a reason for this. Some of us spent four of what should have been our best years in the trenches.

'At the risk of boring I will put my own case before you.

'When the War broke out I was twenty-eight. I had adopted literature as my profession and was at that time art critic on several newspapers. I had also written and published two books involving a great deal of hard work and serious research—the first, a life of Don John of Austria, the second, an exhaustive treatise on the life and work of Cervantes. Both were well received and, encouraged by this, I was, in 1914, engaged upon an extensive history of Spain in the time of

Philip II, dealing in some detail with, for instance, the art of Velasquez and El Greco, the events which led to the battle of Lepanto, the religious struggle in the Netherlands, and so on. I had been working hard at this for three years and had collected most of my material.

'On the 5th August, 1914, whether rightly or wrongly, but true to the tradition in which I had been brought up, I enlisted in the army. Later in that year I received a commission. I will not enlarge upon the ensuing years, but I can't say that I found them very enjoyable.

'When, in 1919, I was demobilized, I found that, as far as my work was concerned, my life was over—at the age of thirty-three. I was well off financially. I had leisure at my disposal. I had my copious notes. Perhaps—no doubt, in fact—it was a question of nerves. Whatever the reason, I can assure you that I was truly incapable of such concentrated hard work as that book would have required. I had lost interest in my subject and faith in myself. The result is that I am now an oldish man, of certain culture, I hope, but unproductive, an amateur and a dilettante. I know it. I despise myself for it, but I cannot help it.

'And that, I am convinced, is more or less the story of hundreds of my contemporaries.

'Everybody knows—you are at no pains to conceal it—that the young people of to-day despise and dislike the men and women of my age. I suppose that never since the world began have two generations been so much at variance. You think us superficial, narrow-minded, tasteless and sterile, and you are right. But who knows what we might have become if things had been different?

'That is why I do earnestly beg of you not to speak sarcastically, as you did just now, of the men who fought in the War. Leave us, at any rate, the illusion that we were right to do so.'

'Oh dear!' said Albert. 'How you do misunderstand me! I suppose I must express myself very badly. Of course I feel the greatest respect and admiration for the men who fought. I am only criticizing those unprincipled members of the governing

83

classes (of all nationalities) who made it necessary for them to do so—men to whose interest it is that there should be wars. Professional soldiers, for instance, must naturally wish for war or all their work and training of years would be for nothing. Many politicians find in it a wonderful opportunity for self-aggrandizement. Certain business men make vast fortunes out of it. These are the people who are responsible. They educate the young to believe that war is right so that when they have manufactured it they are supported by all classes.

'But they ought to be regarded with the deepest distrust by their fellow citizens, instead of which they are set up as national heroes. I would have their statues removed from all public places and put where they belong—in the Chamber of Horrors—thus serving the cause both of Art and of Morals.'

He glared at the general, who returned his black looks with interest, but could not trust himself to speak.

'General Murgatroyd,' continued Albert, 'provoked this discussion by actually boasting (though I don't know how he can dare even to admit such a thing) that he is doing his best in every way to make another war. Not content with rising in his bloody profession over the dead bodies of hundreds of innocent men, he evidently continues to be a propagandist of the most insidious and dangerous type. Happily, however, mankind is beginning to realize that war is of all crimes the most degraded; and when, which will soon happen, the great majority holds that view, peace will be permanent and universal. Generals, on that rapidly approaching day, will become as extinct as the dodo, relegated to the farcical side of drama and the films.'

'Come!' exclaimed Mr. Buggins, feeling that enough had now been said, 'come, Mowbray, and have a game of billiards.'

But the general, deeply incensed, retired to the study, where he listened to *Iolanthe* on the wireless and read his favourite book, *Tegetmeer on Pheasants*.

Admiral Wenceslaus, having finished the port, tottered off to bed, eye in hand, singing, 'The more we are together.'

12

After this rather acrimonious dinner, Albert, noticing that there was a very lovely full moon and that the air outside was warm and mellow, suggested to Jane that they should go out for a little walk. She thought that it would be a good idea. The evenings at Dalloch were apt to be rather boring. Lady Prague had introduced a particularly odious form of paper game, called briefly and appropriately 'Lists,' which consisted of seeing who could make the longest list of boys' names, fishes, kinds of material, diseases and such things beginning with a certain letter. As Lady Prague herself always chose both the subject and the letter, and as she invariably won, it was felt, no doubt unjustly, that she sat up for hours every night with a dictionary preparing herself for the next game. The only time they had played anything else it had been at Albert's suggestion—Consequences, but this was not an unqualified success.

For the erotic Lady Prague to meet the sobered-up Admiral Wenceslaus in a bedroom, undressing; for her to say to him, 'What about it?'; for him to say to her, 'My eye!'; for the consequence to be that they had nine children in three lots of triplets; and for the world to say, 'The only compensation for regurgitation is re-assimilation,' had been considered too embarrassing to risk repetition. (Albert, accused afterwards of cheating, had hotly denied the charge.)

'I couldn't have faced "Lists" again,' said Jane as they walked away from the castle. 'Somehow I seem to get worse and worse at it. Last night, for instance, I couldn't even think of one vegetable beginning with "c", of course—*cabbage*. It was too idiotic; all I could think of was brussels sprouts and broccoli; and I knew they were wrong.'

'Yes; indeed; it is ghastly. The diseases are the most embarrassing, though.'

'And the vices. I think it's a horrid game.'

Albert told her of the conversation that had just taken place in the dining-room and asked what her feelings were on the subject.

'Oh! the same as yours! All young people must surely agree about that except, I suppose, young soldiers, but I don't count them anyway.'

Jane had once been in love for a short time with an officer in the Guards and had looked upon the army with a jaundiced eye ever since. (She had treated him abominably.)

'Mr. Buggins agrees with us, too. Of course, he had to qualify his approval with the general listening like that, but I could see exactly what he really meant. I think him so charming; at first he seemed a little tiresome with all his culture and folk-lore and good taste, but now I'm becoming very fond of him. He told us a lot about himself after dinner, but never mentioned anything about his wife. I wonder when all that happened?'

'Poor man! He looks dreadfully sad, I always think. He's the only nice one among the grown-ups here, isn't he?'

'Yes, indeed he is. I don't know what would have happened this evening if he hadn't been there. I should probably have insulted General Murgatroyd even more than I did, and then have been obliged to leave the house, the very last thing I wish to do at the moment.'

Jane suddenly began to feel embarrassed. It had come upon her lately with a certainty born of experience that Albert was falling in love with her, and now she began to think from the absent-minded way in which he spoke and his general manner that he was about to make some sort of declaration. This was the very last thing Jane wanted to happen.

She had been considering the situation and had decided that although she liked Albert more than anybody she had ever met, and although she would probably marry him in the end, she was not at present in love with him. On the other hand she did not at all want to lose him entirely, which might happen if he proposed and was refused. She was anxious for things to go on as they were at present. So she kept up a sort of barrage of rather foolish, nervous chatter.

'Do you know,' said Albert interrupting her in the middle of a sentence, and standing still, 'that I'm in love with you, Jane?'

Her heart sank.

'Are you, Albert?' she said faintly, wondering what the next move would be.

There was a silence. Albert, taking her hand, kissed her fingers one by one.

'Well?'

Jane said nothing. He took her in his arms and began kissing her face.

'Do you love me, darling?'

Jane felt frightened suddenly of committing herself to anything and said in an unnatural way:

'Albert, I don't know—I'm not sure.'

He let go of her at once, saying rather coldly: 'No, I see. Well, if you change your mind you'd better tell me, will you? Let's go on walking, it's such a lovely night.'

She thought this would be almost too embarrassing, but soon felt curiously at her ease, as though nothing had happened at all. They were in a wood of little fir trees which reminded her of a German fairy story she had been fond of as a child. She told it to Albert as they walked along. Presently, they came out of the wood on to the open moor. The moon, which was enormous, shone in a perfectly empty sky; the moor looked like the sea. There was a very complete silence.

As they stood there for a moment before turning back, Jane suddenly realized with a wave of feeling how much she loved Albert. She passionately hoped now that he would take her in his arms and kiss her, but he did not do so and a strange feeling of shyness prevented her from making an opening for him.

After standing there for some time in silence they returned to the castle, talking quite naturally about everyday things. They found that all the others had gone to bed, and crept up the back stairs in complete darkness, saying good night affectionately when they reached their bedrooms.

Jane lay awake for hours that night, tingling all over with excitement and trying to concentrate on the foregoing events with some degree of calmness.

'He never said anything about marriage,' she thought. 'Probably he has no intention of marrying me: artists seldom want the extra responsibility of a wife. And then he probably has very modern ideas on the subject. No, he evidently means it to be just an *affaire*. Anyhow, to-morrow I shall tell him that I love him. Then, if he wants me to be his mistress, we can run away to Paris together when we leave here, but not before. I can't have Sally involved.'

Jane was delighted with this idea. Marriage had always seemed to her rather a dull and pompous business, but to run away to Paris as the mistress of a handsome young artist would be the height of romance, and would probably scandalize her parents and relations. (Jane's one mission in life seemed to be to alienate her family, of whom she was, if she had only realized it, extremely fond, and nobody would have been more upset or annoyed than she herself if she had succeeded.)

As she lay watching the flickering firelight she suddenly had a mental vision of Albert's good-looking face as it had appeared when he said, 'Do you love me, darling?'

'Yes! yes! yes! Albert, sweetest, I do! And I'll tell you so to-morrow.'

And Jane fell rapturously asleep.

She was awakened at a very early hour by the sound of furious voices in the hall. She knew that this indicated the departure of the shooters (or guns) for another happy day on the moors.

'But why "guns",' she thought sleepily. 'After all, one doesn't speak of people as "paint brushes" or "pens". And why does it always make them cross when they are supposed to enjoy it so enormously? Of course, they simply loathe it really, poor things, and no wonder.'

General Murgatroyd and Lady Prague came out of the

front door and stood just underneath Jane's open window talking angrily.

'Young puppy, I call him! Should like to give him a good thrashing. I couldn't speak, I was so angry, and Buggins more or less stood up for him, too. But I shall certainly write to Craig and tell him the sort of thing that's happening here.'

'Yes, I should. I think of writing to Madge myself about the goings-on. All in and out of each other's bedrooms and the gramophone playing till two and three in the morning. Then, another thing is, the servants won't stand it much longer, you know—champagne for breakfast, and so on! Mind you, the Monteaths aren't so bad. It's those other two. But that young man, my dear, he's *dreadful*.'

'Don't tell me. What d'you think he said to Brenda yesterday—didn't you hear? He said: "What a drenching colour your dress is!" Poor Brenda said afterwards: "Well, I've heard of drenching a cow!"'

'Yes, she told me. Well, I daresay we shall be able to laugh at all this when it's over, but I hardly find it amusing at the present moment, personally.'

'Oh, it's too shocking! It's the downfall of England, mind you. . . . Mons! will you come here.'

At this moment the others came out, and climbing into the 'bus they all roared away up the drive. Jane lay in bed shaking with laughter, but she felt rather sorry for Sally and Walter. 'Still,' she thought, 'it can't be helped. We've done nothing wrong that I know of.'

She began slowly to dress, manicured her nails, took particular pains with her face and hair, and at about eleven she strolled downstairs. She looked into the billiard-room, half hoping that Albert would be there, but it was empty. Coming back into the hall she saw Sally sitting on the bottom step of the staircase.

'Oh, my dear, I'm feeling so awful!'

Jane dashed forward, put her arm round Sally's waist and half carried her to a sofa, where she went off into a dead faint. Jane, thoroughly alarmed, called out loudly for Walter, who ran downstairs in his dressing-gown.

'Oh, God!' he said on seeing Sally. 'What! She's not . . .?'

'She's only fainted. Pull yourself together, Walter, and fetch some brandy or something. Look, though! she's coming round now.'

Sally opened her eyes and smiled at Walter, who was rubbing her hands in a distracted sort of way. Presently she sat up and drank some brandy, which Albert, appearing from nowhere, produced in a tumbler. Walter finished what she didn't want.

'Goodness, darling, what a turn you gave me! But what on earth's the matter with you? You were as right as rain a minute ago. D'you feel better now?'

'Yes, quite better, thank you. I'll just stay here for a bit, I think. . . . Walter. . . .'

'Yes, my angel.'

'Promise not to be cross.'

'Yes. What?'

'No, but promise really and truly.'

'Of course I promise, funny; but what is it?'

'Well, I'm afraid this means I'm in the family way. You're not cross? You see, I've been suspecting it for some time now and hoped for the best, you know; but this is rather conclusive, isn't it. Are you terribly shocked, my sweet?'

'No, naturally not, darling precious. But how careless of us. Never mind, I think it will be rather sweet, really—I mean, the baby will. But it's too awful for you, though.'

'Oh, I don't mind. I am rather pleased. You are divine not to be cross. It is an anxiety all the same, isn't it, because how are we ever going to clothe the poor angel? I mean, babies' clothes are always covered with lace, just like underclothes. They must be frightfully expensive. Oh, gosh!'

'Well, my treasure, you'll have to be like pregnant women in books and sit with a quiet smile on your face making little garments. It is a bit of a shock at first, isn't it, the idea of your being a pregnant woman? But I suppose one will get used to it. Will it be a boy or a girl?'

'Both, perhaps.'

'*Really*, darling!'

90

'I mean twins, you idiot! But if not it'll be a girl, naturally: at least, I hope so.'

'You mustn't,' said Albert. 'I read somewhere that if you have been hoping for a girl and then it turns out to be a boy, it will have a nasty, perverted nature.'

'How awful! And does the opposite hold good?'

'Yes, I believe it does.'

'Oh, poor sweet: we must be careful. We'd better say "he" and "her" alternately: you couldn't call the angel "it", could you? You know I feel quite friendly towards him already. I think she will be a great comfort to us, Walter.'

'Yes, we were needing something to draw us together. Morris will be a bond between us.'

'Oh, need it be Maurice? It's not a name I have any feeling for.'

'M-o-r-r-i-s.' He spelt it out. 'If we call him that, we might get one free for an advertisement. You never know your luck.'

'Why not Bentley, then, or Rolls?'

'No good. We couldn't afford to keep it up if we had one. Suppose the angel's a girl?'

'Minerva, and pop it. Morris Monteath: Minerva Monteath. Not at all bad.'

'Well, if we are going to do that, we'd better call her lots of things and have them all free. Minerva, Sanitas, Electrolux, Chubb, Ritz (then we could live there) Monteath. And I could think of dozens more.'

'Talking of living, where are we going to keep her: there's precious little room in the flat for him.'

'I can't think. What an awful idea!'

'I know,' said Walter, 'we can turn the cocktail chest into a cradle. My dear, what a good article for the Sunday papers:

TURN YOUR COCKTAIL CHESTS INTO CRADLES!
England Needs More Babies
and
Fewer Cocktails!

———

PRACTICAL and PATRIOTIC.

91

No, but seriously, where do people keep their babies: one never does see them about, somehow.'

'I,' said Albert, 'am extremely shocked. I thought that when a woman discovered herself to be—well, "in an interesting condition," as they say in the papers, that she beckoned her husband into the conjugal bedroom and whispered shyly into his ear: "Baby's coming." I didn't know people went on like this, even in these days. I find it most painful and disillusioning, and shall leave you to what should, in my opinion, be your confidences. In other words, you are a pair of clowns, and I must go and work. It's my great chance, as those Murgatroyds are out for the day and I shall have the billiard table to myself. I suppose I ought to congratulate you, Sally?'

He kissed her and left the room.

Jane had expected that he would ask her to go with him, but as he did not even look in her direction she forebore from suggesting it, and went for a dreary little walk alone till luncheon time.

During the next three days Albert completely neglected Jane, who was thrown into a state almost of frenzy by his behaviour. Ever since their midnight walk she had been eagerly awaiting an opportunity to tell him that she had now changed her mind, or rather that she knew her mind and was very definitely in love with him; but the opportunity did not come and it was Albert himself who prevented it. He not only took no particular notice of her, but actually went out of his way to avoid her.

Jane's natural reaction to this treatment was to appear more than indifferent and cold towards him, whereas really she was in a perfect fever wondering what could so have altered his feelings. She began to think she must have dreamt the whole affair.

On the third morning Albert announced that he was going to begin his portrait of Sally. Jane felt that this was almost more than she could stand. Ever since Sally's announcement of her pregnancy, Albert had paid attention to no one else. He and Walter had sat with her for hours on end discussing what the baby would be like, whether it would grow up to be an artist or a writer: ('In point of fact, of course,' said Albert, 'he will probably be a well-known cricket pro.') how much Sally would suffer at the actual birth, and various other aspects of the situation; and Jane was beginning to feel if not exactly jealous, at any rate, very much left out in the cold.

The thought of them closeted together all day—Albert occupied with gazing at Sally's lovely face—was almost too much to bear. The fact that the Monteaths were completely wrapped up in each other was no consolation: it was more Albert's neglect of herself than his interest in Sally that was overwhelming her. She thought that she had never been so unhappy.

All day she avoided the billiard-room where Albert was painting. She tried to read, and write letters, but was too miserable to concentrate on anything. At luncheon Albert sat next to Sally and appeared unable to take his eyes from her face. Immediately the meal was over he carried her off to resume the sitting. Jane, too restless to remain indoors, wandered out towards the kitchen garden, where she came upon Lady Prague, with a large basket, cutting lavender. Any company seemed in her state of mind better than none and she offered to help. Lady Prague, giving her a pair of scissors, told her to cut the stalks long, and for some time they snipped away in silence. Presently Lady Prague said:

'If I were Walter Monteath I should be very much worried.'

'Why?' asked Jane, absent-mindedly.

'Well, it's rather obvious, isn't it? I mean, I don't want to make mischief, but one can't help seeing that Mr. Gates is violently in love with Sally, can one? And, if you ask me, I should say that she was more interested in him than she ought to be.'

Jane's heart stood still: she thought she was going to faint. All the suspicions which she had entertained, almost without knowing it, for the last two days turned in that black moment to certainties. Others beside herself had noticed: others more

93

qualified to judge than she was were sure of it—therefore it was true!

She muttered some excuse to Lady Prague and ran back to the house, never pausing until she had reached her own room. She lay on the bed and sobbed her heart out. This seemed to do her a great deal of good; and when she had stopped crying, and had made herself look presentable again, she felt so calm and aloof that she decided to go into the billiard-room. She told herself that she would only make things worse by sulking and that the best thing would be to behave to Albert exactly as if none of this had happened.

There was an atmosphere of concentration in the billiard-room. Albert had dragged down from some attic a curious, stiff little Victorian sofa with curly legs, upholstered in wool and bead embroidery, and had posed Sally on this in front of the window with her feet up and her head turned towards the light. He was painting with great speed and enthusiasm. Walter was writing at a table near by. Neither looked round when Jane came in. Sally, however, was delighted to see her.

'Jane, darling, where have you been all this time? We were beginning to think you must be getting off with the admiral. I hope, I'm sure, that his intentions are honourable, but don't marry him, darling. I feel he takes his eye out at night and floats it in Milton, which must look simply horrid. Anyway, I'm terribly glad you've come at last: these creatures have been just too boring and haven't thrown me a word all day. I've done nothing but contemplate that bust of the Prince Consort, and I'm terrified my poor angel will come out exactly like him—whiskers and all; because it's a well-known fact that pregnant women can influence their children's features by looking at something for too long. An aunt of mine could see from her bed a reproduction of the *Mona Lisa* and my wretched cousin is exactly like it—just that idiotic smile and muddy complexion—most depressing for her, poor thing.'

Jane laughed; but the joke about the admiral seemed unnecessary, she thought, and rather unkind considering the circumstances, forgetting that Sally was not aware of them.

She wandered over to where Albert was painting and glanced at the canvas, not intending to make any comment. When she saw it, however, she was startled out of all her sulkiness into crying:

'But, surely, this isn't your style?'

'Not my usual style, no,' said Albert complacently, 'but one which, to my mind, expresses very well the personality of Sally. Do you agree?'

'Oh, Albert, it's too lovely! I can't tell you how much I admire it.' Her voice shook a little. ('Albert, Albert, darling, I do love you so much!')

The picture, which was small and square, was painted with a curious precision of detail which gave it rather a Victorian aspect, but in spite of this the general design could have been achieved at no time but the present.

'It's nearly finished already, isn't it?'

'Very nearly, which is lucky, as I leave on Thursday for Paris.'

Jane felt as though somebody had hit her very hard and very suddenly in the middle of her chest. 'To-day is Tuesday. . . . He goes on Thursday. . . . Only one more day! Albert, oh, Albert darling! He doesn't love me, then: it's quite certain now that he doesn't; but he loves Sally, so he's running away. Lady Prague was right. But if he doesn't love me, why, why, did he pretend to? Only one more day!'

While all these thoughts were racing through Jane's head she was talking and laughing in the most natural way. Nobody could have suspected that she was in Hell.

Lady Prague came in, followed by Mr. Buggins.

'We've come to see this famous picture,' she said, walking up to it.

Albert, who hated the idea of Lady Prague criticizing his work, stood aside reluctantly.

('Only one more day!')

'How very sympathetic that is, Gates, or do I really mean *simpatica*?' said Mr. Buggins. 'I feel it to be so exactly right. I can't tell you how much I admire it, really too delightful.'

'Quite pretty,' said Lady Prague, half-shutting her eyes

and putting her head on one side as she had learnt to do years ago at an art school in Paris. 'The face, of course, is a little out of drawing. But it's so difficult, isn't it,' she added, with an encouraging smile. 'And when you've once started wrong it hardly ever comes right, does it? One fault, if I may say so, is that Mrs. Monteath has blue eyes, hasn't she? And there you can hardly tell what colour they're meant to be, can you? But perhaps your brushes are dirty.'

('Only one more day!')

13

Jane dressed for dinner that night with unusual care, even for her. She put on a white satin dress that she had not yet worn, feeling that it was a little too smart for a Scottish house party. With it she wore a short coat to match, trimmed with white fur. She spent almost an hour making up her face and looking in the glass before going downstairs, and felt that, at any rate, she appeared at her very best. This made her feel happier until she went into the drawing-room.

Albert was talking to Sally by the fire when Jane came in. He looked up for a moment and then, not rudely but as though unintentionally, he turned his back on her.

Jane felt that she would burst into tears, but, controlling herself, she talked in a loud, high voice to Walter until dinner was announced.

She sat between Admiral Wenceslaus and Captain Chadlington. The admiral poured a torrent of facts and figures relating to the freedom of the sea into her all but deaf ears. She caught the words: 'Prize Courts. . . . Foreign Office. . . . Nearly two millions. . . . International law. . . . Page. . . . Permanent officials. . . . Blockade.' . . . And said: 'No' . . . 'Yes' . . . and 'Not really?' from time to time in as intelligent a voice as she could muster.

When the grouse was finished she was left to the mercies of Captain Chadlington, which meant that she could indulge in her own thoughts until the end of the meal. He had given up asking what pack she hunted with in despair, and that was his only conversational gambit. Albert was sitting next to Sally again and Jane hardly even minded this. She was worn out with her emotions.

After dinner Lady Prague suggested 'Lists.' Sally said she was tired and would go to bed. Walter settled down to the piano, and Albert pleaded that he had work to do.

'Very well, if nobody wants to play we might as well go and listen to the wireless.'

'It's a wonderful programme to-night,' said the general. 'A talk on how wire-netting is made from A to B—Z, I mean—and selections from *The Country Girl*. I wouldn't miss it for anything.'

They all left the room except Walter, who was playing some Brahms, and Jane and Albert who stood by the fire laughing.

'Why are you going away so soon?' she asked him, almost against her will.

'I am wasting time here. I must return to Paris,' he said. And then, abruptly: 'Come with me. I've something to show you.'

Jane's heart thumped as she followed him into the billiard-room.

Albert shut the door and looking at her in a peculiar way, his head on one side, he said:

'Well?'

Jane put up her face to be kissed.

'Darling, Albert!'

He took her in his arms and kissed her again and again.

'Oh, Albert! I was so miserable. I thought you'd stopped loving me.'

'Yes, I know. I meant you to.'

'Oh, you monster! Why?'

'Because it was the only way for you to make up your mind. I won't be kept on a string by any woman.'

'But I'd made it up completely after that walk. Yes, it's no good shaking your head. I had, and I was going to tell you as soon as I got a chance to. Oh, *darling,* how I do love you!'

'Come and sit here.'

Jane put her head on his shoulder. She had never been so happy.

'When did you fall in love with me?'

'The first time I saw you at Sally's.'

'Did you? Fancy, I thought you seemed so bored.'

'How beautiful you are!'

'Am I?'

'Don't say "Am I?" like that, it's disgusting. Yes you are—very!'

'Oh, *good*. Albert?'

'Yes?'

'Shall I come and live with you in Paris?'

'Well, wives quite often *do* live with their husbands, you know, for a bit, anyhow.'

Jane sat up and stared at him.

'Do you want to marry me?'

'But, of course, you funny child. What d'you imagine I want?'

'I don't know. I thought you might like me to be your mistress. I never really considered marrying you.'

'Good gracious, darling! What d'you suppose I am? An ordinary seducer?'

Jane grew rather pink; it sounded unattractive, somehow, put like that.

'And may I ask if you're in the habit of being people's mistress?'

'Well, no, actually I'm not. But I should love to be yours. Albert, don't be so childish. Have you *no* modern ideas?'

'Not where you're concerned, I'm afraid.'

'I don't think I believe in marriage.'

'Now you're being childish. Anyway, why don't you?'

'Well, none of my friends have made a success of it, except Walter and Sally, and they're such very special people.'

'So are we very special people. If you can't make a success of marriage you're no more likely to make a success of living together. In any case, I insist on being married, and I'm the grown-up one here, please, remember.'

'I'm not so sure. Still I expect it would be rather nice, and I do look terribly pretty in white tulle. You'll have to meet my family, in that case, you know. You're not really going to Paris?'

'No, of course not—now. Let's stay here for a bit and then we'll go and see your parents. Will they disapprove of me?'

'I expect so, most probably,' said Jane hopefully. She had refused to marry at least two people she was quite fond of, on the grounds that her family would be certain to approve of them. 'They simply hate artists. But we need never see them once we're married.'

'I think that would be dreadful,' said Albert. 'After all, you are their only child, think how they will miss you. I shall have to spare you to them occasionally.'

'Darling, how sweet you are! Have you ever had a mistress?'

'Two.'

'Do you love me as much as them?'

'I might in time.'

'Will you love me for ever?'

'No, I shouldn't think so. It doesn't happen often.'

'Do you love me a lot?'

'Yes I do. A great lot.'

'When shall we be married?'

'After my exhibition, about the end of November.'

'Where shall we live?'

'Somewhere abroad. Paris, don't you think? I'll go back and find a flat while you're buying your trousseau, or you could come, too, and buy it there.'

'Albert, you're such a surprise to me. I should have imagined that you were the sort of person who would like to be married in the morning, and never think of a trousseau.'

'Well, my angel, you know how I hate getting up, and after all, I've got to see your underclothes, haven't I? No, I'm all for having a grand wedding I must say; one gets more presents like that, too.'

'My dear, you've never seen any wedding presents or you wouldn't call that an advantage.'

'Still, I suppose they're marketable?'

'Shall we be frightfully poor?'

'Yes, fairly poor. I have just over a thousand a year besides what I make.'

'And I've four hundred. Not too bad. Walter and Sally have to manage on a thousand between them. I must say they're generally in the deep end, though. I simply can't think what they'll do now, poor sweets. How soon shall I tell my family?'

'Not till we leave here, if I were you. You might change your mind.'

'Yes, I quite expect I shall do that. We won't tell the Murgatroyds, either, will we? Just Walter and Sally.'

'Yes, I think so.'

'How many children shall we have?'

'Ten?'

'Albert! You can consider that our engagement is at an end.'

'About four, really. Of course, you may have three lots of triplets like Lady Prague in the Consequences.'

'You do love me, don't you?'

'Yes, I do. How many more times?'

'As many as I like. You know I'm very glad I came to Scotland.'

'So am I. Come on, funny, d'you realize it's past one; we must go to bed or there'll be a hideous scandal.'

14

The days which followed were spent by Jane and Albert in a state of idyllic happiness. It was quite easy to keep their engagement a secret from all but the Monteaths as the heartier members of the house party were so seldom indoors; when there was no shooting to occupy them they would be fishing or playing tennis. The evenings were no longer brightened by the inevitable 'Lists'; nobody dared to thwart Lady Prague by refusing to play, but at least Albert, who could bear it no longer, read out a list of diseases so shocking and nauseating that the affronted peeress took herself off to the study and the game was never resumed.

One day they were all having tea in the great hall. This was an important meal for the shooters, who ate poached eggs and scones and drank out of enormous cups reminiscent of a certain article of bedroom china ware. Albert, who detested the sight of so much swilling, seldom attended it, preferring to have a cup of weak China tea or a cocktail sent into the billiard-room, but on this occasion he had come in to ask Walter something and had stayed on talking to Jane.

'Tomorrow,' said Mr. Buggins to the company at large, 'there are to be some very good Highland games at Invertochie which is about thirty miles from here. I have been talking to the general and he sees no reason why we shouldn't all go over to them. There are two cars, his own and Craig's Rolls-Royce, so there'll be plenty of room if everyone would like to come. We think it would be advisable to take a picnic luncheon which we could eat on the way at a very well-known beauty spot called the Corbie's Egg.'

There was a murmur of assent and 'That will be lovely,' from the assembled guests.

'The Corbie,' went on Mr. Buggins, 'is the local name for a

crow. It is not known how that particular mountain came to be called the Corbie's Egg, but the name is an ancient one: I came across it once in a sixteenth-century manuscript.'

Mr. Buggins's audience began to fade away. The 'grown-ups,' as Albert called them, were frankly bored by folk-lore, which, it is only fair to add, was already well known to them, they had all been fellow-guests with Mr. Buggins before. The others, who had not, politely listened to a long and rather dreary account of how he, personally, was inclined to think that sacrifices might have taken place on the mountain at some prehistoric date, first of human beings, then, when people were becoming more humane, of animals, and finally the whole thing having degenerated into mere superstition, of a Corbie's Egg.

'I do hope you will all come to the games,' he added rather wistfully. 'Of course, I know you don't really much like that sort of thing, but I feel that it would be a great pity for you to leave the Highlands without having seen this typical aspect of national life. And it would make my day very much more pleasant if you came. We could all pack into the Rolls, and the others could drive with the general in his Buick.'

Mr. Buggins had so evidently been thinking it all out and was so pathetically anxious for them to go, that the Monteaths, Albert and Jane, who had each inwardly been planning a happy day without the grown-ups, were constrained to say that there was nothing they would enjoy so much, that they adored picnics, and could hardly wait to see the Corbie's Egg, let alone the Highland games.

'And what games do they play?' asked Albert.

'Actually, in the usual sense of the word, no games. It is what you would call in the South, sports.' (Mr. Buggins identified himself so much with the North that he was apt to forget that he also was a mere Englishman. He had once seriously contemplated adding his grandmother's maiden name to his own and calling himself Forbes-Buggins.) 'The programme consists of dancing, piping, tossing the caber, and such things. The chieftains of the various neighbouring clans act as judges. It is all most interesting.'

'It must be,' said Albert. 'I long to see the chieftains.'

At dinner the subject was once more discussed at some length, and it was finally decided that the whole party should go, starting punctually at half-past twelve; and Lady Prague, who to Sally's great relief had taken upon herself all questions of housekeeping, gave the necessary orders for a picnic luncheon.

The next morning at twelve o'clock Albert had not put in an appearance, and kind Mr. Buggins, knowing his customary lateness and aware that Lady Prague and General Murgatroyd wait for no man, went to his bedroom to see if he had awakened.

Albert was sitting on the edge of his bed, wearing a pair of exquisite sprigged pyjamas. A gramophone blared out 'The Ride of the Valkyries'; the whole room smelt strongly of gardenias. He stopped the gramophone and said:

'This is a great pleasure, Mr. Buggins. So early, too; your energy never ceases to amaze me. I am in a state of intense excitement. Look what I received this morning from a friend in London.' He held out a Victorian glass paper-weight.

'Look into it carefully.'

Mr. Buggins did so, and was immediately rewarded by the sight of Gladstone's memorable features.

'Now,' said Albert excitedly, 'turn it round just a little.'

Mr. Buggins obeyed, and lo and behold! Mr. Gladstone changed before his very eyes to Mr. Disraeli. He made a suitable exclamation of gratified surprise.

'It is unique!' cried Albert. 'Unique in the iconographie of Gladstone and Disraeli and also as a paper-weight. I regard it as a find of the greatest significance.'

'Very interesting. To what date do you think it belongs?'

'Mr. Buggins, I have a theory about that paper-weight; but this, of course, is just my own idea, and must not be taken too seriously, as I am by no means an infallible authority on the subject, though it is one which I have studied deeply. You have guessed, of course, that I refer to Gabelsburgher.'

Mr. Buggins had guessed no such thing, but he bowed courteously.

'In other words, I believe this paper-weight to be an original Gabelsburgher. It will, of course, be some time before I shall be able to proclaim this as an established fact. You ask what date it is? I reply that if, as I think, it is by the hand of the master, it would almost certainly have been made between the years 1875 and 1878. Gabelsburgher, as you know, came to England for the first time in '75. In '76 Elise was taken ill, in '78 he laid her remains in the Paddington cemetery and came away a broken man. Many of his best paper-weights were buried with his beloved, and from that time his work deteriorated beyond recognition. It is easy to see that this jewel belongs to his very greatest period, and I should myself be inclined to think that it was created in the March or April of '76 while Elise was still in the heydey of her youth and beauty. But, as I said just now, I am very far from infallible.'

Mr. Buggins, who knew nothing and cared less about Gabelsburgher, and who heard the cars arriving at the front door, became a little restive during this speech, repeating at the end of it:

'Very interesting. I really came to tell you that we start in about ten minutes for the Highland games.'

'Ah! good gracious! I had quite forgotten!' cried Albert, leaping out of bed and seizing his black taffeta dressing-gown. 'But have no fear, I shall not be late.'

Albert, Walter, Mr. Buggins, Jane and Sally went in the first car, the Craigdallochs' Rolls-Royce, and with them, as they had the most room, was packed the luncheon: one large picnic basket, two thermos flasks and several bottles of beer and whisky.

In the general's Buick, which he drove himself and which was to start a few minutes later than the Rolls, were Lady Prague, the Chadlingtons and Admiral Wenceslaus. Lord Prague was in the apparently moribund condition which characterized him on non-shooting days, and stayed behind.

The Rolls-Royce drove along with a pleasantly luxurious motion. Mr. Buggins pointed out many places of interest as they passed through typical Highland scenery, among others the 'banksome brae' where 'Ronnie waur killed i' the ficht,'

105

and the lodge gates of Castle Bane, let at present to some rich Americans who had installed (Mr. Buggins shook his head sadly) a cocktail bar in the chief dungeon. Sally was much excited to hear this and wondered if it would be possible to make their acquaintance.

'I should so *love* to see the inside of Castle Bane!' she cried. 'And I simply *worship dungeons*, of course!'

'I believe the public are admitted every Thursday, but I will make inquiries,' said Mr. Buggins.

Presently the Rolls-Royce arrived at the Corbie's Egg, a large yellowish mountain commanding an interminable prospect of other mountains, valleys, streams and pine woods. They all got out of the car and were induced by Mr. Buggins, an ardent picnicker, to drag the hamper, rugs, and bottles half-way up a sort of precipice, the idea being that they would thus enjoy a slightly better view. What, however, they gained in that respect they lost in comfort, as they were perched on a decided slope and had some difficulty in preventing basket and bottles from slipping down it.

Having unpacked the luncheon they waited politely for the others; but when a quarter of an hour passed by with no signs of the Buick, Sally suggested that they should begin. 'I'm pretty peckish,' she said, 'eating for two now, you see.'

Albert remarked that the Murgatroyds certainly would not have waited for them, and they all fell upon the food, munching away in a happy silence.

It was only when they had quite finished and were drinking their coffee with the delicious feeling, so rare at picnics, that even if there were any more food it would be difficult to eat it, that Sally noticed, to her extreme horror, that there was absolutely nothing left for the others.

She announced this fact in a voice shaking with hysteria. There was a ghastly silence.

Mr. Buggins said: 'Surely they are bringing their own,' without much conviction.

'No,' wailed Sally, 'this was for everybody.'

Another silence. Walter tried to speak, but no words came. Mr. Buggins gulped down some neat whisky and said:

'Wait a minute. We'll see what's left. Hum—yes, one leg of grouse. Three tongue sandwiches. Look! What's this? A packet of something! Oh dear! Petit-Beurre biscuits, rather cold comfort. Fourteen apples (curious how the cook here seems to think we are all fruitarians). No beer at all. Half a bottle of whisky. A thermos of hot milk. Yes, this is very awkward indeed.'

Another dreadful silence descended upon them. Sally wrung her hands in despair.

'Oh, goodness, goodness me! What *are* we to do?'

Albert poured the remains of the whisky down his throat. Suddenly he shouted:

'I know, of course! The only thing we can do is to hide the picnic basket and pretend it fell out of the car. Quick! quick! before they come!'

With shaking hands and furtive glances down the road they packed the debris of their lunch into the picnic basket, which they proceeded to hide between two large boulders. They then seized the rugs and scrambled down a precipitous slope to the motor-car, explaining matters rather breathlessly to the bewildered chauffeur, who, when he grasped what they were driving at, was only too pleased to aid and abet their little plan as he had a private grudge against the general.

Hardly were all these preparations completed when the Buick bore down upon them and drew up just behind the Rolls-Royce.

General Murgatroyd was the first one to get out and walked briskly up to where the guilty ones were waiting by the roadside. He looked hot and cross, his hands were covered with oil.

'How's this?' he said in a loud angry voice. 'We thought at least you'd have the lunch all ready for us by now. We've had a beastly time with a slipping clutch. Got it put right now but it's been the hell of a journey, I can tell you, and, personally, I'm ready for my food. Come on, let's get it out.'

There was a gloomy silence. At last Walter, prodded from behind by Sally, cleared his throat and said:

'I'm afraid, sir, that a rather—er—disappointing thing has

107

happened to the lunch. Albert found that there wasn't quite enough room for his legs with the basket on the floor of the car, so we stopped and put it on to the carrier. When we arrived here we found to our dismay that it had disappeared —it must have dropped off as we drove along. We hoped that you might perhaps have come across it and picked it up. No such luck, I suppose?'

'This is damned annoying,' said the general violently. 'Who strapped it on to the carrier?'

'Albert and I did, sir.'

'Then you must have done it damned inefficiently, that's all I can say.'

He glared at Albert.

The admiral here came forward and said, not unkindly:

'Well, it can't be helped now. Let's have a drink while we're waiting.'

'Unfortunately, sir, the bottles seem to have been forgotten. I thought when I woke up this morning that Friday the 13th is seldom a lucky day.'

'It happens to be Friday the 12th to-day, though,' said Lady Prague.

The admiral at first appeared stunned by this piece of news, but, suddenly galvanized into life, he cried:

'Forgotten! What do you mean? I saw them into the car myself. I always see to the drinks.'

'Yes, he does: I can vouch for that.' The general looked again at Albert as he spoke.

Nobody answered.

'This is all most peculiar and extremely annoying,' said Lady Prague. 'What makes it worse is that the picnic-basket with fittings was Prague's silver-wedding present from the tenants—with his first wife, of course. We shall certainly have to inform the police of this loss. Meanwhile, what shall we do for luncheon?'

'If I might make a suggestion, Lady Prague,' ventured Mr. Buggins timidly, 'perhaps you had better go to the Auld Lang Syne at Invertochie and have your luncheon there?'

'And what about all of you? Aren't you hungry?'

'Yes, indeed, we are starving—starving. I meant, of course, for all of us to go, but thought that if only a few can get in, owing to the large crowd which is always attracted there by the games, that you should in justice come before us, as it was partly owing to our carelessness that the basket was lost.'

'Oh, I see; yes. Well, there's no point in waiting here, we might as well push on to the Auld Lang Syne. Most inconvenient and tiresome.'

They all climbed back into the cars and when they were once more under way, Albert said:

'Really, Walter, you are a sneak. Why did you say it was my legs that hadn't enough room: surely you could have chosen someone else. I'm in such disfavour with the general and I feel now that he will never look on me kindly again.'

'I'm sorry; I couldn't think of anyone else.'

'Well, there was yourself.'

'I never think of myself.'

'I suppose you all realize,' said Jane, who was tightly holding Albert's hand under the rug, 'that we are fated to eat another enormous lunch. Personally, I couldn't face a small biscuit at the moment.'

They gazed at each other in horror at this prospect, but Mr. Buggins assured them that there was no need for anxiety as the hotel was certain to be full on that particular day.

'I am even rather perturbed,' he added, 'as to whether those poor hungry things will get a bite or sup.'

'I'm quite sure that Lady Prague will get a bite, and don't doubt that the admiral will somehow find a sup,' said Albert; 'but think how awful it would be if there did happen to be enough for all of us. Hadn't we better pretend to have a breakdown and let the others go on?'

'You forget it's the general behind us, who obviously knows all about cranking plugs and things: he'd see in a moment that nothing was wrong. No, we shall have to risk it.'

When they arrived at the Auld Lang Syne it presented, to their dismay, a singularly empty and welcoming appearance.

'Lunch for ten? Certainly. This way, please.'

The waiter led them through a stuffy little hall bedecked

with stags' heads, up some brown linoleum stairs to the dining-room which, though empty, smelt strongly of humanity.

'No, sir; no crowd now. There has been, sir; oh, yes, but they're all to the games. Will you start with fish or soup, sir?'

At this moment the rest of the party appeared, headed by Lady Prague, who said:

'As we are in such a hurry I will order for everybody,' and took the menu card from the waiter.

'Tomato soup, roast mutton, two vegetables, rice pudding and prunes, Cheddar cheese, celery and biscuits. That will do nicely. I shall drink ginger beer. What about everybody else?'

'Whisky,' said the admiral, quickly. 'I wish I could understand what happened to those bottles.'

He looked suspiciously at Albert.

Very soon the tomato soup arrived. It tasted strongly and unnaturally of tomatoes, was hot, thick and particularly filling. Lady Prague fell upon it with relish and crumbled bread into it.

Albert, Jane, Walter, Sally and Mr. Buggins never forgot that lunch. Seated in a row, their eyes fixed upon a print of the Battle of Khandi Pass (underneath which hung a key so that members of the British aristocracy portrayed there should easily be recognizable), they miserably waded through the bill of fare ordered by Lady Prague.

They suffered.

First the soup, followed by enormous helpings of congealing mutton with boiled vegetables; then—except for Albert—mountains of tepid rice pudding floating about in brown prune juice and studded with the prunes. Albert firmly refused this, saying:

'It is my peculiar misfortune that from a child I have been unable to digest rice. Prunes I find so disintegrating that I seldom touch them.'

'Traitor!' whispered Jane, kicking him under the table.

'No biscuits, thank you,' said Mr. Buggins; adding in a jocular voice, 'I have always been told that one should rise from a meal ready to eat a penny bun.'

'And are you ready to now?' asked Albert doubtfully.

At last the nauseating meal drew to a close, and Walter (who luckily had some money with him) was obliged to put down twenty-eight shillings for his own, Sally's, Jane's and Albert's share of the bill. This was felt by some to be the saddest moment of the day.

'My spirit is broken,' said Albert, as they walked downstairs again, 'or I should certainly bargain with the innkeeper for that exquisite aspidistra. I covet it. But I have no energy left in me for such exertions. Mr. Buggins, do tell me, I have always so much wanted to know, who *was* Auld Lang Syne?'

It was past three o'clock when they arrived at the enclosure where the games were taking place. Each member of the party had to pay five shillings to go in.

'I knew it would be cheaper, in the end, to go to the Lido,' said Walter bitterly.

There was an enormous crowd in the enclosure consisting of very large strong-looking people; the men mostly wore kilts and the women dull but serviceable tweeds.

Albert bought a programme which he shared with Jane. It was printed on thin pink paper and informed them that they were about to witness:

TUG OF WAR. VAULTING WITH POLE.
PIPING. DANCING.
THROWING THE HAMMER. TOSSING THE CABER.
FOOT RACES. CYCLE RACES. RELAY TEAM RACES.
PIPING COMPETITION.

Albert began explaining this to Jane as they were separated from the others:

'"Tossing the caber". Now that will be worth seeing; the caber is Scottish for a young bull and this ancient sport was introduced into Scotland by the survivors of the Spanish Armada, who settled in many of the islands. "Throwing the hammer". Two men, I believe, are given six hammers each to throw and they see who can knock out the other one first.

111

Dangerous, but what is that to these wild clansmen?'

'How d'you know all this?' asked Jane suspiciously.

'My dear, of course I know all about it. Don't be tiresome, but come and see for yourself.'

As they drew near to the arena their ears were greeted by a curious medley of sounds, the results of two brass bands playing different tunes, a band of bagpipes and a man walking drearily round alone, piping.

'So like *Le Pas d'Acier*,' murmured Albert, who had long entertained an unreasonable dislike for that ballet.

The arena, which was railed off from the crowd by ropes, was a large piece of flat ground like a football field. At one side of it there was a raised platform, on which sat several ancient men in kilts.

'The chieftains,' Albert explained, 'of neighbouring clans. Although they look so friendly, each in reality is fingering his dirk; their hearts are black with age-old hatreds of each other. Meanwhile, their brave clansmen are striving with might and main to win the games. Let's get up closer, I can't see anything.'

The arena presented an extraordinary spectacle of apparently meaningless activity. People seemed to be doing things quite by themselves in every available corner of the field, while, encircling the whole, about seven skinny little men in shorts were quickly cycling round and round, followed by a crowd of even skinnier little men, running. They mostly looked like Whitechapel Jews. Some girls in Highland dress and long flowing hair were dancing a fling in one corner; in another an enormous giant appeared to be balancing a tree on his chest. The tug-of-war went on the whole time, neither side gaining an inch, and the vaulting also was incessant.

'I am bitterly disappointed!' cried Albert, when he had gazed for some time upon this medley of sports. 'I had imagined that I was going to see savage Highlanders, in philabeg and bonnet, performing unheard-of feats. And what do I find? Men of more insignificant physique than myself cycling, running, jumping, and doing it rather worse than little boys at their private school sports. As for the noise, I cannot condemn it too heartily. I am suffering real physical pain and, also, I feel most dreadfully sick.'

'Well, can you wonder?' said Jane. 'Personally, I've never felt so ill in my life before. What I'm wondering, though, is how we are to account for the picnic-basket being found again.'

'Oh, easily. We can say that some rough man brought it back.'

'Yes, but that's so unlikely; because how is the rough man to know whom it belongs to? Presumably, if there is an address inside, it will be that of the Prague home, as they say in films.'

'We shall have to advertise for it. Oh! the boredom of these games! I've never known anything so oppressive. And as for those *cyclistes* they make me feel positively giddy, round and round like rats in a cage. Can't we go home soon? There's Alfred Sprott! Doesn't he look awfully jolly? Let's go and embarrass him.'

Albert gracefully approached Lord Alfred, who was standing with a pretty blonde young woman.

'De-ar Alfred,' he said, placing a hand on his shoulder, 'why are you not playing in these delightful games? I remember so well the day you won *all* the sports at Eton.'

Lord Alfred turned scarlet, muttered something, and hurried away into the crowd.

'Always so *gauche*, the darling boy,' said Albert sadly. 'Here comes Mr. Buggins.'

Mr. Buggins was walking with a tall, oldish man in a kilt, whom he introduced as Sir Alexander McDougal.

'Sir Alexander,' he said, 'is the convener of the games this year. He has just been judging the piping competition.'

'In other words, I suppose,' said Albert, 'the producer. Well, sir, I must congratulate you. Seen as a sort of out-door ballet these games must command the highest praise. The music, too, although at first unmelodious, seems now a very fitting background to these fantastic gestures. Charming! Charming!'

113

Sir Alexander walked quickly away, followed by Mr. Buggins.

'Why did you say that,' asked Jane (a truthful girl), 'when you know how bored you are feeling?'

'Well, darling, I always think that any artistic endeavour, however unsuccessful, should be encouraged. These games do show a certain amount of enterprise; when looked at impartially there is a sort of pattern to be discerned in them. In time they might become most interesting and unique. Meanwhile, they are, of course, far too monotonous.'

'And do you realize,' said Walter, who, with Sally, now joined them, 'that they are still doing the very things that they were doing at ten o'clock this morning?'

'The same people?'

'The same, or others so similar to them as to be indistinguishable.'

'Don't you think,' said Sally wearily, 'that we might go home, as we're all here?'

This suggestion was felt to meet the situation quite admirably, and Walter was sent off to find Mr. Buggins, while the others waited in the car.

'Sicker,' said Albert, as they finally bowled off towards Dalloch Castle, 'I have never felt.'

After dinner that evening the party assembled in the hall to take leave of Captain and Lady Brenda Chadlington, who, to nobody's very great regret, were leaving the castle for the jolly cosy little lodge where Lord Alfred Sprott and others made such a cheery crowd. When they had gone the butler came up to Lady Prague and informed her that the picnic-basket had just been brought back by a rough man.

'Most peculiar,' said Lady Prague; but she let the matter rest at that.

15

Jane sat talking to Sally in her bedroom after tea. Poor Sally had spent most of the day being sick. Morris (or Minerva) was beginning to make his (or her) presence felt in no uncertain way.

'What is so unfair,' she said, 'is that I'm not only sick in the morning, which one expects to be, but sick in the afternoon and evening as well. However, I'm quite pleased we're going to have him, you know. I think a little squawking baby will be great fun, and Walter's been divine about it.'

'Albert and I are going to have four, all boys. One thing I'm *not* looking forward to is telling my family about Albert. Think of their feelings when they hear that he's an artist, who lives abroad and was sent down from Oxford. They'll blow up, that's all. Oh, how I dread it!'

Sally, who knew that Jane enjoyed nothing so much as a scene with her parents, murmured words of sympathy.

'I expect they'll be delighted when they see him. Albert gets on very well with older people. Look at Mr. Buggins.'

'Yes, and look at General Murgatroyd,' said Jane quickly, frowning at the idea that they might approve of Albert. 'He's much more like daddy than Mr. Buggins is.'

'My dear Jane, how absurd you are! Two people couldn't be more different than Sir Herbert and General Murgatroyd. Your father has a great sense of humour, for one thing, and then he's a very cultivated man. Anyhow, you shouldn't talk like that: you get all your brains from him.'

'No, indeed, I don't. I get them from my maternal grandmother, Judith Trevor. Brains often skip a generation, you know, and come out in the grandchildren. Poor mummy and daddy are both terribly stupid: darlings, of course, but narrow-minded and completely unintellectual.'

'I simply don't understand your attitude towards your parents, and, what's more, I believe the whole thing is a pose. Why, when you're at home you always seem to be so fond of them, and anyone can see that they adore you.'

'Think what you like, my dear Sally, you won't alter the truth. Of course, I know how charming they are and how grateful I ought to be for everything they've done, and so on, and in a way I am fond of them. We have a different outlook and that's all there is to it.'

The door opened and Walter came in with a telegram in his hand.

'Too extraordinary,' he said. 'Here's a wire from Ralph to say that he and Mrs. Fairfax are coming to dinner. Can you understand it?'

Sally read it out loud:

May Loudie and I come to dinner to-day? Will arrive about eight on chance of finding you.

RALPH

'How very mysterious! Why are they in Scotland?'

'I know, so peculiar and why together? However, we shall hear all about it this evening. How pleased Albert will be to see Ralph. Do you imagine they'll be wanting to stay the night?'

'Certainly, I should think. We'll get rooms ready in case. Anyway, it's very exciting. I'm always pleased to see Ralph, myself, and Mrs. Fairfax is such heaven. But I'm longing to know what it all means, aren't you?'

'What *will* the Murgatroyds think of Mrs. Fairfax?'

'I expect they probably know her already. But I imagine that Ralph will be a bit of a shock to them.'

'Oh, this is going to be fun!' said Jane, and she ran off to tell Albert.

Dinner was well advanced before there was any sign of the newcomers.

As Sally had conjectured, Mrs. Fairfax was well-known to all the Murgatroyds. A much-married lady, she had in turn been the wife of an English duke, an American millionaire and an Italian prince; and now, in theory, if not in fact,

116

shared the bed of a rather depressing Colonel Fairfax. Lady Prague, in common with many of her contemporaries, still remained on bowing terms with her despite these moral lapses; as the mother of an English marquess, an American heiress and an Italian duke, Mrs. Fairfax could always command a certain measure of tolerance even from the most strait-laced dowagers.

Lady Prague was in the middle of explaining to the general that dear Louisa had always been such a high-spirited girl and could, therefore, hardly be blamed for her actions. 'Not that I approve of her, of course. I don't, but somehow one forgives things to her that one couldn't put up with in others' —when the door opened and Ralph Callendar swayed into the room. He kissed Sally's hand, blew kisses to Jane and Albert, bowed to the rest of the company, and explained:

'Loudie is making up her face in the hall. She thinks that she's looking tired, but that if she is sufficiently *maquillée* everyone will think: "How painted she is!" instead of: "How aged she is!" which is naturally preferable. The angel! Here she comes!'

The door opened again to admit an immensely fat Pekinese, with bulging eyes and a rolling gait, followed by his mistress and human counterpart, Mrs. Fairfax. Short and plump, waddling rather than walking, her little round face inches deep in paint, her little fat hands covered with rings, her stout little body enveloped in a sable coat, she resembled nothing so much as a rather prepossesing giant Pekinese. The moment she was inside the room she let loose a perfect flow of inconsequent chatter:

'Sally, darling, what *must* you think of us, forcing ourselves on you like this? We heard you were here quite by chance and couldn't resist coming. Florence, what a surprise! And Mowbray, too, and the admiral, and dear, nice Mr. Buggins! Albert such an age since I've seen you. Jane—looking so beautiful. What's happened to you, my dear? In love, I suppose, as usual? Well, I must say this is a delightful party. And the poor Craigdallochs are away, I hear.'

She sat down next to Walter and continued:

'Of course, I suppose you all think Ralph and I are eloping? Well, no. Though to be frank, this is the first time I've made a journey of the sort without eloping. I ran away with all my dear husbands, you know, even with poor Cosmo, though I can't remember why that was necessary. Oh, yes, of course I know, I was under age and my father said we must wait for three months. Three months! As though anyone could. So we just ran away to Paris: only for a night and it was all most innocent (dear Cosmo—so pompous!); but we were seen by several people—we took care to be, of course—and after that it was plain sailing and we were married in the rue d'Aguesso, I remember. Really, it made a vivid impression on me at the time. The Ambassador was there and poor father gave me away, and poor Cosmo took me away, dear thing, to Rome or somewhere, and it was all very different from what I had expected. And now I've shocked Florence. But what was I talking about? Oh, yes, of course. Well, Ralph and I are not eloping: merely escaping.'

'Escaping?'

'From Linda May. From the West Coast of Scotland really. You tell them about it, darling, while I get on with my fish.'

'You see,' said Ralph, shutting his pained eyes and speaking in a voice which gave the impression that he had lived a thousand tiring lives, 'Linda, the poppet, seems to have gone mad. It is a great tragedy. She invited us to go for a cruise in her yacht. She said we would go to the Islands. Naturally thinking she meant the Greek islands, we accepted, intending to leave her quite soon for the Lido. Two days before we were to start I discovered, to my horror and amazement, that we were being taken to visit some islands on the West Coast of Scotland. Well, you know, Albert, Scotland is all right for you, but it's not my *period*. So I telephoned to Loudie and told her this agonizing news. I begged her to come straight to the Lido instead. But no, obstinate as a mule. She insisted on going with Linda. Imagine my mental sufferings faced with the prospect either of not seeing Loudie for weeks, or of facing these ghastly hardships in her

118

company. I begged, I implored her to change her mind; and when, at last, I realized that she was absolutely bent upon going, I made the great sacrifice and accompanied her. But I did beg, didn't I, Loudie?'

'Yes, darling, you did, indeed,' she replied, with her mouth full.

'To continue: It was even more horrible than I had anticipated. The scenery—my dear Albert—forgive me if I say that the scenery made one feel physically sick whenever the eye strayed out of the porthole. I kept my curtain drawn all day and even then I couldn't help seeing those mountains sometimes—they haunted me. To make matters worse, Linda, it appears, is madly in love with a monster of a Scotsman, who came to dinner last night in his kilt. Those hairy old knees decided us. "The mountains I can bear," said Loudie. "Natives in the semi-nude at dinner-time is another matter. I leave to-morrow." Luckily the angel had her Austro-Daimler sitting at Oban, so here we are! But I tell you—'

At this moment there was a piercing shriek from Lady Prague. The Pekinese was seen to have his teeth firmly embedded in her right ankle.

'Doglet!' said Mrs. Fairfax in a gently reproving voice, *'what* do I see you doing, my own? Somebody give him a piece of grouse and he'll leave go at once.'

General Murgatroyd, however, seized the dog roughly by its tail, whereupon it turned round and bit him in the hand. The general shook it off and, crimson with rage, demanded that it should instantly be destroyed.

'My little Doglet destroyed? Oh, what a dreadful idea! Such a horrid word, too. You cruel old general! Besides, a dog is always allowed his first bite, by law, isn't he?'

'First fiddlesticks! Anyhow, it's had two bites this evening—Florence and myself. The animal is not safe, I tell you.'

'"The animal," indeed! Fancy calling my Doglet "the animal"! Come here, my precious. The general isn't safe: he wants to *destroy* you. Ralph dear, be an angel and put Doglet

119

in the car, will you, till after dinner? Thank you so much. I do hope you're not hurt, Florence?'

'Yes, Louisa, the skin *is* broken and he has torn my stocking rather badly. A new pair! Of course it doesn't signify. I must go and paint it with iodine. I only trust the animal has not got hydrophobia.'

She left the room angrily, General Murgatroyd opening the door for her with a gesture of exaggerated chivalry. Lord Prague, who had noticed nothing, went on eating.

'I'm so sorry that Doglet should have caused all this commotion,' said Mrs. Fairfax. 'The angel! So unlike him! I've never known him really to lose his temper before, but you wouldn't believe how sensitive he is to dress. I ought to have remembered that pink georgette is the one material he simply cannot abide. In fact, all georgette is inclined to upset him; and dear Florence's shoes, with those long pointed toes, would drive him distracted. Poor little sweet! He'll be utterly miserable after this, I'm afraid.'

'And he'd have reason to be if I had anything to do with him,' muttered the general.

'You must find this house very interesting, Albert,' said Ralph, returning from his mission. 'So exactly your period.'

'Indeed, yes, I do,' replied Albert earnestly. 'And I would love to show you the wonderful things I have found here and collected together.'

'No, dear Albert, I think I have suffered enough during the last few days from Victorian taste crystallized by the Almighty into the extraordinary scenery with which I have recently been surrounded. Not at all my period, dear. Corbusier, now—'

Here Sally gave the signal, as they say in books, for the ladies to leave the table, and presently took Mrs. Fairfax upstairs to powder her nose.

'You'll stay the night, of course?' she said.

'Alas! no, my dear. Very sweet of you, but we've taken rooms at Gleneagles for to-night. I really must push on. I should like to reach London, if possible, to-morrow, as my husband is passing through for one day on his way to America

120

and I want to see him about being divorced, you know.'

Sally's murmured sympathy was waved aside.

'It's not been too successful, really—our marriage, I mean. I'm getting rather old for all the fuss and worry of having a husband, that's the truth. And how's yours getting on, my dear: still happy, are you? Has Walter settled down at all? I know you were rather worried about him at one time.'

'We're divinely happy,' said Sally, 'and it's wonderful being here. He hasn't a chance to spend money and he's been working harder than I've ever known him. You know, people are too hard on Walter. Of course he gives the impression of being all over the place, but that's only because of his high spirits. And then, poor darling, he has *no* idea of the value of money, which is sometimes very annoying for me as I'm by nature rather stingy.'

'I've hardly ever met a man who has any idea of the value of money,' said Mrs. Fairfax. 'It's one of the nice things about them. Now, women are nearly always mercenary creatures.'

'Oh! And, by the way, of course, I'd quite forgotten it—I'm going to have a baby.'

'Are you, Sally? Well, it does happen. Torture, my dear, but one looks lovely afterwards, which is a great consolation. I've had three, you know, and they all cut each other dead now; but they're devoted to me, specially dear Bellingham. By the way, I'm told that Potts (my second husband) has taken a house near here—Castle Bane. Dreary creature, Potts, but Héloïse is a dream. She's at the Lido now. I'm going out there really to see her. How lovely Jane was looking at dinner!'

'Yes, wasn't she? It's a great secret, so don't say I told you, but she's engaged to Albert.'

'My dear, you amaze me! Will that be a success?'

'I really don't know. They are very much in love at present; but Jane is terribly sensitive, and Albert so much wrapped up in his work that I can't help feeling there will be trouble. So long as she understands his temperament—but I'm not sure how much she does. However, even if they're

121

happy for a year or two it's more than lots of people get out of life.'

'Yes, you're perfectly right. I've lived through it and I know. I had two years of complete happiness with Cosmo, and about eighteen months with Campo Santo, and I can tell you that it makes all the rest of one's life worth while. But I don't really advise too much chopping and changing for most people: gets one into such restless habits. I couldn't have stayed with Cosmo after. . . . Well, never mind. So I thought if I can't be happy I might as well be rich, and made off with Potts. Then, of course, I was bowled over by Campo Santo in ten minutes. Well, I always think that would have lasted, only the angel died on me quite suddenly: and there he was—Campo Santo in good earnest. It was dreadfully depressing. Still, there was little Bobs to cheer me up: quite the nicest of my children. Have you seen him? He's still at Eton, the precious. He's meeting me in Venice, too, when Héloïse leaves. They can't endure each other. Not frightened about this baby, are you?'

'Well, no, not really.'

'You needn't be; nobody dies in childbirth now, my dear. It's considered quite *vieux jeu*. And it may be a consolation to you to hear that the medical profession makes an almost invariable rule of saving the mother's life in preference to that of the child if there's any doubt about it. Sick much?'

'Yes, a whole lot.'

'Excellent! A very good sign. Now can we go and collect Ralph? I think we should soon be making off.'

They found the others standing round the drawing-room fire, the 'grown-ups' having taken themselves off to the study to hear a talk on Timbuctoo. Walter had happened to be passing the door when it began, and declared that the opening words, delivered by the evidently nervous speaker in a sort of screech, had been;

'PEOPLE who take their holidays abroad seldom think of Timbuctoo. . . .'

'Very seldom, I should imagine,' said Albert. 'Loudie dear, I wonder if you would sing us this little song which I found in an album here? The words are by Selina Lady Craigdalloch (the genius who collected in this house so many art treasures), and the music is "By my dear friend, Lord Francis Watt." It has been my greatest wish to hear it sung by somebody ever since I found it.'

'I have often noticed,' said Ralph languidly, 'that all accompaniments between the years 1850 and 1890 were invariably written by the younger sons of dukes and marquesses. They seem to have had the monopoly—most peculiar.'

'I should love to sing it,' said Mrs. Fairfax, settling herself at the piano, 'and then we must go. Where is it—here? Oh, yes. . . .'

To Bxxxxxxxxxxx

———

(Morte Poitrinaire)

She began to sing in a small, pretty voice:

> *When my dying eye is closing,*
> *And my heart doth cease to beat;*
> *Know that I in peace reposing,*
> *Have but one, but one regret!*
>
> *Leaving you, my only treasure,*
> *Bitter is, and hard to bear,*
> *For my love can know no measure;*
> *Say then, say for me a prayer!*
>
> *Lilies, darling, on me scatter,*
> *And forget-me-nots, so blue;*
> *What can this short parting matter?*
> *We shall surely meet anew!*
>
> *We shall meet where pain and sorrow,*
> *Never more assail the breast;*
> *Where there is nor night nor morrow*
> *To disturb our endless rest.*

'Beautiful!' cried Albert. 'And beautifully sung!'
'Well,' said Mrs. Fairfax, 'a very pretty little song. You

know, Ralph dear, I think that we shall *have* to be going. Unfortunately we are still in the realm of night and morrow, and if we don't push on to Gleneagles we shall get no rest at all.'

There was a perfect chorus of dismay, but Mrs. Fairfax was adamant.

'Your figure is a dream, Ralph!' said Albert, as they followed her into the hall. 'Are you on a diet?'

'Yes, dear, most depressing. I got muscles from dancing too much, they turned into fat—*et voilà*! . . .'

'Do muscles turn into fat?'

'Of course they do. Haven't you noticed that all athletes become immense in their old age?'

'But this is very serious!' cried Albert, in a voice of horror. 'It should be brought to the notice of public schoolmasters. I myself shall give up walking and buy a little car. I sometimes walk quite a distance in Paris.'

'Nothing,' said Ralph mournfully, 'develops the muscles so much as driving. Good-bye, Albert. I hope to see you in London, dear.'

16

That night Jane found herself unable to go to sleep. Her brain was in a particularly lively condition and she tossed and turned thinking first of one thing and then of another until she felt she would go mad. 'Albert! Albert! Albert!' was the refrain.

'Shall I be happy with him in Paris? Will he be the same after we're married? Shall I interfere with his work? That, never,' she thought; 'I am far more ambitious even than he is and will help him in every possible way to achieve fame.

'If I lie quite still and breathe deeply I might manage to drop off to sleep. What shall I put on to-morrow? Not that jumper suit again. I wasn't looking so pretty to-day. I shan't look pretty to-morrow if I have no sleep. Perhaps if I get out of bed and walk up and down. . . . Yes, now I'm feeling quite drowsy. I must write to mamma to-morrow, I haven't written for over a week. What shall I tell her? Oh, yes! the games would amuse her.'

Jane began to compose a letter in her head and was soon even more wide-awake than before. She had hardly ever in her life experienced any difficulty in going to sleep and it made her furious.

'I'll stay in bed till lunch-time to-morrow to make up for this,' she thought.

After about two hours of painful wakefulness she at last fell asleep, soothed, as it were, by a delicious smell of burning which was floating in at her bedroom window and of which she was only half conscious.

Hardly, it seemed to her, had she been dozing for five minutes when she was suddenly awakened by a tremendous banging on her door, which opened a moment afterwards.

125

The electric light blazed into her eyes as she was struggling to open them.

'What is it?' she said, very angry at being awakened in this abrupt manner when she had only just gone to sleep with so much difficulty.

The butler was standing just inside the room.

'House on fire, miss. Will you please come downstairs immediately?'

Jane sat up in bed and collected her wits about her.

'Have I time to dress?' she asked.

'No, I think not, miss; the flames are spreading very rapidly to this part of the house, and Mr. Buggins wants everyone in the hall at once; he is holding a roll-call there.'

Jane leapt out of bed, put on some shoes and a coat, and taking her jewel-case from the dressing-table she ran along to Albert's room. She noticed that it was just after five o'clock.

The butler was still talking to Walter as she passed and Albert had not yet been awakened. Jane put on the light and looked at him for a moment as he lay asleep, his head on one arm, his hair in his eyes.

'How beautiful he is,' she thought as she shook him by the shoulder.

'Wake up, darling, quick! The house is on fire. We've no time even to dress; so come with me now to the hall.'

Albert stretched and got out of bed. He was wide awake and perfectly calm.

'Go back to your room,' he said, 'and throw your clothes out of the window, or you'll have nothing to go home in. I'll do the same and come along for you when I've finished.'

'What a brilliant idea!'

Jane flew back to her room and in a very short time had thrown all her possessions on to the gravel outside. Presently Albert came running down the passage and they went, hand in hand, to join the others in the hall.

'Here they are! That's everybody, then.'

Mr. Buggins was cool and collected; it seemed perfectly natural that he, and not General Murgatroyd, should be taking charge of everything.

'Now,' he said in a firm voice. 'This part of the house is quite safe for the present, so as we are all here I think we might begin to save what we can.

'I must beg you all not to go upstairs again. The wing in which your bedrooms are situated is in a very dangerous position and will be the next to go. The dining-room must also, of course, be left to its fate, but we can safely collect things from the drawing-room, billiard- and smoking-rooms. I telephoned some time ago for the fire brigade, but I'm afraid it will be at least an hour before they can possibly arrive. When they come they will naturally decide for themselves where they can go; we *must* be on the safe side. The servants are all engaged with a chain of buckets in trying to prevent the garages and outhouses from catching, in which I think they may succeed. It would be useless for amateurs to attempt saving the house, the fire has much too firm a hold.'

The party dispersed into the various sitting-rooms leading out of the hall and began to work with a will.

Albert, at great personal danger, put a damp handkerchief over his mouth and dashed into the dining-room which was dense with smoke. Cutting them out of their frames with some difficulty he managed to save the portraits by Winterhalter of Selina, Lady Craigdalloch and her husband, the fourth Earl.

(The present Lady Craigdalloch was never able to forgive him this when she heard about it afterwards. It became her pet grievance.

'The dining-room,' she would say, 'was full of beautiful Raeburns, and what must the young idiot do but risk his life to save the two ugliest pictures in the house. It drives me mad.')

As he ran out of the castle to bestow the Winterhalters in a place of safety, Albert was amused to observe General Murgatroyd carrying with great care an enormous coloured print which had hung in the place of honour over the smoking-room mantelpiece. It was entitled 'The Grandest View in Europe,' thus leading one to expect a view of Mont Blanc, the Doge's Palace, Chartres Cathedral or some such popular beauty-spot, instead of which it depicted the back of a horse's head as it would appear to the rider, with two large grey ears sticking up in the immediate foreground. Beyond the ears could be seen a stone wall which was being negotiated with success by two horses and with no success at all by a third. Hounds running across an adjacent field gave the clue to the whole thing; a hunt was evidently in progress. 'The Grandest View in Europe' having been reverently deposited among the rapidly growing collection of objects on the lawn, its saviour trotted back to the house, bent upon rescuing the head of a moose which hung in the hall.

Admiral Wenceslaus now staggered forth with a load of miscellaneous objects, including a chronometer, a model of the *Victory* in silver, a book entitled *The Triumph of Unarmed Forces*, which he had been trying for some time to lend to various members of the party, and several whisky bottles. Mr. Buggins followed him with Prince Charlie's boot, several old family miniatures and a lock of Bothwell's hair.

Sally, looking rather green, sat tucked up on a sofa and watched these proceedings with some amusement. Albert stopped for a moment to ask her how she felt.

'Oh, quite all right, longing to help, but Walter made me promise I'd stay here.'

'D'you know how the fire started?'

'No; Haddock, the butler, says he has no idea at all. He discovered it, you know. The smoke was pouring in at his window and he says he only got some of the maids out just in time.'

When Albert went back to the house he noticed that flames were already beginning to envelop his own bedroom. Meeting Jane in the hall he kissed her hurriedly and said, 'Take care of yourself, my precious, won't you?' She was carrying the Jacob's Ladder.

He then saved his portrait of Sally and several albums containing water-colours from the billiard-room. Lady Prague was busy showing two men how to take the billiard-table to pieces. They had been managing far better before she came along.

Albert and Jane made many journeys and succeeded in

saving all the plush chairs, bead stools, straw boxes, wax flowers, shell photograph-frames and other nineteenth-century objects which they had collected together from various parts of the house.

(When Lady Craigdalloch, far away in Africa, had recovered from the first shock of hearing that Dalloch Castle was razed to the ground, she said that, at any rate, all the Victorian rubbish there would now have vanished for ever and that this was a slight consolation. Her horror and amazement when, on her return, she was confronted by every scrap of that 'Victorian rubbish' which had always been such a thorn in her flesh, knew no bounds.)

At last all the furniture that it was possible to move reposed on the lawn in safety, and there was nothing left to do but sit 'like Lady Airlie in the ballad,' as Mr. Buggins remarked, and watch the house burn down.

A ghastly early morning light illuminated the faces of Lord Craigdalloch's unfortunate guests as they sat surrounded by the salvage from his home, which looked like nothing so much as the remains of an auction sale before the buyers have removed their purchases.

Lot 1.—Fine old Jacobean oak table suitable for entrance hall. Two assegais and a waste-paper basket.
Lot 2.—Bust of the younger Pitt. Large sofa upholstered in Heal Chintz. Gong of Benares brass-work.
Lot 3.—Case of stuffed grouse in summer and winter plumage. Chippendale writing-table. Large print of Flora McDonald (etc., etc.).

Albert and Jane looked round with some amusement at the different varieties of bedroom attire displayed upon other members of the party. Sally looked lovely in crêpe-de-chine pyjamas, over which she wore a tweed coat lined with fur. Lady Prague was also wrapped in a tweed coat over a linen nightdress and a Shetland wool cardigan. She wore goloshes over her bedroom slippers. Lord Prague, who had collapsed into an armchair, was shivering in a Jaeger dressing-gown which had a sort of cape elaborately trimmed with pale blue braid, and the general stood near him in khaki pyjamas and a manly overcoat. The admiral wore a mackintosh. His bare, white and skinny legs sticking out from beneath it bore witness to the fact that Admiral Wenceslaus was a devotee of the old-fashioned, but convenient, nightshirt.

Albert went to the other side of the castle and picked up the clothes which he and Jane had thrown out of their bedroom windows. Jane and Sally, on seeing them, gave high cries of delight, and retiring behind an adjacent wardrobe they began to dress. Walter and Albert did likewise, and Albert was also able to lend a jumper and a pair of grey flannel trousers to Mr. Buggins. Everybody else secretly wished that they had had sufficient forethought to throw some clothes out of the windows; the morning air was distinctly chilly.

'I've still two pairs of trousers left,' said Albert, holding in one hand the orange tartan ones he had worn upon the moor, and in the other his bright blue pair. 'Won't somebody wear them? General, can I tempt you? Lady Prague, come now! No?'

'Will you lend them to me, young man?'

'Admiral—but, of course, how very kind of you, and how lucky that I have the *matelot* ones. You will feel quite at home in them. Here is a real fisherman's jersey, too, why, you'll be thinking you are back on the dear old flagship—with "Yo! ho! ho! and a bottle of rum."'

The admiral, who seemed rather overwhelmed by the foregoing events, retired behind a zebraskin screen to put on the trousers. He stayed there for some time, and when he finally emerged, carried his eye in his hand. Creeping up behind Lady Prague, he suddenly thrust it into her face, yelling out:

'Peep-uck-bo!'

Lady Prague uttered a piercing scream and ran away as fast as the clinging draperies of her night-dress would allow until, tripping over her goloshes, she fell heavily on the gravel and grazed her knees rather badly. General Murgatroyd and Mr. Buggins assisted her to a chair. After this she became more acid than ever.

Meanwhile the admiral again withdrew behind his screen, where he was found much later by Mr. Buggins and Sally, fast asleep on the ground.

'Poor old boy,' said Sally kindly, 'it's been too much for him.'

'Humph! I think I can guess what has been too much for him.' And Mr. Buggins produced from under the cast-off night-shirt three empty whisky bottles. 'Might as well leave him there,' he said. 'Got a head like a horse; he'll be all right soon.'

The whole castle was now enveloped in flames, which rose to almost double its height—a terrifying spectacle. Even more alarming was the noise, a deafening roar like the sound of huge waterfalls, broken every now and then by the crash of falling masonry. Birds and bats, fascinated by the glare, were to be seen flying to their doom; and two huge beech trees which stood near the house were completely blackened.

The little party on the lawn sat in a dazed silence, over-awed by the sight of this catastrophe.

When the firemen arrived they were far too late to save anything but some outhouses. Not to be deprived of their fun, however, they were soon playing the hose indiscriminately upon the huge flames, the beech trees and the general, who unobserved had strolled up towards the house in order to have a better view. Dripping wet and speechless with rage he rushed back to the others, and was obliged to swallow his pride and borrow Albert's tartan trousers and orange sweater. The sight of him thus attired was too much for Sally and Walter, who became perfectly hysterical with laughter which they were unable to control, and finally they had to go for a long walk in order to regain their composure.

'I wonder what the effect of all this will be on Morris-Minerva?' said Sally.

'Are you feeling all right, my own—'

'Yes, quite now, thank you, darling. Will the poor angel have red hair and a fiery nature as the result of it?'

When they got back to the others they found that quite a little crowd was collected on the lawn, constantly augmented by people from neighbouring villages, who straggled by twos and threes up the drive.

Those members of the house-party who were not clothed were beginning to feel rather self-conscious. The sight-seers all followed the same procedure. They stood for some time gazing at the fire, saying: 'Hoots!'—'Wisha!'—'Mon it's gran'! and other unintelligible phrases of the kind, after which they had a good look at the survivors, coming up quite close and breathing heavily. They then inspected the *lares* and *penates* on the lawn, piece by piece, admiring or criticizing. Having taken their time and seen everything of interest, they sat about the place in little scattered groups and ate.

'Oh! I'm so hungry,' said Sally, breaking a long silence.

The others agreed miserably. Although it was in fact only seven o'clock they all felt as though it must at least be luncheon time. It never occurred to any of them to wonder what the next step would be, but they felt instinctively that they must now see the thing through and wait there until the last beam had fallen.

Sally asked the butler, who was busy counting silver, whether any food had been saved, but he replied that both kitchen and larder had been in flames by the time that he had discovered the fire. Lord Craigdalloch's factor came and spoke to Sally. He was in his shirt-sleeves, having been hard at work nearly from the beginning.

'Good morning, Mrs. Monteath. This is a very sad business, is it not? His lordship will be most terribly upset, I'm afraid.'

'Oh! it's too dreadful. Of course, one can hardly realize yet what it means, one is only so thankful that nobody was hurt. Is the house properly insured?'

'It is insured, but I doubt whether the policy will anything like cover the loss. And then, you see, for sentimental reasons it is such a terrible tragedy. We hoped at first to be able to save Lady Muscatel's tower, but we were too late. I think, if I may say so, that you all did wonders in rescuing so much furniture. I have sent to the home farm for waggons, it must be put in safety as soon as may be. I don't like the looks of all these people: I'm sure they would think nothing of removing a few souvenirs here and there.'

Soon after half-past eight the house was a blackened ruin and the fire practically over. Walter and Mr. Buggins were just discussing what they should do next, when a large old-fashioned Daimler drove up, and a middle-aged man in a very long kilt got out of it. Mr. Buggins greeted him warmly and introduced him as Sir Ronald McFea.

'Should McFea show the knee?' whispered Albert to Jane. 'You see, he doesn't show it at all. Isn't it too fascinating?'

'This is a fearful thing,' said Sir Ronald. 'A fearful thing. My gillie came in just now and said Dalloch Castle had been burnt to the ground, he said. I couldn't believe it—couldn't believe it. Well, there it is. Poor old Craig. It will be a most terrible blow for him when he hears it; shouldn't wonder if it kills him—shouldn't wonder at all. He worshipped the place, every stick and stone of it. Poor old boy.

'Now, my wife says you must all come over to Castle Fea and have some breakfast. She says you must be simply starving so she's getting it ready.

'Dear, dear! It must have been a near thing, too, for hardly any of you to have saved your clothes even—and the general in fancy dress. Never mind, we shall be able to fix you up all right, I don't wonder. Hadn't you better come along now?'

Brightening somewhat at the prospect of breakfast, they accepted Sir Ronald's invitation with joy. Even the admiral stopped trying to put on Prince Charlie's boot, and staggered with the rest of them towards the Daimler, which seemed by some miracle to hold them all. Sally arranged with the factor and Haddock that the servants should be boarded out in neighbouring cottages for the present, and said that she would come back later and make plans for them.

Castle Fea, though a sufficiently welcome asylum to the dazed and hungry survivors of the fire, proved to be a perfect temple of gloom. It in no way resembled a castle, being a large square house with Gothic chimneys and a Greek portico, situated in the midst of a perfect tangle of fir trees, laurels and other evergreens which grew nearly up to its windows. Mr. Buggins pointed out the ruins of the ancient fortress upon an adjacent mound.

'I should think the McFea who built this house must have shown his knee quite often,' murmured Albert as they got out of the car.

The inside of the house was, if anything, more oppressive than the outside. It was a mass of badly-stuffed animals, stained glass and imitation French and old oak furniture. The pictures were of a terrifying realism.

However, the breakfast to which the party now settled down in grateful silence was more than excellent, and Lady McFea, an ugly, dowdy, but thoroughly nice woman, tactfully refrained from asking questions about the fire until all the poached eggs and scones had been consumed. It was indeed a heavenly meal and, when it was over, the Dalloch Castle refugees felt more able to cope with their immediate future.

Sir Ronald and Lady McFea begged that any who would care to do so should stay on at Castle Fea for a few days. Walter and Sally, after a short consultation with Mr. Buggins, decided to accept this kind offer, feeling that it was more or less their duty to remain on the spot until they should hear from the Craigdallochs.

All the others, however, decided to leave by the four-thirty train for London that afternoon, and sleepers were ordered for them by telephone. These arrangements having been made, the McFeas took those who had lost their clothes upstairs, and fitted them out as best they could.

Albert and Jane found themselves alone in the drawing-room and kissed each other quite a lot. Presently Jane said in a gloomy voice:

'I suppose I shall have to go home now; what shall you do, darling?'

'Well, Mr. Buggins most angelically says I can stay with him in London for as long as I like, so I think I shall do that. But hadn't I better go and see your parents fairly soon? After all, I shall have to meet them sometime, shan't I? And then we

134

can be properly engaged if they approve of me. How far is it by train to Stow-on-the-Wold?'

'Oh, the beastly hole! don't mention it to me or I shall burst into tears. About two-and-a-half hours, I suppose. And you needn't think they'll approve of you, darling, because they're quite certain to kick you straight out of the house.'

'Anyhow, I can but try: if I'm kicked out we'll elope. It's perfectly simple. Then I think you'd better go straight home to-morrow and more or less prepare them, and I'll come down for lunch on Thursday. If they like me I'll stay the night, and if not we'll both go back to London together. Good plan?'

'Yes, very good, I think. Sweetest!'

The rest of that day was spent in wandering about rather gloomily in the grounds of Castle Fea, and they were all quite pleased when the time came for them to say good-bye to kind Sir Ronald and his wife. The Monteaths, terribly depressed at the prospect of many more such days, waved to them from under the Gothic portico until the car was out of sight.

Jane, Albert and Mr. Buggins dined together in the train that evening. At the opposite table Lord and Lady Prague, Admiral Wenceslaus and General Murgatroyd made a congenial foursome.

Albert was tired and in a very bad temper. Jane, who had never seen him like that before, felt miserable and rather resentful, but Mr. Buggins was in excellent spirits, and when they confirmed his suspicion that they were engaged he ordered a bottle of champagne to celebrate the occasion. Albert insisted on reading a book between the courses which were very slow in coming.

'Albert, darling, please don't read. After all, I shan't be seeing you after to-morrow, I do think you might talk to me; besides, it's so rude.'

Albert took no notice but went on with his book, a very boring history of the Angevin kings. Mr. Buggins, seeing that he was really not himself, tactfully tried to draw Jane into conversation, but she could not leave Albert alone.

135

'Albert, do stop reading. Mr Buggins, *isn't* it rude and disgusting of him?'

Mr. Buggins felt like shaking them both, but went on quite calmly with his dinner.

'Albert, really I do think even if you must read between the courses, honestly you needn't read while you're eating. Oh, well, of course, if you prefer those beastly old Angevin kings to conversation that's one thing. . . .'

At last she quite lost her temper, and snatching the book from him she threw it out of the window. Albert behaved extremely well about this, but none the less he was furious with Jane, who, in her turn, was completely miserable. They each felt that they had been stupid and childish, but rather less so than the other, and were both longing secretly to make it up.

'Isn't it a pity,' said Mr. Buggins, 'for two people with as much sense of humour as you have to behave like this?'

'Well, I may have a sense of humour, I hope I have,' said Albert, 'but I see nothing funny in throwing an expensive book away like that; and, as we've paid the bill, we might as well go to our sleepers.'

'Here's my share for dinner,' said Jane, offering it to Albert, who had paid for the two of them.

'I don't want it.'

Mr. Buggins got up and left them alone at their table.

'Don't be so silly, Jane.'

'Well, I'm not going to be your kept woman, thank you.'

'Oh! really! I thought that was just what you did want to be.'

'Certainly not; I happened to be in love with you and offered to be your mistress. That's quite different.'

'Exactly the same.'

'Quite different. Of course, I should have earned my own living.'

'Oh! I see. May I ask how?'

'Well, I'm not sure.'

'Nor am I; not at all sure.'

'I suppose I could be a model.'

Albert had a sudden vision of the fastidious Jane posing to a lot of half-washed French art students and burst out laughing.

'Darling, how absurd you are.'

'Well, it was horrid of you to be so cross and *horrid* of you to read, wasn't it?'

'Yes, beastly. And horrid of you to throw my book out of the window, wasn't it?'

'Yes, quite.'

'Yes, *very*.'

'Yes, very, then. Look, we're the last people left, we'd better go.'

'Well, give me a kiss.'

'Not in front of that waiter.'

'He's not looking.'

'He's coming to turn us out. We really must go.'

As Jane rolled into her sleeper she just stayed awake for long enough to think luxuriously of the contrast between her journey to Scotland three weeks ago and her present one.

'I know now for certain,' she thought, 'that I've never been really happy before.'

17

To Jane's amazement, real or pretended, her parents
remained perfectly calm when she told them that she was
engaged. The fact was that it had long been their greatest
wish to see her married, and almost any respectable young
man of reasonable fortune would have been received by them
with open arms. When, the following day, Albert made his
appearance, they took an immediate liking to him.

He, on his side, was very agreeably surprised. Even
allowing for a good deal of exaggeration, Jane's account of
her father and mother had been far from encouraging, and all
the way down in the train he had been bracing himself up to
meet a pair of cruel old lunatics who would probably attempt
to murder him at sight. Instead of this he was greeted by two
charming and good-looking people who were not, as far as he
could judge, particularly put off by his appearance.

Jane took him for a little walk in the garden before lunch. 'I
told them all about it,' she said, 'and they weren't nearly so
horrified as I thought they would be, but I dare say they think
it's a cleverer plan to pretend not to mind at first. Apparently
mamma used to know your mother quite well when they were
girls. She says she was a great beauty.'

'Yes, she was very beautiful.'

'But they don't know yet that you're an artist. I expect that
will upset them, all right.'

'Really, darling! To hear you talk one would think you
wanted them to be upset. I believe you've got a totally wrong
idea of your parents, you know. I've only had a glimpse of
them so far, it's true, but they seem very nice and kind—quite
different from what you led me to expect.'

'Oh, well, I suppose now you're going to take their side,'
said Jane pettishly. 'Anyway, there's the bell for lunch, so

come along. Perhaps you'll see my point when you know them better.'

During luncheon Albert realized that, as he had always been inclined to suspect, Jane's pretended hatred of her parents was the purest affectation. She was evidently very fond of them as they were of her. He thought it a curious anomaly that a person with such a straight-forward nature as Jane seemed to him to possess should be capable of deceiving herself to this extent upon any subject, but consoled himself by thinking that marriage would bring home the real truth to her.

The Dacres did not in any way show that they knew of Jane's engagement, but behaved to Albert quite as they would have to any other visitor. They were anxious to hear every little detail of the Dalloch house-party and laughed heartily at Albert's description of Lady Prague.

Encouraged by this he broached the subject of General Murgatroyd, delicately, as he imagined from what Jane had said that no officer in the British Army would be considered a fit subject for jest. Great, therefore, was his amazement when Sir Hubert Dacre cried out:

'Not really! Was Mildew Murgatroyd there? Jane, you never told me that! Well, I'm sure you got plenty of fun out of him, didn't you?'

'What did you call him, sir?' asked Albert, hardly able to believe his ears.

'Mildew Murgatroyd. They called him that in the South African War because he was so untidy and slovenly. People used to say that even his revolver was coated with mildew. Why, he's a perfect joke in the army, you know. During the last War they wouldn't have him in France at all. He was given some job in connexion with the Inland Water Transport, I believe.'

'Oh *good*!' said Albert; 'only I wish I'd known it before. I pictured him leading his men like anything, from the way he talked. He told us a most blood-curdling story about how he and twenty privates held a kopje in South Africa, alone and unaided for a fortnight.'

139

'Yes, and did he tell you that when the relieving force came up in answer to his urgent messages they found there wasn't a Boer for thirty miles, hadn't been the whole time, you know, except in his own imagination.'

'Oh, why didn't we know all this before!' sighed Albert.

'I hear Buggins was up there,' went on Sir Hubert. 'Such a very nice, cultivated man, and a great authority on Scottish history.'

There was a silence. Albert began to feel very much embarrassed; the end of the meal approached rapidly and he dreaded the moment when he would be left alone with Jane's father. He looked helplessly round the room for something to talk about, and presently said:

'What a lovely Richmond that is, Sir Hubert!'

'Yes, quite a pleasant picture in its way, I think. Those two children are boys, though with their long hair and frilly skirts one would rather suppose them to be girls. The one on the left is my father.'

'I see that it is painted in his earlier manner. I am inclined myself to prefer his middle period. Did Jane tell you that I was fortunate enough to be able to save two very beautiful pictures from the fire at Dalloch? Winterhalters. Is he a favourite of yours?'

'How funny,' said Lady Dacre, 'that it should be the fashion to admire those Victorian artists again after so many years.'

Albert, who rather particularly prided himself on being quite uninfluenced by such things as fashions, looked down his nose at this remark.

Lady Dacre now rose to her feet and Albert, with a sinking feeling in the pit of his stomach, was left alone with his future father-in-law.

He thought, 'Better get it over quickly,' and was beginning a beautiful and well-constructed sentence which he had made up in the train, when Sir Hubert interrupted him with:

'Have some more port?'

'Thank you, sir. The thing is,' Albert said hurriedly,

140

forgetting all the rolling periods which he had been about to pour forth, 'Jane and I think . . . that is, we know . . . that we would like to get married.'

'Be married,' said Sir Hubert severely. 'I very much dislike the expression "to get married."'

'So do I,' replied Albert earnestly.

'Then why use it? Well, so you and Jane wish to be married, do you? And isn't this a little sudden?'

'Sudden, sir?'

'How long have you known each other?'

'Oh, for a very long time—quite six weeks altogether, and we've been engaged for nearly a fortnight.'

'Yes, I see—a perfect lifetime! And have you the means to support her?'

'I have a thousand a year, beside what I can make.'

'And what is your profession?'

Albert felt his nerve vanishing.

'If I say "artist" he will kick me out of the house. I can't face it. I shall have to tell a lie.'

'I am in business, sir.'

'What business?'

'In the city.'

'Yes; but what is your business in the city?'

'Oh, I see! Yes, I'm a pawnbroker—did I say pawnbroker? I mean, stockbroker, of course.'

Sir Hubert looked deeply disgusted.

'I'm sorry to hear that,' he said, 'although in these days people must take what work they can get. I have always felt myself—no doubt wrongly—that stockbroking is a very unproductive sort of profession. If I had a son I should have wished him to choose almost any other, and I always imagined that Jane would end by marrying a man of talent, say, a writer or an artist. However, that's neither here nor there, and I don't see that there can be much objection to your engagement. Jane is of an age to know her own mind. Personally, I should advise you to wait for a few weeks before announcing it. Let's go to the drawing-room, if you've quite finished your port.'

141

Albert now wished that the earth would open up and swallow him. He also felt quite furious with Jane; and as soon as they were left alone together he fell upon her, tooth and nail.

'You little idiot! We can never be married now, and it's all your fault. I can't face your father again. I must go away this instant.'

'Albert darling, what d'you mean? Was he awful to you?'

'No, he was charming; but *why* did you say he hated artists?'

'Because I'm sure he does. It's the sort of thing he always hates.'

Albert told her what had happened.

'You see,' he cried miserably, 'it's impossible for me to stay here after that!'

Jane burst into fits of laughter. She laughed and laughed. Then, she kissed Albert on the tip of his nose and ran out of the room. Presently she returned with both her parents, who were laughing so much that the tears ran down their cheeks.

The Dacres were frankly delighted at Jane's engagement. It would hardly be fair to say that they were anxious to get her off their hands, but, fond as they were of her, there was no doubt that she had lately caused them an unending amount of worry. Her constant and violent flirtations with the most curiously unsuitable people, her doubtful friends, wild behaviour and increasingly bad reputation, all these things were driving them demented, and they both felt that the only hope of steadying her lay in a happy marriage.

'I think we are very lucky,' said Sir Hubert, talking it over with his wife that night in bed. 'When you think what some of Jane's friends are like! Suppose, for instance, it had been Ralph Callendar, not very probable, I admit, but one never knows. Now this boy is of good family, has nice manners, was at Eton and all that, and at the same time he is intelligent. Jane could never have been happy with a fool. If he is a trifle affected—well, I don't know that that's such a terrible fault in a young man. Tiresome, of course, but pardonable. Altogether it seems to me quite satisfactory, far more so than I should ever have expected.'

The engagement was announced in the papers a few days later and as at that particular moment there happened to be a scarcity of news, Albert and Jane for one day vied with the Sudbury Murder Trial in holding the attention of the public.

'ROMANCE OF YOUNG ARTIST AND BARONET'S DAUGHTER.

SEQUEL TO FIRE AT DALLOCH CASTLE'

blared forth on the front page of the *Daily Runner* in type only a shade smaller and less black than that used for:

> *'Tragic Widow's Eight-Hour Ordeal in Dock.'*

The gossip-writers, who have little or no use for tragic widows unless they are titled as well, gave the couple their undivided attention.

Jane was described as tall and beautiful with artistic tastes, and was credited with having designed her own bedroom at her father's house in Wilton Crescent. (In point of fact, the bedroom had not been redecorated since they bought the house.)

Much capital was made out of the fact that they had both been staying at Dalloch Castle, the beautiful and historic seat of the Earl of Craigdalloch, when it was so tragically and mysteriously burnt to the ground.

'I hear, by the way,' said one paragraph, 'that Lord and Lady Craigdalloch (she, of course, was a daughter of the late Sir Robert Barns) are shortly returning to Scotland to superintend the rebuilding of the castle. As Lady Craigdalloch is renowned for her exquisite taste, the new castle will probably be an immense improvement on the old, which was built in 1860, a bad year—as some wit is said to have remarked—for wine, women and houses.'

Albert shuddered when he read this.

'My dear Jane, I can absolutely *see* the house that she will build. It is too horrible to think of that heavenly place gone for ever, but even more horrible to imagine, rising out of its ashes, a building in the best cenotaph style. I really believe that Lady Craigdalloch would pull down the Albert Memorial if she had a chance.'

Jane received, among others, the following letters of congratulations:

'Dear Jane,

'Many congratulations on your engagement. I admit that it was a great surprise to me when I read it in *The Times* this morning.

'My husband has been far from well since the fire. He sends good wishes.

'Yrs. sincerely,

'Florence Prague.'

'She doesn't seem wildly enthusiastic,' said Albert, who read this over Jane's shoulder, 'but I rather think she was in love with me herself,' he added complacently.

'Marlborough Club.

'Dear Miss Dacre,

'Congratulations.

'I caught a nasty chill after the fire so please excuse this short note.

'Yrs.,

Mowbray Murgatroyd.'

'Bachelors' Club.

'Dear Miss Dacre,

'Hearty congratulations. After all we went through together I shall always remember you with great affection.

'What a gallant deed of yr. fiancé, saving those Winterhalters. I did not know of it until afterwards.

'Yrs. sincerely,
'Stanislas Wenceslaus.'

'Castle Fea.

'Darling Jane,

'I'm *so* glad everything has passed off all right. I was certain your parents would like Albert myself, but I know that it was an anxiety

144

to you, feeling that they might not approve. The McFeas have been angelic to us. We leave here to-morrow as everything seems to be fixed up now. What d'you think we found yesterday among the ruins of Dalloch? The admiral's spare eye. It was hollow inside and veiny, and I can't tell you what a really nasty look it gave us! Walter insists on wearing it hanging from his watch-chain, which is so disgusting of him.

'It's too awful all our things being burnt; as Walter says, it would have been cheaper in the end to go to the Lido. Still, if we had you'd never have met Albert, so it's all to the good, really.

'Morris-Minerva is making my life sheer hell at the moment. I throw up quite constantly.

'Best love. Come and see us soon.

'SALLY.'

Poor Jane found that it took her the best part of that day to answer these—and some thirty-five other letters, and Albert felt himself rather neglected. When the next morning she received not thirty-five but sixty-five, he announced that he would go to Paris until this influx of congratulations was over.

'But my dear,' said Lady Dacre, 'when the letters come to an end the presents will begin, and that is much worse, because it is such an effort pretending to be grateful for absolute horrors.

'Hubert and I were discussing your plans this morning, and we think that if you want to be married in November we had better go back quite soon to Wilton Crescent. There is Jane's trousseau to be ordered, for one thing.'

'If you do that I can stay with Mr. Buggins, but meanwhile I really think I had better go over to Paris for a bit. I ought to be getting rid of my present studio, and have several things that must be seen to sometime soon. I won't bother to look for a new flat yet. We can stay in an hotel after our honeymoon, until we find a nice one, but I must wind up my affairs, and this seems to be a good moment. Jane is far too much occupied to need me about the place now.'

18

Albert went to Paris meaning to stay there for a fortnight, but in a week's time he was standing outside the Dacres' front door in Wilton Crescent. Frankly, he had not enjoyed himself and had spent his time counting the hours to when he should see Jane again. This worried him a great deal. Always before he had been perfectly happy in Paris and he had expected to be so still—had thought that he would hardly miss her at all and that he might even find it quite an effort to come back to her, instead of which he found himself restless and miserable and unable to stay away. He began to realize that nothing would ever again be as it had been for him, and the realization annoyed him.

He found Jane alone in the downstairs drawing-room; she was not expecting him and flew into his arms.

'Darling sweetest,' she said after a few minutes, 'don't go away again. It was dreadful, I had to be thinking about you the whole time.'

'I got so bored with thinking about you that I had to come back.'

'Angel, did you really? I am pleased. Come and see the presents, they're simply unbelievable!' And she dragged him upstairs to a large empty room which had been set aside for the wedding presents.

'There are masses for you, too. I put them all over there. Shall we unpack them now?'

'Let's look at yours first. My dear, what a lot, though! You must know a quantity of people. But how absolutely horrible they are! What on earth shall we do with all these atrocious things? And where do people go to buy wedding presents? Is there a special shop for them, because these things are all exactly alike? Have you noticed that? Oh, look at the

Lalique, and all that dreadful glass with bubbles in it! I shall burst into tears in a moment.'

'Oh, well,' said Jane, 'don't take it to heart too much. It only needs a good kick.'

'I know what we'll do,' said Albert, 'we'll have a wedding-present shoot, and get General Murgatroyd to arrange it for us. You see, the drivers can throw the things over our heads and we'll shoot at them. Then, when it's all over, we'll be photographed with the bag. Haven't you any nice presents, darling?'

'Not one,' said Jane, sadly. 'Now let's open yours.'

They set to work, and soon the floor was covered with brown paper, shavings and pieces of string. Whereas Jane's presents were nearly all made of glass, Albert's seemed to consist mainly of leatherwork. Leather blotters, waste-paper baskets and note-cases were unpacked in quick succession, and lastly, a cigarette box made out of an old book. This present, which was sent by someone he had known at Oxford, perfectly enraged Albert: it had originally contained the works of Mrs. Hemans.

'My favourite poetess. Why couldn't he send me the book unmutilated? He must remember that I never smoke, in any case. Still, sweet of him to think of me.'

The maid came in with some more parcels for Jane, containing a Lalique clock from Lady Brenda. ('How kind! considering we've only met her once. It will do for the shoot, too.') A lampshade made out of somebody's last will and testament, and a hideous little glass tree, growing in a china pot, from Lady Prague.

'I'm beginning to understand about wedding presents,' said Albert. 'It seems to me that they can be divided into three categories: the would-be useful, the so-called ornamental, and those that have been converted from their original purpose into something quite different, but which is seldom either useful or ornamental.'

'I think,' said Jane bitterly, 'that they can be divided into two categories: those that have been bought in a shop, which are beastly, and those that have been snatched off the

147

mantelpiece and given to the butler to pack up, which are beastlier. Look here, Albert darling, I'm getting really sick of this wedding. I do nothing all day but thank for these revolting presents, which I would pay anybody to take away, and try on clothes I don't want. Couldn't we chuck the whole thing and be married quietly somewhere? If I have to face another two months like this I shall be ill. Really, I mean it. Please, Albert.'

'Well, darling, personally, I think it would be heaven, but I must be in London for my exhibition, you know.'

'When does that open?'

'In three weeks to-morrow.'

'That gives us heaps of time to have a honeymoon and everything. Please, let's do that. Go and see about a special licence, now, this minute.'

'But, darling, listen to me. . . .'

'Oh, well, if you are going to be tiresome. . . .'

'Very well, I'll see what can be done, but first we must ask your parents. No, I absolutely insist on that, darling.'

Sir Hubert and Lady Dacre, as might have been expected, showed no enthusiasm at all when told of Jane's little plan.

'Don't be stupid,' said Lady Dacre scornfully, 'of course you can't do any such thing. People would say at once that Jane is going to have a baby. The presents will get better soon, I dare say: probably you won't have a great many more, and anyhow, the nicest ones generally come at the end.'

'Why not advance the date a little,' suggested Sir Hubert, 'to, say, the middle of October, about a month from now? That would be much more sensible than rushing off in such a hurry, and after all, a month does go fairly quickly.'

Jane and Albert felt the justice of these remarks and decided that they would definitely settle on the sixteenth of October, by which time Albert's exhibition would be well begun.

'If only,' said Jane, 'when announcing a marriage, one could put, "No presents, by request," how much more bearable the life of engaged couples would become. Look what I've got to thank for now. A pair of bellows made from the timbers of the *Victory* and sent by Admiral Wenceslaus. Oh, dear!'

'Very kind of him, I think,' said her father reprovingly.

'Oh, well; yes, so it is. Very kind of all the people who send these inferior things. I only wish they wouldn't, that's all.'

'How much better it would be,' sighed Lady Dacre, 'if *everybody* would send cheques.'

'Or postal orders,' said Jane.

'Or stamps,' said Albert.

For the next week or two, Jane and Albert had to make up their minds that they would only see each other once a day. They generally dined together and sometimes went to a play, but were often too tired even for that. Presents poured in for both of them, over and above which Albert was now very busy arranging about his exhibition .

He found that he had not brought over quite enough pictures for it, and embarked on a series of woolwork designs for six chairs, based on the theme of sport in the Highlands. He also completed his 'Catalogue of Recent Finds at Dalloch' (having wired for and obtained the consent of the Craig-dallochs), intending that a specimen copy should be on view at the exhibition.

With Albert thus kept so busy that anyhow he would have had no time to play with her, Jane found her own jobs far less disagreeable. As Lady Dacre had predicted, the presents she received greatly improved in quality as time went on and she found it much less boring to write letters thanking for things that she really liked. Her trousseau now became a source of great interest, especially the wedding dress, which she could not try on often enough and which was extremely lovely. As for the other things, tiring as it undoubtedly was to stand for hours every day being fitted, there was a certain excitement about the idea that by the time she began to wear them she would be a married woman, and this sustained her.

19

Walter and Sally Monteath, on their return to London, found themselves financially in a very bad way indeed. They had lost almost all their personal effects in the fire. Although they replaced these as economically as they could, it took most of their available money to do so. At this inconvenient moment the accumulated bills of months began to rain upon them, more numerous and insistent than ever before. The bank refused to allow them a further overdraft, all Sally's jewellery had long since been sold, and she began to have difficulty even in paying the household books.

Sally felt desperately ill and worried, and even Walter was obliged to give up taking taxis everywhere; but, apart from that, the situation did not appear to weigh on him at all until, one evening, he came in with some books that he was going to review and found her crying bitterly.

'Sally, darling angel! What *is* the matter?' he said, kneeling down beside her and stroking her hair. When, through her tears, she explained to him that she could bear it no longer, that she literally didn't know how to raise money for the week's books, and that she had been adding up what they owed and found it amounted to nearly a thousand pounds, Walter was enormously relieved.

'I thought something frightful must have happened,' he said. 'But if that's all you're worrying about, I can easily get some money. Why, anybody would lend us a hundred pounds or so to carry on with till our next quarter comes in. As for the bills, they can wait for years, if necessary.'

'Walter, they *can't*. Why, some of them have lawyer's letters with them already. And it's no use borrowing a hundred pounds—that won't really help us at all, permanently, I mean. Then think of Morris-Minerva. How

150

expensive all that business will be, and how are we going to educate him, or anything?' She burst into fresh floods of tears and said wildly that she must have been mad to marry him on so little money but that she had thought they would be able to manage, and that so they would have, except for his idiotic extravagance.

Walter, who had never before in his life known Sally to utter a cross word, was amazed by this outburst and began to feel really worried. His was the sort of mentality which never apprehends an unpleasant situation until it is presented so forcibly that it can no longer be ignored. Now, for the first time, he began to see that their position was, in fact, very parlous, and he was plunged into extreme despair.

'Anyhow, darling,' he said, 'I can't have you worrying like this. Leave it all to me. I'll find a job and support you properly. I'll go out now, this minute, and find one,' he added, and seizing his hat he dashed out of the house, saying that he would come back when he had some work, and not before.

Sally felt strangely comforted by his attitude, although not very optimistic about the job. She sat by the fire and thought that, after all, these bothers were very trifling matters compared to the happiness of being married to Walter.

While she was sitting there thinking vaguely about him, there was a resounding peal on the front-door bell.

Sally remembered that the daily woman had gone home, and was half-considering whether she would sit still and pretend that everybody was out, when it occurred to her that it might be Walter, who was in the constant habit of losing his latch-key. The bell rang again, and this time Sally, almost mechanically, went to the door and opened it.

She was a little bit alarmed to see, standing in the passage, three tall bearded strangers, but was soon reassured by the unmistakably gloomy voice of Ralph Callendar which issued from behind one of the beards, and said:

'Sally, dear, I hadn't realized until this very moment that you are *enceinte*. How beautifully it suits you! Why had nobody told me?'

Sally laughed and led the way into the drawing-room. She

now saw that the other men were Jasper Spengal and Julius Raynor, very efficiently disguised.

'Yes,' she said, 'but how *could* you tell? It's really very exciting, due in April. Morris, if a boy, Minerva, if a girl, and we haven't the slightest idea where she's going to live (there's no room here, as you know) or how we can afford to educate him. But Walter's out now, looking for a job. Have a cocktail, Ralph dear, be an angel and make one; the things live in that chest. But why fancy dress so early in the evening, and why haven't we been asked to the party?'

'No, dear,' said Ralph sadly, taking some bottles out of the chest. 'Not fancy dress at all—disguise.'

'Are you—not wanted by Scotland Yard for anything, I hope?'

'No, dear, curiously enough. No; we are going, simply in order to please Jasper, to the Savoy Theatre, where we shall see a Gilbert and Sullivan operette, called—what is it called, Jasper?'

' "I Gondolieri." '

'Yes, "I Gondolieri." Jasper has a new philosophy, which is that one should experience everything pleasant and unpleasant, and says that nobody ought to die until they have seen one Gilbert and Sullivan operetta and one Barrie play. Last night he begged us to accompany him on these grim errands, and after much talk, we allowed ourselves to be persuaded. But as it would be impossible to explain this to all the casual acquaintances whom we might meet at the theatre, we decided to take the precaution of a disguise.

'It is one thing to see a Gilbert and Sullivan, and quite another to be seen at one. We have our unborn children to consider, not to mention our careers.

'It has taken us nearly all day, but I think the result satisfactory. To complete the illusion we intend to limp about during the *entr'acte*. Jasper, as you see, has a slight hump on one shoulder, and Julius a snub nose.

'I myself, have not been obliged to go to such lengths. Nobody would ever suspect me. Even if I went undisguised, they would only say, "We didn't know Ralph had a double."

Did you mention, Sally, that Walter is looking for a job?'

'Yes, poor lamb, he is.'

'He won't find one, of course. But never mind, there are worse things than poverty, though I can't for the moment remember what they are, and we'll all take it in turns to keep the baby for you. A poet of Walter's ability has no business with money troubles and jobs and nonsense like that. Are you very hard up at the moment, Sally?'

'Yes, terribly, you know. We've got such debts and then our people simply can't help. They give us more than they can afford as it is.'

'Well, then, my dear, I'll tell you what to do, straight away. Come and live with me till Christmas and let the flat to an American woman I know for twenty guineas a week. Would that help?'

'Ralph, what an angel you are! But, of course, we can't do that, and we're not really so hard up, you know, only one likes a little grumble. Anyway, who would pay twenty guineas for a tiny flat like this? What are you doing?'

'Hullo! Regent 3146,' said Ralph into the telephone, his eyes on the ceiling. 'Hullo! Mrs. Swangard? Ralph here. Yes, I found you the very thing—a jewel, 65 Fitzroy Square. Belongs, you know, to the famous poet Monteath. Yes, I had the greatest difficulty. . . . Oh, no, no trouble. I knew at once it would be *the* place for you. Heart of Bloomsbury. . . . Oh, most fashionable, all the famous people. . . . Yes, all round you, roaring away. What? I said "roaringly gay" . . . My dear, you'll be astounded when I tell you . . . only twenty guineas! A *week*, not a day.

'Wonderful, yes. Of course, they wouldn't let it to just anybody, as you can imagine. . . . No. . . . As soon as you like—to-morrow if you like. . . . To-morrow, then. . . . Yes, I'll come round and see you about it after the play to-night. . . . Yes, perfect . . . good-bye.'

'Oh, Ralph!' said Sally, almost in tears. 'How sweet you are! That means more than a hundred pounds, doesn't it, and almost at once? Think what a help it will be. That is, if she likes the flat; but perhaps she won't?'

'My dear, that woman will like just exactly what I tell her to like. So pack up and come round some time in the morning. There's a good-sized bedroom you can have, if you don't mind sharing my sitting-room. Oh, nonsense, darling, you'd do the same by me, as you know very well. The poor are always good to each other. Are you going to Albert's private view?' he added, as though anxious to change the subject.

'Oh, that's to-morrow, of course, I'd forgotten. Yes, we're supposed to be lunching with him first.'

'I hear he's given Jane for an engagement ring a garnet with Queen Victoria's head carved on it.'

'No! has he? Have you any idea at all what his pictures will be like?'

'Absolutely none; but Bennet, I believe, thinks well of them.'

Jasper and Julius, who had been looking at *Vogue*, now came over to the fireplace. Feeling that they had so far not quite earned their cocktails, they began to pour forth a flood of semi-brilliant conversation, mostly in Cockney, told two stories about George Moore, one about Sir Thomas Beecham, asked if there was any future for Delius, and left, taking Ralph with them.

Sally resumed her meditations. How right she had been to marry Walter after all. Nobody could have made her so happy; life with him was very nearly perfect. The same tastes, the same friends, the same sense of humour and, above all, no jealousy. She dropped happily into an almost voluptuous doze. The rain was falling outside, which made the room seem particularly warm and comfortable.

Her thoughts became more and more misty, and chased each other through her head in the most inconsequent way until they were nonsense and she was on the edge of sleep—'When the rain is falling thickly there should be long white hands waving in it.'

Walter, finding her fast asleep on the floor, her head buried in a cushion, wondered whose were the empty cocktail glasses. He found a thimbleful of cocktail left in the shaker which he drank, and then woke up Sally by kissing her.

'It's no good, darling,' he said, 'I cannot dig, and to write gossip I'm ashamed, but I've borrowed ten pounds from Albert, and I love you dreadfully, and I'll write some articles for the Sunday papers. We'll get rich somehow. Meanwhile, I'm going to take you out to dinner at Quaglino's because you haven't been there and it might amuse you. And who's been drinking out of my cocktail glasses, I should like to know?'

'I made a hundred pounds while you were out, my angel, by letting the flat to an American friend of Ralph's from to-morrow, and Ralph says we can go and live in Gower Street while it's let; he's got a bedroom all ready for us. So what d'you think of that, sweetest?'

'Well, I think that beggars can't be choosers. If it's a load off your mind, I'm glad and, of course, it's divine of Ralph. Still, of course, really it's too bloody, because we shall never have a single minute to ourselves. You know what it is in Ralph's flat—one long party.'

'I know, darling, but it's only for six weeks, and it will be such a saving. Also, I didn't like to hurt his feelings by refusing, it was so sweet of him to think of it. As a matter of fact, we could go for some of the time to my family: they're always asking us to stay with them.'

'I believe it would be cheaper in the end,' said Walter crossly, 'to stay on here. Couldn't you telephone to Ralph and say that we've changed our minds?'

'No, darling, I couldn't. If you can't support me, somebody must, you know, and as we're both devoted to Ralph why not let it be he? We needn't really go to the family, of course; I only said that to annoy you, although I shall have to go sometime. By the way, too, remind me to tell mother about Morris-Minerva. I'm sure I ought to have told her ages ago, because it's the sort of thing it drives her mad to hear from somebody else.

'Darling Walter. And I'm sorry I said all that about supporting me, because I know you would like to be able to. And anyway, we're so much happier like this than if you had some horrid sort of job which you hated. And if we're really going to Quaglino's hadn't you better telephone for a table, my sweet?'

20

Albert had decided that the private view of his pictures should take the form of a giant cocktail-party at the Chelsea Galleries, where they were being exhibited, the afternoon before they were to be opened to the public. Guests were invited from half-past three to seven, and at three o'clock Albert and Jane, supported by the Monteaths and Mr. Buggins, with whom they had all been lunching, arrived at the Galleries in a state of some trepidation.

Walter and Sally, who had not seen the pictures before, gasped with amazement as they entered the room, and for several moments were left quite speechless. The pictures were indeed, at first sight, most peculiar and Albert appeared to have employed any medium but the usual. Some of them stood right out like bas reliefs, while various objects such as hair, beards, buttons and spectacles were stuck on to them. Others were executed entirely in string, newspaper and bits of coloured glass.

The first picture—*Child with Doll*—had a real doll stuck across it. The child also had real hair tied up with blue ribbons. The next on the catalogue, '*No 2; Fire irons, formal design*,' represented a poker and tongs and was executed in small pearl buttons, varying in shade from dead white to smoke-grey. This was framed in empty cotton-reels.

The most important picture in the exhibition was '*No. 15. The Absinthe Drinker.*' This was tremendously built out, the central figure—that of a woman—being in a very high relief. On her head was perched half a straw hat with black ostrich feathers. In one hand was a glass filled with *real* absinthe. This was felt by Albert himself to be his masterpiece.

The only painting in the ordinary sense of the word was his

portrait of Sally, which, hung between two huge still-lifes with surgical limbs, stuffed birds and ukuleles stuck all over them, hardly showed up to its best advantage.

Mr. Buggins was rather shocked at this travesty of painting, but was nevertheless obliged to admit that there was a great deal of force in the pictures, while the Monteaths, when the first sensation of surprise had left them, pronounced themselves in raptures.

Albert was evidently in a state of nerves and hardly listened to what was said, but went from picture to picture, adjusting the feathers of *The Absinthe Drinker* at a slightly less-tipsy angle, retying one of *Child with Doll's* hair-ribbons and borrowing Jane's comb with which to tidy its hair. Finally, he ran round combing all the hair and beards that he could find.

The others stood about rather gloomily wishing that the party would begin. Albert's nervousness had imparted itself to them and especially to Jane, who was terrified that the pictures (much as she personally admired them) might be a most dreadful failure.

If this happened, she thought selfishly, a gloom would certainly be cast over their whole wedding.

Albert, from having always before been perfectly indifferent as to what people might think of his work, now that the pictures were about to be exhibited had become almost childishly anxious for them to have a success.

The first guest appeared in the shape of Ralph, who was received with exaggerated cries of joy.

'Ralph dear, how nice of you to come so early! We *were* hoping someone would come soon. You will try and make the party go, Ralph, won't you? We're all simply terrified, and it's sure to be sticky at first, so promise to help?'

Ralph smiled sadly.

'So these are your pictures, Albert,' he said, and very slowly walked round the Gallery, carefully examining each one from various angles. Having completed the tour he went up to Albert and said earnestly, '*Go on* painting, Albert. I mean that. Go on with it and one day you will be a very

157

considerable artist indeed. Good-bye, my dears, I must go home to bed.'

'Don't go!' they cried in disappointed voices; but he took no notice of their protestations and left the Gallery.

Albert wiped his eyes. He was more than touched and flattered by this attitude of Ralph's, and followed his friend out into the street to tell him so.

Jane broke rather an awkward silence by wondering who the next visitor would be. It was felt that Ralph had not exactly proved the life and soul of the party.

'I think this is quite awful,' said Walter. 'I'm not easily frightened myself, but the beginning of a party is always apt to upset me; and now in addition to the social fear I'm suffering, there is this enormous empty room with Albert's terrifying pictures. The whole atmosphere is painful to a degree. Not that I don't think the pictures very clever, mind you, Jane, because I do, and they will certainly cause a great sensation, but you must admit that they *are* terrifying, specially for that child. Sally, darling, I beg you won't look at it for too long, because if Morris-Minerva even faintly resembles it I shall commit infanticide on the spot.'

Sally now had a brainwave.

'Why don't we begin the cocktails?'

This brilliant idea was immediately acted upon, and when Albert came back a more cheerful atmosphere was pervading the whole place. He felt glad of a drink himself after an emotional scene with Ralph in the street.

The next arrival was Admiral Wenceslaus, who came in rather jauntily, saying:

'And don't offer me a cocktail; I never touch the things. How are you? How are you all?'

He took the cocktail which Albert was rather diffidently holding out towards him and drank it off at a single gulp.

'My dear Gates, I have brought back your trousers which I have had well pressed for you. They needed it. And also a little wedding present in the shape of a book which I thought you might read on your honeymoon. It is by an old friend of my own, Admiral Sir Bartelmass Jenks, and is entitled *The*

Prize Courts and Their Functions or The Truth About Blockade. The prize courts, my dear Gates, as you know, investigate the case of ships captured in times of war. . . .'

At this moment, as so often happens at parties, about twenty people all came in a lump together and the admiral, deprived of his audience, settled down to some more cocktails.

Soon the room was buzzing and humming with talk. The pictures, as Walter had foreseen, were causing a real sensation. People were, for the most part, very guarded in their criticism, asking each other rather anxiously what they thought about them.

Not so, however, Lady Prague, who, imposing but dowdy in a coat of Paisley pattern with brown fur, was accompanied by General Murgatroyd and Lady Brenda Chadlington.

She walked round the Gallery rather flat-footedly, pausing here and there to inspect the more outstanding pictures rather closely with her nose almost touching them, and then at an exaggerated distance (a trick she had learnt while visiting the Royal Academy).

When she had completed this tour she turned to Lady Brenda.

'Of course, Brenda, I expect it's my own fault, but I really think these pictures are very ugly. Not the sort of thing I should care to have in a drawing-room at all. In fact, I don't see that you could call this Art. I mean, when you think of those wonderful Dutch pictures we saw last year. These are so terribly out of drawing. And then, all that hair! Well, I suppose they're very clever, but—'

Lady Brenda said, 'Ssh! they will hear you,' and General Murgatroyd said loudly and angrily that it was another art hoax and that he was not the least taken in by it.

'If you want to see some really good pictures,' he said, 'go to the Army and Navy Stores. There's one I saw yesterday—some sheep going into a little birch wood with a mist—early morning, I should say. I think of buying it for Craig's silver wedding—silver birches, you know; makes it rather suitable.'

159

'Personally, I'm glad I have a sense of humour,' went on Lady Prague, warming to her subject. 'That controversy about Rima now: what I said was, "Why be angry? Every time you want a good laugh in future you only have to go into Hyde Park and there it is!" Killing! A perfect scream!

'Ah! here's Jane. Well, my dear, congratulations on your engagement. We are just admiring your fiancé's pictures— quite pretty, aren't they? No cocktail, thank you, dear, I'm *not* very modern, I'm afraid.'

The Gallery was suddenly and surprisingly invaded by a large crowd of people dressed in the deepest mourning and carrying wreaths; among others, Jasper Spengal, who rushed up to Albert saying breathlessly:

'Such heaven, my dear! We've just been having a mock funeral. We bought a plot at the London Necropolis and we drove for miles and miles through the streets in carriages with black horses, and all the time Julius was in the coffin in grave-clothes which we bought at Harrods. And, did you know that one has grave-stockings, too? Then, when we reached our plot in the Necrop., he just pushed up the lid and walked out, and we all picked up the wreaths and ran for dear life.

'Oh, I wish you could have seen the gravediggers' faces! It was a really beautiful moment. Then we all packed into my car and Rosie's car and came on here, and we've brought the flowers for you and Jane because you are engaged. So suitable, we think,' and he laid his wreath at Albert's feet. An enormous card was tied to it, bearing the inscription:

'Sweets to the Sweet. In memory of a noble life.
R.I.P.'

Lady Prague, who had been drinking in every word of all this, said loudly and angrily, 'Those are the Bright Young People, no doubt. How very disgusting! Come along, Brenda, I'm going. Can I drop you anywhere, Mowbray?'

'Yes, if you happen to be passing the Marlborough. . . .'

'Oh, darling!' cried Jasper. 'Did you hear what she called us? What a name! Bright Young People! Oh, how unkind to suggest that we are bright—horrid word—I see nothing bright about a funeral, anyway, do you? What a nasty old woman! I'm so—so glad she's gone!

'Now, darling, I must telephone—may I?— to the *Daily Runner* and tell them all about it: they'll just have nice time to write it up. We had six photographers and a cinematograph at the graveside, and the light has been very good to-day, luckily. Would you like to be photographed among the wreaths, darling? It might give quite a good boost to the exhibition.'

'I think not, Jasper, thank you so much. The Press people were here this morning and this is by way of being serious, you know, not a "freak party,"' said Albert rather crossly. His nerves were on edge, and the mock funeral, which would at any other time have amused him a lot, struck him as being a painfully stupid idea.

He was thankful when they all dashed away to hear the Will read at Jasper's house, leaving the wreaths piled up underneath *The Absinthe Drinker*, especially as Jane's father and mother came in a moment later.

The Dacres, of course, thought Albert's pictures perfectly raving mad, although they were too polite to say so. They had come with every intention of buying one, but decided in whispers that they were too dreadful—even for a lavatory, so they ordered copies of 'Recent Finds at Dalloch Castle' instead. While they were doing this, they noticed that Mrs. Fairfax had arrived, and Lady Dacre, remarking that she refused to shake hands with that woman, left the Gallery, taking Sir Hubert in tow.

'My dear!' said Mrs. Fairfax to Albert, 'I had to come round for a moment to support you, but I am most frightfully busy. Have you heard the news? Well, I'm going to marry Cosmo again, which is lovely, because I do enjoy being a duchess when all's said and done, and now, with any luck, I shall be one for the rest of my life. You can't think what a difference it makes in shops and trains. Aren't your pictures divine? Especially the one of Florence in tweed.

'Ralph and I were furious to miss the fire, but it was lucky I

161

went to Gleneagles, because that's where I met Cosmo again—in the swimmingbath—and we got on so well comparing notes about our various husbands and wives that we fixed it up there and then; so I must fly now and get on with my trousseau. If I have another baby, what relation will it be to Bellingham? Good-bye, darling, then. I really have to go.'

Isaac Manuel, the art critic and collector, now put in an appearance, and Albert spent nearly an hour going round the pictures with him. He was greatly soothed and comforted by the older man's intelligent appreciation of his work.

'You are very young,' he said to Albert as he was leaving, 'and your style is often crude and bombastic, but all the same, Mr. Gates, I must admit that I am very favourably impressed. I have not enjoyed an afternoon so much for some time. I predict a future for you if you realize, as I can see you do, that these methods are, in themselves, far from satisfactory and only a means to an end. Keep the end always in view and you may become a very good artist indeed. I shall certainly see that you have an excellent notice in my paper, and shall most probably present one of your pictures to the Nation. Good day.'

When Albert returned to the Gallery from seeing Mr. Manuel into the street, he found that everyone had gone except Jane, Sally, Walter and the admiral who appeared to have fallen asleep among the funeral wreaths, a terrifying sight as his glass eye remained open, fixed upon the ceiling in a fearful stare.

'What do you think that horrid old admiral has done?' cried Jane. 'To start with he drank so many cocktails that there weren't nearly enough to go round, and then when they were finished he got a straw from one of the wreaths and drank all the absinthe out of the glass in your picture. Sally actually saw him do it.'

'No, really that's too much,' said Albert, who couldn't help laughing all the same. 'I suppose in future I shall be obliged to fill that glass with coloured water, otherwise people will make a habit of drinking it, and you can see for yourselves how terribly the colour values are disturbed when the glass is empty.'

'Well, my dear Albert, I congratulate you,' said Walter warmly. 'The whole thing was a great success, a really good party. And everyone thought the pictures quite brilliant. Manuel was very much impressed. I heard him tell Mr. Buggins that he intends to buy one for his collection, and most probably one for the Nation.'

'Clever Albert,' said Jane. ' Darling, I'm so pleased, aren't you? What's the time, by the way?'

'Past seven. We'd better go, I think. No one's likely to come now, and we'll have to be rather quick if we're really dining at eight.'

They picked up their bags, hats and other belongings and began to move towards the door, when Walter said:

'Look here! What about the admiral? He seems to have passed out completely among those lilies. We can't very well leave him like that, can we?'

Albert considered.

'No, I suppose we can't. Hadn't we better put him into a taxi and send him home? I expect we could carry him between us, Walter; or if he's too heavy I'll call the commissionaire to help.'

They advanced upon the admiral, Walter taking his shoulders and Albert his legs, and half-carried, half- dragged him to the street. Jane hailed a taxi into which they bundled him and shut the door.

'Where to, sir?'

'Oh! Walter, where does he live?'

'How should I know? I haven't an idea.'

'Well, where shall we send him?'

Silence.

'Wait a minute,' said Walter. 'Isn't there a special place somewhere for admirals? Now what *is* it called— Oh, yes! I remember, of course.'

He gave the taxi-driver half-a-crown and said:

'Take this gentleman to the Admiralty, please.'

21

The front page of next morning's *Daily Runner* was full of interest to members of the recent house-party at Dalloch Castle. Jane read it, as she always did, while breakfasting in bed; and for once in her life she pored over its columns with absolutely breathless attention, reading every word, instead of merely skimming down the more sensational columns and then turning over to see if she was mentioned in the gossip page, which I regret to say was her usual method.

To-day, the first paragraph which met her eye was:

AGED PEER DIES IN HARNESS

LORD PRAGUE LIFELESS IN UPPER HOUSE

NIGHT WATCHMAN'S STORY

We regret to announce that Lord Prague, G.C.B., C.V.O., etc., was found dead late last night in the House of Lords. It is stated that his body was discovered just before midnight by Mr. George Wilson, the night watchman.

Mr. Wilson, when interviewed by the *Daily Runner*, said:

'I always go into the House at least once during the night to clear up any pieces of paper, orange peel, or empty bottles that happen to have been left underneath the seats. I had been tidying for some time last night when I noticed the figure of a man half-lying on one of the benches. This did not really surprise me, as the peers often sleep on late into the night after a debate. So I went up to him and said: "Twelve o'clock, m'lord. Can I get you a cup of tea?" He took no notice and, thinking he was fast asleep, I was going to let him stay there till morning when something in his attitude made me pause and look at him more closely. I then realized that he was stone dead, so I went and fetched a policeman.'

Mr. Wilson was much shaken by his experience and says that

although he has often known the peers to die in the corridors and refreshment rooms of the House he cannot recall one to have died in the House itself before.

Dr. McGregor, who was called in by the police, said that death, which was due to heart failure, had taken place some six or seven hours previously: therefore Lord Prague must have passed away in the middle of the debate on Subsidized Potatoes (which is reported on page 13).

It was stated at an early hour this morning that Lady Prague is utterly prostrated with grief.

Lord Rainford, a cousin of the late peer, said in an interview:

'I saw Prague for a moment yesterday afternoon, and he seemed in his usual good form. It has been a terrible shock to all of us, and the loss to the Nation will be irreparable.'

DASHING MORE

Absalom More, fourth Baron Prague, was born in 1838. Educated at Eton and Sandhurst, he first distinguished himself as a boy of eighteen in the Crimea, where he earned the soubriquet of Dashing More—true to his family motto, *More to the Fore*. When peace had been declared he was warmly applauded by Queen Victoria, with whom he was always a great favourite. In 1859 he succeeded to the title on the death of his father, and in 1860 he married one of the Queen's Ladies-in-Waiting, Lady Anastasia Dalloch, daughter of the Earl of Craigdalloch; who died in 1909. In 1910 he married as his second wife, Florence, daughter of Mr. Leonard Jackson of Dombey Hall, Leicestershire, who survives him. Both marriages are childless, and the peerage devolves upon a distant cousin, Mr. Ivanhoe More, of Victoria Road, Kensington.

The very deepest sympathy will go out to Lady Prague, but her sorrow must needs be tempered by the thought that Dashing More died as he would have wished to die—in harness.

(Picture on the Back Page.)

Jane was entranced by this piece of news and read the paragraph over and over again. She was just about to turn to the back page for the promised picture when her eye was caught by:

THE 'BRIGHT YOUNG PEOPLE' GO TOO FAR

MOCK FUNERAL IN LONDON NECROPOLIS

NOT FUNNY—General Murgatroyd.

It is felt that the Bright Young People have had their day and that their jokes, often in the worst possible taste, should come to an end. Yesterday afternoon a 'Mock Funeral' was held in the London Necropolis at Brookwood, where a site had been purchased in the name of Mrs. Bogus Bottom to hold the remains of Bogus Bottom, Esq. The funeral cortège, including six carriages full of weeping 'mourners,' travelled for several miles through the London streets, often causing the traffic to be delayed while it passed, and finally boarded the special Necropolis train. At Brookwood the coffin was reverently conveyed to the graveside and was just going to be lowered carefully into the grave, when the lid opened, and Mr. Julius Raynor stepped out of it, dressed as for tennis. The 'mourners' then picked up the wreaths, which were numerous and costly, and fled to waiting motor-cars.

(Pictures on the Back Page.)

Heartless

The *Daily Runner*, feeling that the only way to stop these heartless pranks is by means of public opinion, sent an interviewer to the following representative men and women, who have not scrupled to express their disapproval:

Miss Martha Measles (well-known novelist):
'I have never heard that it is either clever or amusing to jest with Death. . . .'

Sir Holden Crane (sociologist):
'If these young people would bear more children, they would hardly have the time for such foolishness. . . .'

Bishop of Burford:
'I think it is most shameful, especially as I hear that many people doffed their hats to the cortège as it passed through London. . . .'

Mr. Southey Roberts (satirist):
'Are these people either "Bright" or "Young"? . . .'

General Murgatroyd:
> It's a damned nuisance, and not funny. . . .'

It is understood that the authorities at Brookwood are taking action, and they are very anxiouis to know the address of Mrs. Bogus Bottom.

Jane now turned to the back page and was rewarded by a photograph of Lord Prague in youth; and one of Julius Raynor, a ghastly figure dressed entirely in white, leaping from his coffin.

She then casually glanced at the middle page, where her attention was rooted by a photograph of Albert and a paragraph headed:

AMAZING FEAT OF YOUNG ARTIST

CRITICS ASTOUNDED BY NEW GENIUS
PICTURE FOR THE NATION?

Mr. Albert Gates (herewith) has astounded the art critics and half social London with his exhibition of amazing pictures (now on view at the Chelsea Galleries). They are composed in many cases round real objects stuck to the canvas, such as, for instance, eyeglasses, buttons, hats, and even surgical limbs; and are of a brilliance and novelty impossible to describe, particularly No. 15, *The Absinthe Drinker*, which it is rumoured, has been bought for the Nation by Mr. Isaac Manuel. Another interesting picture is entitled: *Impression of Lady P—* and is executed entirely in bits of tweed cut into small squares. This is framed in beige mackintosh.

Mr. Gates, who left Oxford four years ago, and has since been studying art in Paris, is a tall, good-looking young man of a modest disposition. When a *Daily Runner* representative called on him after the private view of his pictures yesterday, he seemed unaware of the sensation his work has caused in art circles. 'I think it was quite a good party,' he said, referring to the private view.

Mr. Gates recently became engaged to Miss Jane Dacre, the beautiful daughter of Sir Hubert and Lady Dacre of Stow-on-the-Wold, Gloucestershire.

Jane, on reading this, became very thoughtful. She was not at all sure that she liked this sudden blaze of fame which had come so unexpectedly upon Albert. The picture which she had framed in her mind of their married life had been imagined without this new factor. She had thought of herself as being all in all to him: his one real friend, sticking to him through thick and thin, encouraging, praising and helping. Much as she admired, or thought she admired, Albert's work herself, it had never occurred to her that he might have a real success with the critics; she had imagined that such revolutionary ideas would remain unnoticed for years, except by a few of the ultra-moderns.

The telephone-bell interrupted her train of thought. She put out her hand rather absentmindedly to take off the receiver, wondering who it could be so early. Albert's voice, trembling with excitement, said:

'Have you seen the papers, darling? Yes, they're all the same. Buggins says he can't remember any exhibition to have had such notices for years and years. And I've just been talking to Isaac Manuel. He's buying *The Absinthe Drinker* for the *Tate*, my dear! and two still lifes for himself; and he's commissioned me to fresco some rooms in his new house. What d'you think of that? So it looks as if we shall have to live in London for a bit, after all. Do you mind, darling one? Of course, I said I could do nothing until our honeymoon is over, but we may have to cut it short by a week or two, I dare say. Isn't it splendid, darling? Aren't you pleased? I never for a moment thought the English critics had so much sense, did you? Where are you lunching to-day? Oh, yes, I'd forgotten. Well, meet me at the Chelsea, will you, at about one? You're not feeling ill or anything, are you? Oh, I thought you sounded rather subdued, that's all. Well, good-bye. I must go round to Manuel's now.'

As Jane hung up the receiver her eyes were full of tears.

'I couldn't feel more jealous,' she thought miserably, 'if it were another woman. It's disgusting of me not to be pleased, but I can't help it.'

She began working herself up into a state of hysteria while she dressed. She saw all her dreams of Albert's struggle for fame, with herself helping and encouraging, of a tiny house in Paris only visited by a few loyal friends, and of final success in about ten years' time largely brought about by her own influence, falling to earth shattered.

Albert, with his looks, talents and new-found fame, would soon, she thought, become the centre of that semi-artistic social set which is so much to the fore in London. He would be courted and flattered, his opinions accepted, and his presence eagerly sought after: while she, instead of being his one real friend, the guiding star of his life, would become its rather dreary background. She imagined herself growing daily uglier and more boring. People would say: 'Yes, poor boy, he married her before he had met any other women. He must be regretting it now that it's too late.'

Jane, who at all times was inclined to take an exaggerated view of things, and whose nerves had been very much on edge since the fire in Scotland, was now incapable of thinking calmly or she would have realized that a few press notices, however favourable, and a commission from Sir Isaac Manuel, although very flattering to a young artist, do not in themselves constitute fame. She had a sort of wild vision of Albert as the pivot of public attention, already too busy being flattered and adulated to speak to her for more than a minute on the telephone. She imagined herself arriving at the Chelsea Galleries for their luncheon appointment and finding that he had forgotten all about her and gone off with some art critic and his wife instead.

At last Jane believed that all these things were quite true, and by the time she had finished dressing she was in a furious rage with Albert. Unable to contain herself, she wrote to him:

'Darling Albert,

'I have been thinking about you and me, and I can see now that we should never be happy together. You have your work, and now this tremendous success has come you won't be wanting me as well, and I think it better from every point of view to break off our engagement, so good-bye, darling Albert, and please don't try to see me any more as I couldn't bear it.

'Jane.'

Quickly, for fear she should change her mind, she gave this note to the chauffeur and told him to take it round at once to Mr. Buggins' house.

She then went back to her bedroom and cried on the bed. She cried at first because her nerves were in a really bad state. After about half an hour she was crying for rage because Albert had not come round to see her or at least telephoned; but soon she was beyond tears, and her heart was broken.

'If he loved me he wouldn't let me go like that. This silence can only mean that he accepts: that the engagement is really broken off. Oh, God! how can I bear it? I can't go on living! I shall have to kill myself.'

The telephone-bell rang and Jane, with a beating heart, took off the receiver. 'This must be he!' It was her mother's sister asking what she wanted for a wedding present.

'China,' said Jane feverishly, 'china! china! china! Any sort of china! Thank you so much, Aunt Virginia.'

After this she felt that she had reached depths of despair which she did not even know to exist before. She sat in a sort of coma, and when the telephone-bell rang again, she knew that it could not be Albert.

But it was.

'Darling Jane, it's a quarter-past one. Have I got to wait here for ever?'

'Oh! is it really so late? Didn't you get my note, Albert?'

'No, what note? Can't you come, then?'

'Yes, in a moment. I wrote to say I should be late, but I won't be long now.'

'Well, hurry!'

'Yes, sweetest. Oh, I do love you!'

Jane rang up Mr Buggins.

'If there's a note from me to Albert, will you be an angel and burn it? Thank you so much. Yes, isn't it splendid! No. I've not seen him yet. We're lunching together so I must fly.'

170

CHRISTMAS PUDDING

PROLOGUE

Four o'clock on the First of November, a dark and foggy day. Sixteen characters in search of an author.

Paul Fotheringay sat in his Ebury Street lodgings looking at the presentation copies of his book, *Crazy Capers*, which had just arrived by post. He thought of the lonely evening ahead of him and wondered whether he should telephone to some of his friends, but decided that it would be of little use. They would all be doing things by now. He also thought of the wonderful energy of other people, of how they not only had the energy to do things all day but also to make arrangements and plans for these things which they did. It was as much as he could manage to do the things, he knew that he would never be able to make the plans as well. He continued sitting alone.

Walter Monteath was playing bridge with three people all much richer than himself. He was playing for more than he could afford to lose and was winning steadily.

Sally Monteath was trying on a dress for which, unless a miracle happened, she would never be able to pay. She looked very pretty in it.

Marcella Bracket was ringing up a young man and hinting, rather broadly, that he should take her out that evening.

Amabelle Fortescue was arranging her dinner table. She wondered whether to put a divorced husband next to his first wife, and decided that it would be a good plan; they always got on famously with each other now that this was no longer a necessary or even a desirable state of things.

Jerome Field slept in his office.

Miss Monteath, nameless as yet, slept in her pram.

Bobby Bobbin, at Eton, was writing a note to an older boy.

Philadelphia Bobbin sat in her mother's drawing-room

and looked at the fire. She hoped that death would prove less dull and boring than life.

Lady Bobbin tramped Gloucestershire mud and cursed the foot and mouth disease which had stopped the hunting that beautiful, open winter.

'I loved thee in life too little, I loved thee in death too well,' sang Lord Leamington Spa at a concert in aid of the Jollier Villages Movement. Later on he sang 'Fearful the death of the diver must be, and for an encore, 'Under the deodar'. Lady Leamington Spa agreed with the chairwoman of the movement that her husband had a charming voice. 'Our son is musical like his father,' she said proudly.

Squibby Almanack, the said son, sat with the three fair and slightly bald young men who were his friends at a Bach concert, in Bond Street.

Major Stanworth drove his Morris Cowley along the high road between Oxford and Cheltenham. He was on his way to the preparatory school where his little boy was having mumps rather badly.

Michael Lewes was sending out invitations for a garden party at H.B.M. Residency, Cairo. He thanked heaven several times aloud that he was leaving the diplomatic service for good at Christmas.

The Duchess of St. Neots was talking scandal with an old friend. Any single one of the things she said would have been sufficient to involve her in an action for criminal libel. Her daughter by a former marriage, Miss Héloïse Potts, was listening from an alcove where she very much hoped to remain undiscovered.

Sixteen characters in search of an author.

1

There is a certain room in the Tate Gallery which, in these unregenerate days, is used more as a passage-way towards the French pictures collected by Sir Joseph Duveen than as an objective in itself. There must be many lovers of painting who have hurried through it countless times and who would be unable to name or even to describe a single one of the flowerings of Victorian culture which hang there, so thoroughly does the human mind reject those impressions for which it has no use.

Indeed Paul Fotheringay, until, on the second day of November, he found himself sitting in this room, had been unaware of its very existence. He now observed that it was mostly hung with large and unpleasant works of the 'Every picture tells a story' school, interspersed with some rather inferior examples of pre-Raphaelitism and a few careful drawings by Ruskin. He sat on a hard and shiny bench and gave himself up to the contemplation of an elderly lady who was struggling, with but little success, to reproduce the handsome but unprepossessing features of Mrs. Rossetti. For it was copying day in the Tate. Paul wondered how she managed to keep the paint so beautifully smooth. He thought it very clever of her. Whenever he had tried to express himself on canvas, the result had invariably been a mass of dirty bumps; his own particular style of course, and, he liked to think, a not unpleasing one. Nevertheless, he was perfectly aware that even if he wished to do so he was incapable of producing that oleographic smoothness which seemed to come so easily to the elderly copyist.

Soon, however, his thoughts left the exterior world and turned upon his own inward wretchedness. When a man is harassed beyond endurance through the two most important aspects of life; when the labour of months bears a bitterer fruit than that of failure; and when, at the very same moment, she whom he adores shows herself once and for all unworthy of adoration; then indeed is that man unhappy.

So thought Paul; and writhing beneath the duplicated gaze of Mrs. Rossetti he considered for the hundredth time the two causes of his present depression, namely, the behaviour of his fiancée, Marcella Bracket, and the reception by the public of his first novel, *Crazy Capers*, which had been published that week. It would be difficult to say which was the more wounding. The reception accorded to his novel, indeed, appeared at first sight to have been extremely gratifying. The critics, even those of them who had been neither at Eton nor at Oxford with him, had praised it extravagantly, and with a startling unanimity; the cheque which he would eventually receive from his publisher promised to be a great deal larger than those which must so often (and so fortunately) prevent young authors from ever again putting pen to paper. The book, in fact, was an undoubted success. Nevertheless how could praise or promise of glittering gain compensate in any way to the unhappy Paul for the fact that his book, the child of his soul upon which he had expended over a year of labour, pouring forth into it all the bitterness of a bitter nature; describing earnestly, as he thought, and with passion, the subtle shades of a young man's psychology, and rising to what seemed to him an almost unbearably tragic climax with the suicide pact of his hero and heroine, had been hailed with delight on every hand as the funniest, most roaringly farcical piece of work published for years. He who had written with one goal always before him, sincere approbation from the very few, the exquisitely cultured, was now to be held up as a clown and buffoon to jeers and senseless laughter from the mob.

His eyes, fixed upon Lizzie's face, filled with tears, so that her features became blurred and her hair more woolly than ever, as he recalled with a sinking heart that one critic after another had described him as the new humorist and his book as the funniest of the month. Sadly he drew from his pocket a sheaf of press cuttings. He knew them by heart already, and to look at them again was like pressing upon the tooth that aches in the hope that after all it perhaps does not ache unbearably.

REALLY FUNNY BOOK BY NEW WRITER

A welcome contrast to the unrelieved gloom of Miss Lion's *Tragedy in a Farmyard* is provided by Paul Fotheringay, whose first novel, *Crazy Capers*, is the most amusing piece of work to be published for many months. This delicious whimsy maintains a high level of humour throughout, and should certainly find its way to the bookshelves of those who enjoy a quiet chuckle.

AMUSING FIRST NOVEL

. . . I myself paid Mr. Fotheringay the very sincere tribute of laughing out loud several times over the absurd adventures of his hero, Leander Belmont. . . . If *Crazy Capers* bears little or no relation to the experiences of actual life, one cannot but be grateful to its author for such a witty fantasy.

EX-UNDERGRADUATE'S DÉBUT AS HUMORIST

Paul Fotheringay's first novel, *Crazy Capers* (Fodder & Shuttle-cock, 7s 6d.) is one of the most entertaining books which it has ever been my good fortune as a reviewer to read. It reminded me sometimes of Mr. Wodehouse at his funniest, and sometimes of Mr. Evelyn Waugh at his most cynical, and yet it had striking originality. I could scarcely put it down, and intend to re-read it at the earliest opportunity. *Crazy Capers* is the story of a penniless young aristocrat, Lord Leander Belmont, who on leaving Oxford with a double first is unable to find any career more suited to his abilities than that of a pawnbroker's assistant. . . . Lord Leander is an intensely funny character, and so is his fiancée, Clara. The last chapter, in which they attempt to commit suicide by drowning themselves in the Thames, but are unable, owing to the vigilance of the river police, to achieve anything more tragic than a mud bath, is in particular a masterpiece of humour. I laughed until I was literally driven from the room. . . .

With great bitterness Paul remembered how he had written that last chapter, working through the night until he felt that he had arrived at that exact blend of tragedy and pathos for which he searched. As he wrote, the tears had poured down his cheeks. The frustration of two souls, battered beyond endurance by circumstances over which they had no control, unable even to make good their escape from a world which now held nothing for them, had seemed to him a noble, beautiful and touching theme. And nobody else had even remotely apprehended his meaning, not one person.

Putting the press cuttings back into his pocket he pulled out of it a letter which turned his thoughts towards an even more painful subject.

'PAUL DARLING (it ran),

'How sweet of you to send me a copy of *Crazy Capers*—I was perfectly thrilled at the dedication, it was indeed a lovely surprise. I hope it will be a wild success, it certainly deserves to be, personally I couldn't have thought it funnier. I roared with laughter from beginning to end. I never knew you were capable of writing such a funny book. Must fly now, my sweet, as I'm going out with Eddie, so all my love and lots of kisses from

'MARCELLA.

'P.S.—See you sometime soon.'

Paul sighed deeply. That the girl whom he so distractedly adored had thus mocked his book was a wound indeed, but not a death blow; he had never, if the truth be told, entertained a very high regard for her mind. It was her unkind and neglectful conduct towards his person that was causing him so much unhappiness.

Considering her youth (she was twenty-two), Marcella Bracket had all the worst characteristics of the lion hunter developed to an extraordinary degree. She belonged to that rare and objectionable species, the intellectual snob devoid of intellect. Poets and painters were to her as earls and marquesses are to the ordinary snob; the summit of her ambition was to belong to what she considered a 'highbrow' set of people, to receive praise and adulation from the famous. Unfortunately for her, however, whilst knowing through her parents several earls and marquesses, she had not as yet managed to scrape even the most formal acquaintanceship with any great man of letters, nor had the only artist of merit to whom she was ever introduced been at all insistent that he should paint her portrait. Therefore, when poor Paul fell in love with her, which he did for some unaccountable reason at first sight, she saw in him a promising bottom rung to that particular ladder of social success which it was her ambition to climb. She even allowed him to think that they were unofficially engaged in order that she could go about with him, meeting his friends, nearly all of whom were people she had long wished to know, and at the same time picking up from him certain clichés and ideas that might be regarded as a passport to that society of which she hoped to become a member. In time, of course, she intended to marry some rich and colourless man so that she could settle down in Chelsea—a hostess; meanwhile it pleased and flattered her to feel herself the object of hopeless passion in one who had already a certain reputation for brilliance amongst the younger people.

Paul, who although he suspected something of this, only partly apprehended the situation, and moreover thought himself very much in love, was constantly plunged into a state of gloom and depression by her treatment of him. That very day, thinking thus to buy her company for the afternoon, he had invited her to luncheon at the Ritz, a luxury which he could ill afford. He had arrived there, admittedly a few moments late, to find that she was accompanied by the mindless body of Archibald ('Chikkie') Remnant. They were drinking champagne cocktails. When Paul appeared she hardly threw him a word, but continued to gossip with this moron for at least twenty minutes, after which 'Chikkie', having thrown out several unheeded hints that he would like an invitation to lunch, strolled away leaving Paul to pay for his cocktails. The meal which ensued gave him very little satisfaction; Marcella proved to be in her most irritating mood. In the intervals of ordering all the really expensive items on the menu, for it was one of her principles in life that the more you make people pay the more you can get out of them in the end, she chattered incessantly about her success with various young men unknown to Paul. He gathered that, so far from it being her intention to spend the afternoon with him, she had planned to leave him the moment that lunch was over and go down to Heston for a flying lesson with another admirer. The feeling that he was so soon to lose her from his sight again made him cross and restless, and he was almost glad when she did finally depart in a large Bentley for her destination of loops, spins and jupiter wapities. He knew quite well that by now an aerial flirtation would be in progress, for Marcella was an inveterate flirt.

Meanwhile he had come to Millbank for consolation, only to discover, as so many must have done before him, that there is in good art a quality which demands contentment if not happiness in its observer, its very harmonies serving but to accentuate disharmonies within. On the other hand, contemplation of the second-rate, by arousing the mind to a sort of amused fury, can sometimes distract it a little. Hence Mrs. Rossetti. Paul felt, however, that his present unhappiness was too deeply seated to be much shaken, and that even time would be powerless against such a situation as his. There seemed to be no hope, no ray of comfort. The career for which he had longed from childhood, that of a writer, was evidently closed to him; he never wished again to face a chorus of praise uttered in such lack of comprehension. Nor could his affair with Marcella come to any more satisfactory conclusion, for although he loved her, he knew that he would always dislike her.

The copyist now came down from her high stool and began to pack up. Lights appeared, making the place look more dismal than before, and a little fog seemed to have penetrated, although outside the day had been clear and beautiful. Paul's thoughts returned to his present surroundings. He looked at his watch, which had stopped as usual, and decided that he would go home. Marcella might telephone, in which case he would like to be there—his landlady was bad at taking messages. He rose to his feet, and was about to wander towards the door when he noticed the unmistakable figure of Walter Monteath hurrying through the Turner room on his way, no doubt, to the French pictures. He looked round on hearing his name, and catching sight of Paul, said:

'Hullo, old boy, fancy seeing you here. I am pleased. Sally and I have just laughed ourselves ill over your book by the way; it is heavenly. Those policemen! Honestly, my sides ached. And the pawnbroker was divinely funny too. How did you think of it all? I'd give a lot to write a book like that, everyone's talking about it. Well, and where are you off to now?'

'I don't know,' said Paul, trying to look pleased at this praise. 'What are you doing? Can't we have a drink somewhere?'

'Yes let's. As a matter of fact, I'm just on my way to Amabelle's for a cocktail, so why don't you come along too. I know she wants to see you; she was asking about you only yesterday. If you don't mind waiting a moment while I have a look at the Puvis we'll go straight away. I've got a car outside; for once it's not being repaired at the works.'

Whilst Walter, who apparently was going to write an article on Puvis de Chavannes, was examining the picture of John the Baptist, Paul gazed at the large Manet and wished he were dead. He felt, however, that like the hero of his own book, he would be too cowardly and ineffective to achieve a satisfactory suicide; he was no Roman soldier to lean upon his sword.

Presently, as they drove towards Mrs. Fortescue's house in Portman Square, Walter said, shouting to make himself heard above the twitterings, groanings and squeakings of his ancient motor car:

'Sally and I met your Marcella last night; she was out with that poor mut Remnant and they joined our party later. We thought she was rather a dreary old do. Whatever do you see in her, Paul?'

'Heaven knows,' said Paul, drearily.

2

Amabelle Fortescue, unlike so many members of her late profession, was an intelligent, a cultured and a thoroughly nice woman. The profession itself had, in fact, been more a result of circumstances than the outcome of natural inclination. Cast alone and penniless upon the world at eighteen by the death of her father, who had been a respectable and well-known don at Oxford, she had immediately decided, with characteristic grasp of a situation, that the one of her many talents which amounted almost to genius should be that employed to earn her bread, board and lodging. Very soon after this decision was put into practice, the bread was, as it were, lost to sight beneath a substantial layer of Russian caviare; the board, changing with the fashions of years, first took to itself a lace tablecloth, then exposed a gleaming surface of polished mahogany, and finally became transformed into a piece of scrubbed and rotting oak; while the lodging, which had originally been one indeed, and on the wrong side of Campden Hill, was now a large and beautiful house in Portman Square.

Amabelle, without apparently the smallest effort, without arousing much jealousy or even causing much scandal, had risen to the top of her trade. Then just as, at an unusually early age, she was about to retire on her savings, she had married a charming, well-known and extremely eligible Member of Parliament whom she lost (respectably, through his death) some three years later. After her marriage she became one of the most popular women in London. Her past was forgiven and forgotten by all but the most prudish, and invitations to her house were accepted with equal satisfaction by pompous old and lively young.

The house itself was one of Amabelle's most valuable assets, and its decoration, calculated as it was to suit the taste of the semi-intelligent people who were her friends, showed a knowledge of human nature as rare as it was profound. What could be more subtle, for instance, than the instinct which had prompted her to hang on the walls of her drawing-room three paintings, all by Douanier Rousseau? Her guests, on coming into this room, were put at their ease by the presence of pictures, and 'modern' pictures at that, which they could recognize at first sight. Faced by the works of Seurat, of Matisse, even of Renoir, who knows but that they might hesitate, the name of the artist not rising immediately to their lips? But at the sight of those fantastic foliages, those mouthing monkeys, there could arise no doubt; even the most uncultured could murmur: 'What gorgeous Rousseaus you have here. I always think it is so wonderful that they were painted by a common customs official—abroad, of course.' And buoyed up by a feeling of intellectual adequacy, they would thereafter really enjoy themselves.

The rest of the house was just as cleverly arranged. Everything in it belonged to some category and could be labelled, there was nothing that could shock or startle. People knew without any effort what they ought to say about each picture, each article of furniture in turn. To the Victorian domes of wool flowers in the hall they cried, 'How decorative they are, and isn't it quaint how these things are coming back into fashion? I picked up such a pretty one myself at Brighton, and gave it to Sonia for a wedding present.' To the black glass bath those privileged to see it would say, 'Isn't that just too modern and amusing for words, but aren't you frightened the hot water might crack it, darling?' And to the Italian chairs and sideboards, the exquisite patina of whose years had been pickled off in deference to the modern taste for naked wood, 'How fascinating, now do tell me where you get all your lovely things?'

Amabelle's own personal charm operated in much the same way. She was clever enough only to open up, to put, as it were, on view, those portions of her mentality to which whomsoever she happened to be with could easily respond.

All her life she had before her one ambition, to be a success in the world of culture and fashion, and to this end alone her considerable talents and energy had been directed; from a child she had played to the gallery quite consciously and without much shame. If the fulfilment of this ambition brought with it the smallest degree of disappointment, she managed very successfully to conceal the fact from all but herself—herself and possibly one other, Jerome Field.

Jerome Field was Amabelle's official friend, so to speak, appointed by her to that position, and for life. Their friendship had already lasted over twenty years, and had been a most satisfactory one on both sides; for while Jerome was necessary to Amabelle's comfort and happiness, her only confidant, the one person who thoroughly understood her character and yet never questioned anything that she might do, she, supplying much of brightness and domesticity to an otherwise lonely existence, was no less indispensable to him. The fact that there had never been the smallest hint of love in their relationship (he being frankly in love with his business affairs and she with social life, and neither of them capable of any other real or lasting passion), lent it a peculiar flavour for which she at least was grateful.

On the afternoon of Paul's sad vigil at the Tate, Jerome Field took tea, as was his almost invariable custom, in the Douanier Rousseau drawing-room.

'The worst part of getting old in these days,' he said, 'seems to be that those of one's friends who are neither dead, dying nor bankrupt, are in prison. It is really most depressing, one never knows when one's own turn may not be coming. I said to my directors only to-day, "Now mind, if I go to the Old Bailey I don't intend to stand in the dock alone. I asked all of you to be directors on the distinct understanding that you know as well as I do how to add, substract and even multiply, and I count on you to be equally responsible with me for any slips that are made." That shook 'em, I can tell you, especially that fat old fool, Leamington Spa; he practically asked me how long we could expect to be at large.'

'But I do hope,' said Amabelle with some anxiety, 'that

you're not in immediate danger of arrest, are you? Do try and put it off till after Christmas anyhow.'

'Why, do you need me for something special at Christmas time?'

'Not more than usual, darling. I always need you as you know perfectly well. The thing is that I hope you'll come and stay with me for Christmas—I've taken a house in the country then.'

'Not in England?'

'Yes, in Gloucestershire, to be exact.'

'Good gracious, Amabelle!'

Jerome Field was one of those rare and satisfactory people who always play the exact part that would be expected of them. At this particular juncture it was obviously indicated that he should register a slightly offended amazement. He did so.

'The country in England, my dear. What a curious notion. Whatever could have made you think of such a thing? Do you say you have actually taken a house?'

Amabelle nodded.

'Have you seen it?'

She shook her head.

'How long have you taken it for, may one ask?'

'Two months. I signed the agreement to-day.'

'Without even seeing the house?'

'Yes, I couldn't be bothered to go all that way. The house agents seem to think it's very nice and comfortable and so on, and after all it's only for such a short time. I thought of moving in just before Christmas. The Monteaths are coming down with their baby, and naturally I want you too. I think it will be rather fun.'

'But it's such an extraordinary idea. Whatever will you do in the country for two months, at that time of year too? I'm afraid you'll be bored and wretched.'

'I don't know. After all, hundreds of people live in the country, I believe, and presumably they must occupy themselves somehow. Besides, it's patriotic not to go abroad now. I've heard you say so over and over again.'

'Abroad, yes. But there's nothing to stop you from staying

in London, which would surely be more pleasant than to traipse down to Gloucestershire in this weather.'

'You're not very encouraging, are you?'

'Where is this house, anyway?'

'It's called Mulberrie Farm, and it's in the Cotswolds, near Woodford—incidentally, it's quite near Compton Bobbin, so I shall expect to have little Bobby trotting round most days, and you know how I dote on that child. Apparently Mulberrie Farm itself is very old and lovely. I'm awfully excited about it.'

'Now why, apart from the obvious attractions of young Bobby (horrid little brat) do you choose the Cotswolds of all places? Anything more dreary in winter can hardly be conceived. I dare say that Devonshire or Dorset would have been quite pleasant, but the Cotswolds—!'

'Oh, it wasn't on Bobby's account in the least, much as I shall love having him so near. I didn't even discover that he lived there until after I had signed the lease. No, I read a book about the Cotswolds once when I was waiting for a train at Oban, I don't know why, but I bought it off a bookstall. I suppose I wanted change for a pound note. Anyhow, I read it, and apparently the Cotswolds are naked, grey hills with lush valleys and Saxon churches and Elizabethan farm houses and lonely wolds, which sound so entrancing, lonely wolds, don't you agree? In fact, if I like it as much as I know I shall, I might easily buy a house there and settle down among the lonely wolds for ever.'

Jerome snorted.

'Not cross, are you darling?'

'No, of course I'm not. But, frankly, I don't think you'll enjoy yourself much.'

'Then I can come straight back here, can't I?'

'Yes, that's true.'

'There's one other reason why I don't want to be in London at present,' said Amabelle slowly. 'Michael is coming back for good at Christmas, and I can't, I can't, face all that business over again. There are limits to one's powers of endurance, you know.'

'You managed him quite all right before,' said Jerome drily.

'I'm three years older now and more easily bored by that sort of thing. Besides, Michael makes such appalling scenes and I really don't feel quite equal to them any longer.'

'Who says you'll have to feel equal to them? May I remind you, my dear, that three years at Michael's age is a lifetime, and I should think it more than doubtful that he will still be in love with you when he gets back.'

'Oh, well, if you're merely going to be disagreeable—'

At this moment Paul and Walter were announced.

3

Amabelle got up to shake hands with them and began moving tables and chairs into different positions.

'Darlings, I couldn't be more pleased to see you.'

'Let me help with that.'

'Months and months since I saw Paul last.'

'If you'd just say where you want it put.'

'All right, I can manage. There that's perfect. Now Jerome and Walter can settle down to a game of backgammon, which I know they're longing to do, while I have a little chat with Paul. Come over here to the fire, darling, and tell me a whole lot of things I'm dying to know about. First of all, was your book really meant to be funny when you wrote it?—don't answer if you'd rather not; secondly, why did you cut me dead in the Ritz to-day; and thirdly, who was that very repellent female you were lunching with?'

'What a clever woman you are, Amabelle,' said Paul admiringly. 'It's perfectly terrifying how nothing ever escapes those tiny yellow eyes.'

'Large green in point of fact.'

'There's nobody like you—luckily. The book was intended as a horrible tragedy, the female was my fiancée, Marcella Bracket, and the reason I cut you was that if I hadn't she would certainly have insisted on being introduced and I know just how she would bore you.'

'Oh, I see. She's a bore as well as being hideous, is she? I must say, she looks it all right.'

'I think she's maddeningly beautiful.'

'She's certainly not that, poor girl. I can see that we shall have to get you out of this.'

'I wish you could, but unfortunately, I happen to be in love.'

'That won't last,' said Amabelle soothingly. 'It never does with you. As for the book, it's no good writing about the upper classes if you hope to be taken seriously. You must have noticed that by now? Station masters, my dear, station masters.'

'I know, I know. Of course, I have noticed. But you see my trouble is that I loathe station masters, like hell I do, and lighthouse keepers, too, and women with hare-lips and miners and men on barges and people in circuses; I hate them all equally. And I can't write dialect. But you must admit I had a pawnbroker in my book.'

'Yes, and such a pawnbroker—those Gibbon periods! Pawnbrokers, my dear, don't often talk like that in real life, at least, I can't imagine that they do. No wonder he was taken for a comic figure. What between your book and your young woman you seem to be in a pretty mess, poor darling.'

'I am indeed,' said Paul gloomily. He was enjoying this conversation as people can only enjoy talking about themselves.

'Though what it is you can see in her I don't know.'

'Go on saying that. Say that she's awful and hideous and stupid and unkind, you don't know what a lot of good it's doing me.'

'All right, I will, only don't cry if you can help it, there's a sweetie. I expect you'll get over her quite soon, you know; it's happened before, hasn't it? Still, of course, it must be hellish for you while it lasts, having to look at that penny bun face every day. The poor girl's certainly no oil painting.'

'Oh, I am glad to hear you talk like this, Amabelle: it's cheering me up no end. It makes things much less awful if you honestly think her plain, because perhaps one day I shall see her as you do, and then everything will be all right again.'

'Well, just you bring her round here some time and I'll tell you all about her.'

'Ha, ha, she'd bore you to death, she's the most cracking bore I've ever met.'

'Are you going to marry her?'

'No such luck, I'm not rich enough. Her mother's out to

191

catch a guardsman for her.' To Paul the word 'guardsman' was synonymous with millionaire. 'Besides, it's not as though she cared for me in the least. She only got engaged to me because she thinks I have some clever friends she would like to meet. She's a terrific intellectual snob among other things.'

'You seem to have her pretty well sized up, don't you?'

'Oh, she's driving me mad.'

'Now, don't cry, or I shall stop talking about you. Do you intend to start another book soon?'

'What's the good of that? I only get laughed at; I don't care to be made such a fool of again, I can tell you. It has hurt me terribly—terribly. Look at these.' He drew the press cuttings from his pocket. 'They mock at me, they make fun of my sacred feelings. It's not very nice for me, is it?'

'Poor sweet.'

'It's the most appalling disappointment, I must say. All my life I have wanted to write; I love it. Now I don't know what I am going to do. It is hell—hell!'

'I should keep off fiction, if I were you. People don't understand tragedy in these days, only sentiment; and quite frankly your book was a bit melodramatic, darling, wasn't it? Now, why don't you try your hand at something else, some different form?'

'Yes, perhaps I should.'

'Biography, for instance. I've always been told that it's very good mental exercise, and it can be quite profitable into the bargain.'

'What a nice woman you are, Amabelle,' said Paul, cheering up visibly. 'Thank goodness I came to see you. I never thought of biography, but of course that's the very thing for me. Yes, but whose? May I be your Boswell, darling?'

'I believe books are still censored in England, old boy, and I don't much fancy the idea of being burnt by the public hangman, thanks awfully, just the same. No, you choose carefully some really sympathetic character—and talking of sympathetic characters, here's darling Sally. How's the mother?'

'Very well considering,' said Sally, who looked enchanting in a seal-skin tippet. 'Pleased to see you, Paul—not so pleased to see Walter at the backgammon table again. What did you promise me, darling?'

'It's all right, darling. I'm throwing doubles the whole time to-day. There, you see, I've got old Jerome on the run again. Backgammoned, in fact. That's a sixteen game,' he said, leaning back in his chair and putting an arm round Sally's waist. 'Anyhow, my sweet, it's hardly fair to grumble, considering that that most peculiar garment you've got on now was bought entirely out of my winnings last week, eh? So go away, or you'll spoil the luck.'

'How's my goddaughter, Sally?' asked Paul.

'Good heavens, are you going to be its godfather too?' said Amabelle. 'Whatever induced you to ask him of all people, Sally? And how many godparents does that make?'

'Altogether about twelve, I think,' said Sally vaguely. 'We thought it would be silly not to ask Paul, as he is literally the only religious maniac we know.'

'I'm not a maniac,' said Paul angrily.

'Aren't you, darling? I think you are, though.'

'Just because I happen to be a Buchanite—'

'What's that you're saying?' said Amabelle; 'I never thought an old highbrow like you would admit to such a thing. I read them in trains myself when there's nobody looking.'

'I was not,' said Paul with dignity, 'referring to the novels of John Buchan, if that is what you mean. Of course I don't read them. Buchanism is the name given to a religious sect founded by Mrs. Elspeth Buchan, a Scotch and vastly superior prototype of Mrs. Eddy and Mrs. Besant. In fact, she started that fashion for the founding of religions by untitled married ladies which has since become almost universal. The last of her followers died in 1848, and I have constituted myself head of the N.B.M. (New Buchanite Movement.) As her teachings died with her followers I am able to make up the rules as I go along, which is pleasant. When's the christening, Sally?'

'Well, if the poor little sweet is still with us then we thought next Tuesday week (suit you?), but she's most awfully ill to-day, she keeps on making the sort of noises Walter does after a night out, you know.'

'D'you think she's likely to live or not?' said Paul. 'Because if there's any doubt perhaps I could use your telephone, Amabelle, to call up the jewellers and see if I'm in time to stop them engraving that mug. It's such an expensive sort, and I don't want it spoilt for nothing, I must say.'

'I believe she's expected to pull through. But tell me, Paul, how could you have it engraved, we haven't even decided what her name's going to be ourselves. I want Henrietta Maria and Walter wants Dora Mildred, and we don't seem to be able to strike anything we both like.'

'It's being engraved Elspeth (after Mrs. Buchan) Paula (for obvious reasons) Monteath, from her loving godfather, Paul Frederick Fotheringay.'

'Well, really, all the cheek! Walter, did you hear that?'

'Yes, I did. I'll offer you a double, Jerome. I think those names are O.K., don't you? It saves trouble if someone settles them for us, because perhaps now we shan't have to be quarrelling all day. Only I vote we use Paula, I'm not so wild about Buchanism myself.'

'Thanks, old boy, a very delicate compliment, if I may say so.'

'By the way,' said Walter, 'why Paula and not Pauline?'

'Cheaper. The thing is, you pay for engraving by the letters. I say, I do hope she lives all right, Sally.'

'So do I, you know. After all the trouble I've had, one way and another, it would be extraordinarily souring if she didn't. However, nanny and the charlady between them are battling for her life, as they say in the papers, like mad, so I expect she will. The charlady knows all about it, too, she has lost six herself.'

'Sounds a bit of a Jonah to me, but I don't want to depress you. Anyway, I hope you won't be sparing expense in this matter. Remember that I didn't over the mug.'

'One of your own, I suppose, with the name taken out?'

'Not my name, that's left in, you see. I had "From his loving godmother, Eliza Stratford" (the Countess of Stratford, carriage folk) taken out. That came after my name, and they're putting the words "Elspeth Paula Monteath from her loving godfather" in front of it. Such a brainwave, don't you agree? And who thought it all out for me? Dear little Marcella, bless her heart.'

'We saw Marcella last night with that man Chikkie. She's a nasty piece of work, if you like. Walter finds her so repellent that he says he can only suppose he must really be in love with her.'

'I expect he is, too. Did you ask her to be Paula's godmother?'

'No, I did not.'

'That lends her a certain distinction, doesn't it? She must be the first person in London you haven't asked.'

'How careless you Protestants are of your children's souls,' said Jerome looking up from his game. 'That poor little wretch was born months ago, and there she is, still wallowing in original sin, without mentioning the horrid risk she would run if she should die before next Tuesday week—I call it a shame. Double you, Walter. What does it feel like to be a mother, Sally?'

'Childbirth,' said Sally, 'is an unpleasing process. It must be quite awful for the father who, according to Walter, suffers even more than the mother. I don't quite understand about that, but of course I take his word for it. To be honest, I should like the baby a good deal better if she wasn't the split image of Walter's Aunt Lucy; all the same I am getting quite attached to her in a sort of way, and Walter's so impressed by being a father that he's actually looking out for a job. You know, motherhood is an enormous financial asset in these days; to begin with you get pounds and pounds for publishing a photograph of a child twice or three times her age and saying she's so well-grown because of Gatebury's food, then you get more pounds for saying that no nursing mother would care to retire without her cup of Bovo, and finally I can now edit the Mothers' and Kiddies' Sunshine Page in the *Daily Runner* under my own name, so I get an extra pound a week for that. Oh, yes, the little dear is pulling her weight in the home and no mistake.'

Later that evening Paul escorted Marcella to a party given by one of her Slade friends. For Marcella, like so many girls, studied Art in her odd moments.

'It is to be a Russian party,' she told him as their taxicab threaded the mazes of S.W.14, 'in honour of Peter Dickinson, who has just come back from Moscow.'

Paul thought that under the circumstances Mr. Dickinson would most probably have preferred any other sort of party, but he refrained from saying so.

'There is to be some interesting conversation,' said Marcella.

'I hope there'll be something to drink,' said Paul.

They arrived at a basement flat decorated with tasteless frescoes. All Marcella's arty friends lived in basement flats decorated with tasteless frescoes. There were hardly any chairs, but the floor was covered with the semi-recumbent forms of dirty young men in stained and spotted grey flannel trousers and dirty young women with long greasy hair. One of the young men, presumably Peter Dickinson, was holding forth when they arrived.

'Yes, I went to see the timber camps; they are fine, wonderful, a triumph of organization. A clean, healthy outdoor life, think what that must mean to these city clerks, people accustomed only to the fetid air of offices. They are as happy as little children, and in everything that they do, their work, their play, they keep always before them their wonderful ideal of communism.'

Paul thought that they sounded rather like Boy Scouts, and was unattracted by the idea. He soon wished he could go home. Marcella had disappeared almost at once accompanied by a tall young man with side-whiskers, and he saw nobody else that he knew. Although the party was by way of being Russian he could find neither vodka, caviare nor Russian cigarettes to cheer him; in fact, the only noticeable attribute of that great country was the atmosphere of dreariness and hopeless discomfort which prevailed. The chains of love, however, kept him there until past three in the morning, when Marcella appeared and announced that she was quite ready to go home. Paul felt too tired to make a scene about the young man with side-whiskers, and devoted his remaining supply of energy to finding a taxi. These are rare in S.W. 14 at three a.m.

'How all your friends do dislike me,' said Marcella complacently as they bumped away in the ancient vehicle which he had eventually procured. 'Those Monteaths were horrid to me last night. But perhaps she's jealous, poor thing, of me being so young and pretty.'

'Sally?' said Paul. 'Sally's incapable of jealousy, I assure you. Besides, she quite honestly thinks you very plain and boring indeed,' he added in an attempt at revenge for the terrible evening he had just undergone. This reply was so unexpected that Marcella was for once quite unable to defend herself, and was quiet and affectionate during the remaining part of the drive to Gloucester Square where she lived. She snuggled as close to Paul as the patent leather covering to the springless seats would allow, and in the hall of her house she gave him a long, hot and sticky kiss, saying, 'Anyhow, you think I'm beautiful, don't you?'

'The poor girl is admiration mad,' thought Paul. 'Apart from that she's not a bad little thing, though heaven knows how I can be in love with her.'

4

The more Paul considered the idea of writing a biography, the more it seemed to offer him an ideal medium for self-expression, and one into which he could pour his heart and soul without risk of ill-timed mockery. Even the most hardened and callous critic could scarcely shake his sides over the description of a deathbed scene that had really taken place. He felt that in this branch of literature lay his opportunity to establish himself as a serious writer, and to shake off the humourous reputation which he had so unwillingly acquired. Once thus established he would surely be able to publish another novel with less danger of being misunderstood. The difficulty now before him was that of finding a suitable subject; one whose work should be thoroughly sympathetic to himself and whose outlook in life should be comprehensible to him.

He considered this problem for several days, but with no result. Those people whose lives he would have enjoyed writing, notably Maria Edgeworth, Miss Austen, Elizabeth Barrett Browning and Mrs. Carlyle, seemed already to boast a formidable bibliography. Others that occurred to him, such as Dorothea Felicia Hemans, Mary Russel Mitford, and Mrs. Livingstone (the mother of Dr. Livingstone—I presume), presented almost insuperable difficulties in another direction, as little or nothing seemed to be known about them by anybody. It would be hard, in fact, to find exactly what he wanted, which was a woman of breeding, culture and some talent, living towards the last half of the nineteenth century, who was not already the subject of a 'life'.

At last, in despair of ever finding his ideal, he wandered into the London Library, where he began, in a desultory manner, to read through the opening pages of the *Dictionary of*

National Biography. Unhelpful as it appeared to be, he waded on through the Adam brothers, Prince Adolphus Frederick, Aelfred Aethling, Anerium the Welsh poet, Bishop Baggs, Praisegod Barebones, Boate de Boot, and Bertulf. Having arrived by this weary pilgrimage of the mind as far as Beorhtric, King of the West Saxons, he was just going to abandon his search for the time being when, turning over two pages at once, his eye lit upon the name Bobbin, Lady Maria.

Lady Maria Bobbin. The only wonder was that he had never thought of her before. Here, indeed, was a life worth writing, a sermon waiting to be preached. This woman, this poet, brought up amid the conventions and restrictions of the mid-Victorian era, wife of a country squire, mother of twelve children, who found time among her manifold duties to sing in noble, deathless verse such songs as 'The Redbreast's Lament', 'Prayer of a Grecian Warrior' and 'Wales in Captivity', was surely the very heroine for whom he had been searching. There was not much information about her in the *Dictionary of National Biography*, only enough to whet Paul's appetite for more, but there was an allusion to her vast correspondence and copious journals which led him to hope that these might still be extant at her home in Gloucestershire, Compton Bobbin.

In the *Dictionary of National Biography* he discovered the following bare facts of her life:

'Lady Maria Almanack, daughter of the eighth Earl of Leamington Spa, was born in 1818, and married in 1837 Sir Josiah Bobbin, M.F.H., of Compton Bobbin, Gloucestershire. From her earliest childhood she displayed an astonishing talent for writing verse, and in 1842 her parents were foolish enough to publish her "Poems" in a quarto volume. She soon recovered from the adverse criticism which these met with, and published in 1844 "Autumnal Tints", a collection of short poems including the famous "Farewell to Mount Ida". In 1845 she had her first real success with "Elegant Elegies, Tasteful Trifles and Maidenly Melodies". The following year an epic poem, the well-known "Martyrdom in Mercia", came from her pen, and after that date, in spite of her many duties as châtelaine of Compton Bobbin and mother of twelve children, she never failed to produce an annual volume, generally far from slim, of poems, ballads, sonnets, odes or romantic plays. She was, in fact, as prolific as she was gifted a writer, for, besides her published works, she found time to conduct a vast correspondence and to keep a journal which extended into 14 volumes. This treasure is now in the possession of her descendants at Compton Bobbin. During her lifetime her works enjoyed an almost world-wide popularity, and she was intimate with many of the most famous among her contemporaries, including Meredith, Carlyle, Lord Tennyson (who often spoke of the exquisite sensibility of her writing) and Queen Victoria herself. In 1896 she died from a chill which she caught at the christening of her fiftieth descendant.'

At the end of this paragraph there was no bibliography, no hint as to how or where further information was to be sought. The mention of a journal, however, was enough to spur Paul on to further action. He returned to its shelf the *Dictionary of National Biography* and had recourse instead to *Debrett's Peerage, Baronetage and Knightage*; from which he gathered that Compton Bobbin was now held by Lady Bobbin, M.F.H., J.P., in trust for her son, Sir Roderick, a minor, her husband, the late Sir Hudson Bobbin, having been drowned in the *Lusitania* disaster. Paul needed no more information. It only remained now for him to write to the present châtelaine of Compton Bobbin and ask that he might be allowed to read the journal and letters of her predecessor. In a state of excitement and enthusiasm he returned to his rooms, where he composed the following letter.

155 Ebury Street, S.W.

'Dear Madam,

'I am most anxious to write a life of the late illustrious Lady Maria Bobbin, a task which, I understand, has never yet been attempted, and one which I would devote all my energy and my poor talent to completing in a manner worthy of its subject. To do this with any degree of accuracy would however be impossible without access to those of her private papers, notably the fourteen volumes of her journal, which I assume still to be in existence at Compton Bobbin. It would be most kind and gratifying to me if you would consider lending me the said volumes—or, should you very naturally object to the idea of parting, even for a space, with documents so invaluable, perhaps you would give permission for me to reside in the local hostelry that I may study them in your house, whose atmosphere must yet I feel be redolent of Her. I would naturally work at this life in entire collaboration with yourself, submitting all proofs to you before publication.

'If I trouble you, please forgive me and remember that I do so in the interests of Art and to the perpetuation of a memory which must ever be sacred to you, to me, and to all lovers of Verse.

'Yours sincerely,

PAUL FOTHERINGAY.'

It was unfortunate that Paul, in writing this letter, had allowed himself to fall victim to the intoxication of his own style. Lady Bobbin, M.F.H., J.P., opened it together with several appeals for new hens from farmers whose old ones had been removed by Mr. Reynard. She read it over twice, found herself unfamiliar with such words as hostelry, redolent and collaboration, and handed it to her secretary, saying, 'The poor chap's batty, I suppose?' The secretary, who occasionally read book reviews, said that Paul Fotheringay was a comic writer, and would be a most unsuitable person to undertake a life of Lady Maria. She was then instructed to answer his request, as well as those of the farmers, in the negative.

Meanwhile, Paul, never doubting the success of his letter, walked on air. His fingers itched to take pen in hand, to prove once and for all to those idiotic critics that he was a serious writer; and at the same time he looked forward greatly to the perusal of Lady Maria's journal, feeling that it would provide the rarest intellectual treat. He went out and bought himself a collected edition of her works, so that he might re-read some of his favourites—'The Lament of Llywark Hen', 'Moorish Bridal Song', 'On the Deathbed of Wallace', 'To my Brother', etc., which he did with his usual appreciation of her genius. Altogether his outlook on life became far more cheerful and optimistic than it had been before he went to see Amabelle Fortescue.

Alas, how dashed were his hopes when the letter for which he had been so eagerly waiting was found to contain the following abrupt refusal in the third person:

'Compton Bobbin,
'Compton on the Wold,
'Gloucestershire.

'Lady Bobbin regrets that she is unaware of the existence of any documents at Compton Bobbin which could interest Mr. Fotheringay. She cannot enter into further correspondence on this subject.'

Paul was stunned by this blow.

'And then,' he said to Amabelle, to whom he had gone immediately for consolation, 'it is so rude and horrid, I feel terribly snubbed.'

'From what I've always heard of that woman I'm not in the least surprised,' said Amabelle. 'I don't want to be governessy, darling, but I do think it was a mistake for you to write off in such a very violent hurry. It would have been more sensible to find out what sort of person she was first, and what was likely to be the best method of approach.'

'Yes, I see that now. But I was so excited when I thought of the journal in fourteen volumes that my one idea was to get hold of it as soon as I possibly could.'

'It's a pity you didn't consult me, you know. Little Bobby Bobbin (Sir Roderick) is a great buddy of mine, and I'm sure he could have fixed it for you easily. After all, the journal belongs to him, doesn't it?'

'You don't think he could smuggle it out of the house for me?'

'He'd never dare to now, it wouldn't be safe. You see, Lady Bobbin is in a very strong position as far as he is concerned because she has every penny of the money, and he's terrified of getting into her bad books. She was a great heiress, a Miss Swallowfield (tea), and if old Hudson Bobbin hadn't married

202

her the place would have gone long ago, I believe. But surely you know Bobby, don't you? Why didn't *you* ask him about it?'

'D'you mean that comic child from Eton who's always here? Of course I know him quite well, but how could I have guessed his other name was Bobbin? It's unnatural, Bobby Bobbin. Oh, dear, I do feel wretched.'

'Poor old boy, it is boring for you.'

'It's far worse than boring,' said Paul vehemently, 'it's the end of my literary career. From now onwards I am condemned to the life of a social parasite. If I can't write the life of Lady Maria I shall never set pen to paper again. She is not only my favourite poetess, but my affinity, my period, my ideal heroine. I understand her mentality, I could write the most beautiful life of her. Oh, it is too hard to bear. I tell you that since I had this idea I have thought of nothing else night and day, not even of Marcella. However, I can't despair yet, it means too much to me. I shall get inside Compton Bobbin by hook or by crook, even if I have to disguise myself as a housemaid to do it.'

Amabelle looked at him thoughtfully. There was nothing in the world she enjoyed so much as getting herself involved in other people's affairs, and she was beginning to see here a good chance to indulge in this hobby.

'Are you quite serious, Paul?'

'Yes, Amabelle. More serious than you would believe. I honestly think I could write a first-class book on Lady Maria, and I want to do it more than I've ever wanted anything.'

'Really and truly?'

'I promise you.'

'In that case, my dear, and especially if it's going to cure you of that dreary little Marcella, I think I must try to help you. I'll go down to Eton at once and call on Bobby, I expect that between us we could think out some scheme for getting you into Compton Bobbin.'

'Oh, Amabelle, if only you could,' said Paul, but he went away feeling depressed and not very hopeful.

The next day, at one o'clock punctually, Amabelle, dressed

in pale beige furs, stepped out of her pale beige Rolls-Royce into the High Street of Eton, where she was met with noisy acclamations of delight by Sir Roderick Bobbin, Baronet, of Compton Bobbin, in the county of Gloucestershire.

'Cad, cad, Amabelle darling! First of all you haven't written to me once as you promised you would, and then you send me a wire only this morning to say you're coming down. If you had let me know a tiny bit sooner I could have ordered a decent lunch, but as it is I don't know what we shall get, something uneatable probably. Two days' notice in future, please, my sweet!'

'I'm sorry, duckie, I simply couldn't. I only had to-day free, and I must see you about something very particular. I'm sure the luncheon will be perfect, anyway, it always is. In here?'

She followed Bobby into a little old house that was half curiosity shop, half restaurant. It was stuffed so full of antiques that every step had to be taken carefully for fear of knocking down some fragile object, while interspersed among the curios were luncheon tables covered with check cloths and arty crafty earthenware. Bobby passed these by, however, and led the way up a dark and narrow staircase, hung with Indian fabrics, to a miniature room at the top of the house, where luncheon for two was laid out in front of a lattice window. A peat fire burned in the open hearth, giving off a delicious smell. The room was cosy and comfortable in the extreme, and seemed to have the very definite atmosphere, unexpected in a shop, of belonging to one particular person. This was indeed the case. Sir Roderick (who had been born with an unerring instinct for living in the greatest available comfort, and who always seemed to know exactly how that comfort could be obtained with the least amount of trouble to himself) had, by dint of showering boyish charm upon the proprietress of the shop, appropriated this room to his own use, and the objects that were strewn about it in casual disorder belonged to him.

A guitar, that he could not play (lying beside a red leather gramophone that he could and did), a tasteful edition of *A la Recherche du Temps Perdu*, the complete works of Messrs.

Ronald Firbank and Aldous Huxley, together with reproductions of two of Picasso's better-known aquarelles, bore testimony to the fact that young Sir Roderick liked to associate himself with modern culture. The possessor of keen eyes, however, observing some well used bridge markers, the masterpieces of Wallace, and a positive heap of social weekly journals, might suspect that the child was in no real danger at present of overtaxing his mind.

Amabelle, who had had many opportunitites of drawing her own conclusions on these matters, sat down at the table and picked up an enormous bunch of orchids that lay beside her plate. 'Are these for me? Thank you, darling, so much.' During the excellent luncheon that followed Bobby chattered incessantly, telling her with immense gusto the latest scandals from London as viewed at Eton, generally through the prejudiced eyes of son or brother to the person concerned.

'By the way, Felton's sister, the pretty one, has run away with her chauffeur—did you know?'

'Barbara Casement? Really, darling, do be careful what you say; it sounds most unlikely to me. Are you quite certain?'

'Oh, yes, rather. Felton and I saw them driving through Slough together the day before yesterday. We rocked with laughter, I must say.'

'Well, people generally do drive with their chauffeurs, it's quite usual.'

'No, I promise it's true. Felton says she never could resist a peaked cap.'

'I can't believe it—those lovely babies, she couldn't leave them.'

'Oh, heavens,' said Bobby, suddenly whispering. 'The most awful thing—I quite forgot. Felton's people are down to-day and they're certain to be lunching in the next room. You can hear every word. Gosh, that's just about torn it.'

'We don't hear them, though.'

'I know. They never speak, that's why. But people always hear their own name, don't they? Isn't it too ghastly—what can we do?'

'Pretend I've got a dog here called Melton.'

'Oh, what a good idea. Lie down, Melton,' he shouted. 'Stop eating my bootlaces, you little devil. There, good boy, Melton—want a drinkie water?' He made loud noises intending to imitate a dog drinking until, overcome with hysteria, he and Amabelle were forced to bury their heads in cushions to smother the sound of their giggles. Presently they ascertained from the waitress, greatly to their mutual relief, that Sir Oswald and Lady Felton and their family had left about half an hour previously.

When the bill came, Bobby said, 'You can pay that, darling, if you'd like to. I don't see why I shouldn't trade on my status as a schoolboy for as long as I possibly can. All too soon I shall be the one to pay, and that will last to the end of my life, worse luck.'

'When are you leaving Eton for good?'

'I shall trail away clasping (we hope) my little leaving book and draped in my tiny Old Etonian tie at the end of the summer half, unless, of course, the beaks should happen to find out before then that you are my dentist, darling. Such bad teeth. But I don't expect they will, I'm hardly ever unlucky.'

'Is it settled what you're going to do after that?'

'Well, mother keeps on droning about Sandhurst, but I fully intend to go to Oxford, and I usually get my own way with the old girl in the end, you know, so I expect it will be all right.'

Presently they went for a walk. It was a beautiful day, sunny and windy; little golden leaves like small coins, earnest of a treasury to come, blew about the school yard; one of those days at Eton when Windsor Castle has all the appearance of the better type of Victorian water-colour painting, clean, clear and romantic. Specimens of the British aristocrat in embryo were to be seen on every hand running, or lounging about the place in and out of 'change'. They were hideous, pathetic little boys for the most part, with one feature, whether nose, ears, chin, Adam's apple or eyebrows out-stripping its fellows which, having apparently forgotten how to grow, were overshadowed quite by their monstrous neighbour. They all stared hard at Amabelle, whose beauty was of the obvious, mature description that children always admire, and looked enviously at Bobby. He was considered a bit of a masher by the younger ones; his own contemporaries, although for the most part quite fond of him, merely thought him an extremely funny joke.

As they strolled among those playing-fields whose connection with the Battle of Waterloo had been cause for so much facetious comment, Amabelle said:

'How about this holiday tutor you mentioned in your last letter—has your mother engaged one yet, d'you think?'

'Not yet, thank goodness,' said Bobby sulkily. 'It is a bit hard, you know. I saw my sister, Philadelphia, last Sunday, she came over with darling Aunt Loudie, and she says that mother is still quite determined to have one who will "get me out of doors". This out of doors idea is a perfect fetish with mamma; she quite honestly believes that there is something wrong about being under a roof unless you have to be for purposes of eating or sleeping. Last summer hols were unbelievably horrible. I was made to be out of doors from dawn till dark, and then mother and Uncle Ernest used quite often to drag me out after dinner and make me lay traps for crayfish. Cruel and boring it was.'

'I shouldn't be surprised if that's why you have such a lovely complexion; you ought to be very glad you're not like all these spotty little wretches.'

'I know,' said Bobby with alluring archness. 'But you see, I was born with that, anyhow, it's one of my natural attributes. But do say you think this tutor business is the last straw; it's such a ghastly idea.'

'Yes, in a way. But supposing it was somebody you liked very much yourself?'

'My dear, have you met many tutors?'

'Somebody you knew already—Paul Fotheringay, for instance.'

'Of course that would be heaven. But I can't quite imagine it happening, can you?'

Amabelle then expounded her plot.

When she had finished speaking Bobby cried in tones of high delight: 'It's a divine idea! You mean that Paul shall come to Compton Bobbin disguised as my tutor so that he can read up the old girl's journal without mother knowing. Oh, yes, it's there all right, neatly bound in red morocco—it takes up a whole shelf of the library. I rather think there are some bags full of letters, too. How marvellous you are to think of it, darling. Oh, what heavenly fun it will be!' and Bobby vaulted over some fairly low railings and back, casting off for a moment his mask of elderly roué and slipping on that of a tiny-child-at-its-first-pantomine, another role greatly favoured by this unnatural boy. 'Only it's too awful to think you won't be there, joining in the riot.'

'Don't be too sure of that,' said Amabelle darkly.

'You're not coming too by any chance, disguised as my nanny?'

If Amabelle flinched inwardly at this remark she showed no signs of it and merely said, 'But why the disguise? As a matter of fact though I shall be in your neighbourhood then, because I've taken a little house for Christmas time which can't be very far from you—Mulberrie Farm.'

'Oh, it's not true! You haven't taken Mulberrie Farm, have you? It's only two miles from us. You *are* an angel, Amabelle. I say, though, have you seen it?'

'No, why? Is it horrible?'

'No, no,' said Bobby hastily, 'quite attractive. Very comfortable and all that. Tee-hee, though, this will ginger up the hols for me top-hole, it will. Do you really think you can persuade m'tutor to recommend Paul to mother?'

Bobby's house-master was Amabelle's first cousin and one of her greatest friends.

'I can't see why not,' said Amabelle, 'because I honestly do think that Paul will have a very good influence on you.'

'Personally I can't imagine Paul having influence over man, woman or child.'

'Anyhow, it can do no harm and may do good, as Geoffrey said when he joined the Embassy Club. And as we are here I

208

think I might as well go in and see Maurice about it now, so good-bye, darling, try to be good, and buy yourself some sausages with that, will you?'

Amabelle, as always, had her own way, and the upshot of her visit to Eton was that Bobby's house-master, Maurice Pringle, wrote off to Lady Bobbin highly recommending one Paul Fisher as holiday tutor to her son, Roderick.

'I am not actually acquainted with this young man, but I have received from mutual friends a most glowing account of his character and attainments, and I feel certain, from what I hear, that he is in every way qualified to fill your post. I understand that he is a particularly sportsmanlike young fellow, devoted to outdoor pursuits, and at the same time (which is important), a first-class coach. Should you wish to interview him, I shall be most happy to arrange this for you. . . .'

Lady Bobbin, however, who was at that time busy hunting five days a week, did not wish to waste one of them by spending it in London, and engaged Mr. Fisher by return of post with no mention of an interview. She merely remarked in her letter that he would be expected to ride, shoot and play golf with 'the boy', as well as to coach him in whatever subjects Mr. Pringle might think advisable, and ended up by saying that Roderick would be hunting three days a week. Paul wondered with a shudder whether he would also be obliged to participate in this unnerving sport.

The five weeks which still remained before Christmas were unpleasantly strenuous ones for Paul. His mornings were spent clinging in a frenzy of fear to the back of ancient hirelings in the Row, mild, drowsy animals which were in his eyes monsters of fire and speed, savagely awaiting an opportunity to hurl him to his doom. His afternoons, less fraught with actual danger than with the horror of an almost equally distressing boredom, alternated between a shooting school at Richmond and golf lessons in Putney. By the evening he could hardly either stand or see. He regarded himself, however, as a martyr in the cause of Art, and this sustained him. Marcella, piqued by a sudden cessation of his advances, was now seldom off the telephone, a state of things which would have seemed unbelievably blissful two or three weeks before. But, although he still fed her loyally at the Ritz every day, he was beginning, if the truth must be known, to find her beauty less maddening and her lack of intelligence more so than formerly.

5

Walter and Sally Monteath, accompanied by Miss Elspeth Paula Monteath, now an accredited member of the Church of England, and her nanny, travelled down to Gloucester-shire by train a few days before Christmas. They had temporarily solved their always pressing money troubles by letting their flat for a few weeks, during which time they intended to live entirely at Mrs. Fortescue's expense, and by selling the ancient motor car. This had from the first proved to be more in the nature of a luxury than an economy, and latterly it had cost them endless money and bother owing to what Walter was pleased to call 'Sally's incurable habit of ploughing her way through human flesh.' Walter, while showing a greater respect for life where pedestrians were concerned, was all too much addicted to tearing mudguards, headlights and other gadgets from onrushing vehicles. In fact, the sale of the car was regarded by all their friends as an undisguised blessing, and they themselves were highly relieved to see the last of it.

'Isn't this too perfect,' said Sally as she settled herself into the corner seat of a first-class carriage. 'Now, just run along and buy me all the weekly papers, will you, darling. Oh, you have already. Thanks so much. Do you realize,' she added, opening the *Tatler* and throwing a copy of the *Sketch* over to Walter, 'that from this moment we literally shan't have to put hand to pocket for six whole weeks. It's a beautiful thought. Such a comfort too that Amabelle's taken a small house, so that there'll only be her and Jerome for Christmas presents. Yes, I got them on Monday, hankies. Quite nice and very cheap.'

'I must say I rather hope they won't retaliate with diamond links and things. D'you remember the Liberty boxes?' said Walter.

Two years before, Walter and Sally, then newly-married, had spent Christmas with a millionaire and his wife. On Christmas Day Sally had duly presented them with chintz handkerchief and tie boxes from Liberty, which she had chosen with some care as being suitable gifts. Slight embarrassment had been felt even by the ordinarily shameless Monteaths when they were given in return enamel waistcoat buttons, gold cigarette and vanity cases, and a handbag with a real diamond clasp.

'Oh, I'm past minding about that sort of thing now,' said Sally cheerfully. 'I'm only so thankful Elspeth Paula did well at her christening, the angel. We ought to get quite a lot for that pearl necklace, and I suppose the mugs will fetch something. I say, here's the most ghastly photo of Paul and Marcella at a night club. Do look. Aren't they exactly like deep-sea monsters! What a girl!'

They were met at Woodford station by the beige Rolls-Royce, and on the doorstep of Mulberrie Farm by Amabelle herself, exquisitely turned out in that type of garment which is considered suitable for *le sport* by dressmakers of the Rue de la Paix.

'Thank God you've come at last,' she said in her gloomiest voice. 'Darling Sally, looking so lovely, the angel. Oh, Paula! Isn't she sweet? Well, come in. You won't like it, but I can only hope you'll be amused by it, that's all.'

'My dear Amabelle,' cried Walter in tones of horror as he followed her into the hall, 'what a house!'

'Yes, you don't have to tell me that; I've been here now for a week, kindly remember. And do you know that from what the agents said I honestly thought it was going to be really old and attractive. They never stopped talking about its old-world charm, mullioned windows, oak beams and so on. Look at it—how could I have guessed it would be anything like this?'

'You just made the mistake,' said Walter soothingly, 'of confusing old world with olde worlde. You should have been more careful to find out whether or not there was an "e"; so much hangs on that one little letter. In any case, I must submit, with all deference, that the very name of the house, Mulberrie Farm, ought to have aroused your worse suspicions. I never heard anything so art and craft in my life, and I bet the yokels have no idea it's called that, they probably knew it as The Grange before all these inglenooks and things were put in. You must be crackie-boo, poor sweet, to go and take a house you've never even seen.'

'Don't tease her,' said Sally. 'I think it's divinely funny; just like those Paris restaurants made for Americans that we saw on our honeymoon.'

'I think it's very beautiful, Amabelle. I didn't know so much crooked wood existed in the world. I wonder if it was the architect's wife who bored all those worm-holes in her spare time instead of knitting jumpers. Oh, I say, too, look at the way the doors open. You just pull that little string and walk in—I do call that a dainty thought. And I adore that ironwork that looks like cardboard meant to look like ironwork; a very original touch that is. Now, I think, if you don't mind me saying so, that you ought to send up to Soloman's for some rushes to strew about the floor; then, when you've hung a couple of Fortmason hams on to those hooks in the ceiling and dressed all your servants in leathern jerkins, you'll have arrived at the true atmosphere of Ye. If I think of any other homey touches I'll let you know. It's no trouble at all to me.'

'Shut up, Walter, you fool,' said Sally. 'Anyhow, I'm sure it's a very comfortable little house.'

'That's what everybody says,' wailed Amabelle. 'Personally, I could never feel comfortable in a hideous place like this. However, now we're here I suppose we must make the best of it. Sit down, angels, and you shall have some cocktails in a minute.'

Presently Walter said: 'And how d'you think you'll enjoy life in the country, Amabelle?'

'Well, it will be better now you've come, but I can't describe to you what I've suffered so far. Frankly, I doubt whether I shall be impelled to settle down here for good, which was rather my idea in taking this house, although I

213

suppose I shall have to stay on till the end of the lease because of Jerome saying, "I told you so." The old boy was dead right, just the same.'

'Why, what's happened? You've been bored, I suppose?'

'I've nearly gone mad, that's all. Everything seems to be so queer and awful. To begin with, the lonely wolds I was so excited about are no more wolds than my hat. Ordinary fields full of mud, that's what they are. And as for their being lonely I never heard such bosh; they are covered with cows and awful staring men in filthy clothes and huge motor things which drive slowly up and down them. And in any case I think it's dangerous to go out alone here. Only yesterday I came across the bodies of two dear little rabbits which must have been killed by some lynch-maniac. It's terrifying to think there are such men wandering about. I brought the poor mites home and gave them decent burial in the garden.'

'The lynch-maniac must have been delighted when he came back for his dinner,' said Sally. She had spent her childhood in the country. Walter remarked that the amount of sadism among the lower classes was truly terrible.

'Now, listen, Sally,' went on Amabelle. 'You've lived in the country—I want you to tell me what people do all day. I simply can't find anything to occupy myself with. Your mother, for instance, what does she do?'

'Let me think now. She always seems to be extremely busy. For one thing she grows a lot of bulbs in the winter, in a dark place.'

'Don't forget to add that they always get immensely tall and thin and finally bend over like croquet hoops,' said Walter spitefully. He was not devoted to his mother-in-law.

'Be quiet. They are very pretty.'

'But that can't take up much time,' said Amabelle. 'What I want to know is how do people fill all those hours every day; there seem to be twice as many here as there are in London.'

'Mother, of course, takes a lot of exercise, walks and so on. And every morning she puts on a pair of black silk drawers

214

and a sweater and makes indelicate gestures on the lawn. That's called Building the Body Beautiful. She's mad about it.'

'And is it really beautiful—her body, I mean?' Amabelle asked with some show of interest.

'It's all right, I think. I never really look at it much. Then, of course, she does some gardening.'

'I thought of that myself, but when I got into the garden I couldn't see anything to do. There were no flowers at all, either, only some dying chrysanthemums.'

'I think flowers are so vulgar,' said Walter. 'It sounds a nice garden to me.'

'And she orders the food every morning.'

'Oh, I could never do that, the cook would give notice at once.'

'And she's district commissioner for the Girl Guides.'

'I can't quite see myself in khaki shorts,' said Amabelle. 'I think I must be resigned to playing the gramophone and gossiping. When Jerome and Bobby arrive there'll be some bridge for you, Walter. By the way, Major Stanworth is dining here to-night.'

'Who's he?'

'A sweet man, one of my neighbours. I met him in a field yesterday opening up a dead ewe to see what she died of. It was very interesting, we made great friends at once. I expect we ought really to go and have our baths; dinner is at eight-thirty.'

Major Stanworth, whose alien presence that evening Walter and Sally had rather dreaded, turned out to be a charming person. At the beginning of dinner he seemed shy and silent, but Walter presently let loose a perfect flood of conversation by saying: 'And what was the matter with the dead ewe? I gather you were having an autopsy when Amabelle came along the other day. I hope there was no suspicion of foul play?'

Major Stanworth shook his head sadly. 'Nearly as bad, I fear,' he said; 'she was suffering from a disease known as the fluke, and once that gets among our sheep it is a knockout blow to us farmers. However, as that is the only case I have had so far I must hope for the best.'

'Oh, yes, I know,' said Walter brightly; 'fluke and mouth, I've heard of that before, but I thought only foxhounds had it.'

The major looked rather surprised, and was about to speak when Sally said, 'Don't pay any attention to Walter, he's as ignorant as a bat, poor sweet. I remember quite well when one of our farmers at home was nearly ruined by the fluke; it's a horrible scourge. Something to do with the sheep's liver, isn't it?'

'The fluke,' said Major Stanworth, sipping his sherry, 'is really a small insect. It has the most curious and interesting life history—I wonder whether you would care to hear it?'

'Indeed we would,' said Walter enthusiastically. 'I always think that one half of the world knows too little of how the other half lives.'

Thus encouraged, Major Stanworth proceeded:

'The fluke begins life as a little worm. It is born into the sheep's liver and there it reaches maturity, marries, and has an inordinate number of children,' he paused impressively, '*totally* different from itself.'

'How extraordinary,' said Amabelle.

'I don't think so at all,' said Sally. 'Look at Elspeth Paula.'

'These children,' continued the major, 'are almost immediately passed out by the sheep and find their way, as soon as may be, into the lung of—the water snail. Here they in their turn marry, reach maturity, and in due course have an inordinate number of children *totally* different from themselves.'

'What a romance!' said Walter. 'And pray where are the next wedding bells to be heard?'

'In the snail's liver. The children who were born in its lung find their way to the liver, where they reach maturity, marry, and have an inordinate number of children *totally* different from themselves, who are passed out of the snail, on to a blade of grass, and so back once more into the sheep's liver.'

'Well, I do call that a tasteful roundelay,' said Walter.

Sally choked.

'Have some fish,' said Amabelle, tactfully changing the subject. 'It's very good for the brain. I have seen it reported that Lloyd George eats great quantities of fish.'

'No fish, thank you,' said the major.

'When does your little boy begin his holidays?' asked Amabelle. Major Stanworth was a widower with an only son. His wife had died the preceding year.

'Comes back to-morrow.'

'Do you go down often and see him at his school?'

'About twice a term, you know. Unsettles the boy if one goes oftener. As a matter of fact I went down last week for the annual sports, and rather a ghastly thing happened. The father of one of the boys died in the fathers' race—just collapsed, poor chap, and died. We carried him into the gymnasium—he was a stoutish cove, too—but it was no good; he was quite dead before the doctor could get at him even.'

'What an awful thing,' said Amabelle. She was arriving at an age which no longer regards death as a funny joke.

'At my private,' said Walter, 'we had a most handy little cemetery for the fathers, just behind the cricket pav. But of course, we had a fathers' three-legged race which used to finish them off in shoals. I have even known them die at the prize-giving, from shock, I suppose, if their boys got prizes.'

'Not a bad idea that about the cemetery, what?' said the major. 'I always have said "where the oak falls, there let it lie". This poor bloke was lugged off to Suffolk in a motor hearse, I believe.'

'Why *oak*, I wonder?' said Walter. 'Why not sycamore or monkey puzzle?'

Amabelle frowned at him and asked Major Stanworth whether he had been hunting that winter.

'I have been, of course, but this beastly foot and mouth has stopped us for the present. However, Lady Bobbin tells me that if there's no fresh outbreak we should be able to start again in about ten days' time, she thinks.'

'Is Lady Bobbin a good Master?'

'Foul mouthed, very foul mouthed, you know. Scares all

the young 'uns out of their wits, but she's very good with the farmers, they understand her. Do you hunt, Monteath?'

'I love it,' said Walter. 'Unfortunately, I only did it once. Before that I used to write articles in the newspapers saying that it was cruel and ought to be stopped and so on. But when I found out what jolly fun it is I gave that up in no time.'

'Oh, well done, splendid. Still, I mean to say, you couldn't really call it cruel, now, could you? Ever seen an old dog fox hunted out of covert on a fine sunny morning? Crafty old devil, he enjoys it right enough. I know he does.'

'I'm perfectly certain he doesn't,' said Walter. 'But that's not the point. The point is that *I* do, so I very soon stopped writing the articles and spent the money I got for them on a pair of topboots. But it was awful waste really, because since then I've never had another opportunity to hunt.'

'Oh, but I call that good! Now, I'll tell you what, Monteath, as soon as this something foot and mouth has stopped I'll lend you a horse. Yes, yes, it would be a pleasure—I've got more than I can ride myself as it is. And besides that I'll give you a ride in the point-to-point, if you like.'

'No, thank you,' said Sally, firmly intervening. 'I've got nicely used to being married to Walter now. There was a time when I thought the only ideal state would be that of widowhood, but now, what with the shortage of marrying men and one thing and another, I'm not at all sure about it. I believe I should miss the old boy a whole heap, you know. Besides, I need a man's help with the little one. And Walter popped his riding boots last week.'

The major winked at Walter and announced that he himself was a prominent member of the husbands' union, and would see fair play. This remark scarcely seemed, in view of his own recent widowhood, to be in the best of taste, and was received in a somewhat embarrassed silence. This he broke himself by asking Amabelle how she had enjoyed her visit to old Mrs. Cole that morning.

'Rather moderately, to tell you the truth,' said Amabelle. 'She looked so sweet and picturesque in her garden, feeding

218

the chickens, that I simply had to go in; but poor old thing she is filthy, isn't she? However, that can't be her fault, because when I asked if I could send her anything from here she said she'd like some soap. So I sent some along at once, and I only hope she uses it.'

The major began to laugh.

'Are you sure it was soap she asked for?' he said.

'Quite sure. Yes, of course, what else could it have been?'

'How about soup?'

'Soup? Oh, no, it wasn't soup; it was soap all right, I'm certain.'

'Well, you're wrong. She asked for soup, as a matter of fact.'

'My dear! I mean my dear Major Stanworth, how awful, I sent soap.'

'Yes, I know you did. And the big joke is that the poor old soul thought that you had sent soup tablets, so she boiled one for her dinner. The story was all round the village this afternoon. Leverett, my cowman, told me.'

'Oh,' said Amabelle, in tones of deep dismay. 'Soup! Yes, I see. But I shall have to leave for London at once, shan't I? I couldn't stay on here after doing a thing like that. How awful!'

'Now, Mrs. Fortescue, don't you worry about it. I would never have told you, only I thought it was too good a joke for you to miss.'

'I quite agree,' said Walter.

'Joke!' cried Amabelle faintly.

'Besides, I've fixed it all right for you. I went round to see her and took a couple of rabbits and told her that you were a bit hard of hearing. She was as pleased as Punch.'

'Yes, but the other people in the village must think I'm such a monster.'

'Oh, no, they're all frightfully pleased. They hate old Granny Coles like fifteen different kinds of hell because in hot weather she uses the village water supply for her garden and nobody else can get any.'

'She certainly doesn't use it for any other purpose. But it is a bit embarrassing because that's the second awful thing I've done here already.'

'What's the first?'

'The parson came to call, you see, and asked me if I would give a pound towards the bier—he said they wanted if possible to collect forty pounds for it. I said I would give five pounds, and then I thought it would be polite to take a little interest, so I asked who was going to drink all that beer. What made it worse was that he thought I was trying to be funny, and he was fearfully annoyed.'

6

Compton Bobbin is one of those houses which abound in every district of rural England, and whose chief characteristic is that they cannot but give rise, on first sight, to a feeling of depression in any sensitive observer. Nevertheless, a large, square and not unhandsome building, it bears testimony, on closer acquaintance, to the fact that it has in the past been inhabited by persons of taste and culture. But these persons have been so long dead, and the evidences of their existence have been so adequately concealed by the generations which succeeded them, that their former presence in the place is something to be supposed rather than immediately perceived. Supposed, however with some degree of certainty after a sojourn, however short, with their descendants.

It must have been, for instance, a person of taste who introduced the Chinese Chippendale mirror now hanging where only housemaids can see it in the back passage, the tails and wings of its fantastic birds sadly cracked and broken, victims of the late Sir Hudson Bobbin's addiction as a child to indoor cricket. For whom, if not for a person of taste, did Fragonard paint those pastorals, now so dirty and neglected as to be little more than squares of blackened canvas, and which must be examined in the strongest light if the grace of their composition is even faintly to emerge? They hang unnoticed in dark corners of a spare dressing-room. Again, whose were the negro slave boys in black and gold wood with which the Bobbin children have for generations terrified a new governess, and who now inhabit the big lumber-room? Whose Hepplewhite chairs on which the servants place their underclothes at night? Whose the Venetian glass chandelier, ruined by electric wiring carelessly and locally performed, which hangs, draped in dust sheets, in the disused ballroom? Whose the enamelled snuff-boxes, whose the Waterford glass jumbled together with so much horrible junk in glass-fronted cupboards on the landing? And, oh! to whom belonged the Empire crown of blue diamonds and pink pearls, transformed in 1910, the year of her marriage, into the brooch, bracelet and two rings which now adorn the unpleasing bosom, wrist and fingers of Gloria the present Lady Bobbin?

Persons of taste there have been. The eighteenth century statue of Apollo, hidden quite by dowdy evergreens; the domed temple on the island in the lake; the lake itself; the rococo bridge whose curious humped shapes are only permitted to appear beneath a tangle of ivy; the walled garden with its Italian gates and sundial; the classical lay-out of trees in the park; all testify to their charming and cultured existence. And after them persons some of whose taste might, not edify perhaps, but at any rate amuse. Those who bought the gay and touching little chintzes, beaded fire-screens, Stafford pottery, Berlin wool-work, gaudy flower paintings, and many strange products of a budding Empire; those who crowned a ram's head with silver and cairngorms and set it in triumph upon the mahogany sideboard. It is sad that of their possessions only the stuffiest should remain, nothing that might amuse, much that must appal. Stained glass windows, for instance, in each clouded amber pane of which leaps fierily the ruby Bobdgin, that legendary creature half unicorn half jackal from which the family (perhaps) derives its name. The hideous furniture and stuffy curtains in the dining-room, the stamped leather chairs and table in the study, the embossed wallpaper in the passages, and—let us speak of it quickly and never think of it again—the feudal fireplace with its load of heraldry in the hall. These, characteristically enough, remain, suffering in their turn and rendered even more horrible than they would otherwise appear by modern lighting, modern arrangement, and the exile to the boxroom of their jaunty fellows so patently designed to brighten their gloomy aspect.

The châtelaine of Compton Bobbin sat, a few days before

Christmas, reading the *Morning Post* beneath the prancing Bobdgins. It was to her, or rather to the talent of her forebears in picking and packing the strongest brand of Indian tea, that the Bobdgins owed their continued existence, for it is hardly to be supposed that any alien purchaser of the house would have tolerated for long those active little creatures. Lady Bobbin was the type of woman best described by that single adjective so explicit of its own dreary meaning, 'plain'. As a girl she had been the greatest heiress of her time and even then nobody could find a happier epithet with which to describe her looks than 'handsome', and that to the loudly expressed mystification of those of her fellow débutantes whose faces were their fortunes. At forty-five she was tall and thin but heavy of movement, her fuzzy hair uncut, her muddy skin unaided by any condiment, and with a voice like the worst sort of loud-speaker, imitating and aggressive and perpetually at work. She was without any kind of grace, either mental or physical.

At twenty-four she had married Sir Hudson Bobbin, a weak but rather charming character. To those who knew her it was a perpetual mystery, not indeed that she had married at all, as, but for the packages of tea, it must have been; but that having married she should have produced children of such charm and beauty as were possessed by her son Roderick and her daughter Philadelphia. She herself, if she had ever considered their undoubted attractiveness, would have felt it to be profoundly unimportant. (Actually, in her eyes, Roderick was merely a tiresome little schoolboy and Philadelphia a pert and disagreeable girl.) She knew that every woman has in life two main duties, to marry well and to produce a son and heir; having achieved both it was of no consequence to her whether or not the marriage was a happy one or the heir a young man of looks and distinction. Except for one terrible period, when between the sinking of Sir Hudson in the *Lusitania* and the birth of Roderick, she had been submitted to the suspense of not knowing whether the child would indeed prove to be of the required male sex, she had never known much disquietude on the score of her family life. Her daughter, beyond the initial disappointment caused by her sex, had never interested her at all, her one wish in that direction being that Philadelphia should marry as quickly and as advantageously as possible. The only thing which afforded her a real and lasting satisfaction was her pack of foxhounds. These meant to her what husband, children or artistic expression may mean to other women; they were her vanity and her delight. A hard day's hunting was to her the most exquisite of joys, and when this happiness was rendered temporarily impossible by frost, flood, or, as at present, an outbreak of foot and mouth disease in the district, her bitterness of spirit would be beyond all bounds; she would be as one mourning the untimely loss of a beloved, shut up within herself and inaccessible to sympathy.

Philadelphia Bobbin balanced a few pieces of rather dreary holly on the frame of her great grandmother's portrait by W. Etty.

'And now,' she said, getting down from the chair on which she had been standing, and viewing without satisfaction the results of her handiwork, 'I suppose I had better go and meet this hellish tutor. God, how I do hate Christmas.'

'Don't speak like that, Philadelphia,' said Lady Bobbin sharply, looking up from her perusal of the *Morning Post*, a perusal which at present was a daily torture to her since it consisted entirely in reading about the good runs of other packs of hounds which, more fortunate than hers, were not haunted by the grim spectre of foot and mouth disease. 'May I ask what else you want to be doing at this particular moment? The truth is you never do a hand's turn for anybody except yourself—self, self, self with you, all day long. You ought to be very grateful to have a motor car of your own instead of making all this fuss when you are asked, occasionally, to do some little errand for me with it. Another time I will hire a car when Fred is away. I would much sooner do that than have all these complaints. And if you're going to be in such a disgustingly bad temper, I'll thank you to keep to yourself and not spoil Christmas for everybody else. It is a time which means a great deal to some of us, I may tell you.'

'Oh, all right,' said Philadelphia. 'I can't see that having a car is anything to be so grateful for, even the butcher's boy has one, you know. And I wasn't grumbling at having to take it out; I just hate meeting strangers, that's all. What on earth am I to talk to him about all the way from Woodford?'

'It's quite unnecessary for you to talk. I suggest that you should occupy yourself with driving rather more carefully than you usually do around those Hogrush corners. The man is being paid to teach your brother, not talk to you, and I may say, whilst we are on this subject, that one of the chief reasons why I engaged a tutor these holidays is that I am not anxious for you to see a great deal of Roderick just at present. He is going through a very tiresome phase indeed, quite beyond himself with all this nonsense about not caring to go into the army and so on. I only hope that this tutor (who is, I understand, a sportsmanlike young fellow) will be able to make him see sense and get him out of doors a bit. You'd better go now, or you'll be late for that train—don't forget to ask if there are any packing cases for me at the station.'

Philadelphia stumped out of the room, banging the door as loudly as she dared, dragged on an old fur coat, fetched her car from the garage, and drove at a perfectly reckless speed to Woodford Station, where she found to her further annoyance that she was a quarter of an hour too early for the train. It was a clear night after a day of drenching rain, and as she sat looking through the open window of her car at a tiny new moon surrounded by twinkling stars and listening to the distant church bells practising, no doubt, their Christmas peal, her temper gradually improved. By the time that she heard the train approaching, so far off at first that the noise it made seemed almost to come from inside her own head, she was feeling quite well disposed towards the world in general. Presently the noise of the train grew much louder, then stopped altogether, and she knew that it had arrived at the next station. At last it came puffing through the tunnel, all lights and bustle. She could see people reading or sleeping behind the misted glass of the windows, and a man, probably, she thought, the tutor, taking luggage down from the rack. There was a long pause, then as the train heaved itself, groaning and creaking, towards its destination, a porter came up to the car with two suitcases, followed by a small young man who was fumbling in his pockets, no doubt for change.

'Are you Mr. Fisher?' said Philadelphia. 'I'm Philadelphia Bobbin. How do you do?'

'Excuse me, miss,' said the porter; 'there are two large packing cases for her ladyship. Will you take them now?'

'No, thank you,' said Philadelphia. 'They can wait.'

'I'm so sorry you had all the bother of turning out on such a cold evening,' said Paul as they drove away.

'It doesn't matter in the least; I love driving. The chauffeur's wife is in hospital and he's gone to be with her, and Bobby went out after lunch to see an Eton friend who lives near here and he isn't back yet. I expect he's found some sort of gambling, bridge or backgammon. You know Bobby, do you?'

Paul wondered whether she was in the secret and decided that she was not. 'Yes, I have met him once or twice. Have you any more brothers and sisters?'

'No, thank goodness. I expect we should have had, only father was drowned, you see, just before Bobby was born. But on Christmas Eve all my aunts and uncles and cousins come for a week, with masses of children, so the house will be quite full.' She said this almost apologetically, as though she thought that Paul might otherwise feel bored.

'Nice uncles and aunts?'

'Oh, not too bad on the whole. Uncle Ernest Leamington Spa is rather a trial because he always has such jolly ideas for a Merry Yule, but nobody pays much attention to him.'

'Do you live down here always?' He looked at a face which seemed to him, in the faintly reflected headlights of an oncoming car, to fall very little short of perfect beauty.

'Yes, we do,' she said abruptly. 'Nobody knows how horrible it is to live in the country always, you might just as well be in prison. I hate the country.'

'Would you prefer London?'

'Well, I went to London once for the season; I was coming out, you know, and I can't say I enjoyed it very much, but there must be other sorts of life there that I should enjoy.'

'Why do you think that?'

'One knows certain things about oneself.'

'You ought to marry,' said Paul. 'Girls are always happier married, I believe.'

'So my mother tells me,' said Philadelphia drily. She looked at him as though she had remembered that he was a stranger and her brother's tutor, and said no more. Presently they separated, Paul to make his first entrance into Compton Bobbin and Philadelphia to put her car away in the garage.

When he saw her again in the drawing-room before dinner he thought that she was not really as beautiful as she had seemed to be at first. Her features were certainly very good, her eyes large and of a remarkably bright blue colour; but her hair, complexion and clothes were dull and looked uncared-for. This he thought might be due to the fact that she evidently had no idea of how to (as the French say) arrange herself. A London girl with far less to go upon in the way of looks would have made twice as good an effort. He decided that she had better be handed over to Amabelle's care as soon as possible.

As Bobby had not yet put in an appearance, Lady Bobbin said that they would not wait, and began dinner without him. Half-way through the meal he strolled into the dining-room in day clothes and said, 'How *are* you?' in his most affected manner to Paul, winking at him with the eye away from Lady Bobbin. 'Sorry, mother,' he added as he took his place at the head of the table.

'Is it quite necessary to be so unpunctual for meals?' inquired Lady Bobbin in her most rasping tone of voice. 'And I think I have mentioned before that I insist upon you dressing for dinner. I can remember my dear father telling me that even when he was on one of his most strenuous safaris in the African bush he *never* omitted to dress for dinner.'

'Well, but we're not in the African bush now, are we?' said Bobby with his mouth full.

There seemed to be no reply to this piece of logic. Lady Bobbin turned to Paul with an air of effusion obviously intended to accentuate her displeasure with her son and said, 'You come here at a very unlucky moment, Mr. Fisher; our hunting has been stopped by an outbreak of foot and mouth disease on the edge of my country. I am glad to say that we are allowed to hack about in this district, but of course, nothing can make up for the season being spoilt in this way, just when the weather is so beautifully open too. It is really heart-breaking. You do hunt, I fancy?'

'No, no,' said Paul, who was bent on making a good impression; 'I hack, though.'

Lady Bobbin took this to mean that the tutor had no clothes for hunting, and nodded graciously.

'And of course,' Paul went on, 'I love to see others hunt. But how rotten about the foot and mouth—so wretched for the poor cows, too.'

'What cows?'

'The ones with feet and mouths.'

'Oh, the cows,' said Lady Bobbin vaguely. 'But they're all right. The Government slaughters them at once; humanely, too. The terrible thing about it is the way it stops hunting. Of course, it's quite obvious to me that it's all done by the Bolsheviks.'

'Now, really, mother, what do you mean by that?' said Bobby impatiently.

'Florence Prague was saying only yesterday, and I am perfectly certain she is right, that the Bolsheviks are out to do anything they can which will stop hunting. They know quite well, the devils, that every kind of sport, and especially hunting, does more to put down socialism than all the speeches in the world, so, as they can't do very much with that R.S.V.P. nonsense, they go about spreading foot and mouth germs all over the countryside. I can't imagine why the Government doesn't take active steps; it's enough to make one believe that they are in the pay of these brutes themselves. Too bad, you know.'

'Never mind,' said Bobby, throwing a look of mock despair

in the direction of Paul, who sat open-mouthed at this theory; 'the great thing is that we are allowed to hack.'

'Yes, you can hack to within a radius of five miles of Woodford. Oh, I don't fancy you will want for occupation; the golf course is in excellent order, I believe. You are very fond of golf, I hear, Mr. Fisher?'

'Yes, indeed, I love nothing more than golf. In fact, I am devoted to everything in the way of open-air sports, even hiking and biking. So long as I can be out of doors, away from stuffy houses, I am perfectly happy.'

Lady Bobbin looked at him with approval. 'Then you will like the life here, Mr. Fisher. It is a pity you do not hunt, but you can ride all day; there are plenty of horses to be exercised while the foot and mouth continues.'

Bobby, who hated to be ignored by anybody, even his mother, for long, now tried to ingratiate himself by asking, very politely, if everything was quite as it should be in the village.

'I'm sorry to say that we've had a good deal of trouble lately,' she answered. 'The new parson has proved far from satisfactory, far. Very high church indeed. I should not be at all surprised to find that he is in the pay of Rome, his services are nothing but lace and smells and all that nonsense about changing clothes every now and then. In fact, I have been obliged to give up going to church here at all. It is monstrous that this living is not in our gift. Why should some Oxford college choose a parson for us? I have written to the dear bishop about it, but I fear that he is powerless to intervene.'

'I say, that's too bad,' murmured Bobby, mentally resolving that he would go to church next Sunday.

'Another thing,' continued Lady Bobbin, 'which is causing me great anxiety is this new law allowing people to marry their uncles. It is a perfect scandal, I consider. Three of our women have done it already. It is really most discouraging just when one was beginning to hope and think that morals were improving in the village at last.'

'But if it's allowed by law, surely it cannot be immoral?'

said Bobby, in just that reasonable tone of voice which he knew would annoy his mother most.

'It is immoral—immoral and disgusting. That sort of thing can't be made right just by passing a few laws, you know. Besides, the Church will never countenance it. The dear bishop came to lunch not long ago, and he was saying, and of course I entirely agreed with him, dear, good old man, that a measure of this kind must be the ruin of family relationships.'

'On the contrary,' said Bobby, 'I think it will ginger things up top hole. I expect that Philadelphia already begins to look on Uncle Ernest in a new and far more fascinating light, don't you, Delphie? I must say I'm looking forward to some very matey doings this Christmas.'

'Bobby!' said his mother sharply, 'you are not to talk like that. Please get on with your food; we are all waiting for you. Silly little schoolboys like you can't be expected to understand these things, but it is unnecessary and not in the least clever to make flippant remarks about them. Mr. Fisher, I am sure, will agree with me.'

'Yes, indeed I do,' said Paul fervently. 'I can't think of a single one of my aunts whom I wouldn't sooner be dead than married to.'

'That, if I may be allowed to say so, is very much beside the point, Mr. Fisher. In any case, I don't feel at all certain that aunts are allowed. I rather fancy it is uncles only. Why they want to pass such filthy laws I cannot imagine, but there, it's so like the Government. They waste their time over useless and even harmful measures of that sort, and do absolutely nothing to wipe out Bolshevism. I said as much to our member, Sir Joseph Jenkins, last time he was here, and he quite agreed with me. A very sound man, Sir Joseph,' she added, turning to Paul; 'very much interested in all questions of drainage, sanitation, and so on—in fact, I believe he is nearly always chairman of drains committees in the House.'

'Ah,' said Paul.

There was a silence. Bobby began to giggle, but was fortunately able to conceal this fact from his mother, as there was a large bowl of holly on the table between them. Paul looked self-consciously into space, wondering whether or not he should mention passing angels, and Philadelphia took a second large helping of steamed pudding with hot plum jam. Presently Lady Bobbin spoke again.

'By the way, children, I went over to see Florence Prague this afternoon. She has quite recovered from that nasty little toss she took, but poor old Sagrada strained a ligament and has had to be put down.'

Bobby and Philadelphia made suitable comments upon this piece of news, and Lady Bobbin continued:

'Florence and I had a long chat about your holidays, and we agreed that as there is to be no hunt ball this winter it would be a good idea for me to give a little dance here for you both. I had been thinking of it for some time, but I thought that perhaps it would be wrong, in view of the present crisis, to spend money on pure amusement. Florence, however, says very sensibly that so long as we have neither champagne nor a proper band there could be no great harm in it, and of course it would give an immense amount of pleasure.'

'Not, I may say, to me,' remarked Bobby sourly. 'My dear mother, I really don't know what you can be thinking of. How can you possibly have a dance without either champagne or a band?'

'Of course you can, perfectly well. There is a young man in Woodford, the butcher's son, who plays dance music very nicely; he would play all night, I am told, for thirty shillings, and I suppose even in these days everyone likes a good cider cup. The truth is, Roderick, that you are too disgustingly spoilt for words. It is perfectly sickening trying to make plans for your amusement, because one knows quite well beforehand that nothing will be right and that you will grumble unceasingly at whatever is arranged. I said so to Florence Prague this afternoon. I said: "Now, Florence, you'll see I shall get no thanks for all this from Roderick, nothing but complaints." But all the same I see no reason why, just because you happen to have these large ideas, Philadelphia and all the other young people in the neighbourhood should be deprived of their fun. I'm afraid, my boy, that you will

231

soon find out that nowadays it's a question between taking what is offered in the way of amusement and going without it. Very few people can afford unlimited champagne, and even if they could such extravagance would be most harmful and unpatriotic, just the very sort of thing that breeds socialism in the country.'

Everyone now looked embarrassed. Bobby turned crimson with annoyance, but did not dare answer back, and Paul said, helpfully but tactlessly: 'Why not have champagne cocktails instead? They are very economical, because you need only buy the cheapest sort of champagne, to which you add a little brandy and sugar, and people do seem to like them most awfully.'

'No, Mr. Fisher, no cocktails in this house, thank you. I regard the cocktail habit as a most pernicious and disgusting one. Besides, people get rowdy enough on champagne alone, without adding brandy to it. Why, last year, at Lady Jenkins' party, the most disgraceful things happened. I actually saw that awful Hood boy, at supper, cramming a sausage down his ear, for a bet, I suppose. Perfectly revolting, we don't want that sort of behaviour at Compton Bobbin. No, we will have good British beer and cider cup, quite sufficient for young people. Nobody need be half drunk before they can enjoy themselves, or at least I should very much hope not.'

And Lady Bobbin rose with majesty to leave the dining-room. It will be noticed that during this entire meal Philadelphia Bobbin never once opened her mouth to speak. She was a silent girl.

7

After dinner it was quite kindly indicated to Paul that he was expected to retire to the schoolroom, which he did with alacrity, most willing to exchange the physical presence of Gloria Lady Bobbin for the intellectual proximity of her predecessor. He knew that the thoughtful Bobby, who showed him the way to his appointed sanctuary, had hidden all the fourteen volumes of Lady Maria's journal and a vast quantity of her letters behind the schoolroom radiator; a spot less calculated than might, perhaps, be imagined to harm the precious documents, the central heating apparatus at Compton Bobbin never having been known to affect the temperature of the atmosphere by so much as one degree.

The moment he was alone Paul fell, with a thrill of the most exquisite anticipation, upon his prize. The journal consisted of large manuscript volumes handsomely bound in red morocco. Lady Maria's handwriting was small but very legible, and of an extreme neatness, not one correction or erasion appearing in any of the pages that Paul looked at. After browsing indiscriminately for a while, examining the little water-colour drawings that were interspersed among the text, Paul settled down to read the fifth volume, which began with the following words:

Jan. 1st, 1878.
Another year, with its store of tribulations and sufferings, its trials and grievous disappointments, is now before us. Thought much last night, while listening to the New Year bells, of the Dear Dead, and was thankful for all they will have been spared. Felt how *willingly* I could join them should the Call come to me. As Mr. Landor has said, so truly and so touchingly. 'I warmed both hands before the Fire of Life, it sinks, and I am ready to depart.' Thought of Dearest

233

Papa and all his sufferings so patiently borne, and of the Loved Grave at Margate. Prayed for strength in the coming year that I and my Dear Ones may be able to bear everything that is in store for us. (N.B.—Must remember to tell Mrs. Craven that the beef was overdone yesterday. It makes Josiah so very sad and angry when this is the case, and I feel that it must be *quite* unnecessary.) As I write poor Ivanhoe lies at my feet. Dear faithful beast, I fear that he may not be spared to see many more New Years; how dreary, how different this house will seem without the feeble, friendly wag of his old weatherbeaten tail. . . .

Hardly had Paul read so far when Bobby came back into the room, shut the door and settled himself down by the fire in the evident anticipation of a good gossip.

'Look here, old top,' he said, 'put down great-grand-mamma for a few minutes and listen to a very natty piece of news. No, really, something too incredible is going to happen.'

'Oh, is it? What?'

'My cousin Michael Lewes is coming to stay here to-morrow for a fortnight.'

'What is there incredible about that? Your sister told me in the car that all your aunts and uncles and cousins were coming for Christmas.'

'Oh, didn't you know? Why, Michael left England three years ago and got a post in Cairo simply because of Amabelle, because she refused to marry him. She was the love of his life. He's only been home for exactly a week, and now he'll find himself in the next house to hers—you must say it's pretty odd. They're bound to meet.'

'They may not.'

'Likely tale! I shall certainly make it my business to see that they do,' he added mischievously, giving Paul the benefit of that smile with which he had already launched, as it were, a thousand ships.

'Good gracious,' said Paul suddenly, forgetting to smile back and shutting up Lady Maria's journal with a bang. 'Lord Lewes. Yes, of course I remember all about it now. I'd no idea he was any relation to you though.'

'My first cousin. Father's sisters all married well, as it happens, which leaves me quite nicely connected.'

'You're a damned little snob.'

'I know; I glory in it.'

'Oh, you do, do you? Tell me some more about your cousin though. How old is he now?'

'Michael is thirty-two or -three I suppose. Amabelle's what? Nearly forty-five should you think? He was crazy about her, I believe, begged and implored her to marry him, but the old girl had too much sense to do that. And anyway she was frightfully bored by the whole affair. I don't wonder either. Michael's awfully sweet, you know, but not exactly a hero of romance.'

'What did his people think of it?' asked Paul.

'His father and mother are both dead, you know. My mother got hold of the wrong end of the stick, as she always does, and thought that poor darling Amabelle was a scheming old tart trying to lure him into her clutches. But Michael settled the whole thing by getting another post abroad when he saw that she was determined not to marry him.'

'D'you think he'll have got over it by now?'

'Would one ever get over being in love with Amabelle?' asked Bobby sententiously. 'I doubt it. I don't imagine Michael would anyway; he took it very hard at the time; besides, he's a sentimental old thing. It's lucky you happen to be an author, Paul, my boy. This house is going to be a perfect hotbed of copy for the next week or two. Another frightfully funny thing has happened, by the way. Mamma has left cards on Amabelle. I can only suppose she has no idea it's *that* Mrs. Fortescue.'

'How d'you know she has?'

'I've been over at Mulberrie Farm the whole afternoon playing bridge with Jerome and the Monteaths.'

'Oh, so that's your Eton friend. I thought as much. How does Amabelle like the country?'

'Loathes it, of course. She's so bored that she's taken to going out farming every day with old Major Stanworth. It's frightfully funny, I must say, to hear her talking about Runner Ducks and Middle Whites. Apparently she helped to *accouche* a cow yesterday.'

'I must go over and see her to-morrow. How am I going down with your mamma?' asked Paul, rather nervously, glancing at the precious journal.

'Quite O.K. so far. She likes the look of you she told me. But for heaven's sake keep off the subject of hunting, or I know you'll put your foot in it. Oh, and by the way, she's going to talk to you about a daily programme for me this hols., so mind you arrange that we finish all the work in the morning, then we can get out after lunch and spend our afternoons at Mulberrie Farm under the pretext of riding or playing golf. D'you see the idea? I'm going back there now—you coming?'

'I don't think so, thank you. Now that I am here I'm longing to get down to the journal. It looks too entrancing. Does your mother know you're going out?'

'No, of course she doesn't, you loopy old thing. What d'you suppose? I said good night to her ages ago, and what's more I've put a lay figure in my tiny bed in case she comes to look—it's been done before. Leave this window open for me, will you?—so long, then, see you in the morning.'

He jumped out of the window, and a few moments later a car was heard starting up in the road outside. Paul continued his perusal of the journal.

Jan. 3rd, 1878.

Went out in the donkey chaise accompanied by Edward and his dear children, who are here paying us a very happy visit. We took some pudding to poor old Mrs. Skittle; she is not, I fear, likely to be with us much longer, poor old soul, and she herself reminded me of the country proverb, 'A green Christmas makes a fat churchyard.' This Christmas has certainly been the greenest that I can remember for years past, and Josiah says the same. (N.B.—The soup was not very warm at dinner last night; this must not occur again, as it makes darling Josiah very sad.)

Little Hudson, darling Edward's eldest boy, looked so very pretty to-day in his blue dress and little pink ribbon shoes. As we

236

approached Compton Bobbin down the oak avenue I said to him, with a wave of my hand, 'This will be yours one day, my darling,' thinking it right that he should learn his responsibilities thus early in life. He looked at me earnestly for a while, clasped together his little pink hands, and said: 'Then I must be very, very good.' This reminded me so much of the dear Queen who, when first told that she was in the succession to the throne, said with charming resolution, 'I will be good.' Heaven knows that she has kept her word.

Jan. 8th, 1878.

Heard to-day from darling Edward, who left us on Tuesday in anticipation of this happy event that dearest Feodora has been brought to bed of a lovely little girl. This makes the fourth addition to their family. Heaven grant that in time they will have a quiverful. The news came by the telegraph, and as soon as I had imparted it to darling Josiah I went up to the nursery, where little Hudson, Mildred and Millicent sat at breakfast. I nodded to Mrs. Darcy, their most excellent nurse, who was made aware by this signal of the news that I had received. I then sat down next to Hudson and said: 'Darling, the storks have brought you a little sister.' 'Where?' he cried, clapping his hands in glee. 'Does mamma know?' At this remark Mrs. Darcy and I had great difficulty in keeping our countenances.

Jan. 16th, 1878.

Alas, the little daughter born last week to Feodora passed away from us on Tuesday night. This dreadful news reached me yesterday morning by the telegraph, and for the rest of the day I was too much upset to write in my journal. Poor darling Edward, and poor, poor Feo, only a mother can guess at what she must be feeling now. Edward wrote me a dear note to say that he had been able to baptize the little one, which he did with the names Mary Ursula Christian Margaret, so I am thankful to think that the beloved little remains will be able to repose in sanctified ground. He tells me that dearest Feo is still very weak and most dreadfully sad, but beautifully resigned. She is allowed to sit up for a few hours every day and occupies herself embroidering a little shroud. How inscrutable are the ways of Providence, that He should give us this dear one to add brightness to our lives for a few days, only to take her from us in so short a space. I went up to the nursery as soon as I had received the news and found, as before, the three babies sitting at breakfast. Mrs. Darcy, observing my black garments, knew the worst at once. I sat down next to baby Hudson and told him that his new sister had gone to Heaven. 'Did the storks come and fetch her away?' he asked innocently. 'No, my darling, it was the angels who took her away,' I replied.

8

The next morning after breakfast, which took place punctually at the unalluring hour of half-past eight, Lady Bobbin sent for Paul. Sleepy and rather unnerved, he found his way to her study, a room which so exactly, in every respect, resembled a man's typical smoking-room that Paul looked round for the pipe rack without which it did not seem complete. Lady Bobbin herself, dressed in a riding habit, flannel shirt and soft felt hat, looked almost human. She was one of those women who are only tidy and presentable when wearing some kind of uniform. She sat bolt upright on a hard chair and indicated another to Paul.

'I thought, Mr. Fisher,' she said, tapping her booted leg briskly with a riding whip, 'that it would be a good plan if you and I together were to arrange a kind of daily programme for Roderick to carry out during the time that you are with us. I am a great believer in strict routine for young people, especially now that they have these ridiculously long holidays, and Roderick badly needs discipline, as you will very soon find out.'

Here she paused, looked at her watch, then out of the window, and finally at Paul, as though expecting him to make some comment.

'I think you are right. He evidently does need discipline. It seems to me that he is the sort of boy who should spend a great deal of time out in the open,' said Paul, remembering Bobby's little plan for bridge parties at Mulberrie Farm. 'Plenty of exercise and fresh air would do him a world of good, both mentally and physically; nothing like it for building character, you know. In fact,' he went on, warming to his subject, 'in all the years that I have had boys in my charge I

239

have adhered to the motto, *Mens sana in corpore sano*. I have never found a better.'

'There is no better,' said Lady Bobbin approvingly. The tutor was making an excellent impression. 'If more young people would realize that we could do away with a great deal that is bad nowadays, and especially this unhealthy modern art, I feel certain.'

'I think we could, too.'

'Some of these artists, you know (if you could call them artists, which, personally, I don't) would be different beings after a day's hunting, do them all the good in the world, take their minds off those hideous atrocities that they pretend to like. Diseased minds, that's what they've got, diseased minds in unhealthy bodies.'

'Poor wretches,' said Paul, in tones of withering contempt.

'However, that's beside the point,' said Lady Bobbin, again looking at her watch. 'Now I had very much hoped that Roderick would be getting four or five days a week with hounds these Christmas holidays, but of course the wretched foot and mouth has stopped all that for the present (although between ourselves I have an idea that, if there are no fresh outbreaks before the new year, we shall be able to carry on just as usual in January). Luckily, however, we are not prevented from hacking on the estate, so you and he will be able to help keep the hunt horses fit. Then I shall be arranging one or two shoots for him, nothing much, you know, as we have given up rearing since my husband's death, but just rough days. Besides that there is quite a nice little golf course outside Woodford, and Major Stanworth, who is farming near here, has a squash court, so as you see there will be no lack of sport for you. Now would you be so good as to cast your eye over this piece of paper on which I have written out a daily programme for Roderick, subject, of course, to your approval, Mr. Fisher.'

'Let me see, let me see,' said Paul, fixing on to his nose a pair of pince-nez through which, in fact, he could hardly see anything at all, but which he felt to be in keeping with his new character as tutor. (Amabelle had with great difficulty restrained him from making his appearance at Compton Bobbin arrayed in a platinum blonde wig, moustache and eyebrows.)

'Ah! Hum! Hem! Yes! "Breakfast at eight-thirty, work from nine to eleven, ride from eleven to one." That won't do, you know, Lady Bobbin, won't do at all, I fear. Let me see now, "luncheon at one o'clock, ride or play golf from two till four"—that's all right—"from five till seven-thirty more work or a game of squash rackets". Yes, a very excellent programme, if I may say so, but there is one thing about it which I shall be obliged to alter. We *must* have the whole morning for work.'

'Has Mr. Pringle given Roderick so much to do?'

'Yes, indeed. A very great deal. I am afraid from what Mr. Pringle tells me that Roderick is an idle, a backward boy.'

'I know he is.'

'Mr. Pringle doubts whether Roderick will pass into Sandhurst at all unless we read the whole of Horace, selections, which he has made for us, from Pliny and Virgil, the letters of Julius Caesar, the *Iliad*, most of the Greek Anthology, Gibbon's *Decline and Fall of the Roman Empire*, Burton's *Anatomy of Melancholy*, and Froude's *Essays*,' said Paul wildly, and at random. 'And besides all that he urged on me the importance of coaching Roderick thoroughly in mathematics and European history. Personally I think it seems rather a pity to pin the boy down to his lessons when he could be reaping so much benefit from fresh air and exercise, but you know what these schoolmasters are like. Besides, you must yourself be anxious for him to pass into Sandhurst, and if he is to do so with any degree of certainty we shall, I fear, be obliged to give up more time to our work than you have allowed for on this programme.'

'Very well,' said Lady Bobbin, 'I'm sure I don't wish the boy's work to suffer, and as you say, I am very anxious that he should pass for Sandhurst. And that reminds me of something I wanted to mention to you—please do all that you can to persuade Roderick that he wants to go into the army. He has an absurd idea of becoming a diplomat, which I should

241

very much dislike. I myself am a soldier's daughter and a soldier's wife—'

'So am I,' said Paul. 'At least I am a soldier's son and my mother was a soldier's wife.'

'And I particularly wish Roderick to become a soldier, to carry on the tradition in his father's regiment, so that I shall be very much obliged to you for any influence you may bring to bear in this direction. Now tell me how you intend to arrange your day, and then I must go out.'

'I fear that it will be necessary for us to work from nine to one a.m. Personally, I am a great believer in morning work for young people. I think it most valuable. The whole afternoon will then be free for outdoor exercise—I am glad to hear that there are some squash courts near-by, as we shall be able to play them after it is too dark for riding or golf. We will see how the work is going, but I expect that I shall be obliged to call upon a couple of hours of his time after dinner as well.'

'I see that you intend to be very severe with Roderick, so much the better. The boy has needed a man's hand for some years. I'm afraid I have been rather inclined to spoil him myself. All right, then, we'll leave it at that. I should be obliged if you would let me know from time to time how the work is getting on.'

So saying, Lady Bobbin hurried away to the stables.

'That's grand,' said Bobby, when Paul had told him with a good deal of unseemly merriment, the results of his interview. 'I'm thankful you were quite firm about the morning work. Actually, of course, what I shall do is to tuck up on this sofa; it doesn't suit my constitution to be awake before lunch time, while you get on with great-grandmamma's journal. You might read out any juicy bits that you happen to come across. Then the moment lunch is finished we'll hack over to Mulberrie Farm. Amabelle says there is a groom who can exercise the horses for us, while we play bridge and gossip with her—I'll tell him to jolly well tire them out, too. If we get back late we'll pretend that we stopped at Woodford Manor (that's Major Stanworth's) for a game of squash and some tea.

Mother will be awfully pleased. Well, thanks to you, Paul, old boy, I'm looking forward to the decentest hols. for years.' And Bobby flung himself on to the sofa, where he immediately fell asleep.

Meanwhile Paul returned to the journal, and was soon in the middle of that part of it which describes at immense length and in great detail the last weeks and hours of Sir Josiah Bobbin, who died, at the age of sixty-one, evidently from chronic over-eating.

Aug. 6th, 1878.

Spent many happy hours to-day in the Beloved Sick Room. I occupied some of them by reading aloud from the 'Idylls of the King', a work combining such noble sentiments with such an interesting narrative (both of which are, in my opinion, and that of Josiah, a *sine qua non* of *really great* poetry) that it is truly pleasant and edifying to read. How different from *so much* that is written in these days! My Dear One slept most of the time. He still has, I am most thankful to say, a good appetite, although so unwell, and it is by the means of constant feeding with nourishing foods that we are able to maintain his Precious Strength. It is now very late, almost midnight, the hour always consecrated to my journal. Ah! Faithful Page, to thee how many sorrows have I confided, safe in the knowledge that thou at least will never misconstrue my meaning, never repeat my secrets to a hard, uncomprehending world. To-night I will unburden more of myself to thee, as I sit beside the Beloved Bed. For the day which is just dawning is the anniversary of the death of Dearest Mamma, who passed away when I was but an unthinking babe of four months old. Oh, cruel Fate which robbed nine little ones of their Guiding Star at such an early age, leaving them to reach maturity without a Mother's care.

At such sacred moments I sometimes think that I myself could have made a truer Wife, a more attentive Mother, if I had been less devoted to my Art. Alas! Can it be so? Would Arthur, George, Edward, Albert, Frederick and William, Alice, Julia, Maud, Eva, Louise and Beatrice have been *better* men and women, had I given up my writing? The very thought is a knife in my heart! Would darling Josiah have had a *more perfect* helpmeet but for the cultivation of my Gift? The knife turns! And yet I console myself with remembering that Nature teaches us a different, and, I hope, a truer lesson. The gentle Nightingale can ever find time for the duties of her home in

the intevals of charming the woodlands with her silvery note; the
merry lark, soaring above the cornfields, the perky robin hopping
among the evergreens, each has its little song to sing, yet is not
therefore a *neglectful* Mother! And surely it has ever been thus with
me? Surely I have no cause for self-reproach on that dread score? I
know that I have not, otherwise how could I survive another
moment at such a melancholy time? Sometimes it comes upon me
with a fearful shudder that I am soon to be left a Widow. Widow!
Hateful word, how could these fingers fashion thee? Surely I must
be spared that unbearable, that fatal blow awhile? And yet I saw in
the doctor's eye to-day a look of cruel foreboding as he said: 'Give
Sir Josiah anything he likes to eat, we must not cross him now.' That
word 'now', I shuddered as I heard it, nor dared to ask its meaning.

> *Ah! Leave, my darling, leave me not awhile,*
> *Lonely upon this planet sere and grey;*
> *Spare my poor heart such melancholy trial,*
> *Lest frail my courage faint and fade away.*
>
> *Forget that thou art ill and tired of woe,*
> *Think rather of the day when first we met.*
> *Forget the hateful burdens here below,*
> *Sorrow, ingratitude and loss, forget!*
>
> *Think only, love, upon our wedding day,*
> *The lilies and the sunshine and the bells;*
> *Of how, the service o'er, we drove away*
> *To our blest honeymoon at Tunbridge Wells.*
>
> *Think of our life together all these years,*
> *The joys we've shared, the sorrows we have known;*
> *The laughter of our children, and their tears,*
> *The happiness of duty bravely done.*
>
> *But if with longing thou art overcome*
> *To leave forthwith this sad and tearful earth,*
> *E'en should my heart with poignant grief be numb,*
> *It yet would not begrudge thee Heavenly birth!*
>
> *Then song of nightingales in the wet leaves*
> *Of churchyard yews shall be thy heavy dirge;*
> *Though for a space alone my bosom heaves,*
> *It everlastingly with thine shall merge!*

Paul recognized these as being the first verses of what later became one of Lady Maria's best known and most popular poems, 'At a Husband's Death-Bed, or The Passing of a Beloved', set to music by her son-in-law, Lord Otto Pulman, and published shortly after Sir Josiah's death. Presently he came to the following entry:

Aug. 26th, 1878.

'Tis o'er. All is over, and I a Widow. Little Hudson came to me just now as I sat by the Loved Remains in a kind of sad trance.

'Granny,' he said, in his little lisping voice, 'what is a widow, granny?'

'Alas! I am a widow, my love,' I replied.

'And granny,' went on the poor innocent, 'what is a corpse granny?'

'Look there,' I said in awful tones, pointing to the Bed.

'But, granny, I want to see a corpse. That's only grandpa, gone to sleep.'

At this I quite broke down, and I think that the tears have done me some little good. Now I must collect my thoughts and try to recall, while it is yet fresh in my memory, every incident connected with The End.

At four o'clock, or it may have been a few minutes later, I went to my room, to rest before tea time. I removed some of my garments and lay down on the couch, and I think I must have dozed for a few moments. At any rate, I remember nothing more until I saw, with a *fearful start*, that darling Alice was standing near me, pointing with her hand towards Heaven. I realized, as soon as I observed this significant and awful gesture, that The End *must* now be very near, so hastily throwing a shawl around my shoulders I returned to the Bedside, where I found dear Arthur, George, Edward, Albert, Frederick, William, Julia, Maud, Eva, Louise and Beatrice standing around it in various attitudes of pious resignation very beautiful to see. As I approached my darling Josiah he turned over in bed, a smile of happy anticipation o'erspread his features and he spoke, not very coherently, a few words. In my agitation I thought at first that he was saying 'Bring me the oysters,' a dish to which he has ever been most partial, but of course, as dearest Edward remarked when speaking of it to me afterwards, he must really have said, 'Bury me in the cloisters,' a curious fancy as there are no cloisters in this neighbourhood. There was a long silence after this, which my Loved One broke himself. He looked darling Edward full in the face, said, very loudly, 'Pass the Port,' and fell lifeless to his pillow. Edward said immediately, in low but ringing tones, 'Safe past the Port indeed, Life's perilous journey done.' A moment later dearest Alice very reverently took my blue shawl from off my shoulders and replaced it with a black one. Then and only then did I realize that it was all over, and I indeed a Widow. The *best*, the *noblest* husband that woman ever had—I can write no more at present.

Aug. 31st, 1878.

I have just returned to the house from attending My Angel's funeral. Such a long, and such a very beautiful service, how he would have rejoiced in it had he but been there to participate. Afterwards I sent for Mr. Brawn, our incumbent, and spoke with him upon the subject, now most dear to my Poor Widowed Heart, that of erecting some Gothick cloisters in the churchyard as a memorial to Him. It was His dying wish. Mr. Brawn, I am thankful to say, is delighted with the idea and has made one or two very feeling suggestions. He thinks, and this shows him to be a man of true sensibility, that the cloisters should have fourteen arches, one for Darling Josiah, one for myself, and one for each of our dear sons and daughters. The Dear Tomb can then repose in the middle.

The children have been very kind and considerate, and so have the poor people, who for miles around came with their little offerings of flowers, most touching. Baby Hudson's has been the only smiling face on which I have looked for days. I would hardly have it otherwise; he is mercifully too young as yet to know the dreadful anguish which he must else have felt at the loss of Such a Grandfather.

Paul read on for the rest of that day. (It was pouring wet, and even Lady Bobbin conceded, at luncheon time, that their first ride had better be postponed until slightly more reasonable weather should have set in. Bobby and Philadelphia went instead to Oxford to do some Christmas shopping, and to bring back Lord Lewes, who had telephoned to say that his car had broken down there.)

Lady Maria Bobbin, after the death of her husband, retired to a dower house in the park, where she lived for some years with her only unmarried daughter, Eva, as a companion. Her life there appeared to have been singularly uneventful, except for certain little disagreements with her daughter-in-law, Lady Feodora Bobbin, whom she too evidently detested, until, in 1888, Paul came upon the following entry:

June 3rd, 1888.

A most extraordinary and agitating event occurred this afternoon. A person of the name of Hardysides came to see me and made a proposal for dear Eva's hand. I very naturally said that I could not possibly consider this matter, and bid him good day; but the whole affair has upset me dreadfully. Supposing that Eva were in time to marry? Not Hardysides, of course, the idea is ridiculous, but supposing (which God be thanked is unlikely owing to our very retired position) that some young man of family and fortune were to make an offer for her? What could I say? For Eva's presence here is very necessary to me. If she left me, who would copy out my poems ready for the publisher? Who would order the food, arrange the flowers, attend to the linen and perform the hundred and one little odd jobs which it is a daughter's plain and joyous duty to do for her Mother? I *cannot* believe that dearest Eva would be so *base* and *selfish* as to leave me alone for the few years that remain before I join my beloved Josiah on High. Who are these Hardysides? A family with which I seem to be unacquainted. I very much hope that *no more* will be said on the subject, as these shocks are *most* injurious to my health.

June 4th, 1888.

Dearest Eva herself broached the subject of Mr. Hardysides (whom she *most* improperly refers to by his christian name of Horace) during the time which I always devote to my correspondence. I kindly, but very firmly, explained my reasons for objecting to this marriage, *absurd, preposterous, unthinkable,* and indicated to the dear child that I should be much obliged if, in future, she would refrain from taking up my valuable time with such foolishness. I feel *quite tired* and done up, but I am thankful to think that this will not occur again. (It appears that Mr. Hardysides is an artist, an acquaintance of dearest Feodora's, and has several times lately been to stay at Compton Bobbin. I must speak to darling Edward about this.)

June 8th, 1888.

I feel so much agitated that I can hardly even hold my pen, to communicate my feelings to *this* Sacred Page. That any child of mine should behave with such ingratitude, such selfishness, such rank inconsideration for others, and such utter lack of modesty or self-restraint, is hard to record. This Little Book has been the recipient of *many* sorrows and *some* joys, but never before has it chronicled a Deed of this description. Let the facts then speak for themselves, for who am I to judge another sinner?

This morning, as I was pondering over the proofs of my 'Peasant Children on Mount Snowdon', Eva came into my morning-room, wearing as I noticed somewhat to my surprise, a new bonnet and shawl.

'Are you going out, dearest child?' I said, intending, if this should indeed prove to be the case, to give her one or two little commissions for me in the village.

'Yes, dear mamma,' she replied, a guilty flush o'er spreading (and, alas! with what reason) her usually somewhat pallid cheeks. 'I have just come to acquaint you with the fact that I am now going out to be married, by special licence, to Horace Hardysides.'

I flatter myself that I maintained, on hearing these insolent words, an admirable composure.

'Then Go!' I said, in very *awful* tones, which I fear may ring in poor Eva's ears to the hour of her death. 'Go! But do not seek to return! When your Hardysides has proved himself false and unfaithful, *this* roof shall never shelter you again!'

'Mamma!' she said, imploringly, the full sense of her guilt coming over her, no doubt, for the first time.

'Go!' I reiterated. 'Pray go!'

Hesitatingly, she turned and went.

Without another word, without even so much as a glance, she left her lonely, *Widowed* Mother for the embraces of a stranger. May *he* never use *her* so! How sharper than the serpent's tooth—

I have sent in haste for dear Edward and told him to summon dear Arthur, George, Albert, Frederick and William, Alice, Julia, Maud and Louise. (Darling Beatrice is shortly expecting a happy event, and I refused to have her informed, as I fear that the shock might have *disastrous consequences* and jeopardize a little Life.) No doubt they will all, as ever, be very kind, but ah! how I long on such occasions for the guidance and wisdom of my own Sainted Josiah—I can only hope that in a very little while we shall once more be united—Above! This Happy and Dreadful thought has made me wonder how Eva will be enabled to meet her Father's eye when her day shall come—if, indeed one so selfish and untruthful be granted entrance to the Heavenly Spheres. Poor, poor misguided Child.

Later.

My darling Edward has just been round to see me. He is very much perturbed, not only upon my account, though, naturally, I am his chief preoccupation in the matter, but also because of the disgrace which poor Eva's dreadful action will have brought upon the whole Family. Dearest Feodora is immeasurably distressed (he says) and well she may be, at her share in this matter. It appears that she met this Mr. Hardysides in London and asked him down to Compton Bobbin to paint a group of herself and the five eldest children. The picture was never finished, as darling Edward, when in Town, was taken to see some of the artist's works; and finding that they were most dreadfully secular and unedifying, besides being devoid of the smallest genius, whether of composition, style or design, and finding also that Mr. Hardysides had a most *unsavoury* and *immoral* reputation, he gave him his immediate *congé*. Since then it would appear that the wretch has been staying in the neighbourhood in order to complete his seduction—already half begun—of poor Eva. I am saddened and amazed, and can write no more for to-day.

9

Lord Lewes, who arrived that evening, was the true type of Foreign Office 'young' man. (Men remain, for some reason, 'young men' longer in the Foreign Office than in any other profession.) He was tall, very correctly dressed in a style indicating the presence of money rather than of imagination, and had a mournful, thin, eighteenth-century face. His correct and slightly pompous manner combined with the absence in his speech of such expressions as 'O.K. loo', 'I *couldn't* be more amused', 'We'll call it a day', 'lousy', 'It was a riot', 'My sweetie-boo' and 'What a poodle-pie' to indicate the barrier of half a generation between himself, Paul and Bobby; a barrier which more than any other often precludes understanding, if not friendship, between young and young-ish people.

He appeared, in a totally undistinguished way, however, to be a person of some culture, and since being *en poste* at Cairo, had interested himself mainly in Egyptology. He told Paul that he had recently spent much time and money on excavations, and had been rewarded, just before he had left, by finding the tomb of some early and unknown (he did not use the word 'bogus') Shepherd King, the unearthing of which had caused a certain stir amongst Egyptologists.

'Isn't it supposed to be unlucky to dig up tombs?' asked Philadelphia, who had languidly been listening to Michael's conversation.

'Who was it said that "only shallow men believe in luck"?' he replied, smiling sadly. 'Emerson, I think. In any case, it is certain that if luck exists I have had a very small share of it in my life, either before digging up poor old Papuachnas or since. Besides, I haven't kept any of the things I found for myself, not a single scarab, and I think that might make a difference, don't you?'

250

Paul, who had a practical side to his nature, thought that he himself would easily be able to endure the kind of lucklessness that brought with it a marquisate, a superb Adam house and fifteen thousand pounds a year. He felt sure that Michael Lewes still believed that he was in love with Mrs. Fortescue; he evidently considered himself to be an unhappy person, hardly used by Fate.

'It is curious,' went on Lord Lewes, 'to consider the hold that Egyptology takes on people. Nearly everyone seems to be more or less interested in it, more so, I believe, than in any other ancient history, not excepting even that of Greece herself. The most unlikely people used to ask if they could come to see my little collection in Cairo; débutantes from London, for instance, and their mothers, people you would think had no feeling for such things.'

'It is the human interest,' said Paul. '(And I don't mean only in the case of the débutantes.) I believe that most people have felt it at one time or another. Of course, it is very romantic to think of those tombs, found exactly as they were left at the beginning of the world, full of art treasures and jewels, the pill of historical research is gilded with the primitive and universal excitement of a treasure hunt. Personally, I have always thought that as a rule it is people of more imagination than intellect who feel drawn towards Egypt. Whereas the Philhelene, for instance, is less concerned with how the Greek lived than with how he *thought*, the average Egyptologist always seems to be rather too much fascinated by the little objects of everyday life which he has found, and rather too busy reconstructing the exact uses to which they were put, to look below the surface for spiritual manifestations of the age in which they were made.'

'Perhaps on the whole you may be right,' said Lord Lewes. 'One does not, however, have to look very far for such manifestations; they are all around one in that country. The Egyptian was a superb artist.'

'Ah! But for such a short time when measured by the length of his civilization . While the art was strictly formalized, I admit that it was good, almost great. Under Aknahton—

correct me if I am wrong—the representational school came into being. After that, to my way of thinking, there was no more art in Egypt.'

'There, I am afraid, I cannot possibly agree with you,' said Lord Lewes with his charming smile. 'I must regard Aknahton and his artists as very wonderful reformers, and their art as some of the greatest that can be found anywhere in the world.'

'Yes, you see we have a different point of view. I cannot possibly admire purely representational art,' said Paul, thinking how few people there were so tolerant and easy to get on with. For the first time since his arrival at Compton Bobbin he found himself wishing that he had been there under slightly more creditable circumstances. It occurred to him that if Michael Lewes knew the truth he might easily regard him as quite an ordinary thief, since he was evidently a person rather lacking in humour. Lord Lewes broke in upon this train of thought by saying, after considering the matter for some moments, 'I think, you know, that the Egyptians themselves were more human than the Greeks, who always appear to have been so coldly perfect, like their own statuary, that it is difficult to credit them with the flesh and blood of ordinary human beings. "Fair Greece, sad relic of departed worth,"' he added mournfully, '"Immortal though no more, though fallen, great."'

Paul looked at him in some amazement. He had never, since his Oxford days, met anybody so fond of quoting.

'And presumably,' said Lord Lewes, 'that is how the Byzantinist must feel, otherwise I see no way to account for him. Attracted beyond words to the Archipelago itself, and repelled, I suppose, by the sheer perfection of the art which he finds there, he is obliged to search the islands for something which he thinks he can honestly admire. He ends, of course, by valuing the Byzantine quite absurdly high, far higher than its actual merit deserves.'

Paul, who was himself an ardent Byzantinist, and, like all such, extremely sensitive on the subject, was disgusted by this speech, which revealed in his opinion an intellectual

252

dishonesty too dreadful to contemplate. He was just about to inform Lord Lewes that he was the author of a small and privately printed monograph entitled *The Byzantine Break-away* when he remembered for the second time that evening that his position in the household was not of the most genuine, and that his name was now no longer Fotheringay but Fisher. Too angry to continue the discussion he walked quickly out of the room, saying over his shoulder to Philadelphia, 'I'll fetch that book I said I would lend you; I particularly want to know what you think about it.'

'Nice, isn't he?' said Michael as soon as he was out of the room.

'Awfully sweet,' said Bobby.

'He's an angel, I think,' said Philadelphia dreamily.

Later Lord Lewes said to his Aunt Gloria, 'What a really charming, cultured young man, that Mr. Fisher, it is a real pleasure to have made his acquaintance. I think you were so clever to find him. He is just the very person for Bobby, too; full of brains and yet most human.'

'Yes, he seems all right,' said Lady Bobbin. 'He was very much recommended to me. I only hope he will get the boy out of doors and make himself useful with Brenda Chadlington's brats. She announced to-day that she is bringing them again; most thoughtless and inconsiderate of her to my mind, but still—!'

Paul looked forward with no feelings of delight to his first ride to Compton Bobbin. He was, in fact, extremely terrified at the idea of it. Bobby, noticing his aversion to that form of exercise, tried to reassure him by pointing out that the distance to Mulberrie Farm was well under three miles, that it would be unnecessary for them to proceed at any pace more desperate than a walk, and that Boadicea, the mare which had been allotted to him to ride, was as quiet as any old cow; but in vain. Paul, most unfortunately for his own peace of mind, had happened to see the said mare out at exercise the day before, and had noticed in her a very different aspect from that of the ancient hireling on whose back he had spent so many painful hours jogging up and down the Rotten Row. To compare her to an old cow was simply silly. It was, in fact, only too apparent that here was a beast of pride and pedigree, who would almost certainly consider it a point of honour to cast the trembling tyro from her back. Paul knew, alas! how fatally easy, in his case, this would be; the smallest jerk, nay, even the transition between trot and canter, often proved sufficient to unseat him. He visualized with a shudder that horrid moment when everything would fly from his grip, the universe become black and roll several times round him, while the earth would suddenly rise up and bang him in the kidneys. It had happened in the soft and friendly Row and had been extraordinarily painful; what of the tarmac road, hard, black and shining like ebonite, which lay between Compton Bobbin and Mulberrie Farm? Poor Paul spent a wakeful night pondering these things, and by the morning had quite made up his mind that he would return to London sooner than court an end so sudden and unpleasing.

After breakfast, however, he felt more of a man again, and the sight of the precious red morocco volumes peeping from behind the schoolroom radiator put new courage into him. Besides, it would be a pity not to see a little more of Philadelphia. He was looking forward with some interest to hearing her verdict upon *Crazy Capers*, which he had lent her to read, saying that a friend of his had written it. Unsophisticated but intelligent, he thought, it was just possible that she might prove to be the one person who would put a proper construction on it. Possible, not likely. If she joined in the chorus of laughter he knew that he would be hurt, far more hurt than when Marcella had, who was always a hard, unimaginative little thing with a mind like a tennis ball. Meanwhile, fasting, for he felt too nervous to touch food at luncheon time, he prepared to face his ordeal.

By the most unlucky accident of fate Lady Bobbin happened to be talking to the stud groom in the stable yard when Paul and Bobby arrived there, and waited to see them mount. Paul, sadly conscious of the newness of his clothes, which had elicited roars of delight from the heartless Bobby as they left the house, stood a quaking and, no doubt, he thought bitterly, a pathetically comic figure, as he waited for Boadicea to be brought from her dark and smelly lair inside the stables.

'Cold, isn't it?' he said between chattering teeth to Lady Bobbin, who took no notice whatever of this remark. At that moment the snorting animal was led out, tossing her head from side to side in what seemed to be an ecstasy of rage and contempt, and showering little bits of froth in all directions. Paul, his unreasonable terror of horses now quite overcome by his unreasonable terror of Lady Bobbin, whose cold gimlet eye seemed to be reading his every emotion, decided that here was one of the few occasions in a man's life on which death would be preferable to dishonour, and advanced towards the mounting block with a slight swagger which he hoped was reminiscent of a French marquis approaching the scaffold. Grasping the reins and the pommel of the saddle firmly as he had been taught, he placed his left foot in the stirrup, when the animal, as indeed he had feared it probably would, began to wriggle its hind quarters away from him. When this had happened in the Row it had been his invariable custom to remove his foot from the stirrup and begin all over again. Now, however, feeling (he dared not look) that Lady Bobbin's eyes, not to mention the eyes of the stud groom, two under grooms, the stable boy, Bobby and two men who were carting away manure, were upon him, he rather lost his head and with the courage of despair gave a tremendous leap in pursuit of Boadicea's retreating back. To his immense astonishment, this piece of bravura was rewarded with complete success, and he found himself sitting fair and square in the saddle, with the stable boy placing his other foot in its appointed stirrup. Alas, he had not time to enjoy the fruits of triumph, as no sooner did the under groom, who was holding her, release Boadicea's head from his grasp than, despite Paul's frenzied tugs at the reins, she departed at a brisk trot out of the stable yard, and with a series of sickening slithers on to the tarmac road outside. Making a desperate effort, and by dint of counting out loud, one-two, one-two, Paul did manage to 'rise' in the approved Row style until he felt himself to be well out of Lady Bobbin's sight, when, abandoning all pride and self-respect, he clung with one hand to the saddle, jerked at the reins with the other and sobbed out in pitiful gasps: 'Stop, stop, dear Boadicea, whoa, whoa, Boadicea whoa, oh, please, please, stop!' The insensitive Boadicea, however, paid no attention to his pathetic cries, but continued to trot on, very nearly pulling him over from time to time by suddenly throwing her head right forward with loud and terrifying snorts. At last, when Paul felt himself to be at the end of his tether and, having long since abandoned both reins and stirrups, was looking out for a soft piece of grass on which he could hurl his aching bones, he heard another horse come up behind him. Bobby's outstretched hand seized the reins and, with a painful and alarming bump, Boadicea came to a standstill. She immediately began to eat grass at the side of the road, leaving, in the place where her head and neck had formerly been, a hideous gaping chasm. This was, for poor Paul, the last straw.

'I can't bear it, I can't bear it. I knew I should hate it. Lousy horse! Please, please let me get off and walk. Oh, what Gehenna!'

'It's all right,' said Bobby, who was laughing so much he could hardly speak. 'Oh, you did look too entrancing. I hope you'll do it again for me. No, no, don't get off, she'll walk quite quietly now as far as Amabelle's. Besides, you've got to get used to it, haven't you? But, you know, I can't think why she didn't come down, spanking along the tarmac like that. You should have taken her up on to the grass.'

'It's all very well for you to talk,' said Paul, who was still on the verge of tears; 'but I can't guide the beastly thing at all, it's as much as I can do to stay on its back.'

'My God, you looked funny,' said Bobby, rocking and guffawing. 'I'd give anything to see that again.'

Paul felt that, considering he had just been rescued from the jaws of death, he was not receiving that sympathy which was his due, and for some time he maintained a dignified silence. Presently, however, his sense of humour asserted itself, and he began to giggle too.

'I say, what will your mother have thought?' he asked rather nervously when he had recovered his breath.

'Well, by the mercy of Providence she was having a look at this horse's fetlocks when you got up, so I don't believe she noticed much. She did mutter something about "Why can't the blasted idiot wait a minute; what's all the damned hurry for?" But that doesn't mean a lot from her. No, you had a lucky escape this time, old boy. If you had let Boadicea down on the tarmac it would have been the end of Compton Bobbin and the journals for you, believe me.'

10

'One heart.'

'I double a heart.'

'Really, Sally, my sweet, don't you ride that convention to death just a little? It seems to be your one and only idea of a bid.'

'Well, I don't want to have to play the hand any more; I'd much rather you did, then there's no grumbling afterwards, you see.'

'I should have thought it would be more useful,' said Walter, ostentatiously looking at the score, 'at this stage in the proceedings, if you would show a suit.'

'Well, I've said before and I'll say again that I can't play bridge, and I don't like playing bridge. I only do it, as you know quite well, to make up a four. I think it's a horrible game, it makes everyone too bad-tempered and beastly for words—especially you, Walter darling, and you're apt to be quite nice at other times,' she added, for even when goaded to madness by Walter she always found it impossible to be unkind to him. 'Thank goodness Jerome comes to-morrow, and I shall be able to go back to my kiddies for Christmas like Mrs. Culbertson.'

'Darling, now don't be sour, please, my angel. I only meant that when you're playing you might try to concentrate a tiny bit more?'

'Concentrate! My head's aching with trying to concentrate, and all the thanks I get from you are these everlasting lectures, or else you sit there looking so reproachful and swallowing every time I play a card, as though I were doing it on purpose to annoy.'

'I said a heart,' murmured Bobby, who, having a superb hand, was anxious to get on with the business and had become rather restive during this family argument.

'Well, now, I've got to show a suit, have I?' said Sally.

'No, no! Of course not *now*,' cried Walter in that agony of impatience only known to the good bridge player obliged to suffer the vagaries of an absolutely incompetent partner. 'Not now, you can't. You've doubled a heart, haven't you? And you must stick at that. Paul says?'

'Two hearts,' said Paul.

'Two spades,' said Walter. 'Now, if Sally would only sometimes show a suit instead of sitting there saying double—'

'Oh, I'll show you the whole of my hand if you go on like this,' said Sally, 'and much good may it do you!'

'Four hearts,' said Bobby with an air of finality.

'Tee-hee,' he said as Paul put down a hand with six hearts to the ace, queen and an outside ace; 'now wasn't that just too psychic of me for words. Thanks ever so much, Paul, old boy—of course, you should have given me a double rise really, shouldn't you? But still—'

'What an extraordinary lead, Sally darling. Are you in your right senses?'

'Well, in that ghastly little book you made me read it said, "never lead from an ace, queen, never lead from a king, and never lead from a doubleton, it is a rotten lead". So that's the only thing for me to do, as far as I can see.'

'That's right,' said Bobby good-naturedly, 'tell him exactly what you've got in your hand; don't mind me, will you?'

Paul wandered over to the old world inglenook where Amabelle was sitting with Elspeth Paula on her knee.

'That's right, darling, have a good gurk,' she was saying, 'makes us all feel better, that does. Isn't she a treasure? Look at those huge goggling eyes. She's going to be a one with the chaps, she is. Aren't you, sweetikin. Boo!'

A confused murmur came from the bridge table.

'Now, Sally, out with it. There's only one lead you can possibly make.'

'I don't see that. I've got six cards in my hand and I can lead any of them, can't I? Oh, dear, I wish I knew.'

'Now, *think*. There's only one possible lead. Oh, my God,

you are a vile player, Sally. Well, now, that makes it all very
O.K. for you, Bobby, game and rub—'

The butler opened the door and announced:

'Lord Lewes, madam.'

A perfectly stunned silence fell on Amabelle's drawing-
room as Michael Lewes walked into it. Amabelle herself, who
hardly ever showed emotion of any sort, turned crimson and
nearly dropped the baby; Paul, feeling as he had not felt
since, when at Eton, he was caught by the 'beaks' in the
Slough cinema, made half a movement to escape through the
garden door, but decided that this would only make matters
far worse and that it would be better to stay and brazen it out;
and the Monteaths gave each other long glances, fraught
with meaning, over their cards. Bobby alone remained
unshaken and went on playing the hand in his usual brisk and
businesslike style. Such was the emotion of his adversaries
that he made as a result not only four hearts giving him game
and rubber, but little slam as well, a fact which he was heard
afterwards loudly to lament. ('You know, Paul, it was
monstrous only putting me up one. After all, you had the
hearts; you knew I was calling on outside cards, didn't you? I
naturally imagined you had a bare rise and wanted me to go
to game. It is too maddening.')

The silence was broken by a shattering gurk from Elspeth
Paula.

'What *savoir faire*!' said Bobby under his breath. 'Anybody
would think I was the father. No more diamonds, Sally? Yes, I
thought you had—no, no, that's O.K. The rest are good on
the table, aren't they? That's one hundred and twenty below,
one hundred overtricks and five hundred for the rubber.
Thirteen I make it.'

'How are you, Michael?' Amabelle was saying. 'Ring the
bell, will you, Paul? How lovely to see you, my dear. I can't
think why, but I imagined you were still abroad. You know
Mr. Fotheringay, do you?'

'Mr. Fisher?' said Lord Lewes.

'What am I thinking of—Mr. Fisher I mean, of course. And
Walter and Sally you know, don't you? And this is the

Monteath heiress, Miss Elspeth Paula, who was born at one of my cocktail parties.'

'Indeed she wasn't,' cried Sally indignantly.

'Well, more nearly than I care to think about; if that taxi hadn't come when it did—'

'My dear, she wasn't born till four in the morning.'

'What a cheesey time,' said Bobby. 'Well, darling, we've finished our tiny rubber and I think we'd better be going. See you all to-morrow and thanks so much for having us. Come on, Paul, to horse, to horse!'

'Where are you off to, Sally?'

'I think I'd better take baby up to her beddie-bye. Come along then, you sweet precious.'

'I'm going to see Paul on his horse,' said Walter, chuckling, 'It sounds too good to be missed.'

Amabelle sighed. There was evidently a conspiracy to leave her alone with Lord Lewes.

'You look very well, my dear,' she said briskly, as the door shut on Walter and Sally. 'Did you enjoy yourself in Cairo?'

'No.'

'Oh, I'm sorry. I thought it all sounded so nice and interesting. I saw photos, in *The Sphere*, wasn't it, of a camp stool four thousand years old (or was it four hundred? I'm so bad at figures). Anyway, a very interesting old camp stool that you had found, and I thought how pleased you would be to find a lovely old camp stool like that,' said Amabelle desperately, making up the fire until it was a sort of burning fiery furnace.

'I shall never enjoy anything, and I shall never have a single moment's happiness in life until I can persuade you to marry me, Amabelle.'

'Oh dear. I hoped so much—I mean, surely Cairo must be full of lovely girls, isn't it? One's always reading about them, anyway. Haven't you changed your mind at all?'

'How could you imagine such a thing? No, indeed, I thought of you every moment of the day. I dreamt of you every moment of the night. I saw no beautiful girls, or if I did they looked to me like dolls stuffed with sawdust. Occasionally I came across people who knew you, they would mention your name in passing and it would go through me like a red-hot sword; if I saw in some illustrated paper a photograph of you it would make me even more wretched than I was already, and for days. Anything of beauty or of interest became intolerable because you were not there to share it with me. I tell you, you have made life very sad for me, Amabelle.'

'Dear Michael,' said Amabelle, stifling a yawn.

Curious, she thought, how some people have this devastating effect of boredom upon one. She had forgotten in three years just how much he did bore her, but the moment he had opened his mouth it had all come back to her in a wave and she was hopelessly, crushingly bored again.

'I'm so sorry, my dear,' she said.

'But I haven't come here to reproach you with that. I am here because I know, I feel quite certain that in your heart, only you won't admit it, you love me too.'

Amabelle was startled by this remark. Had she really behaved so badly as to lead him to suppose that this was the case? Or was it just his own vanity? 'Perhaps you think that because you wish it so much,' she said kindly.

'It's true, it must be true, I know it is. Only you are such an angel that you won't marry me because you think, quite mistakenly, that it would spoil my life, because you are older than I am and because of—'

'My international reputation?' Amabelle was of an age to think of reputation in these terms; in her young days a woman either had a good reputation or an international reputation, and, modern as she was in many ways, she never could quite rid her mind of these nineteenth century *nuances*.

'Yes,' she went on, 'I admit that is partly the reason. If I didn't feel certain that you would soon be very unhappy indeed I suppose I might make the sacrifice of marrying you. But in a short time you would be miserable, your career would be ruined for one thing' (international reputations and ruined careers went hand-in-hand when Amabelle was young), 'and besides that it is important for you to have children, and I'm not Sarah, you know, though in many ways a remarkable woman. But don't you see, Michael dear, that if I *were* in love with you I shouldn't consider any of that for five minutes. I'm far too selfish. I'm not in love with you. I like you I'm fond of you, and we have much in common. All that leads you to suppose that I'm in love with you, so now I must try and make you understand once and for all that I'm *not*. I'm *not*. And in any case I'm sick and tired to death of love. You must remember that for years it was my trade, my shop, my profession. Now I've retired, left my practice or whatever you like to call it, and I won't begin all over again. It bores me. I'm not strong enough to face the wear and tear and racket of a new love affair, with all the business of being your wife into the bargain; your relations who would come and see me, rightly as I think, to dissuade me from such a step, the sneers of the newspapers and of my own friends. Why should I be obliged to put up with all these things for something I don't even want? Because you must see, Michael, that, apart from any other consideration, if I marry you I lose instead of gaining a position. I become neither fish, flesh nor good red herring. In the case of James Fortescue it was quite different; he was an old man of the world when he married me and it was a good bargain for us both. He needed someone to keep his house, amuse his friends and be good company for himself; I needed a home and a name. We were both admirably suited, the best of friends, and, I think, very happy. I certainly was. This case is utterly different; if I married you we should each in our different ways lose much of what makes life bearable, but I honestly believe that I should lose more than you would. Anyhow, Michael, I am telling the truth, I swear to you that I am, when I say that nothing would influence me, none of these worldly considerations would prevent me from marrying you to-morrow if I loved you; but I don't love you. I don't, I don't, I don't. Is it possible that perhaps now at last you understand me?'

After making this speech Amabelle fell back on the sofa with a look of utter exhaustion and there was a long silence between them.

263

'Then what is to become of me?' said Michael bitterly.

'Oh, my dear, really I don't know. What does become of people who have been crossed in love? I never have been myself so I can't say from experience, but I imagine that sooner or later they meet somebody else who attracts them, mentally or physically, *et voilà! L'affaire est morte, vive l'affaire*. In your case let's hope it will be some nice, pretty girl who will make you very, very happy.'

'If you speak like that,' said Michael, 'it only shows that you can't understand the meaning of true love. Some people are made so that they can only love once in their lives.'

'Nobody is,' said Amabelle firmly. 'Unless, of course, they live with the person they love all their lives. Permanent and exclusive affection between married people may be possible but nobody can remain faithful to a person they never see. As for true love, I didn't believe in that until I met Walter and Sally, but I am really beginning to be very much afraid that in their case it does exist. Maddening, because it upsets all my theories about life.'

'You promise, then, that you don't love me at all, and that no argument, no persuasion will ever induce you to marry me?'

'No, Michael, I don't love you. I never have loved you and I never shall love you, and nothing that you can say or do will ever make you marry you. And I beg you, from the bottom of my heart, if we are to remain friends, that you won't bring up this subject any more.'

'Very well. I won't speak of it again. No woman has ever been so much loved as I have loved you, none has ever been so cherished and considered as I would have cherished and considered you if you had married me. Let that pass. I promise that I will never mention this subject to you again as long as I live, if you will promise that we can go on being friends?'

'Yes, of course, Michael dear,' said Amabelle gloomily. It seemed hard that she should have been at such pains to retire from Lewes Park on purpose to avoid this very boring scene, only to find that Michael was staying in the next house to hers.

'Are you staying at Compton Bobbin?'

'I arrived yesterday.'

'How did you find out that I was here?'

'By a fortunate chance. I happened to go for a little stroll before lunch with Bobby, and just as we got on to the Stow Road a large blue Bentley drove past, and Bobby said, "Oh, look, there's Amabelle's car." Not my usual luck, it would have been more like me to have stayed here three weeks without knowing that you were in the neighbourhood at all.'

Amabelle looked pensively into the fire. She did not and never had possessed a large blue Bentley. She thought out a few pungent observations which might be made to Sir Roderick when he came for his next game of bridge.

'Bobby is a very naughty little boy; he needs a thoroughly good spanking,' she said.

'It's really amazing how much he has grown up since I was in England last,' said Michael. 'Of course, it is three years, but even so it seems like a conjuring trick. When I left he was a little boy, rather young for his age. Now he is more like a man of thirty.'

'Eton does that for them. Bobby has a peculiar character, I must say. I suppose he is the one complete egotist of this generation. It is very lucky for him, because it means that he will never, in his whole life, know the meaning of the word boredom. He will always be quite happy so long as he is with other people, because it is wildly interesting to him to watch the effect that he is producing, and their reactions to his personality. If they like him, so much the better; if not, there is the entrancing problem of how to make them. Leave him alone and he would collapse, of course; but in company, of whatever description, he is contented and amused, and always will be. Perfect from his point of view, because he will never have to be alone in his whole life presumably, and for the rare occasions when loneliness will be forced upon him he has a certain weapon of self-defence, an absolutely inexhaustible facility for sleeping.'

'Yes, I should think that sums up his character pretty well,' said Michael, who had taken no great fancy for his cousin.

265

'And now that we are on the subject of Bobby, what's all this mystery about his tutor? Is he Fisher or is he Fotheringay?'

'By the way, yes, I must explain that to you, because it's all my doing really. His name is Paul Fotheringay, a great friend of mine. He very much wanted to read the journal of Lady Maria Bobbin with a view to writing her life. Your aunt wouldn't hear of lending it to him, which he very politely asked if she would do, so Bobby and I between us arranged for him to come down here under another name, as Bobby's tutor. You won't go and muck it all up, now will you, Michael darling?'

'Really, Amabelle, you are a baby. If you can play a trick on anybody you will. Poor Aunt Gloria; what a shame!'

'Honestly, I can't see any harm in it. In so far as anybody can have an influence over Bobby, Paul's will only be for the good, and as for the book on Lady Maria's Life and Works, I think it may be very well done and most amusing.'

'It will certainly be amusing, from what I remember of the journal,' said Michael, 'although it will probably be a case of laughing at and not with my poor great-grandmother. Philadelphia has become extraordinarily pretty since I saw her last, by the way.'

'Paul says she is so intelligent. He says she hardly ever speaks but that she has the most "heavenly instincts". I think he is falling in love with her, you know.'

Michael looked rather thoughtful on hearing this, and presently took his departure, saying, 'Good-bye then, my dear, dear friend. Please allow me to come and see you again soon. "Friendship," Lord Byron said, "is love without its wings," and that is a very consoling thought for me.'

When he had gone Amabelle went up to the nursery, where Elspeth Paula was having her evening meal.

'Oh, you cad,' she said to Sally, 'how could you have left me like that? You must have seen I didn't want to be alone with him; you are a monster, Sally darling.'

'It had to be, sooner or later,' said Sally calmly. 'Well what happened?'

'Oh, it was all most exhausting, you know, and frightfully

dull. The same old arguments over and over again, just like a debate on protection *versus* free trade, each side knowing exactly what the other will say next and neither having any intention whatever of being convinced. Poor Michael, it is quite funny really when you think that probably I would have married him if he'd been at all clever about it. But instead of putting it to me as a sensible business proposition he would drag in all this talk about love the whole time, and I simply can't bear those showerings of sentimentality. Otherwise I should most likely have married him ages ago.'

'Even boring as he is?'

'Yes, I think so. One never can tell, of course. It was all this nonsense about love that put me off so much. And of course he is a cracking old bore, isn't he?'

'When I was a girl,' said Sally, 'and before I met Walter, you know, I fixed a definite price at which I was willing to overlook boringness. As far as I can remember it was twenty-five thousand pounds a year. However, nothing more than twelve seemed to offer, so I married Walter instead.'

'You have always had such a sensible outlook,' said Amabelle approvingly. 'If I had a girl I should say to her, "Marry for love if you can, it won't last, but it is a very interesting experience and makes a good beginning in life. Later on, when you marry for money, for heaven's sake let it be big money. There are no other possible reasons for marrying at all."'

Michael Lewes walked back through the moonlight to Compton Bobbin in a most curious frame of mind. During his three years' absence abroad he had persuaded himself that Amabelle really and in her heart of hearts wanted to marry him; at the same time he was convinced that if (too terrible a thought to contemplate) by any unhappy chance he should prove to be wrong and if she should definitely refuse him, in such a manner as to make him feel certain that there was no hope of her ever changing her mind, under those circumstances he would be so very unhappy that he would undoubtedly feel tempted to commit suicide. He had sincerely thought that for him the prospect of life without her would be more than he would be able to bear. And yet now, strangely enough, he felt almost as though a load had been lifted from his shoulders, happier and more light-hearted than for months.

The truth was that during those three years he had made an imaginary picture of Amabelle in his own mind which had become, the longer he was away from home, the more unlike the real woman; until, on finding himself sitting with her, holding that first interview on which he had built so many hopes, he found himself sitting beside a stranger, and the image of Amabelle in his mind was shattered for ever. The things which he said to her then had little real meaning or conviction behind them. They were speeches which he had been rehearsing to himself for three years, and out of a sort of habit, a sort of loyalty to that self which had invented them, he repeated them to her. It was with no particular feeling, except perhaps that of relief, that he received in reply a final and definite refusal. And now, it seemed that the course of his life was delightfully plain before him. Having left diplomacy, a profession of which he was heartily tired, he would settle down at Lewes Park, take his seat in the House of Lords, and marry some pretty, well-born and delightful girl, someone, in fact, not unlike his cousin, Philadelphia Bobbin. He hummed a little tune as he walked.

11

Lady Bobbin was always most particular that the feast of Christmas should be kept by herself, her family and dependents at Compton Bobbin in what she was pleased to call 'good old-fashioned style'. In her mind, always rather a muddled organ, this entailed a fusion of the Christmas customs brought to his adopted country by the late Prince Consort with those which have been invented by the modern Roman Catholic school of Sussex Humorists in a desperate attempt to revive what they suppose to have been the merrieness of England as it was before she came to be ruled by sour Protestants. And this was odd, because Germans and Roman Catholics were ordinarily regarded by Lady Bobbin with wild abhorrence. Nothing, however, could deter her from being an ardent and convinced Merrie Englander. The maypole on the village green, or more usually, on account of pouring rain, in the village hall; nocturnal expeditions to the local Druid stones to see the sun rise over the Altar Stone, a feat which it was seldom obliging enough to perform; masques in the summer, madrigals in the winter and Morris dances all the year round were organized and led by Lady Bobbin with an energy which might well have been devoted to some better cause. This can be accounted for by the fact of her having a sort of idea that in Merrie England there had been much hunting, no motor cars and that her bugbear, socialism, was as yet unknown. All of which lent that imaginary period every attribute, in her eyes, of perfection.

But although each season of the year had its own merrie little rite it was at Christmas time that Lady Bobbin and her disciples in the neighbourhood really came into their own, the activities which she promoted during the rest of the year merely paving the way for an orgy of merrieness at Yule. Her

269

first step in this direction was annually to summon at least thirty of the vast clan of Bobbin relations to spend the feast beneath their ancestral roof, and of these nearly twenty would, as a rule, find it convenient to obey. The remainder, even if their absence in Araby or Fair Kashmir rendered it palpably unlikely that they should accept, were always sent their invitation just the same. This was called Decent Family Feeling. Having gathered together all those of her late husband's relations who were available to come (her own had mostly died young from the rigours of tea planting in the Torrid Zone) she would then proceed to arrange for them to have a jolly Christmas. In this she was greatly helped by her brother-in-law, Lord Leamington Spa, who was also a fervent Merrie Englander, although, poor man, having been banished by poverty from his country estates and obliged to live all the year round in Eaton Square, he had but little scope for his activities in this direction. Those who should have been Lady Bobbin's prop and mainstay at such a time, her own children, regarded the whole thing with a sort of mirthful disgust very injurious to her feelings. Nothing, however, could deter her from her purpose, and every year at Compton Bobbin the German and the Sussex customs were made to play their appointed parts. Thus the Christmas Tree, Christmas stockings and other activities of Santa Claus, and the exchange through the post of endless cards and calendars (German); the mistletoe and holly decorations, the turkeys, the boar's head, and a succession of carol singers and mummers (Sussex Roman Catholic); and the unlimited opportunity to over-eat on every sort of unwholesome food washed down with honest beer, which forms the groundwork for both schools of thought, combined to provide the ingredients of Lady Bobbin's Christmas Pudding.

On Christmas Eve, therefore, various members of the vast Bobbin family began to arrive from every corner of the British Isles. The seven sisters of the late Sir Hudson, who, be it remembered, had all married well, of course brought with them their husbands and children, and in many cases their

270

dogs. It was noticeable that those who had married the least well came first, by train, while, as the day wore on, richer and ever richer motor cars, bedecked with larger and ever larger coronets, made stately progress down the drive; until the St. Neots Rolls-Royce made its strawberry-leaved appearance, marking the end of this procession, just before dinner time.

Bobby, who for some while had been hovering round the front door, greeted this vehicle with bloodcurdling screams of delight, and rushed forward to assist from it his favourite aunt, the Duchess of St. Neots and her daughter, his favourite cousin, Miss Héloïse Potts. (The duchess had been married five times, and had now settled down once more with her girlhood's husband, the Duke of St. Neots, Miss Potts being the offspring of an intermediate venture with an American millionaire.)

To Paul the day was like an endless nightmare. Wherever he went he met some new, and for the most part, unsympathetic face, upon which the mutual embarrassment would become intense. Lady Bobbin, unversed in social graces, forbore to make any introductions, and Bobby spent most of the day sulking in his bedroom. His mother had instructed him to stay at home to greet his guests, the greater number of whom, however, he was pleased to consider quite unworthy of any notice.

Unluckily for himself, Paul happened to be the first down to breakfast, when, entering the dining-room with a prodigious yawn, he discovered six hungry Mackintoshes just off the midnight express from Perth. They reminded him of nothing so much as a Scotch family he had once seen on the music halls, sandwiched between some performing seals and a thin woman who gave imitations of (to him) unknown actors and actresses. The children, a son of about seventeen and three hideous girls of between ten and fourteen years old, all wore tartan woollen stockings and long tartan kilts. Lady Mackintosh was dressed in one, and Sir Alexander's reddish whiskers fell into the porridge which he ate—Paul could scarcely believe his eyes—standing up. Paul ventured a few polite remarks, inquired about their journey and observed

271

that the weather was beautifully open, a cliché which he had learnt from Lady Bobbin, but as a family they appeared to be incapable of sustaining conversation, and he soon relapsed into that silence which they so evidently preferred. Presently Lady Bobbin came in from her early morning ride, and he was able to leave them to her hospitable ministrations.

Next to arrive were some more distant relations of Bobby's; Captain Chadlington, M.P., his wife Lady Brenda, their children Christopher Robin and Wendy, and a pack of ugly liver and white spaniels. They were being warmly congratulated by the rest of the party on Captain Chadlington's recent election to Parliament. Paul, having listened during lunch to some of his conversation, felt that it would be impossible to extend the congratulations to his electors; their choice of a representative seemed strangely unfortunate. He was evidently a young man of almost brutish stupidity, and Paul, who had hardly ever met any Conservative Members of Parliament before, was astounded to think that such a person could be tolerated for a moment at the seat of government. To hear him talking about Bolshevik Russia was a revelation to Paul, who took it for granted that Communism was now universally regarded as a high, though possibly a boring, ideal. Lady Bobbin's attitude towards it was just comprehensible, as she had evidently been out of touch with the world for years; but anybody who, being perforce in daily contact with persons of a certain intelligence, could still hold the views held by Captain Chadlington, must surely be a monster of denseness and stupidity.

Lord and Lady Leamington Spa came with their son, Squibby Almanack, whose appearance on the scene threw Paul into a fever of guilty terror since they had been at school together. He explained the situation to Bobby, who led his cousin into the schoolroom and told him the circumstances of Paul's presence in the house, upon which Squibby shook his fat sides, laughed a Wagnerian guffaw, and betook himself to the piano where he sat alone, picking out harmonious chords until it was time to dress for dinner.

Squibby Almanack was a person who belonged so

exclusively to one small circle of very intimate friends that any divorce, however temporary, from that circle left him in a most pitiable condition of aimlessness and boredom. In London he was never seen anywhere unless accompanied by 'Biggy' Lennox and 'Bunch' Tarradale, the three of them forming, so to speak, a kind of modern édition de luxe of *Les Trois Mousquetaires*. Of this fraternity that insouciant beguiler of womanhood, Maydew Morris, provided a picturesque if only occasional fourth, a sort of d'Artagnan, who, although of very different character to the others, was drawn to them by that passion for German music which was the dominant note in all their lives. In spite of the fact that Squibby, Biggy and Bunch sought no adventures save those of the questing spirit, while the adventures of Maydew were the talk of London, they being men of words while he was in all things a man of deeds; in spite of many dissimilarities of nature, the four of them got on well together, and there were very few classical concerts and no performances of German opera at which they could not be seen sitting side by side, deep in perusal of the score. They were further made remarkable by an extraordinary physical resemblance to each other. All four were on the large side, blond and with pink and white complexions, all, with the exception of the hirsute Maydew, slightly bald and quite lacking in eyebrows. They walked with the same peculiar gait, swinging rather prominent buttocks in the manner of hockey-playing schoolgirls, and all sat listening to music (which, provided, of course, that it came from the Fatherland, was the beginning and end of their existence) with the same air of rigid concentration.

Nearly always they sat alone, dispensing with female company. Sometimes, however, by mutual consent, each would appear followed by some pretty débutante; these, with gestures of exaggerated courtesy, would be motioned into the intervening seats, presented with programmes, and then be completely ignored. Many unlucky girls were forced to subdue their very natural distaste for highbrow music for hours on end in order that they might sit in this delicious proximity to their heroes, listening with awe to the Olympian

273

breathing and even, if lucky, occasionally brushing a heroic hand. In the case of Maydew things sometimes went further during the dark moments of The Ring, but the other three were most consistently platonic in their friendships, and were rapidly becoming the despair of match-making mammas. Things were indeed beginning to reach such a pitch that the more ambitious mothers of sub-débutantes were obliged to abandon Paris as an educational centre and dispatch their daughters instead to Munich, where they could be trained to endure classical music silently and, in certain cases, even intelligently. For Squibby, Biggy, Bunch and Maydew were all highly eligible young men. After one of these 'mixed' evenings each would sternly criticize the girls produced by the others. Should one of them have yawned, or even sighed a little, her immediate expulsion from her admirer's visiting list would be demanded, while too frequent crossing and uncrossing of legs would be made a cause for bitter complaint. Poor Bunch, always less fortunate in his choice than the others, because more easily beguiled by a pretty face, produced two inveterate leg crossers on consecutive nights during the Wagner season and was very severely spoken to by Biggy, who, seated on the other side of these ladies, had suffered in consequence sundry kicks and knocks, and complained that his attention had been quite abstracted from the stage during several moving moments. It is true that the climax of horror was reached by a girl friend of Maydew who, during the Rhinegold, was heard to ask in a piercing whisper what the heaps of firewood were for, what the story was all about anyway, and whether there wouldn't soon be an interval; but then a certain licence was always allowed to Maydew in matters of the heart.

When the performance was concluded the girls, if any, were obliged to stifle their cravings for food, drinks and the gay sights of the town, and were hurried away in one or two unromantically full taxis to their respective homes. (Maydew's girl, however, always lived in a different part of London from the others and had to be taken home alone.)

After this, Squibby, Biggy and Bunch would foregather in

Biggy's flat, where they drank strong beer and talked of music and philosophy, and where, much later if at all, they might be joined by a complacent Maydew.

These friends were so seldom separated that Christmas time, when from a sense of duty Squibby, Biggy and Bunch would rejoin their noble families, seemed to them the most inhuman of feasts. How, secretly, did they envy the unregenerate Maydew, who had departed with a Balham beauty to Berlin in order to improve his German. Squibby in particular, dreaded all the year round the Christmas house party at Compton Bobbin. This year, however, things might be more amusing; he had been fond of Paul at Eton, Bobby was now a grownup person instead of a child, Michael Lewes, too, might prove to be pleasantly reformed. With less than his usual depression, he picked out some obscure motif from Siegfried.

The presence at Compton Bobbin of these people and others too numerous and boring to mention had the effect for the time being of throwing Philadelphia, Paul and Michael very much into each other's company. All three of them had a profound distaste for noise, crowds and organized pleasure, and they now spent most of their time hiding from the rest of the party. They went for long rides together every morning, Paul mounted, at his own urgent request, on an ancient cob which had long ago been turned out to enjoy a peaceful old age in the orchard, and which he found more to his liking than the aristocratic Boadicea. After dinner they would retire by mutual consent to the schoolroom and thus avoid the games of sardines, kick-the-bucket, and murders with which the others whiled away their evenings.

Bobby was now seldom to be seen; he spent most of his time giggling in corners with Miss Héloïse Potts, a pretty black-eyed little creature of seventeen who substituted parrot-like shrieks and screams of laughter for the more usual amenities of conversation, with apparently, since she was always surrounded by crowds of admiring young men, the greatest possible success. Even Squibby would often leave his beloved piano in order to enjoy her company, while at meal times her end of the table was eagerly sought after by all the men of the party, young and old, except for Paul and Michael. They, understanding neither her attraction nor her language (when she spoke at all she usually inserted the sound 'egi' after the consonants of her words, thus rendering her meaning far from clear to those unversed in this practice) would make their way with unhurried footsteps to the vacant places near Philadelphia. Indeed, everywhere else the conversation was too highly specialized to be very enjoyable. Héloïse, Bobby and their followers ended every sentence with 'egat thegi Regitz', which meant to the initiated 'at the Ritz'; Captain and Lady Brenda Chadlington, whose recent election to Parliament, actual and vicarious, had rather mounted to their heads, could speak of nothing but the P.M., S.B., L.G., the F.O., the L.C.C., the I.L.P., and their fellow M.P.s; the Mackintoshes fell upon their food in a famished silence, relieved, but very rarely, by remarks on the grouse disease; Lady Bobbin spoke to those about her of horses, hounds, and such obscure eventualities as going to ground, eating bedding, pecking while taking off, and being thoroughly well wormed; while Squibby, although quite intelligent, was apt to be a little wearisome with his musical talk or else a little exasperating with his theories on conditioned reflexes and other philosophical data.

Only Philadelphia, having no interests, talked no shop, but merely sat looking beautiful, calm and amiable, while Paul and Michael exchanged across her their cultured confidences, referring politely every now and then to her judgment. They both considered that although totally uneducated she was very far from being stupid, while the fact that what few books she had ever read had been written before the present century began gave to her mind and outlook a peculiar old-fashioned quality which Paul, at least, after the specious and metallic up-to-dateness of Marcella, found extremely restful.

As for Michael, he was consciously and most conveniently falling in love with her. For a day or two after his meeting with Amabelle he had been saddened and depressed. This was chiefly a retrospective feeling of regret for the last three years, embittered on account of what proved to have been a mere dream, a figment of his own imagination. Nature abhors a vacuum, and Michael had so extremely romantic a character that it was impossible for him not to imagine himself in love with somebody. His thoughts, therefore, turned almost immediately to his cousin Philadelphia, who, young, lovely, unsophisticated and intelligent, was clearly the sort of wife that a man in his position ought to have.

'I could never feel for her as I did for Amabelle,' he thought, as, in common with many people, he liked to believe himself only capable of loving once. 'All the same, what a charming wife she will make, and how happy I shall be with her!'

Lady Bobbin, who, with a mother's eye, saw clearly what was taking place, thought so too, as did young Sir Roderick. He had long intended that his sister should follow the example of his aunts in making a creditable alliance, and was delighted with this state of affairs. Philadelphia herself was happy in her new friends. She had a great respect for culture, and felt it to be a privilege that she was included in so many of their fascinating conversations. Of the two, however, she undoubtedly preferred Paul; Michael seemed to be rather grown up and alarming.

12

Christmas Day itself was organized by Lady Bobbin with the thoroughness and attention to detail of a general leading his army into battle. Not one moment of its enjoyment was left to chance or to the ingenuity of her guests; these received on Christmas Eve their marching orders, orders which must be obeyed to the letter on pain of death. Even Lady Bobbin, however, superwoman though she might be, could not prevent the day from being marked by a good deal of crossness, much over-eating, and a series of startling incidents.

The battle opened, as it were, with the Christmas stockings. These, in thickest worsted, bought specially for the occasion, were handed to the guests just before bedtime on Christmas Eve, with instructions that they were to be hung up on their bedposts by means of huge safety pins, which were also distributed. Lady Bobbin and her confederate, Lord Leamington Spa, then allowed a certain time to elapse until, judging that Morpheus would have descended upon the household, they sallied forth together (he arrayed in a white wig, beard and eyebrows and red dressing-gown, she clasping a large basket full of suitable presents) upon a stealthy noctambulation, during the course of which every stocking was neatly filled. The objects thus distributed were exactly the same every year, a curious and wonderful assortment including a pocket handkerchief, Old Moore's Almanack, a balloon not as yet blown up, a mouth organ, a ball of string, a penknife, an instrument for taking stones out of horses' shoes, a book of jokes, a puzzle, and, deep down in the woolly toe of the stocking, whence it would emerge in a rather hairy condition, a chocolate baby. Alas! Most of Lady Bobbin's guests felt that they would willingly have forgone these delightful but inexpensive objects in return for the night's sleep of which they were thus deprived. Forewarned though they were, the shadowy and terrifying appearance of Lord Leamington Spa fumbling about the foot of their beds in the light of a flickering candle gave most of them such a fearful start that all thoughts of sleep were banished for many hours to come.

For the lucky ones who did manage to doze off a rude shock was presently in store. At about five o'clock in the morning Master Christopher Robin Chadlington made a tour of the bedrooms, and having awoken each occupant in turn with a blast of his mouth organ, announced in a voice fraught with tragedy that Auntie Gloria had forgotten to put a chocolate baby in his stocking. 'Please might I have a bit of yours?' This quaint ruse was only too successful, and Christopher Robin acquired thereby no fewer than fourteen chocolate babies, all of which he ate before breakfast. The consequences, which were appalling, took place under the dining-room table at a moment when everybody else was busily opening the Christmas post. After this, weak but cheerful, young Master Chadlington spent the rest of the day in bed practising on his mouth organ.

By luncheon time any feelings of Christmas goodwill which the day and the religious service, duly attended by all, might have been expected to produce had quite evaporated, and towards the end of that meal the dining-room echoed with sounds of furious argument among the grown-ups. It was the duchess who began it. She said, in a clear, ringing voice which she knew must penetrate to the consciousness of Lady Bobbin:

'Yes, the day of the capitalist is over now, and a jolly good thing too.'

'May I ask,' said Lady Bobbin, rising like a trout to this remark and leaning across the projecting stomach of Lord Leamington Spa, 'why you, of all people, think that a good thing? Mind you, I don't admit that the capitalist system has come to an end, of course it hasn't, but why should you pretend to be pleased if it did? Affectation, I should call it.'

'No, not entirely affectation, Gloria darling. What I mean is that if, in a few years' time, people like us have no money left for luxuries we shall all, as a consequence, lead simpler and better lives. More fresh air, more sleep, more time to think and read. No night clubs, no Ritz, no Blue Train, less rushing about. And the result of that will be that we shall all be much happier. Don't you agree?'

Lady Bobbin, whose life was quite innocent of night clubs, the Ritz, and the Blue Train, and who had more time than she wanted in which to think and read, was not impressed by this statement. 'It has never been necessary to make a fool of oneself just because one happens to have money. There have always been plenty of decent people in the world, but unfortunately nobody ever hears about them, because they don't advertise themselves like the others. I wonder, Louisa, whether you will be quite so glad of the end of capitalism when you find yourself without the common necessities of life.'

'I don't anticipate that,' said the duchess comfortably. 'The world at present is suffering from over-production, not under-production, of the necessities of life.'

'Surely, duchess,' began Captain Chadlington ponderously, from his end of the table, feeling that now, if ever, was the time to make use of the information that he had so laboriously garnered from the P.M., the F.O., the I.L.P., S.B., L.G., and his fellow M.P.s, and to assert himself as a rising young politician. The duchess, however, took no notice of him and continued to goad Lady Bobbin.

'Think,' she said, 'how splendid it will be for our characters as a class if we are forced to lead simple, healthy lives, to look after our own children, and to earn our own bread. And then think of all the horrors that will be done away with, all those ghastly hideous country houses everywhere that will be pulled down. We shall be able to live in darling clean little cottages instead—'

'My house,' said Lady Bobbin, always quick to take offence, 'is, I hope, scrupulously kept. If you are implying—'

'Darling, don't be absurd. I only meant that they would be spiritually clean.'

'If you feel like this, Louisa,' said Lord Leamington Spa, now entering the lists with the light of battle in his eye, 'why on earth don't you act accordingly?' Why not shut up Brackenhampton and live in one of the cottages there instead? I don't suppose there's anything to prevent you.'

'Nothing to prevent me, indeed!' cried the duchess. She had been waiting for this argument to be produced like a cat waiting for a mouse. 'There are nearly a hundred living souls to prevent me, that's all. D'you realize that we employ altogether ninety-eight people in the house and gardens at Brackenhampton? I can't, for no reason at all, take a step which would deprive all those old friends of work, food, even of a shelter over their heads. It would be quite unthinkable. I only say that if the whole system by which we live at present were to be changed we ourselves would all be a good deal happier than we are, and better in every way.'

Lady Bobbin said 'Pooh!' and rose to leave the table. She was trembling with fury.

The afternoon was so wet and foggy, so extremely unseasonable, in fact, that Lady Bobbin was obliged with the utmost reluctance to abandon the paper chase which she had organized. Until four o'clock, therefore, the house party was left to enjoy in peace that exquisite discomfort which can only be produced by overfed slumberings in arm-chairs. At four punctually everybody assembled in the ballroom while for nearly an hour the Woodford school children mummed. It was the Woodford school children's annual burden to mum at Christmas; it was the annual burden of the inhabitants of Compton Bobbin to watch the mumming. Both sides, however, bore this infliction with fortitude, and no further awkwardness took place until after tea, when Lord Leamington Spa, having donned once more his dressing-gown and wig, was distributing gifts from the laden branches of the Christmas Tree. This was the big moment of the day. The tree, of course, immediately caught fire, but this was quite a usual occurrence, and the butler had no difficulty in putting it out. The real crisis occurred when Lady Bobbin opened the largish, square parcel which had 'To darling mummy from her very loving little Bobby' written on it, and which to Lady Bobbin's rage and horror was found to contain a volume

281

entitled *The Sexual Life of Savages in Northern Melanesia*. This classic had been purchased at great expense by poor Bobby as a present for Paul; and had somehow changed places with *Tally Ho! Songs of Horse and Hound*, which was intended for his mother, and which, unluckily, was a volume of very similar size and shape. Bobby, never losing his head for an instant, explained volubly and in tones of utmost distress to his mother and the company in general that the shop must have sent the wrong book by mistake, and this explanation was rather ungraciously accepted. Greatly to Bobby's disgust, however, *The Sexual Life of Savages in Northern Melanesia* was presently consigned to the stoke-hole flames by Lady Bobbin in person.

The remaining time before dinner, which was early so that the children could come down, was spent by Bobby and Héloïse rushing about the house in a state of wild excitement. Paul suspected, and rightly as it turned out, that this excess of high spirits boded no good to somebody. It was quite obvious to the student of youthful psychology that some practical joke was on hand. He wondered rather nervously where the blow would fall.

It fell during dinner. Captain Chadlington was in the middle of telling Lady Bobbin what the P.M. had said to him about pig-breeding in the West of England when a loud whirring noise was heard under his chair. He looked down, rather startled, turned white to the lips at what he saw, sprang to his feet and said, in a voice of unnatural calm: 'Will the women and children please leave the room immediately. There is an infernal machine under my chair.' A moment of panic ensued. Bobby and Héloïse, almost too swift to apprehend his meaning, rushed to the door shrieking, 'A bomb, a bomb, we shall all be blown up,' while everyone else stood transfixed with horror, looking at the small black box under Captain Chadlington's chair as though uncertain of what they should do next. Paul alone remained perfectly calm. With great presence of mind he advanced towards the box, picked it up and conveyed it to the pantry sink, where he left it with the cold water tap running over it. This golden deed made him, jointly with Captain Chadlington, the hero of the hour. Lady Bobbin shook hands with him and said he was a very plucky young fellow and had saved all their lives, and he was overwhelmed with thanks and praise on every side. Captain Chadlington, too, was supposed to have shown wonderful fortitude in requesting the women and children to leave the room before mentioning his own danger. Only Bobby and Héloïse received no praise from anybody for their behaviour and were, indeed, more or less, sent to Coventry for the rest of the evening.

Captain Chadlington, secretly delighted to think that he was now of such importance politically that attempts were made on his life (he never doubted for a moment that this was the doing of Bolshevik agents) went off to telephone to the police. Bobby and Héloïse, listening round the corner, heard him say: 'Hullo, Woodford police? It is Captain Chadlington, M.P., speaking from Compton Bobbin. Look here, officer, there has just been an attempt to assassinate me. The Bolsheviks, I suppose. An infernal machine under my chair at dinner. Would you send somebody along to examine it at once, please, and inform Scotland Yard of what has happened?'

Lady Brenda said: 'I have always been afraid of something like this ever since Charlie made that speech against Bolshevism at Moreton-in-Marsh. Anyhow, we must be thankful that it was no worse.'

Lady Bobbin said that perhaps now the Government would do something about the Bolsheviks at last.

Lord Leamington Spa said that he didn't like it at all, which was quite true, he didn't, because on Christmas night after dinner he always sang 'The Mistletoe Bough' with great feeling and now it looked as though the others would be too busy talking about the bomb to listen to him.

Michael Lewes and Squibby Almanack dared to wonder whether it was really an infernal machine at all, but they only imparted this scepticism to each other.

The duchess said that of course it would be very good publicity for Charlie Chadlington, and she wondered—but

283

added that perhaps, on the whole, he was too stupid to think of such a thing.

Captain Chadlington said that public men must expect this sort of thing and that he didn't mind for himself, but that it was just like those cowardly dagoes to attempt to blow up a parcel of women and children as well.

Everybody agreed that the tutor had behaved admirably.

'Where did you get it from?' Paul asked Bobby, whom he presently found giggling in the schoolroom with the inevitable Héloïse.

'A boy in my house made it for me last half; he says nobody will be able to tell that it's not a genuine bomb. In fact, it *is* a genuine one, practically, that's the beauty of it. Poor old Charlie Chad., he's most awfully pleased about the whole thing, isn't he, fussing about with those policemen like any old turkey cock. Oh! It all went off too, too beautifully, egI cegouldn't thegink egit fegunnegier, cegould yegou?'

'I think you're an odious child,' said Paul, 'and I've a very good mind to tell your mother about you.'

'That would rather take the gilt off your heroic action, though, wouldn't it, old boy?' said Bobby comfortably.

The local police, as Bobby's friend had truly predicted, were unable to make up their minds as to whether the machine was or was not an infernal one. Until this pretty point should be settled Captain Chadlington was allotted two human bulldogs who were instructed by Scotland Yard that they must guard his life with their own. A camp bed was immediately made up for one of these trusty fellows in the passage, across the captain's bedroom door, and the other was left to prowl about the house and garden all night, armed to the teeth.

'Darling,' said the Duchess to Bobby, as they went upstairs to bed after this exhausting day, 'have you seen the lovely man who's sleeping just outside my room? I don't know what your mother expects to happen, but one is only made of flesh and blood after all.'

'Well, for goodness sake, try to remember that you're a duchess again now,' said Bobby, kissing his aunt good night.

13

The two children of Captain and Lady Brenda Chadlington took a tremendous fancy to Paul, and he, although in the first place he had been completely put off by the fact that their names were Christopher Robin and Wendy, decided after a day or two that he would overlook this piece of affectation, which was, after all, not their own fault. He addressed them as George and Mabel (his lips refusing to utter their real names) and became very much attached to them.

'You see, it's not as though the poor things had chosen those names themselves,' he said to Bobby, 'and I should like to do what little I can to help them towards some form of self-respect. It is really tragic to see children surrounded by such an atmosphere of intellectual dishonesty. Poor George and Mabel.'

'What d'you mean?' asked Bobby, yawning. He was both bored and piqued, as Héloïse had gone off for the whole day with Squibby.

'In every respect,' went on Paul, 'they are treated as congenital half-wits by their parents. It is really shocking. They tell me,' he added disgustedly, 'that their Sussex house is called "The Cottage in the Wood". Well, I mean to say! I always refer to it as The Cedars when mentioning it to them. "The Cottage in the Wood" indeed; it's nearly as good as "Mulberrie Farm". I don't know what the English-speaking race is coming to.'

'Oh, of course, Brenda is the most affected woman in the world, we all know that, but she seems to be bringing them up quite nicely, I must say. They aren't at all spoilt or naughty.'

'They may not be. All I know is that their poor little minds are simply drowning in a welter of falsehood and pretence.'

'I s'pose you mean,' said Bobby, lighting a cigarette, 'that they are made to say their prayers and discouraged from seeing Brenda and Charlie naked in the bath. Personally, I'm rather old-fashioned about these things, too.'

'They are treated insanely. Not only are their brains being warped by constant application to the most sterile and insidiously unmoral forms of child literature—Barrie, A. A. Milne, Kenneth Grahame, Kipling, and so on—but they are being sternly repressed in every way. Just at this age when they should be opening out to life, assimilating new experiences of every sort, learning to care for truth and beauty in every form, they are subjected to constant humiliations, constant thwarting and hindering. Each little instinct has to be fought back as soon as it appears. How can they be expected to develop? Look at what happened to poor George on Christmas Day!'

'I didn't then and I should simply hate to now,' said Bobby, wondering when was the soonest that he could expect Héloïse back from her outing.

'Poor child, what could be more natural though? It was obviously the first time in his stunted little life that he had had the chance to eat as much chocolate as he really wanted. That incident told a tale of wanton cruelty.'

'Wanton greediness, I should call it. Dirty little pig.'

'As for Mabel, it is tragic to see the way she is chivvied about from pillar to post all day. "Have you washed your hands, Wendy? Did you clean your teeth? Take off your outdoor shoes. Get on with your knitting. Why haven't you brushed your hair? Put on your coat. Go for a walk." And all this, I would have you observe, to a child of inherently contemplative nature, a philosopher, probably, in the making. How *can* she develop properly? Every time she sits down to commune within herself, to think out some abstruse problem or to register some new experience, she is hounded off to perform dreary and perfunctory tasks. My heart bleeds for Mabel.'

'Wendy's the laziest little beast I know. She'd never do a thing if she were left to herself. It's pure idleness with her.'

'I entirely disagree with you, Bobby. That child has ideas and perceptions far beyond her age, and naturally they tire her out. She needs time and leisure in which to tabulate the impressions which she is always receiving from the outer world. Another thing very sad to see is the way her emotional life is threatened.'

'How d'you mean?'

'The poor child has a most distinct father-fixation, haven't you realized that? Very marked indeed.'

'Oh, nonsense, Paul; what extraordinary ideas you do have.'

'Nonsense, is it? My dear Bobby, just you notice the way she copies him in everything—she sits, walks, eats and talks exactly like him. Why, in another year or two she'll be the living image of him, always a sign of morbid affection, you know.'

'Really, you do surprise me. I suppose heredity could have nothing to do with it?' said Bobby sarcastically.

'Oh, no, nothing whatever. Nobody believes in hereditary influences nowadays. No, it's all the result of this mad passion she has, subconsciously, of course, for her father. Most dangerous.'

'Well,' said Bobby, 'I expect you know best. Anyhow, here comes one of the little cherubs, bless his tiny heart.'

'Mr. Fisher,' said Christopher Robin, putting his head round the schoolroom door. 'Please will you come out with us? Mother says we must go up the drive and back before lunch.'

'*Must, must,* always that word *"must"*,' sighed Paul. 'So unwholesome, so stifling. Yes, I'd like to come out with you, George. Where's Mabel, then?'

'She's just looking for still-borns in *The Times*,' said Christopher Robin. 'I'll fetch her—oh, here she comes though.' Wendy Chadlington kept a little red pocket-book in which she wrote down the numbers of still-born babies every day as announced in the Births column of *The Times*. This lugubrious hobby seemed to afford her the deepest satisfaction.

'Any luck to-day?' asked Christopher Robin casually.

'Not to-day. One lot of triplets though. I keep a separate page for them, and there were two still-borns yesterday. One mustn't expect too much, you know.'

'Now George and Mabel,' said Paul, 'if you are quite ready let's go, shall we? There isn't much time, really, before lunch.'

Wendy looked at Christopher Robin and they both giggled. They were not, as yet, accustomed to their new names, and thought that Paul, though both amiable and entertaining, was undoubtedly a little mad.

Paul carefully replaced a volume of Lady Maria's journal behind the radiator, a practice that had but little meaning since Lady Bobbin, for whose deception it had been invented, never came near the schoolroom by any chance.

'What story are you going to tell us to-day?' asked Wendy as they started out.

'Please, Mr. Fisher, tell us a story about animals.'

'A true story about animals, please, Mr. Fisher.'

Yesterday's 'story', a homily on the life history of eels, had not really gone with much of a swing, and it was felt that a true story would be preferable to one which he had palpably invented himself.

'Well, let me think,' said Paul. 'I don't know many stories about animals. What kind of animal?'

'Any kind. *Please*, Mr. Fisher. You told us a lovely one yesterday,' said Christopher Robin encouragingly.

'I really *don't* know any,' said Paul, at his wits' end. 'Unless you'd like to hear one that I read in *Country Life* the other day. That was supposed to be true, I believe.'

'What's *Country Life*?'

'It's a paper your Aunt Gloria takes in.'

'*I* know,' said Wendy in tones of superiority, and added in a stage whisper: 'Christopher Robin can't read, you know, so of course papers aren't very interesting to him.'

'Pig,' said Christopher Robin. 'I *can* read. Anyway, *you*—'

Paul had been treated to arguments of this kind before, and hastily said: 'I'll tell you the story then, if you'll be quiet. A man was walking across a farm-yard—'

'A farmer?' asked Wendy, 'or a labourer?'

'If you interrupt I shan't go on. The man who wrote this story to *Country Life*—I don't know who he may have been—was walking across a farm-yard when he saw two rats running along in front of him. He threw a stick which he had in his hand at the first rat and killed it dead. To his great surprise the second rat, instead of running away, stood quite still as though it were waiting for something. The man thought this was so odd that he went over to look at it, and when he got quite near he saw that it was stone blind and had a straw in its mouth. The rat he had killed had been leading it along by the straw, you see, and the poor blind one thought it had stopped to have a drink or something, I suppose, and was just patiently waiting there for it to go on.'

'Well?' said Wendy after a pause.

'That's the end of the story.'

'But what did the man do with the blind rat?'

'I don't know. He didn't say in *Country Life*.'

'I should have kept it for a pet,' said Christopher Robin, 'and led it about on a straw.'

'I should *love* a dear little blind rat,' said Wendy, and added in a contemplative voice: 'I sometimes wish I were blind you know, so that I needn't see my tooth water after I've spat it.'

'I know what,' said Christopher Robin, 'let's pretend you're a blind rat, Wendy. Shut your eyes, you see, and put this straw in your mouth, and I'll put the other end of it in mine, and I'll lead you along by it.'

That evening Lady Brenda said to Paul: 'I think it is so kind of you to take my wee things out for walks (I'm afraid they *must* bore you rather, don't they?) but—please don't mind me saying this—don't you think that game you taught them with the straw is perhaps just the least little bit unhygienic? Of course if the straw could be sterilized I wouldn't mind, but you see one can't be certain where it came from, and I am so frightened always of T.B. So I've strictly forbidden them to play it any more, I hope you won't be angry; it's too sweet of you to bother with them,' and with a vague smile she drifted away.

*

Héloïse Potts took Squibby Almanack for a ride. She did this mainly in order to annoy Bobby, because she knew that she would be fearfully bored by Squibby before the day was over. They went, in the duchess's black Rolls-Royce, to visit Bunch Tarradale, whose ancestral home, Cracklesford Castle, was some thirty miles away, in Warwickshire.

Bunch was more than pleased to see them, and quickly led off Squibby to the downstairs lavatory so that they could have a good gossip.

'Have you heard from Biggy?' said Bunch, with more than a hint of malice in his voice. 'He's in love again.'

'Not again ! Who is it this time?'

'A girl called Susan Alveston. However, she's refused him, which is all to the good. Very ugly and stupid I hear she is, and only sixteen.'

'Biggy always likes them young though, doesn't he? How d'you know she's ugly and stupid?'

'He said so in his letter. He said "You might not call her strictly beautiful, but she has a most fascinating and expressive little face". That means she must be ugly, doesn't it, and all girls of sixteen are stupid. All the ones I've met are, anyhow. Besides, she must be, to refuse Biggy.'

'You seem to think that girls only have one idea in their heads, and that is to marry a lord as soon as they can.'

'Well, isn't that true?'

'*I* have my ideals,' said Squibby.

'And have you heard from Maydew?' continued Bunch. 'I had a picture post-card saying everything had turned out very satisfactorily.'

'So did I. Balham is evidently a success. What a sensible man Maydew is, to be sure, so untrammelled by feeling. It must be delightful to have a nature of that sort.' He sighed deeply. 'Anyhow, I am very glad about poor old Biggy, only I do feel that he should be more careful. One of these days he will be accepted, and how he would resent that.'

'So should we all. Do you think that perhaps my mother has now been subjected to the maddening prattle of your first cousin for long enough? Shall we relieve her?'

'Just a minute. I knew there was something else I wanted to ask you. What is all this nonsense about a quintet society?'

'Ah! Biggy has written to you about that, too, has he? Mind you, I think it's quite a good idea in some ways, only I'm afraid it's bound to be a failure if Biggy has anything to do with it. Still, I suppose one will have to join?'

'I suppose so. One must support the poor old boy, though, frankly, it seems rather a waste of his time and our money. It's so like Biggy, isn't it? Her always starts these wildly unpractical schemes. As though there were not enough good concerts as it is, besides, I hate listening to music in drawing-rooms. One's always catching people's eyes.'

'He tells me we shall be able to take off our boots.'

'I always do in any case.'

'All the same, I daresay there is something to be said for it, you know,' muttered Squibby grudgingly as they went upstairs. Fond as they were of each other, these friends had a sort of underlying bitterness in their characters which made it impossible for them not to indulge sometimes in a little harmless venom; like certain brothers and sisters, they always pretended to be sceptical of any venture embarked upon by others.

On the way home Miss Héloïse Potts took advantage of the darkness and the undoubted cold to snuggle very close to poor Squibby, who, overwhelmed by her proximity and by the kisses which soon fell upon his lips, responded in no uncertain manner and presently begged of her to marry him.

'No thanks, darling,' said Héloïse. 'I'm not old enough to marry yet. But when I am grown up I'm going to be either a duchess like mummy or a tart like Amabelle. Nothing in between for me. Only,' she added jauntily, 'there are rather few eligible dukes about so it almost looks as though—'

14

'DARLING EVELYN,

'*How* sweet, but oh, how *very* naughty of you to send me such lovely links, at least I s'pose it was you who sent them, wasn't it? Cartier very stupidly forgot to put in a card, but I don't know anybody else who would be likely to do such a divine thing. I just can't tell you how much I dote on them. I look at them all day and think what an angel you are to give me a present like that, although I do feel rather badly about not having sent *you* even a Christmas card! However, I haven't forgotten the date of your birthday, Evelyn dear. I have had a gorgeous Christmas. I do hope you have, too. Amabelle, who has taken a house down here, gave me an evening watch (platinum with diamonds round the edge) and Auntie Loudie St. Neots a pair of gold hair-brushes, rather chi-chi, but very attractive all the same, and I had altogether £60 in tips. But far, far the best of all my presents do I like your exquisite links. See you very soon, I hope. I may be in London for a few days towards the end of the holidays, in which case we might lunch or something? Anyway, mind you come trailing over to Eton some time next term, won't you?

'Many more thanks for the lovely surprise.

'With love from
'BOBBY'.

Bobby folded up this letter, put it in an envelope, addressed it, and laid it in a pile of about six others, all couched in exactly identical terms.

'Think of some more people for me to write to,' he said to Paul, who was deeply engrossed in the journal.

'What sort of people?' asked Paul vaguely.

'The sort that might be taken in by a letter like this and stump up something fairly reasonable.' He read Paul the letter.

'That's rather a good idea, isn't it?' said Paul. 'I wish I was brazen enough to do that sort of thing.'

'But I can't think of anybody else. You see, it must be someone rich, who enjoys giving presents. I won't risk taking all this trouble just to get a New Year's card back.'

'Nobody seems to enjoy giving me presents,' said Paul gloomily; 'and if they do their mothers go and burn the thing in the stoke-hole. It is hard—*The Sexual Life of Savages in Northern Melanesia* is a book I had always wanted most particularly too.'

'You can have *Tally Ho! Songs of Horse and Hound*, old boy. Here it is if you'd like it. I'm still wondering how they could have got mixed up. Do you think darling Héloïse might have had something to do with it?'

'I expect that's exactly what did happen. Thank heaven the little chatterbox isn't here any more. She gets on my nerves with her sudden shrieks and all that egi-egi.'

It was New Year's Day, and the entire house party had gone away that morning except for Lord Lewes, who remained alone and palely loitering, with the intention of very shortly laying his coronet, estates and person at the feet of his cousin, Philadelphia.

'She may be a little chatterbox,' said Bobby sourly, 'but nobody can deny that she is divinely attractive.'

'Indeed, *I* can.'

'And, as a matter of fact, I may quite likely marry her in years' and years' time,' went on Bobby, taking no notice of Paul. 'We are engaged now, if you want to know, secretly, of course.'

'My dear, she'll be married and have children before you're out of the cradle.'

'Oh, I don't expect to be her *first* husband, naturally. And you know, on second thoughts, I'm not at all sure I wouldn't rather marry Aunt Loudie. She's even more my cup of tea in many ways, and now it's allowed by law I shall consider it very seriously indeed.'

'Your mother told me most distinctly that aunts were not allowed. Only uncles, *she* said.'

'Oh, mother! She just makes up the rules as she goes along. I dare say she's guessed my guilty passion for Aunt Loudie and thinks she can throw cold water on it from the start. If one's allowed it's quite obvious that the other would be too. I wonder where Delphie is, by the way?'

'I think I saw her go out with Michael—for a walk, I suppose.'

'That's all to the good. Splendid. I'm very pleased about that.'

'Oh, you are, are you? May one ask why?'

'Well, naturally, I'm delighted when I see Delphie going about with Michael. I'm arranging for her to marry him, you know.'

'Oh, indeed! I thought he was supposed to be in love with Amabelle?'

'Love,' said Bobby pompously, 'has little or nothing to do with a matrimonial alliance. We Bobbins never marry, we contract alliances, and all that is necessary for a successful alliance is mutual respect. Now Michael's a sentimental old thing, and he likes to imagine that his heart is broken irreparably; it gives him a certain kick, I suppose. But that needn't prevent him from wanting to marry and settle down with a family of his own. Naturally he's not *in love* with Delphie, I don't see, personally, how one could be, but she would make him an ideal wife, healthy, well-born, properly educated for that sort of position, and so on. Just the very thing he ought to be looking for.'

'Oh, damn you,' said Paul.

'Now what's the matter?'

'Well, you see, I happen to be in love with her myself.'

'Oh, no! Are you honestly? How too enthralling this is. I wish I knew what you all see in her. But that's perfect. I hope Michael has noticed; it ought to egg him on no end, oughtn't it? A little rivalry and so forth. I must drop him a hint.'

'Do be serious for one minute, Bobby.'

'I *am*, dead serious.'

'You see, I want to marry her myself.'

'You want to marry her? Poor old boy, I'm afraid that's absolutely no cop. Delphie must marry well whatever happens. We Bobbins always do. Not that I wouldn't dote on you for a brother-in-law if things were just a tiny bit different, but—you see?'

'You are a worldly little beast, Bobby,' said Paul gloomily, but without rancour.

'Yes, aren't I? It does pay so much better to be. I'm awfully sorry if you're feeling wretched about all this though, Paul dear, I am truly. I'm very fond of you, though you might not think it. Now I'll put these letters to be posted (let's hope they bring in a good fat return) and then we might ride over to Amabelle's, shall we? It's rather late, but we can always say that we stopped on the way back for a game of squash.'

At this moment Philadelphia wandered aimlessly into the room and asked what they were going to do.

'Where's Michael then?' said Bobby.

'I've no idea at all. Oh, yes, though, hasn't he gone out with mummy to look at that old barrow he's going to excavate?'

'Why didn't you want to go with them?'

'I thought it would be so boring.'

'Barrows,' said Bobby severely, 'are very far from boring, let me tell you. I think you should try to take more interest in such things. You seem to live in a walking swoon.'

'Anyway, what are you doing? Can't I come too?'

'We're only going to ride over for some squash in Woodford.'

'I'll come and watch.'

'All right, do,' said Bobby, in exasperation. 'Only I warn you there won't be much to watch. It's all a blind really, this squash and riding. We're really going over to see Amabelle Fortescue at Mulberrie Farm.'

'Oh, how thrilling. You know I heard mother talking to Auntie Loudie about her, and afterwards she forbade me ever to go near Mulberrie Farm.'

'Just you come along now then,' said Paul. 'Amabelle is longing to meet you, I know, and this is an excellent opportunity.'

On their way to the stables Bobby drew Paul aside and said: 'Now we must try and make her pay attention to that barrow, community of interests is supposed to be an essential of married happiness.'

'Damn you,' said Paul again.

They found the party at Mulberrie Farm scattered about the drawing-room in attitudes of deathlike exhaustion.

'We're awfully tired and ill to-day, darlings,' said Amabelle, 'but it's always lovely to see you, and I'm glad you've brought your sister at last, Bobby dear.' She lay curled up on a Knole sofa and appeared almost unable to open her eyes. Her voice had become a mere whisper, her face a grey mask on which the rouge showed up with startling intensity. Her eyelashes, which she always painted navy blue, were now no darker than the shadows beneath them. Even the tactful Bobby was hardly able to conceal the shock that her appearance had given him. Sally and Jerome lay on other sofas, their ravaged faces half buried in pillows. Walter was nowhere to be seen.

'What on earth is the matter with you all?' said Bobby, after surveying this scene for some minutes in silence. 'I know, you've been having a blind,' he added accusingly.

Amabelle, who had dropped off to sleep again, woke with a start and said, 'That's it, however did you guess? We got to bed at half-past eight this morning, if you want to know, and we should be there still if it wasn't for Sally's perfectly idiotic theory that it makes one feel better to get up for tea. I can't say I've noticed it. I couldn't possibly feel more awful myself.'

'What on earth have you been doing that could keep you up until eight-thirty; and why didn't you invite me to the ball?'

'We went to the New Year party at the Albert Hall. Sally suggested it at dinner last night, so we just bundled ourselves into fancy dress and popped up to London in the car. Oh, how I wish we hadn't, too!'

'Oh, cads!' said Bobby, and his eyes quite literally filled with tears. It was always a very real sorrow to him if he missed a party of any kind. He felt cross and resentful.

Amabelle saw this at once; she knew her little Bobby. 'Darling, you can't imagine how much we all longed for you

296

to come,' she said quickly, 'but I simply couldn't think of taking you, for your own sake, my sweet. You must remember that it never pays to risk quarrelling with one's bread and butter, and you've got to keep in your mamma's good books, especially if you're not to be packed off to Sandhurst, eh? So don't look quite so sad, precious.'

'Oh, well, I see your point, I suppose. Actually, of course, it could have been worked quite safely; still, never mind, it's all over now. Was it lovely?'

'It was lovely,' said Sally, sitting up with an obvious effort, and powdering her nose. 'Simply grand. I got off with a miner from Lancashire, who had just absconded with the local slate club money and was having the time of his life in London on the proceeds. He was a great wit; he said the lady miners are minarets—he made that sort of joke. He was that sort of man, you see. Heavenly. And he said "I know where I've met you before, with Lady Alistair Grayson in her villa at Antibes," and I said "You can't have met me there because I don't know the old trout," and he said, "Oh, nor do I, of course. But I always read about her parties in the papers." That is the sort of man he was—very O.K. I had a great romance with him. And who Walter got off with no one knows because he vanished half-way through the party, you see, and hasn't come back yet. He must be having a gorgeous time.'

Sally rose uncertainly to her feet and staggered upstairs.

'Poor darling Sally,' said Amabelle. 'I must say she does behave well on these occasions. I admire her for it a good deal. It's really too naughty of Walter not to ring her up or something; he must know by now how much she always worries.'

'There's your groom,' said Bobby, who hated hearing about other people's troubles, and had wandered over to the window, 'galloping Paul's horse round and round that field; he is a divine man. Fielden, our groom, told mother that he'd never known me to take so much interest in riding, or exercise the horses so thoroughly before, as I do these hols.; and of course the old girl puts it down entirely to Paul's wonderful influence. Tell me some more about that party you so kindly asked me to.'

'It was just like any other party of that sort. It had every element of discomfort and boredom and yet for no particular reason that one could see, it was divine fun. It's not often one finds English people really gay, is it? And in the Albert Hall of all places, in that odour of Sunday afternoon concerts, it is quite astonishing.'

'Who was there?'

'Everybody in the world. The improper duchess for one.'

'With Héloïse?'

'I didn't see her, but she may have been too well disguised. Jane and Albert were there, just back from Paris.'

'Were they, now?' said Paul with interest. 'And how are they? Happy?'

'Wretched, I believe. Did they expect anything else? What a silly marriage that was, to be sure.'

'Oh dear,' said Paul glomily, 'it really is rather disillusioning. When one's friends marry for money they are wretched, when they marry for love it is worse. What is the proper thing to marry for, I should like to know?'

'The trouble is,' said Amabelle, looking at Philadelphia whom she thought surprisingly beautiful, 'that people seem to expect happiness in life. I can't imagine why; but they do. They are unhappy before they marry, and they imagine to themselves that the reason of their unhappiness will be removed when they are married. When it isn't they blame the other person, which is clearly absurd. I believe that is what generally starts the trouble.'

'I expect that's quite right,' said Paul, sighing.

'In any case,' Amabelle went on, 'the older I get the more I think it is fatal to marry for love. The mere fact of being in love with somebody is a very good reason for not marrying them, in my opinion. It brings much more unhappiness than anything else. Look at Sally. Every time Walter leaves the house for half an hour she thinks he will be run over by a bus and on an occasion like this it's impossible to guess what she must be suffering. Now, supposing she weren't in love with him, she'd be feeling ghastly now, like I am; but she wouldn't be frightfully unhappy as well, and on ordinary occasions she

298

could enjoy her life peacefully. What does Bobby think about it?'

Bobby said, 'Just what I told you, see?' to Paul, and to Amabelle, 'I still think it's lousy of you not to have taken me last night. I shan't get over it for ages and ages. As for marriage, I fully intend to marry you, darling, when I'm a bit older and have had my fling, you know. We'll live where it's hot, shall we? and adopt four black children and be as happy as the day is long.'

'You are a fool, Bobby. I'm very glad you've brought your beautiful sister here at last,' said Amabelle. Philadelphia blushed, she was unused to being thought beautiful. 'She must come again soon, when we're not all so tired and sad. Where's Michael, by the way? Still at Compton Bobbin?'

'Oh, yes, rather,' said Bobby. 'He's gone out to look for a barrow to excavate, I believe.'

'Gosh! how boring.'

'No, no, not at all boring, you know, really. Barrow digging is a fascinating occupation.'

'Is that a car coming up the drive?' said Amabelle languidly. It was getting dark, and the sidelights of a car flashed into the room.

'Yes, it is. A huge Daimler, with Walter in it. Ha, ha, that's funny; the old boy's still in fancy dress.'

Waslter came in rather sheepishly, still wearing his *matelôt* clothes of the night before, and borrowed some money from Jerome to pay for the car, which was a Daimler hire. This done, he came back again, lit a cigarette and said in an exaggeratedly casual voice, 'Sally all right?'

'I suppose so; I don't imagine she's awake yet really. Did you have a good time?'

'No, lousy. Why on earth did you go away like that without me?' Walter flung himself out of the room.

'Hity-tity,' said Amabelle. 'So that's the tone, is it? Well, so long as one knows. How much did you lend him, Jerome darling?'

'A fiver,' said Jerome, who was now sitting up and reading *The Times*.

299

'I'll give it to you myself. It was rather a shame, I suppose, leaving him there. Still, half-past six, you know, and he hadn't been seen by anyone since midnight.'

'There are trains,' said Jerome, pursuing his own line of thought, 'and road coaches.'

'In those clothes? I hardly think he could have.'

'He had an overcoat. He must know he can't afford Daimler hires. It would have been more honest.'

'It would have been most unlike Walter. How goes the journal, Paul?'

'Grand. I'm reading the first volume now. This morning I got to where "Dearest Mamma very kindly gave me permission to go a little way into the shrubbery with Sir Josiah Bobbin, and while there he said that it would make him very happy if I should become his wife. I replied in some agitation, due to the beatings of my poor heart, that my future must be decided by dearest Mamma and dear Papa; whereupon he told me, to my immeasurable joy, that he had already solicited and obtained their consent to our union. We then went back into the drawing-room, where I was embraced by dearest Mamma, dear Papa and all my dear brothers and sisters, also by poor Aunt Agatha, who all said that they hoped I should be very very happy. It was a most touching scene, and I felt quite *faint* from joy and emotion." Isn't it exquisite?' said Paul enthusiastically. 'The account of her wedding is too perfect; I can't remember that exactly, but I'll bring it along sometime. You know, Amabelle, I think I shall be able to write something unusually good after this, thanks entirely to you and Bobby, of course.'

'Don't mention it, old boy,' said Bobby. 'Just remember me in your dedication, though. "To my friend, Sir Roderick Bobbin, Bt., great grandson of Lady Maria, without whose help, encouragement and never failing sympathy this book could hardly have been written." Something on those lines, you know.'

Paul said nothing. He intended to dedicate the 'Life' to Philadelphia Bobbin.

15

Shortly after the New Year, foot and mouth disease vanished from the cow-sheds of Gloucestershire, and the Bobbin hunt was able to resume its season. Lady Bobbin was now rarely to be seen between breakfast, at which meal she would appear booted and spurred to eat vast quantities of meaty foods, and tea-time, when she would loudly re-live the day for the benefit of Philadelphia, Paul and Michael. Her accounts of what had happened were always interspersed with bitter criticisms of the young female members of the hunt, who, according to her description of their appearance, might be supposed to come out hunting in full evening dress and with the sole idea of abstracting the attention of their men friends from the serious business on hand.

'There was Maisie Critchley, in a pink shirt and a satin stock (I know you'll hardly believe me), made up to the eyes and her hair all fuzzed out under her bowler. Perfectly disgusting. I can't imagine why she bothers to get up on a horse at all; she can't go for nuts and she spends her whole time coffee-housing with young Walters. Then, of course, he's too busy holding her horse while she makes up her face and so on to think of anything else. I don't know what the young people are coming to. Lucky thing my poor father is dead, that's what I say. It would have broken his heart to see all these goings-on.'

Paul, hoping to see some painted sirens, went to one or two meets; but the women seemed to him, young and old, to be of a uniform plainness, with hard, weather-beaten faces entirely devoid of any artificial aids to beauty. He could only suppose that Lady Bobbin, in the delirium of the chase, was subject to hallucinations which took the form of satin stocks and pretty painted faces.

Bobby, who, rather against his will, admitted to a fondness for hunting, usually accompanied his mother and stayed out most of the day; but Philadelphia, since having as a child broken nearly every bone in her body when her pony fell at a stone wall out cubbing, had no nerve left. She and Paul now spent their time between Mulberrie Farm, both Sally and Amabelle having taken a great fancy to her, and the barrow, where Michael was busily conducting excavations with the aid of four members of the local unemployed.

'That book you lent me,' she said one morning as they were walking towards the barrow; 'I finished it in bed last night. It's very sad, isn't it?'

Paul looked at her with positive rapture.

'Did you really think so?' he said incredulously.

'Yes, of course. It is dreadful—I cried at the end.'

'Oh, you *didn't*, Philadelphia?'

'Yes, I did. Why, don't you think it's very sad?'

'I do. But nobody else does, you know. They don't understand it; all the reviewers thought it was meant to be a funny book.'

'How could they? How perfectly absurd. I think it's too terrible, and wonderfully written, isn't it? Poor Leander Strutt, he was so happy at Oxford, d'you remember? And so miserable when he was working for the pawnbroker. I'm sure that must be true of certain young men. I'm sure lots of them are happy until they leave their university and then never happy any more.'

'Indeed,' said Paul eagerly, 'you are so right. I was just like that myself. I don't believe I shall ever be as happy again as I was at Oxford.'

'It is different for girls, of course. I had a dreadful childhood; I was wretched the whole time. How I longed to be grown-up!'

'And now that you are grown-up, is it any better?'

'Up to now I haven't thought so. I came out in London, you know, about three years ago, and went to parties, which I simply hated. I didn't like the people I met, and they didn't like me either. Since then I've just lived down here, with nothing to do and no friends, and been even more miserable than I was as a child. But I've always felt that there must be people somewhere in the world whom I could like and get on with, and I see that I was right.' She paused a moment, and then said, 'Now that you and Sally and Amabelle and Michael have all appeared in my life I'm very happy indeed. I don't know what I shall do when you all go away.' Her eyes filled with tears as she said this.

Paul felt rather annoyed at the inclusion of Michael's name in this group of superior beings.

'I've got a great secret to tell you,' he said.

'Have you? What?'

'*I* wrote *Crazy Capers*.'

'*You* did, Paul? Oh, how thrilling. I do feel excited to think that I know a real author at last. But how clever you must be; as clever as Michael I should think, or even cleverer. It is a lovely book. I don't understand, though, why you wrote under another name; I should want everyone to know that I was the author if I wrote something so wonderful.'

'My real name,' said Paul, '*is* Fotheringay. Fisher was my mother's name.' And he told her why he had come to Compton Bobbin. 'Thank God I did,' he added, looking at her lovely face.

After this conversation Paul appeared in a new light to Philadelphia. She had already felt that she might fall in love with him, now she knew that she had done so. An author in disguise is a more heroic figure than a holiday tutor.

They arrived at the barrow to find Michael in his shirt-sleeves, grouting about in the bottom of a hole, now about five feet deep, which had been dug by the workmen.

'We may strike the treasure at any moment now,' he cried, in a voice strangled with excitement. 'At any moment we may come upon the charred bones of the great Viking and his wives, the human ashes, surrounded by great spears and shields and gleaming gold ornaments, painted sherds and jewelled necklaces.'

Paul and Philadelphia, fired by his enthusiasm, leapt into the pit and began feverishly to dig.

'Be careful,' cried Michael, in great agitation. 'All this earth must be properly sifted. I think perhaps you had better leave it to me; you can stand on the edge there, if you like.'

This proved, however, in the bitter east wind that was blowing, to be rather a chilly occupation, and they very soon went home again.

That afternoon, coming in from a visit to Mulberrie Farm, they were met by Michael, who almost screamed, 'Come and see, come and see. I've found him; I've found the Viking with all his ornaments, great painted sherds, gold breastplates—'

'Where—where?'

'On the billiard table.'

They rushed to the billiard-room, where they found, reposing on newspaper, a small heap of earthy objects. There was a bit of bone, a square inch of what looked like broken flowerpot, some apparently meaningless pieces of metal and a tiny gold wire. These were the great skeleton, the sherds, the spears and shields, the jewelled necklaces for which Michael had so perseveringly and so expensively been searching. Such, however, is the power of an archaeological imagination that Michael himself, able to reconstruct out of these bits and pieces the objects of which they had (perhaps) originally formed a part, regarded them as a most valuable and interesting addition to modern knowledge. His gratification knew no bounds when, having dispatched his treasure to the British Museum, that revered institution graciously accepted it. (The piece of bone, however, under expert examination, proved to be not that of a Viking but of a pig.)

16

The point-to-point meeting of the South Cotswold hunt took place in some of Major Stanworth's fields. To celebrate the occasion, Amabelle gave a lunch party which consisted of the Monteaths, Major Stanworth, his little boy Adolphus and Paul. Bobby, who had, of course, been invited, was obliged, greatly to his disgust, to attend a farmers' luncheon in a large, damp and evil-smelling tent on the race-course itself. In the absence of his always cheerful rattle the party at Mulberrie Farm settled down to a meal of unrelieved gloom. Sally made no attempt to conceal her wretchedness and never for one moment stopped crying, her emotion being due to the fact that, in spite of all her efforts to prevent such a thing from happening, Major Stanworth had lent Walter one of his horses to ride in the nomination race. Nobody liked to break in upon her too evident grief with a merry remark, and her tears, though of the unobtrusive variety, stealing down her cheeks one by one instead of gushing forth in uncontrolled abandon, had a most depressing effect on the general spirits. Major Stanworth, a kindly and not insensitive soul, was perfectly well aware that poor Sally regarded him as a particularly low and evil type of murderer, and kept on making pathetic little advances to this unresponsive Niobe.

'Really, Mrs Monteath,' he said nervously, 'you need not feel in the least upset. I assure you, there is no need to worry like this. Old Foxtall, the horse that Walter is going to ride, has never put a foot wrong in his life, never. Please believe me. He may be a bit slow, but there's no safer ride in the country. Surely you must realize that I would never think of putting Walter up on one of my horses unless I knew that it was perfectly safe—would I, Mrs Fortescue?'

'No, of course not, darling,' said Amabelle, looking at him

affectionately; 'but all the same, I do think it's rather dreadful for my poor Sally, and none of us are blessing you exactly, because now, you see, we shall all have to go out in this ghastly east wind to see Walter doing or dying, whereas otherwise we might have drunk our cherry brandy by the fire and imagined ourselves at the point-to-point instead. Now, Walter dear, before I forget, I mean to bet five shillings on you, not that I imagine for a moment that I shall win anything, but just for old sake's sake, don't you know.'

'Each way, or win only?' said Walter professionally. ('If you don't stop crying like this, Sally, I shall divorce you—I wish you'd try to be more controlled on these occasions; think of the women of Sparta, can't you?) It may make all the difference to my tactics when approaching the last fence. You see, if it's win only I might feel obliged to bump and bore a bit, otherwise I should probably sit tight and get a comfortable third. So make up your mind and let me know, will you?'

'That's all right, old boy,' said Paul. 'You ride a really filthy race. Above all, don't miss any opportunity to cross Captain Chadlington; he's riding a horse called Stout Unionist (out of True Blue by Brewery) and I shall die if he wins.'

'Oh, so he's back again, is he?'

'Yes, he came back for the point-to-point last night.'

'How's the Infernal Machine?'

'Grand. He's going to ask a question about it in the House.'

'I think we should be going on out,' said Amabelle, 'although a more unpleasant idea in this weather I can hardly imagine, myself! Just listen to the wind, howling down the chimney—ugh! Come on, Sally, my poor darling, I can lend you a fur coat and a nice big hankie, and we might tie hotwater bottles next to our tummies, don't you think? Very nice and pregnant we shall look, too.' She led the weeping Sally from the room.

'You'll be blind, you know, Walter, old boy, if I may say so,' remarked Paul, who had been watching Walter fill his glass with unusual abandon.

'Yes, I mean to be,' said Walter. 'I'm terrified,' he added

confidentially as Major Stanworth left the room, 'never been so frightened in my life. But nothing hurts nearly so much if you're drunk, does it? I once saw a drunk man fall thirty feet, on to a stone pavement, too; he wasn't hurt a bit. Come on, then; are we all ready for the pretty spectacle of my demise? Cheer up, Sally, think of the Roman matrons, darling. Besides, you're quite attractive enough to get some more husbands, though, of course, I doubt you finding anything quite up to my form again. Have we got lots of cherry brandy in the car?'

The point-to-point course lay on the exposed and wind-swept side of a hill and the cold which assailed Amabelle's party on their arrival at this scene of action was beyond what would be thought possible by anyone not accustomed to the pleasures of rural England in winter. Walter, by now fairly drunk, got out of the car and strode about in his overcoat, accompanied by Major Stanworth, Paul and Bobby. He went down to look at the water jump, had a talk to Major Stanworth's groom, and generally behaved in what he imagined to be a professional manner. Amabelle and Sally huddled up together for warmth in the Rolls-Royce, clasping innumerable hot-water bottles, and refusing to move out of it until Walter's race should begin. This was third on the programme. After the first race, at which there were many accidents, poor Sally was even further depressed by seeing the motor ambulance leave the course with its groaning load. A reserve of pride in her nature, however, prevented her from making any more scenes, and it was with a comparatively cheerful face that she went off to the paddock when the time came for Walter to mount. Amabelle still declared that nothing would drag her from the car, so Paul took Sally under his protection. He pointed out Captain Chadlington, whose ordinarily red face was now mauve from cold and har-monized unpleasantly with his racing colours of black, cerise cap and old-gold sleeves. Lady Brenda, in expensive tweeds and holding a brown leather shooting stick, was talking to friends nearby; it seemed to Sally that she was viewing her

307

husband's approaching peril with unnatural calm.

'You can go into the paddock, if you like, Sally,' said Bobby, who was accompanied by a pretty little Jewess with thin legs and a spotted scarf.

'Oh, I shouldn't dare,' shivered Sally, 'your mother looks too forbidding to-day, doesn't she? Besides, Lady Prague is in there.'

At last the terrible moment came and the crowd round the paddock drew back to make a path for the horses, who jogged off with much tossing of heads and jingling of harness towards the start. They were soon lost to sight over the brow of the hill, and Walter was last seen leading the field at an uncontrolled gallop and fishing madly in the air for a stirrup with his left foot.

'Now,' said Paul, taking Sally's arm in a fatherly manner, 'where would you like to go? Shall we watch the race from the winning post or would you rather be at one of the jumps?'

'Where is he most likely to be killed?' asked Sally, her teeth chattering. She was by now in a state of utter resignation, regarding herself as a widow already; she felt, however, that she would like to be at hand to close Walter's eyes and hear his dying words, if any.

'Sally, dear, please don't be so absurd. Walter rode in several grinds at Oxford. I remember it quite well,' lied Paul, 'and he never had a scratch. I promise faithfully that he'll be all right—do stop worrying. Let's go to the last jump of all, shall we? Giles Stanworth says we can see most of the course and the finish from there.'

'Just as you like,' said Sally in a dull voice. She was wondering vaguely which of her male acquaintances she could bear to marry in the event of Walter's death.

Presently there was a murmur all over the race course, somebody in the crowd said 'They're off,' and a distant thunder of hoofs could be heard.

'There,' said Paul triumphantly, 'what did I tell you? They're all over the first jump. Walter's among the first three; can you see? Would you like these glasses?'

308

'No thanks,' said Sally. 'I never can see anything but sky through them.'

'I believe Walter's bound to win, you know; all over the second jump and he's still leading. Isn't it grand. Cheer up, Sally, it'll soon be over. Now they go round the hill and we shan't see them for a minute or two.'

A voice in the crowd behind was heard to say confidentially: 'Here, photographer—I'm Sir Roderick Bobbin and that's my cousin, Lady Brenda Chadlington, in the beige hat. If you take our photographs you'll get promotion, I should think.' And a moment later, 'Oh, look, Brenda darling, we've been photographed! No, of course I won't tell him our names if you'd rather not.'

'Here they come,' said Paul excitedly. 'Walter's still leading; aren't you thrilled, darling? Over the water jump, only one more now—over that—here they come—come on, Walter—come on, old boy—'

The horses thundered towards them, Walter leading easily. They approached the last fence, rose to it, Walter for some reason lost his balance and fell heavily to earth. Six horses in rapid succession jumped into the small of his back and passed on.

'You see,' said Walter that evening, as they settled down to bridge, 'the great advantage of getting blind before point-to-points. Sober I should certainly have been killed, as it is my left knee is a little sore but otherwise I feel grand.'

'The only thing is,' said Amabelle, 'that if you'd been a shade less drunk you might easily have won the race, instead of losing my five shillings in that careless way.'

'I should like to say that it's hardly the fault of anyone here if I'm not a widow to-night,' remarked Sally coldly. Major Stanworth, who had come, as he generally did now, to spend the evening at Mulberrie Farm, looked rather uncomfortable at this remark, which he took, and with reason, to be directed at himself.

309

17

It seemed to Philadelphia Bobbin that there was too much going on in her life all at once, she had scarcely the time to assimilate one new impression before being faced by another, even stranger and more dazzlingly improbable than the last. She felt a smouldering resentment against fate, which had crowded three weeks of her ordinarily uneventful existence with so many and such varying excitements. How much more satisfactory if they could have been spread out over the months and years of boredom which she had hitherto been obliged to endure at Compton Bobbin. As things were, it was in the course of three short weeks that she had fallen in love, received a proposal of marriage, been precipitated into the strange and dazzling society of Amabelle, and made friends violently and passionately—'best friends', the kind of relationship that girls of her age have usually outgrown—with Sally Monteath.

Any single one of these events would normally have kept her happy and given her food for thought over a period of months; crammed all together like this she was unable to treat them as realities, but behaved rather as though the whole thing were a play in a dream, and she the chief actress.

Philadelphia was twenty-one. She had hitherto led the flat, uninspiring life of many such girls, 'educated' by a governess (Lady Bobbin, for some reason about which she herself was none too clear, disapproved of girls' schools), sent with the same governess to Paris and Florence for six months, and then 'brought out' in London. Her mother took a house for her first season in Eaton Place and escorted Philadelphia to dances nearly every night in Pont Street, Chesham Place, Cadogan Gardens, Queen's Gate or occasionally Hyde Park Gardens or Sussex Square. Also she gave a dance for Philadelphia, for which, the Eaton Place house being too small, she hired a large and dirty mansion in Belgrave Square.

All these dances were as one dance, absolutely and completely identical. Philadelphia, self-conscious and unhappy in her printed chiffon, her pink taffeta or her white and diamanté georgette, her hair too much crimped, her nose too much powdered and her stays much too tight (her beautiful rounded body being a constant source of worry to her) would follow Lady Bobbin, or some other chaperone on duty for the evening, up stairs already crowded to their utmost capacity into the noisy, hot and overwhelming ballroom. It then became her business to make herself agreeable to the young men who danced with her, because it was essential that when she met them in similar circumstances the next night and the night after they should be willing to repeat the experience. She soon realized that to sit in that silence for which alone she felt inclined until it was time to go back to the ballroom was merely to lay up for herself a future of wall-flowerdom, which fate she thought on the whole even more embarrassing and unamusing than that of attempting, usually in vain, to interest the nonentities in whose company she found herself. It was a fate, however, from which she did not entirely escape, despite all her efforts. She had no success in London, her beauty, as produced by Lady Bobbin, never appeared to its best advantage, and in any case was not such as would appeal to the heirs of Cadogan Place, while they were unallured by those long and indifferent silences, that complete absence of small talk which Paul and Michael were later to find so intriguing. Much, indeed, as she hated sitting, an obvious failure, by the wall with her mother, or a girl friend in like case, she was very little happier when perched on the back stairs or at the supper table with some strange man. Dancing she enjoyed; she was a beautiful dancer.

If her evenings were on the whole rather depressing, her days were made positively hideous by the girls' luncheon parties to which her mother forced her to go. 'You must get to know some nice girls; besides, as we are in London, I want you to do everything you are asked to. We need never come up again.' Nearly every day, therefore, at one-thirty p.m., she would find herself in printed crêpe de chine, standing, finger pressed to bell marked 'Visitors', before some house in Pont Street, Chesham Place, Cadogan Gardens, Queen's Gate, Hyde Park Gardens or Sussex Square. She would be ushered into an empty L-shaped drawing-room decorated in the pre-pickled-wood-and-maps period, but brought slightly up-to-date by the presence of a waste-paper receptacle with an olde print stuck on to its plain green surface, a couple of Lalique ornaments and a pleated paper lampshade.

'I will tell Miss Joan (or Lady Felicity) that you are here, miss.' For Philadelphia, owing to early training, was one of those unfortunate people always fated to arrive a little before anybody else.

Presently Lady Joan (or Miss Felicity) would appear, and several pretty, fluffy girls in printed crêpe de chine and they would all go downstairs to a meal consisting of egg rissole with tomato sauce, cutlets with paper frills round the bone, hard round peas and new potatoes, followed by a pinkish jelly served in glasses with a tiny blob of cream on the top of each portion.

The conversation would run on the following lines:

'Which dance are you going to first to-night?'

'I think the Campbell-Parkers', because Archie said he'd meet me there, so I've booked up five and six with him. Besides, Lady Millicent Freke-Williams' is sure to be fearfully crowded at first.'

'I hear she's got thirty dinner parties for it.'

'I know. But I expect it will be fun later on. Which are you going to?'

'Well, I'm dining at the Freke-Williams' so I shall have to go there first, I suppose. Did you have fun last night? I was dying to get asked.'

'Yes, it was marvellous, but, my dear, the most awful thing happened. You see, Teddy asked me for number four and I said yes, and then Claud came up and said could he have number three or four because he had to go. Well, three was Johnny, and I never cut him; so I said "yes, four. But meet me downstairs by the buffet, or else I shall be caught by Teddy.'' So I went to the buffet at the beginning of number four and waited for ages and Claud never came and Angela said she had just seen him leave with Rosemary, so then I dashed upstairs but Teddy had started dancing with Leila, so then, my dear, I had to pick up that awful little Jamie Trent-Pomeroy. I felt so ashamed at being seen with him. But wasn't it awful of Claud—'

Philadelphia, meanwhile, would sit in a stony silence, bored and boring, and when she had gone Lady Joan or Miss Felicity would say to her girl friends, 'Isn't she too awful. Mummy made me ask her.'

Philadelphia's one London season was from every point of view a failure, and it had never, to her great relief, been repeated. Lady Bobbin was far too much wrapped up in all her country pursuits to leave them more than once for the sake of a daughter who neither appreciated nor repaid such sacrifice. She felt that she had done all that duty demanded by the child, and could now rest on her laurels.

Philadelphia herself never had the slightest wish to repeat that particular experience, but all the same she was profoundly unhappy at Compton Bobbin. She was without occupation or interest, the days dragged by each more boring than the last, and she was beginning to think that perhaps she was never to find those people who she felt sure must exist in the world and who would prove more congenial to her than those she had met as a débutante. She longed passionately for even one friend who would not think her plain, stupid and tongue-tied.

It is hardly surprising, therefore, if she was dazed and incredulous on finding herself hailed as a beauty by Amabelle, admitted to the confidences of Sally, treated as an intellectual equal by Paul and asked in marriage by Michael, all of whom were people she felt to be not only far more intelligent and interesting than any she had met, but more thrilling even than those imaginary beings whom, in day dreams, she had longed to have as her friends.

All the attention and praise that she was now receiving had

313

the very natural effect of making her twice as pretty and attractive as she had been before, and with Sally to help and advise her she was even acquiring a certain chic.

'You're so lucky; you've got the sort of face that can be made into anything,' said Sally one day as they sat talking in Elspeth Paula's nursery. 'It's like a sheet of white paper waiting to be drawn on—or, at least, painted. The drawing's there all right; you've got beautiful features. Fancy having real natural platinum blonde hair, too; it's incredible. You'd have a wild success in London, you know.'

'I didn't when I went there.'

'No, of course not, with all those awful debs. I mean, among people who understand what real beauty is. You must come and stay in the flat when we go back there. We can easily make up a bed for you in the bathroom, or Amabelle will put you up, and then we'll arrange some parties. Now, I've got a very good idea: why not tell your mother you want to learn drawing and come to us permanently as P.G.? Do, it would be such fun.'

'Oh, Sally, you are divine to me, only, you see, I can't draw at all.'

'That doesn't matter. It makes a wonderful excuse to be in London. I can't draw a single line, and I was at the Slade for years. My family lived in the country, too, you see, and I had to get away somehow.'

'Mummy would never let me.'

'You and Bobby seem to be very much under your mother's thumb.'

'Yes, even Bobby's frightened of her, really, although he does pretend not to be. Besides, you see, all the money we have comes from her, and that puts her in a very strong position.'

'Yes, of course, I quite see that.'

Michael took Philadelphia for a walk and proposed to her by the statue of Apollo. It was, like everything that Michael did, very much stage managed, very well rehearsed, supremely diplomatic and in the last degree unimaginative. Nevertheless, had he arrived at Compton Bobbin three weeks earlier it is certain that Philadelphia would have accepted him on the spot; she longed for marriage, for escape from her home, which she regarded as a prison, and from her mother, whom she detested, and she had subconsciously imbibed enough of Bobby's somewhat outspoken snobbery to be not at all averse to the idea of being a rich marchioness. Even now, had he employed any other method of approach he would probably have been successful, as Philadelphia's feelings for Paul at this stage were hardly strong enough to outweigh the obvious advantages of marriage with Michael. Besides, she liked him very much.

They went for a long walk, during which he spoke in his cultured Foreign Office voice of his life in Egypt, and before that in Paris, and of his future prospects. Philadelphia, who had a sort of blind veneration for culture and learning in all forms, thought how charming he was and how lucky it was for her that at last she knew somebody who, just occasionally, in a way that never could bore, but quite perfectly, would insert into his speech some happy little quotation that she could often recognize, from various English poets, or even, though more rarely, a few words of Latin, French or German.

'So, you see,' he said, 'I intend to leave diplomacy now. As a career it has proved a great disappointment to me, I must own.'

Philadelphia, whose ideas on the Diplomatic Service were culled exclusively from the works of Maurice Baring and Marion Crawford, said that she had always imagined a diplomat's to be the most interesting life in the world.

'In theory I suppose it must be,' said Michael, 'because you see, in theory one would be in daily contact with the most important, most intelligent people of every nation, and that would be perfect. In practice one is continually being polite to elderly ladies in amethyst brooches, and that is not quite the same thing, is it? Although, I imagine that every life has its amethyst brooch side. All the same, I am inclined now to prefer the English variety to any other, so I am going to settle down at Lewes Park for good, with, perhaps, a *pied à terre* in Westminster from which I can attend, when I wish to do so, the House of Lords. I am told that a certain amount of good work is done there, even in these days, and of course it is very necessary that a few of the younger peers should take their seats,' he added complacently.

They walked in silence for a little. Presently Michael said:

'Here we are at this very exquisite statue of Apollo—I had quite forgotten its existence. How civilized, how charming, is it not? I wonder why Aunt Gloria allows it to be hidden by all these dreary shrubs. It is a perfect example of French eighteenth-century sculpture, and I should never be surprised if it turned out to be a genuine Bouchardon. Most satisfying—most.'

With a slight effort he removed his gaze from the statue and let it rest on Philadelphia's upturned face.

'I am going to ask you a question,' he said, 'and I don't want an answer until I get back from Lewes Park on Tuesday. I expect you can guess what it is going to be?'

'No,' said Philadelphia, honestly enough.

'I want you to marry me, my dear.'

She was as though turned to stone with amazement. Now was Michael's opportunity. If he had taken advantage of her surprise and obvious emotion to make love to her, Philadelphia, young, beautiful and longing to be loved, would probably have accepted him there and then. Unfortunately he had only given rein to his emotions with the one woman who would be alienated by that particular form of courtship, and he thought that he had now learnt his lesson once and for all. Women evidently disliked to be rushed off their feet, they must have time to make up their minds, sentiment in all forms was clearly anathema to them. So instead of taking her in his arms as of course he should have done there and then, he said coldly and rather shyly: 'Don't think of answering me now; you will have plenty of time to consider the matter during the next few days and you can let me know when I return. I feel sure that you will realize how very well suited we are to each other in every way, and indeed I would do my best to make you happy.' With that he embarrassed her rather by kissing her on the forehead, and they went indoors.

Philadelphia parted from him in the hall and ran upstairs to her bedroom. Her mind was in a state of excitement and confusion. She had never had a proposal of marriage before, and she was now thinking less of how she intended to answer Michael than of what she should do immediately and whom she could tell the grand news to. Deciding, as she powdered her nose, that it would be awkward to see Michael again before his departure, which was imminent, and that she must tell Sally first of anybody, she stole downstairs by the back way, got out her little car, and drove over to Mulberrie Farm.

She found Sally wheeling the baby up and down the gravel path. 'The little monster hasn't been asleep the whole afternoon,' she said. 'No, talking doesn't keep her awake; in fact, it seems to send her off, on the contrary. Your odious brother is in there, inducing Walter to waste his time and lose his money at bridge. It *is* so naughty of him. I know he's not written his weekly article yet, and it ought to have gone off by this post at the latest. I wish the game had never been invented.'

'Then who's the fourth?' asked Philadelphia, who knew that, except during week-ends, when Jerome came down from London, poor Sally was usually dragged in, much against her will, to play.

'Giles Stanworth, of course, my dear. He's never out of the house now, you know, night or day. The poor man's quite batty about Amabelle, and he's having to earn his keep by learning contract. Walter's taken a packet off him already, I may say.'

'Isn't it funny? I can't imagine Major Stanworth in love with anybody.'

'Can't you just! You wait till tea-time and then watch the way he goes on. It's pathetic. But the really extraordinary thing is that I believe Amabelle rather fancies him too, I honestly think she does. Yesterday evening—' Sally broke off. She was a very discreet person where her friends were concerned, and decided that for the present she would keep the doings of yesterday evening to herself. 'I dare say we shall

317

see the old girl a farmer's wife yet,' she added hastily to cover her lapse. 'What news from Compton Bobbin?'

'Michael's motoring back to Lewes after tea.'

'He is, is he? That's no great loss anyway. I shouldn't think anyone will miss him unbearably—I never notice whether he's about or not myself, do you?'

'Not much,' said Philadelphia, rather dashed by this remark. She feared that Sally would be unimpressed by her news. There was a short silence. 'He proposed to me before he left,' she said at last.

'Delphie! You don't say so? My dear, isn't that *grand*. When are you going to announce it? Oh, you lucky girl.'

'Oh, I haven't said yes. I mean I haven't given him any answer yet, you see. I'm to think it over until he comes back.'

'But of course you'll accept, won't you?'

'I hadn't thought so. I'm not in love with him.'

'My darling Delphie, you mustn't *hesitate*. Michael is a divine person. We all adore him; he's quite perfect in every way. Attractive, intelligent, everything you could want in the world. Besides just think of all that money. Why, you could afford to have ten children if you liked.'

'That would be nice,' said Philadelphia doubtfully; 'but you see I'm not in love with him.'

'Nonsense, of course you are. One couldn't help being in love with a heavenly person like that if he wanted one to be. Besides, nobody is in love with their husbands before they marry, at least I was, but that's most exceptional. It's hardly ever done. You're not fancying anyone else, by the way, are you?'

'I don't know.'

'Of course you're not.' Sally looked relieved. 'Well, that's too lovely, darling, I do congratulate you. I wonder where you'll be married, Westminster Abbey, perhaps. Shall we go and tell the others? No, no, not unless you like, of course, but I'll tell Amabelle afterwards as a great secret, can I? And you wouldn't be an angel, I suppose, and let me sell it to the press (I mean when it's all quite settled, naturally), because I could get at least a tenner for the news, do let me have it and not

318

Bobby, please. How gorgeous of you, isn't it? I wonder what sort of ring he'll be giving you. You are a lucky girl, Delphie, I must say.'

After Sally had been working on her mind in this manner for about half an hour, Philadelphia began to regard herself quite as the future Lady Lewes, doubts and misgivings faded from her mind and she felt already a delightful new sense of her own importance. If Sally, whom she looked up to in every way, thought that it would be all right for her to marry Michael she herself would raise no further objections. Indeed, Sally had done Michael's own work for him most efficiently, and by the time that they had discussed every aspect of the wedding, from the cheering crowds outside the Abbey to the pattern of nightdress for her trousseau, Philadelphia was feeling quite romantic about him. She had some difficulty at tea-time in keeping the news to herself, and even threw out one or two hints at a mystery to which she alone had a clue, but nobody paid much attention to her. They were all busy watching the latest developments in the situation between Mrs. Fortescue and Major Stanworth.

When Philadelphia returned to Compton Bobbin she found a note from Michael on the hall table.

'MY DEAREST PHILADELPHIA,

'I couldn't find you anywhere to say good-bye. However, I shall be back again in less than a week (next Tuesday at the very latest, D.V.), and shall expect my answer then. Consider the matter very carefully, my dear, remembering that marriage is a state which once entered into, lasts the whole of one's life. I need hardly say how much I hope that you will consent to be my wife, and I truly believe that in trusting me with your future happiness you will be putting it into reliable hands. I spoke of this before I left to Aunt Gloria. Remember, dearest Philadelphia, that if you are in any doubt as to how you should act, there can be no one so well fitted to guide and advise you as your own mother.

'with love from
MICHAEL.'

This peculiar missive probably seemed less chilling to Philadelphia, who had never in her life before received a love letter, than it would have to most girls of twenty-one. On the other hand, it certainly did not arouse in her those emotions which the loved handwriting is usually supposed to evoke, and the reference to Lady Bobbin annoyed her a good deal.

Michael went to Lewes Park to settle up certain matters with his estate agent. He intended to stay there under a week. The day after he arrived, however, he caught a chill which developed into jaundice and kept him in bed for nearly a month. This circumstance very nearly altered the entire course of his life.

Before leaving Compton Bobbin he had an interview with his Aunt Gloria, during which he informed her of his intentions and hopes with regard to Philadelphia. Lady Bobbin was, of course, delighted.

'My dear Michael,' she said, almost with emotion, 'this is the best news I could possibly have. How pleased poor Hudson would have been, too. We will discuss the business side of it another time—I have to go now and speak to the huntsman about a new horse—but I may as well tell you that I have always intended to settle £2,000 a year on Philadelphia if she marries with my approval, and of course when I die she will be fairly well off. I must rush away now, so good-bye, and we meet again on Tuesday?'

'Of course she hasn't accepted me for certain yet,' said Michael with more than a touch of complacency, 'but I may say that I have little doubt that all will be well in that direction. Good-bye, then, Aunt Gloria, thank you so much for my delightful visit.'

Philadelphia herself came back from Mulberrie Farm with her mind quite made up. Sally's way of treating the whole thing as an accomplished fact had made her feel that it was so, and she only wished that Michael had not gone away and that they could begin all the exciting business, as outlined by Sally, of being engaged that very evening. She decided to answer his letter at once, begging him to return as soon as he could, and was going towards the schoolroom with this object in view when she ran into her mother.

'Oh, Philadelphia, come in here a minute. I want to speak to you. Well, darling, Michael has told me your news and I am, I need hardly say, quite delighted. It is far the best thing that could possibly have happened, and we shall be able to announce your engagement at the dance I am giving the day before Bobby goes back to Eton.'

Lady Bobbin had the somewhat unfortunate effect upon both her children of invariably provoking them to argument.

'But I haven't any intention of marrying Michael,' said Philadelphia defiantly. 'He proposed to me, certainly, but I never accepted him.'

'Then I hope that you will do so without delay,' said Lady Bobbin acidly. 'Michael spoke to me as though it was all settled.'

'He may have settled it, but I haven't.'

'You really are a very silly obstinate little girl. Michael will make you a most ideal husband. Surely you like him, don't you? What is it you have against him?'

'Yes, I like him all right, except that I think he's rather a pompous old thing,' said Philadelphia, a phrase she had borrowed from Bobby.

'Nonsense. Michael has a very proper sense of duty, of the responsibilities attached to his position in the world, and I am very glad that he has. You don't want a sort of clown and buffoon for a husband. And in any case, if you don't marry him you'll probably remain an old maid, I should think. I can't imagine that you will ever find anybody else half so suitable or so nice. And I may as well tell you, Philadelphia, while we are on this subject, that I am not obliged to settle a penny of money on you if you marry without my approval.'

'All right,' said Philadelphia sulkily, 'I'll think about it.' She left the room, tearing up Michael's letter into small pieces as she went.

In the schoolroom she found Paul, whom she had hardly seen all day.

'Your grandmother was most certainly a genius,' he said, looking up from the Journal, 'although in some respects her character was not everything that could have been wished for. But her prose seems to me even to transcend her poetry in literary merit, and her metaphysical conclusions are always faultless. Listen to this now:

'One curious and very noticeable feature of the workings of a human mind is that so often it will seize upon and stress the unimportant almost to the exclusion of anything else. This it does most especially in dreams. Last night, for example, I dreamt that I was playing in the nursery with darling Julia when, suddenly seizing her teddy-bear, which I gave her yesterday and which cost me 4s. 6d. in the Baker Street Bazaar, she flung herself upon the blazing fire and was burnt to a cinder. In the dream (and this illustrates my point) I was worried far less by the extinction of poor Julia than by that of the bear, and I wandered about saying very sorrowfully, "It was a four-and-sixpenny bear".'

'Funny reading that just now,' Paul went on, 'because last night I had just such a dream myself. Would you like to hear it?'

Philadelphia stifled the feeling of acute boredom which comes over those about to hear the dreams of others, and said that she would.

'Well, it was a very odd dream indeed. You and I and Michael were going down to Brighton for the wedding of the Prince Regent to Mrs. Fitzherbert. We took first-class return tickets. But when we arrived at the Pavilion, where the wedding was to be held, we found that all the people there were French, and dressed in clothes of the time of Louis XIV, and Michael was very much put out by this. He said to me, loudly and angrily, "This is really too much. These people to begin with are not English, most of them don't know the Regent, even by sight, and they haven't had the common decency to dress in the proper clothes of the period. Besides, Sheridan isn't here, and Mrs. Fitzherbert has gone off to the Y.W.C.A. in a rage. I don't blame her, I must say, but I do feel annoyed that we have been dragged all the way down here, first-class for nothing." So we all came straight back to London, first-class.

'Now in the whole of that dream, which was long and quite involved, I was only really impressed by one important fact, which was that we travelled first-class. I woke up with the words "first-class" on my lips, and can still, although the rest of the dream has practically faded from my mind, see most clearly in my imagination the upholstered seats with arms, clean white lace antimacassars and little views of Bath and Wells in our first-class carriage.'

'Very strange,' said Philadelphia, burning the pieces of Michael's letter. Life itself, she thought, as she went upstairs to dress for dinner, was stranger than dreams and far, far more disordered.

'Jerome,' said Amabelle.

Jerome looked up from his weekly, rather shamefaced, perusal of *The Tatler*.

'Yes, Amabelle?'

'I've got some news to tell you.'

'What's that, my dear?'

'I'm going to marry Giles Stanworth.'

'Oh, my God,' said Jerome, and buried his face in his hands.

'Amabelle—it isn't true, is it?' he said, a minute later; 'you don't really mean it, do you?'

'Yes, you know, it's quite true. The banns are going to be called to-morrow in the village church—not in this village, because Giles says the parson here is really a papist, but in Hogrush. It's jolly exciting, don't you think? We're being married at the beginning of February, down here. I shall wear a hat, of course, and we both hope that you'll give me away, darling.'

'I shall do no such thing.'

'Then Bobby will have to.'

'Are you off your head, Amabelle? I really never heard such scandalous nonsense in all my life. Only think of that poor man dragged up to Portman Square, out of his element, wretched, bored—'

'I don't think of it for a moment. Giles would never leave his precious farm, not even for me; besides, I shouldn't ask him to. I'm looking forward to living in the country myself.'

'My dear, you are being a little bit childish, aren't you?'

'No, darling, not in the least. However, I suppose I had better explain the situation to you quite clearly, then perhaps you'll see my point of view for once. First of all, then, I happen to be very fond of Giles, and I adore his little boy.'

'If you're so anxious to be married, why not marry Michael?'

'Because Michael bores me into fits, and I don't like being laughed at by my friends and acquaintances. People always laugh when a woman marries someone fifteen years younger than herself, quite right, too.'

'I don't understand why you want to marry at all. Aren't you happy?'

'If you would listen to me for one single minute—'

'Oh, all right, go on.'

'The real point is, old boy, that I am forty-five. You didn't know that, did you? Still, there it is. Now what happens to women like me, unattached but not unattractive women, when they are over forty-five? It's very tricky, I can tell you. They gradually begin to get taken up by boys at Oxford, who rather like being seen about with them and all that, but who really regard them as a cross between a fortune-teller, a nanny, and an interesting historical character who has somehow managed to live on until the present day. I've seen it happen over and over again, haven't you, honestly? And at about fifty-five or so people start saying, "How *wonderful* Amabelle looks for her age. Of course she must be well over seventy now, why, when I was a girl she was quite an old woman." It's an awful, and, as far as I can see, an inevitable fate, and it seems to me more dignified to retire before it overtakes one.'

'I think you are wrong,' said Jerome. 'You have been feeling depressed, I suppose, and no wonder in this ghastly house, but that is no reason for making such a terrible mistake. You'll be miserable, bored and miserable living down here always. Giles Stanworth is very nice, of course, I think he is charming, but what interests have you in common?'

'The Fluke, for one. You wouldn't believe how passionately I am interested in the Fluke. There is another fascinating disease called the staggers too, he tells me; horses have that. Then the rotation of crops—'

'Can't you be serious for one minute?' cried Jerome in

exasperation. 'I see nothing to joke about in the fact that you are jeopardizing your whole future happiness for a crazy idea like this. Look here, Amabelle, if you must marry, marry me.'

'Darling Jerome, you *are* sweet. But what would Mrs. Nickle say?' Mrs. Nickle had been Jerome's housekeeper for twenty years. 'No, no, my dear, that would never do. Besides, strange though it may seem to you, I actually do want to marry Giles; and as nothing that you can say will stop me you might just as well look pleasant and wish me happiness.'

'I may be dense, but I still don't see the point in taking this step. It's no good pretending to me that you are passionately in love with Giles Stanworth, or anything so silly as that.'

'Actually I am rather in love with him. But that's neither here nor there. The point, as I've told you already, is that I don't want to be taken up by Oxford undergraduates.'

'I think you exaggerate the danger of these youths, the modern young man is not quite so importunate as perhaps you may imagine.'

'No, that's just it, one wouldn't mind so much if he were. It's the maiden aunt relationship that I object to more than anything.'

'You're incorrigible, Amabelle.'

'Pig-headed, you mean. Anyhow, you might wish me luck, old boy.'

'I do—I do. Oh, how bored you'll be after about six months of country life.'

'You said that before, if you remember, when I took this house. Actually I was at first, terribly bored for about a day, but since then I've enjoyed myself top-hole.'

'For a few weeks, yes. You've had people to amuse you and so on. But think of months and years on that awful farm.'

'It isn't awful at all. It's a sweet little house. I think I shall adore being a farmer's wife. I intend to have a still room and make my own face creams out of herbs, and Giles has lent me a book of sillabubs and flummery caudles and all sorts of art and craft food, and did you know before that ye rhubarbe maketh to go to ye privy? I bet you didn't.'

The news of Amabelle's engagement spread like wildfire

326

after the banns had been read out in church the following Sunday. Bobby came round in a state of high excitement, and after kissing her repeatedly he said to Major Stanworth:

'Amabelle has always been in love with me really, of course, and that's why she's going to marry you, simply in order to live near Compton Bobbin. Darling, darling, you ought to have seen mummy's face in church! She said afterwards, "Poor Giles, I must say I never imagined that he would end up by marrying a woman of the demimonde, but I suppose she has got him into her clutches like so many others. It will be a finisher for him."'

Major Stanworth got rather red. Although by his own lights he was an exceptionally broadminded man, he never could quite accustom himself to hearing Amabelle's friends refer in this light-hearted way to her past.

'You heard what mother said to Auntie Loudie,' went on the tactless child. 'You see apparently she found out somehow that I know you quite well, and she was talking it over with Auntie Loudie, who was divine as usual, and said nothing matters for boys in that sort of way, and mother agreed with her more or less, and finally she said, "Anyhow I am told it costs £10,000 to sleep with Mrs. Fortescue, so I suppose it's all right for Bobby to go over there sometimes."'

'Your mother can't know much about the state of the market in these days,' observed Amabelle drily.

'However, she said at lunch that she will receive you when you're married for Giles' sake, because she always stands by her friends in their misfortunes. It's one of her boasts, like changing for dinner in the bush—she's white all through, my mother is. And she's going to the wedding with the whole hunt, they'll meet at the church and play "gone to ground" over you on the horn and everything. It will be a riot, won't it?'

'Won't it just?' said Amabelle delightedly. 'Will you be able to get away from Eton for it, my sweet?'

'Well, I've been thinking about that. May I be best man? Then they'll simply have to give me leave.'

'No, you may not,' said Giles Stanworth.

19

'I love you, I love you, I love you, I love you, I love you, I love you, I love you, I love you,' said Paul. 'I love you. And if there were anything more to say I should say it, but there isn't, really.'

'Oh, isn't there just,' said Philadelphia rather tartly, drawing herself to the other end of the sofa and smoothing down her ruffled hair. 'Personally, I should have thought there was a good deal more that you might have said by now.'

'That only shows that you don't love me as much as I love you, my sweet poppet.'

'Yes, I do. Much more, as a matter of fact.'

'What makes you think that?'

'For one thing I've never loved anybody in my life before.'

'Nor have I.'

'What about Marcella then?'

'Oh, Marcella! She never meant a thing to me, not a thing. I thought she was rather attractive, but as for loving her—'

'And Susan and Elizabeth and Sheila and Sonia and Rosemary and Joan and Veronica?'

'Sally's been talking to you. I think it's very naughty and horrid of her. I promise you I never cared for any of those girls in the way I care for you. No other woman will ever be the same to me, you're something quite special in my life, quite apart.'

'Well, I believe you, darling, though I expect it's very silly of me to, and you must see it's a risk I'm taking. In any case, it's time we began to think of what we're going to do next.'

'Darling, don't be so practical. Everything will be all right in the end, I promise you it will, only don't fuss.'

'But I am fussing. Here we've been engaged for two whole days, and you've done nothing about it except to kiss me on the sofa and tell me lies about other girls you've been in love with.'

'But, my darling, what d'you expect me to do?'

'I expect you to take steps.'

'What steps?'

'Oh, you are maddening.'

'Yes, but really, what steps? I'm going to marry you, my precious, and that's taking a big step, I should have thought.'

'Marry me!' cried Philadelphia in despair. 'I know, so you say, but how—how—how? How are you going to tell mother, how do you intend to support me; above all, how am I to get disengaged from Michael? You don't seem to realize that if he hadn't caught jaundice, by the mercy of Providence, he would have been back again yesterday, ring and all.'

'I can see quite plainly that you've been talking about this to Sally,' said Paul sulkily, 'and if it goes on I shall be obliged to tell your mother that as soon as her back is turned you are off like greased lightning to Mulberrie Farm. She'll soon put a stop to that.'

'Paul, darling, do you love me?'

'Yes, I do.'

'Then go and tell mother that we're engaged.'

'I'm going to, to-morrow morning.'

'You said that yesterday.'

'I know I did. I felt so awful this morning that I simply couldn't face it. There were brains for breakfast again, and the sight of them always upsets me. But to-morrow I'm going to be brave and heroic. And you're going to write to Michael, aren't you, and I'm going to write a best-seller about your great-grandmother, and we shall be as happy as the day is long, you'll see. So give me a kiss and stop bothering, won't you?'

'No, I won't. Will you go and tell mother this evening as soon as she comes in from hunting?'

'Darling, please not. You don't know the effect your mother has on my nerves; it's positively uncanny. I shiver and shake like an aspirin leaf, whatever that may be.'

'Have a whisky and soda first.'

'That wouldn't really do. Supposing she smelt my breath, like the police in motor accidents?'

'Well, when do you intend to tell her?'

'Darling, you're not being just a shade governessy, are you? If you really want to know, I don't see very much point in telling her at all. It will only mean that I shall have to leave by the next train if I do. Imagine my position. "Oh, Lady Bobbin, by the way, my name is Fotheringay, not Fisher, and I've been here all this time under false pretences, and I've never done a stroke of work with Bobby, but instead I've been collecting material for the life you don't want me to write of Lady Maria, and I should like to marry your daughter, but as I haven't any money I should be glad if you would pay off just a few of my more pressing debts and buy me a tail coat to be married in as I've rather grown out of my old Eton one." It doesn't sound too well, you know.'

'Oh, Paul, whatever are we to do?'

'"The glory of man is in being, not in doing."'

Philadelphia burst into angry tears.

'Don't cry now, darling. Everything will be all right, you'll see.'

'Let's go and ask Amabelle what she thinks, shall we?'

'Oh, very well, if you like. Anything to stop you crying. Not that I imagine she'll be much good to us, but still—'

They found Amabelle wringing her hands in front of the drawing-room fire at Mulberrie Farm. There was a strong smell of bananas in the room.

'It's all right,' she said. 'This is not a sign of mental anguish. Giles hasn't given me the raspberry or anything like that. I've just been varnishing my nails, and I simply can't get them to dry.' And she fell to wringing her hands with even greater vigour than before. 'I wanted particularly to see you, Philadelphia. Walter and Sally left for the south of France yesterday in a wild hurry. Someone was paying for them, and the poor sweets think it will cost them nothing. Sally was miserable she couldn't say good-bye, and left a thousand messages. They're only going for a couple of weeks, but you see they won't be coming back here again as I'm off to

London myself on Saturday to buy my trousseau, dear, for the farm. I think of having corduroy trousers like the ones that Giles wears; they ought to be quite attractive. Lucky I've kept my figure, isn't it? Where's Bobby, by the way?'

'He's staying with Bunch for a shoot; he'll be back to-morrow.'

'Send him along, will you? I want to see him before I go. I don't suppose I shall get out of it under a fiver, but still. *What* it will save me in tips when that child goes to Oxford.'

'Amabelle, we really came to ask your advice about something.'

'Oh, did you just?'

'Paul and I are engaged to be married.'

'I know; Sally told me. You don't expect me to congratulate you or anything like that, do you?'

'I think you're being rather unkind; it's nearly always done, isn't it? And anyway, why not?'

'Because it is no matter for congratulations, my poor sweet. I suppose you think you are in love with each other?'

'We don't think it. We are in love,' said Paul defiantly. He had an idea of what Amabelle was going to say next.

'Then how can I possibly congratulate you? You must both know quite well that this marriage is practically an impossibility. At the best you have endless fusses and bothers in front of you; Lady Bobbin will, very naturally, refuse to give you any money. Paul has nothing but debts, you will both have to be terribly worried and unhappy for ages before you can be married, and miserably poor, probably for years, afterwards. Not a very enchanting prospect, to my mind.'

'Look how poor Walter and Sally are,' said Philadelphia. 'They couldn't be worse off, but they are the two happiest people I've ever seen.'

'Walter and Sally are very exceptional. I am inclined even to think that they are unique; anyhow, I personally have never come across another case like theirs in my life. Nothing that could happen would ever make the smallest difference to their feeling for each other. I suppose a love of that sort can be found once in a generation. I don't want to seem unkind, because I am very fond of you both, but I very much doubt whether either you or Paul has the character which is needed to sustain such a relationship—you won't believe me, of course. It's a funny thing that people are always quite ready to admit it if they've no talent for drawing or music, whereas everyone imagines that they themselves are capable of true love, which is a talent like any other, only far more rare. I don't doubt, mind you, that if Paul were an eligible young man and if you could be married in the usual way without any trouble, you would probably be quite happy. I only say that as things are it's impossible.'

'Oh, Amabelle,' cried Philadelphia, 'unkind, unkind! I thought that you at least would be able to advise us.'

'If you really want my advice here it is, but you won't like it much. Don't say a word to anybody; don't let your mother or Bobby suspect a thing, but have a lovely time together till next week, when Paul is going away in any case. Then, as soon as Michael has finished having jaundice, announce your engagement to him. Please believe me when I say that you'll be very happy with him. I know Michael so well and I feel sure of it. He'll take you for a gorgeous honeymoon, all round the world perhaps, and when you get back you'll settle down at that exquisite Lewes Park and have some nice babies, and entertain a lot, and be the best-dressed marchioness in England. I don't know how you can hesitate, I really don't.'

Philadelphia began to cry again.

'Thank you for nothing,' said Paul loudly and angrily. 'Look how you've upset my poor darling Delphie. Don't cry, my precious; you shan't marry that old bore, he'd drive you mad in a week. I thought at least you would have shown us some sympathy, Amabelle, but I suppose it's too much to expect even that. You women are all the same, a lot of blasted matchmakers, that's what you are.'

'Paul, Paul, don't be so bitter. You must have known that I of all people would take the common sense point of view. Just think for a moment; use your intelligence, my dear. You and Philadelphia have known each other for exactly three weeks. You both think, honestly I'm sure, that you are ready to undergo almost intolerable hardships over a period of years, and possibly for life, in order to be able to remain in each other's company. I say that it would be much easier, more to your mutual advantage and eventual happiness, if you could bring yourselves to part now and lead different lives. That's all.'

'Of course,' said Philadelphia, sniffing rather loudly, 'my mother would probably give us some sort of allowance once we were actually married; she'd be obliged to, really.'

'I doubt it very much,' said Amabelle; 'from what I know of your mother's character I should think it most unlikely. At present she naturally wishes you to marry Michael; when you tell her of your engagement to Paul she will be furious, and doubly so when she discovers the trick that has been played on her all this time. Think of her feelings when you tell her that he is not only not Mr. Fisher, but actually that Mr. Fotheringay whom she refused to have in the house!'

'Yes, that's awful, I must say,' said Paul.

'And what will happen? Angry words will pass of the sort that can never, never be forgotten, and you will find yourselves faced with the alternative of eloping on the spot and living on Paul's £300 a year' (Amabelle had an amazing faculty for knowing to a penny the incomes of her friends) 'or of staying at home and leading an incredibly drab and dreary life, more or less in disgrace with your mother, until he can make enough money to support you in moderate comfort, which, as far as I can see, will be never.'

'Oh, God!' said Paul.

'I'm sorry to be so depressing, but I say again, for heaven's sake, marry Michael. If you don't I see nothing but trouble ahead for you, my poor Philadelphia.'

'Now listen to me, Amabelle,' said Philadelphia, with unexpected firmness. 'I am not going to marry Michael, and I *am* going to marry Paul. Get that clear, and then tell me what I ought to do about it.'

Amabelle frowned. She was incapable of seeing Philadelphia's point of view, and thought that the child was being merely obstinate.

'Thank heaven I haven't got a daughter,' she said impatiently. 'However, if you really mean what you say, I consider there is only one course open to you. Refuse Michael, giving no reason for doing so, keep all this a deadly secret (and by that I mean a secret—no hints or half-confessions to anybody, you understand) and wait for a few months while Paul finds some good, steady job. Then let Bobby go to your mother, tell her the whole story and ask her to give you enough money to be married; he is much more likely to get round her than you are, I imagine. By then she will have lost all hope of Michael as a son-in-law and may be quite anxious to get you off, even to somebody as ineligible as Paul. Only it's essential that he should first get a proper job and keep it for a few months. That seems to me your only possible hope. And of course, Paul, it goes without saying that you must give up the idea of publishing Lady Maria's life, anyhow, until you have got a good marriage settlement tucked away.'

Paul and Philadelphia looked glum. The prospect of a glamorous elopement was far more attractive to them than a course of action which necessitated on his part the daily grind of some regular job, so long and so studiously avoided by him, and on hers the indefinite continuation of her present dreary life. However, they could not but admit that this was the most sensible course to follow, and both felt immensely relieved that it would not, at present, be necessary to beard Lady Bobbin in her den.

'Thank you, dear Amabelle,' said Philadelphia. 'I think you are quite right, although it will be terrible to wait all that time. Still, it won't be so bad when you come to live here for good.'

'Of course not,' said Amabelle cheerfully. 'I'll have Paul to stay every week-end, and I expect Walter and Sally will be down sometimes, so it won't be nearly as lonely for you at Compton Bobbin as it used to be. All the same, I think you're making a terrible mistake, my dear, in refusing Michael. I shall never alter my opinion about that.'

Paul said, as they walked back to Compton Bobbin, 'I'll tell

334

you what I'll do. My Uncle Joseph has some ghastly sort of business in the city. I'll make him give me a job, he has offered to before. I see what Amabelle means; your mother is far more likely to come round to the idea of our marriage if she thinks I have definite work. People of that generation are so extraordinary in those ways; they don't care about self-expression or any of the things that really matter. So long as one has a good solid and respectable job they are quite satisfied about one. The truth is that they have misused leisure themselves for so long that they think of it as a bad thing for anybody to have. Never mind, I will crucify myself for your sake, sweet one, on an office stool, for a month or two anyway, until we see what happens. Something is sure to turn up, it always does. It's a bit souring about Lady Maria all the same. I was looking forward to publishing that.'

'Darling, I hate to think of you making such a sacrifice.'

'There's no sacrifice I wouldn't make for you, darling. Besides, the moment we're married I shall bring it out and show the world that I'm a serious writer of the front rank.'

'Paul, I do love you.'

'Darling, darling Philadelphia. How do you manage to be so heavenly with a mother like that?'

'I believe daddy was rather sweet.'

'That accounts for it then, no doubt.'

As soon as Bobby got back from his shoot he went round to see Amabelle.

'What's all this nonsense about Paul and Delphie?' he said accusingly.

'Oh, so you know about it by now, do you? Who told you?'

'Nobody told me, but I should have to be as dense as my mother seems to be if I couldn't see with half an eye what's happening. They sit holding hands on the drawing-room sofa all day, and Delphie keeps on throwing out dark hints about how wonderful it is to be in love and all that sort of thing. It can only be a matter of moments now before mummy tumbles to it, I should think, and then there'll be the devil to pay.'

'Didn't I know those silly children would never be able to

335

keep it quiet? And what view do you take of the whole thing, Bobby? You needn't tell me, darling. I can guess.'

'Well, naturally, I think it's quite crazy. I only hope and pray that Delphie won't ruin her chances of marrying Michael by her idiocy, that's all. Thank heaven he's out of the way for the present. As for Paul, I really do think it's a bit hard he should behave like this after all the trouble I've taken for him.'

'I must say I agree with you for once,' said Amabelle. 'They came over yesterday to confess it all and ask my advice, and I'm afraid I was rather unkind to them. I've seen Paul wildly in love with too many people to take that very seriously, and as for Philadelphia, why at her age one is in love every other week. I gather that Michael made a mess of everything as usual. He had only to go about it with a little ordinary sense and she'd have been crazy about him by now. Really that young man, I've no patience at all with him; he behaves like a very unconvincing character in a book, not like a human being at all.'

'Yes, doesn't he. The sort of book of which the reviewers would say "the characterization is weak; the central figure, Lord Lewes, never really coming to life at all; but there are some fine descriptive passages of Berkshire scenery." What did you say to Delphie?'

'I told her she was mad not to marry Michael, and then she began to cry, and I really hadn't the heart to go on. I finally told them that if they intend to marry in spite of everything they must keep this affair a deadly secret until Paul has some satisfactory job. Of course they'll do neither the one thing nor the other. They are evidently not capable of keeping a secret, and I can no more imagine Paul in a job than a fly.'

'Good gracious, no; he'd never stick to it for a day.'

'I suppose, in point of fact, that if they did marry your mother would have to give them some sort of allowance, but it's much better that they shouldn't think so, because Paul, who must, after all, have a good idea of what poverty means, isn't likely to elope with her unless he can be fairly certain that there will be some money eventually.'

'Paul's not mercenary, you know,' said Bobby.

'Not in the least, but he's not an absolute fool either. I doubt if he'd risk such a thing, for her sake as well as his own. The worst of it is that I don't believe, apart from the money side of it, that they would be particularly happy together. They are really most unsuited. Paul needs somebody who is very strong-minded and who will manage him. Why, even that repellent girl, Marcella, would be a better wife for him. As for Philadelphia, the darling, she is obviously cut out to have money and position.'

'And I shall do my very best to see that she gets both,' said Bobby with one of his self-conscious smiles. 'What a fund of common sense you are, darling. You've cheered me up enormously. What is my line for the moment, then?'

'You must do all you can to keep this nonsense a secret from your mother. If she finds out it will be fatal. She'll probably say a lot of bitter and unkind things to both of them and as likely as not drive them straight into an elopement. If it can be kept from her I give the whole thing three months at the most before it fizzles out.'

'That ought to be easy. Paul goes away in less than a week now, when I trail back to the old col., and mother is still out hunting most of the time. Besides, several people are coming to stay here over the week-end for this bogus dance she will insist on having. I dare say she won't notice anything much; she's been as blind as a bat so far.'

'We can only hope for the best,' said Amabelle, who was looking out of the window. 'Hullo, here comes my fiancé— whatever is he carrying? Oh, I say, isn't that rather sweet, d'you see; he's bringing two dead hens for the kitchen; he always has some exquisite present for me, the angel.'

'Well, I'll be off,' said Bobby, rather sourly; 'and I don't suppose, if you're really going to London, that I shall see you again until after you're married, which is too awful. Look here, darling, will you promise to go and choose yourself a present at Cartier? I've got an account there, so get something really nice, won't you, not a diamond hen, though, if you don't mind.'

20

The dance at Compton Bobbin was in no way a riot of joyous and abandoned merriment; it was, in fact, even more dreary an entertainment than might have been anticipated, and was long afterwards remembered by Cotswold beaux and belles as 'that frightful party at the Bobbins'. When the guests arrived, cold and dazzled after a long motor drive, they found neither the cheering strains of Terpsichore nor the sustaining draught of Bacchus awaiting them. The young man from Woodford who had been engaged to provide the former came very late indeed, so that for quite half-an-hour the guests stood about in uncertain groups, while Paul and Squibby struggled to make the wireless work. When finally he did arrive, breathless and apologetic, having left his car upside down in a ditch, his playing proved to be of that sort which induces sleep rather than revelry by night. Lady Bobbin had remained true to her resolution that in *her* house there should be no champagne during the national crisis, and on every hand could soon be heard the groans and curses with which British youth greets the absence of any alcohol more fortifying than beer at its parties. The rare and somewhat tipsy appearances downstairs of Bobby, the duchess, and such of their intimates as were secretly invited to the cocktail bar provided by Bobby in his bedroom, merely accentuated the wretched sobriety of the other guests.

The duchess and Héloïse were staying with Bunch for this occasion, as also were Squibby, Biggy and Maydew. The two latter, however, had most ungallantly refused to attend the dance, giving as their excuse that they always felt sick in motor cars. Everybody else was quite well aware that they really wished to stay at home in order to play Brahms on two pianos. As a result of this monstrous behaviour the girls who had been invited by Bunch solely on their behalf spent the greater part of the evening sitting drearily together in the hall. This fact appeared to weigh rather on the duchess, who, as their chaperone, felt that she ought to feel some responsibility for their amusement.

'Those wretched girls,' she kept saying, in the intervals of helping Bobby to mix the cocktails, 'oughtn't I to do something about them? Shall we have them up here, darling?'

'Oh, don't let's. They look so gloomy, and there's hardly enough drink to go round as it is. Anyways, I expect they enjoy being together down there.'

'Of course they don't; they look furious, and I don't blame them either. I think it's simply odious of Biggy and Maydew to get them asked down and then stay behind like that. If I were Lady Tarradale I should be quite furious, especially as they're certain to keep her awake all night with their awful music, and she's been so wretchedly ill lately. Those poor charming girls, looking so sweet in their pink and green, too. I do feel badly about them. Do go and see if they're all right, Bobby, won't you?'

'Darling, you know they're not all right, so why bother? Besides, they're Bunch's guests, not mine. Let him look after them.'

'Bunch has got his own girl here, Sonia Beckett. You can't expect him to do more than dance about once with each of the others. Hullo, Héloïse, darling. Come here, sweetest, I want to whisper. Angel, is it quite necessary for you to wander about with four young men when poor Rosemary and Laetitia have no one at all to talk to them?'

'I don't think anyone wants to talk to them,' said Héloïse; 'they're such cracking bores, aren't they? Give me a cocktail, darling, quickly. This party is quite the bloodiest I've ever been to, personally. How right Biggy and Maydew were to stay behind. I do envy them, don't you?'

'Squibby dear,' said the duchess, waving an empty glass at Bobby as she spoke, 'just tell me something. Have you seen

Rosemary and Laetitia latishly? Are they all right, the sweet poppets?'

'Oh, yes,' said the heartless Squibby. 'I expect so. Sure to be. I saw them having a very jolly little chat with Lady Prague just now.'

'You don't think it would be rather nice if you went and saw how they were getting on?'

'Well, Aunt Loudie, I don't think I need. I'd much rather stay and talk to you. In any case, I've danced with both of them and they are nothing to do with me. It was Biggy and Maydew who insisted on having them asked down.'

Paul and Philadelphia spent most of the evening shut up together in the linen cupboard, bemoaning the fact that tomorrow they must be parted, and reiterating that they intended to be faithful to each other during the months to come.

'Darling, when I think,' said Philadelphia, her voice shaking, 'of all those lovely girls you go out with in London I do feel so terrified that you'll soon forget all about me.'

'I shan't do that. I tell you that you have quite a special place in my heart, and you always will have. Wherever I am I shall be thinking about you the whole time. I expect I shall go about with other girls, because it would be a mistake not to, but they won't mean anything to me really. You are, and always will be, the only woman in my life. I shall never feel about anybody as I do about you. You're perfect, to me.'

The fact that Paul had repeated this sentence, word for word, to at least three other women, did not prevent him, as he said it, from sincerely believing it to be the truth.

'But I feel terrified too,' he went on, 'that you'll decide to give me up after all and marry Michael instead. Remember, I shall never blame you in the least if you do. It would probably be much more sensible. But to me you are the only woman—'

At this juncture the duchess opened the linen cupboard door and popped her head round the corner.

'Oh, you darlings,' she said delightedly, 'I'm so glad somebody's having a lovely time. It does me good to see you. You've no idea what it's been like everywhere else, too

340

gloomy and awful for words. Now, when you've quite finished being happy together in there we've got some cocktails in Bobby's room, so mind you come along and join us.'

She shut the door carefully and went, bursting with her news, back to Bobby.

'There they were, *locked* in each other's arms. I can't tell you how sweet they looked—the lambs. Quite frankly, I never should have thought Philadelphia had so much sense. I must ask her to stay as soon as ever we get back from Switzerland.'

'Now don't you start encouraging her,' said Bobby crossly. 'Amabelle and I are working like niggers to stop all this nonsense and make her get engaged to Michael.'

'Oh, *no,* you awful child, you can't behave like a match-making mamma at your age; it's not natural. For heaven's sake let the poor girl have her fun, besides, it's so good for her. Just think how pretty she's looking now. She is a different being from what she was a month ago.'

'I'm all in favour of her having as much fun as she likes,' said Bobby, 'so long as she'll be sensible and not go on with all this ridiculous talk about marriage—just think, if Michael heard about it, he might quite easily be put off for good.'

'You don't seriously want her to marry Michael, do you? He's such a fearful bore. I wouldn't allow a daughter of mine to marry him, however much she wanted to.'

'That's just very silly and naughty of you, darling Auntie Loudie, because a girl's first husband must be eligible, otherwise she will very soon go downhill altogether. Amabelle agrees with me.'

'Amabelle is so frightfully pompous in these days,' said the duchess with a hiccough. 'I can remember the time when she was just an ordinary tart (a very successful one and all that, of course) and then she really was the greatest fun. We used to go secretly to her parties and think we were being absolute dare-devils, but ever since she married old James Fortescue she's been twice as much of a duchess as I am. It's a great pity, because in those days she used to be too heavenly.'

'I think she is still,' said Bobby stoutly. 'She's one of the sweetest people in the world. Look how divine she has been to the Monteaths ever since that baby was born.'

'Yes, I agree she is very sweet and kind, she always has been. I'm only saying that she's no longer such absolutely rollicking fun. In any case, I think it's absurd for her to take that line about Delphie. Why surely the child is rich enough to marry anybody she likes.'

'She's only rich so long as my mother chooses to make her an allowance.'

'Clearly. But I suppose that even darling Gloria could hardly see her own daughter starve. I don't understand what there is against Paul myself. He seems an exceptionally nice young man, good-looking, polite, everything one could want for a son-in-law.'

'Well, to begin with, if you'd really like to know, his name isn't Fisher at all.'

'Oh?'

'It's Fotheringay, Paul Fotheringay.'

'My dear, that's a much nicer name than Fisher. Most romantic, too. One of Henry VIII's wives was executed at a place called that. I remember all about it in English history.'

'Darling, I don't think you quite understand. His real name, as I said before, is Paul Fotheringay, and he is masquerading here under the alias of Fisher.'

'How divinely thrilling. Wait a moment, though, wasn't there somebody called Paul Fotheringay who wrote that screamingly funny book about pawnbrokers trying to commit suicide?'

'Yes, that's his book, *Crazy Capers*.'

'Oh, but I've never laughed so much at anything before in my life. Wait a minute while I rush to the linen cupboard— it's too bad, I haven't my copy here for him to autograph. It *was* a heavenly book. Bobby, you little monster, why ever didn't you tell me this before?'

'You see he's here in disguise really,' said Bobby, unbending a little, 'because he wants to write the life of Lady Maria. He asked mother in a letter whether he could borrow

342

the journal, and she wrote back awfully rudely, so then he got taken on as my tutor and ever since then he has been studying it for his book.'

'Well I should think that will be a scream,' said the duchess. 'Delphie will be mad if she doesn't marry him, but if she doesn't I shall, that's all. What I do adore is a really good sense of humour. The funny thing is that though I've liked Paul from the very beginning he never struck me as being so particularly amusing, but of course that must have been entirely my own fault. Shake up one more cocktail, won't you, Bobby, my sweet—here's Héloïse back again. Dear, what a pudding-faced young man she has got with her this time. Where can she have picked him up? Héloïse, what do you think, Philadelphia and Paul have been sitting out for more than two hours in the linen cupboard.'

'Oh, where—can I see?'

'No, certainly you can't. It's nothing whatever to do with you. I may say I'm surprised you've not been in there yourself.'

'If Maydew had come I don't doubt I should have been,' said Héloïse, 'but all the young men here seem to be so sexless. I honestly don't think I've ever been to such an awful party as this in my life. Can I introduce Mr. Wainscote to you, by the way. He has been to a lot of jolly shows lately in London, and I expect he'd like a cocktail, Bobby.'

'As a matter of fact,' said Mr. Wainscote, blushing, 'the rest of my party is very anxious to go home—I mean,' he added hurriedly, looking at Bobby, 'ready to leave. We have all enjoyed ourselves immensely, but we have a long cold drive before us, so I think that perhaps I should say good-bye,' and he edged out of the room sideways like a crab.

'My darling Hèloïse, what an extraordinary young man,' said the duchess.

'He's not at all extraordinary,' said Héloïse, 'unless you mean extraordinarily attractive. I'm rather in love with him myself,' and she looked under long blue eyelashes at Bobby.

'No cop, old girl, you can't lead me on like that. I know you're in a temper because I haven't spoken to you the whole

343

evening, but there's no point in making a fool of yourself just the same. Have another cegocktegail?'

'I degon't megind egif egI dego,' said Héloïse, happily settling herself on the edge of the bed. 'Now run along downstairs, mother, if you don't mind, because I want to kiss Bobby.'

'All right, I'll go and see how Rosemary and Laetitia are getting on. Have a lovely time, and don't be too long.'

Shortly after this, Bobby himself came downstairs, and revolted by the sights and sounds of cheerlessness which greeted his eyes, thoughtfully turned out the electric light at the main, thus breaking up the party. By the flickering rays of the only candle that Compton Bobbin possessed, coats were found, adieux were said, and, grumbling to the last, the flower of Gloucestershire man and maidenhood climbed into their Morris Cowleys and drove away.

This contretemps postponed but did not avert Lady Bobbin's furious upbraiding of Bobby and Philadelphia, who, having disappeared at the first dance on the programme, had never been seen again mingling with their guests.

'I know it's all Louisa's fault,' she said angrily, 'and I'm damned if I'll go on having that woman to the house. I'm sick and tired of her rudeness, and as for that little—Héloïse, I'd much sooner neither of you had any more to do with her.'

Paul and Philadelphia parted the next day with tears and promises of eternal fidelity. Their farewells were rendered slightly more bearable than they would otherwise have been by the fact that Aunt Loudie, having given them the only moral support they had as yet received, had promised that she would invite Philadelphia to stay in London as soon as she herself should return from Switzerland.

'See you very soon, my darling,' said Paul, as they stood on Woodford platform waiting for his train.

'Yes, darling. And mind you write to me.'

'Of course I will, every day. And mind you do, too. Take care of yourself, my precious, and don't worry too much. Everything will come all right in the end, you'll see.'

'I don't know,' said Philadelphia, miserably.

'Now come on,' said Bobby impatiently as the train came to a standstill, 'jump in, Paul—good-bye, Delphie, come and see me at Eton some time, old girl. Don't let them forget to send on my letters and parcels. Good-bye—good-bye.'

To Philadelphia, left alone on the cold, wet and empty platform, it seemed as though all happiness had come to an end. She cried so much that she could hardly see to drive her car home.

Paul and Bobby lounged luxuriously in their first-class carriage (it was one of Bobby's talents that he could always travel first-class on a third-class ticket), and argued as to whether they should lunch at the Ritz or the Berkeley, and what film they should go to afterwards. At Oxford they got out and bought all the illustrated papers. Paul felt agreeably sentimental and wretched, but he was glad, on the whole, to be going back to London. The only drawback was that he had promised Philadelphia to look for work, a pastime that he detested, and worse still, to do work if he found it. Much would he have preferred to settle down in a desultory manner to his life of Lady Maria Bobbin. However, he put these unpleasant thoughts from him without any difficulty and was soon deep in perusal of *The Tatler*.

Philadelphia wandered about Compton Bobbin like a lost soul. She could find no comfort in her situation. It was typical, she thought again, of the malignant spirit which apparently controlled her destiny to cram just one month of her life with fascinating people and events, only to remove them all in a single day, leaving in their place a few memories to make everything seem flatter, more dreary than before. Paul had gone, Sally and Walter had gone for ever, Amabelle would not, it appeared, be back before Easter—her plans for a country wedding had been altered; she now intended to get married quietly in London as soon as the lambing season should be over and go to her villa on the Riviera for the honeymoon.

Philadelphia found herself once more without any occupation or interests, and for the rest of that day she sat before the fire in an arm-chair, assailed by the ghastly boredom only known to those who live in the country but have no love for country pursuits, and no intellectual resources on which they can fall back. And in the clutches of that boredom, too boring even to describe, she remained during the weeks to come. She would get up in the morning as late as she dared, and read the papers over and over again, hoping to pass the time until luncheon. In the afternoon she would go for a little walk, and when she came in from that would sit or wander aimlessly about the house, waiting for tea. After tea she would perhaps try to read some improving work suggested to her by Michael, or, more often, play canfield on the schoolroom table (if this comes out it means that he loves me and I shall marry him) until it was time to have her bath and change for dinner. The evenings were occupied with wireless, to which Lady Bobbin was devoted. And so the days dragged on, from one meal to the next. Poor Philadelphia hardly employed the best methods with which to fight depression, but it is difficult to know, under the circumstances, what else she could have done. Her education had not fitted her for study, and in any case, like most women, she was only really interested in personalities. When she received a letter from Paul it would colour a whole day, and she would spend hours reading, re-reading and answering it; but he wrote at the most irregular intervals. Like most people who write for a living he hated writing letters, and moreover seldom had any notepaper in his lodgings.

Michael, on the other hand, wrote from his bed of jaundice nearly every day. Although his letters were, in tone, more those of a father than a lover, he evidently quite regarded himself as engaged to Philadelphia, and she was too indolent, and too much afraid of bringing matters to a climax to disillusion him. Besides, she rather enjoyed receiving and answering his letters. Lady Bobbin also assumed that the engagement was to be announced as soon as Michael recovered.

Meanwhile, Paul was leading his usual happy-go-lucky existence in London. He obtained, without much difficulty, a

346

'job' in his uncle's office. The uncle having flatly refused to give him work, was quite glad to let him sit for a few hours every day in the office, at a pound a week, so that he might obtain that background of respectability which was to prove such a valuable factor in influencing Lady Bobbin. He still loved Philadelphia very much, and wanted nothing more than to marry her, but he felt that since several months must now elapse before it would be in any way feasible to ask her mother's consent, he might as well pass those months as pleasantly as he could. With this end in view he went, a few days after his arrival in London, to a fancy-dress party given in a tiny flat off the Brompton Road. On entering the room, which was a seething mass of travesty, the togas of ancient Rome and the beards of Elizabethan England rubbing against the talc wings of modern fairyland, he was immediately greeted with cries of enthusiasm by Marcella Bracket.

'Here's darling Paul. Oh, how cross I am with you. Where have you been all this time? I've done nothing but ring you up for weeks. You might have sent me a Christmas card, you ogre.'

Paul tried to ignore the girl, he really tried hard. Nevertheless, before the night was over he had abjectly apologized for his neglect of her during the past month, and had finally found himself with her in his arms, her large painted mouth pressed to his as of yore.

The next day he woke up with a bad headache and a worse conscience.

'This is really terrible,' he thought, 'I must pull myself together. How can I, how can I be behaving in this caddish manner whilst poor little Philadelphia is shut up in that dreary house with no one to speak to but Lady Bobbin, and she out hunting all day. It is beginning to look as if Amabelle were right in saying that I have no talent for true love. I am evidently incapable of being faithful to one person. All the same, I do love Philadelphia far, far the best, although Marcella seems to have this extraordinary effect on me.'

And he resolved never to see Marcella again. That

determined young woman, however, was not easily to be put off. She had just suffered a serious reverse in her own love affairs, and it suited her very well to have Paul hanging around her once more. Paul, on the other hand, lonely, worried and very much attracted by Marcella, did not require a great deal of encouragement, and at the end of a fortnight they were inseparable.

21

As soon as Michael was allowed to move again he returned by train to Compton Bobbin to arrange about his wedding. No doubts whatever had crossed his mind as to Philadelphia's attitude towards him, and he travelled as far as London with perfect serenity. On his way through London he took the opportunity to lunch with Amabelle, and she immediately put him in possession of all the facts with regard to Paul and Philadelphia, once more giving it as her opinion that the whole affair was a piece of childish nonsense.

'Everything will be quite all right,' she said, 'if you do as I tell you. First of all, you'd better go round to Cartier this afternoon and buy her a lovely ring and some other little present as well, one of those diamond bracelets for instance. I should give her the bracelet when you arrive, but keep the ring for a day or two to give her when she has been really nice to you—it will seem more romantic like that. Be very sweet and sympathetic, of course, but perfectly firm, make her feel she is definitely engaged to you; and if by any chance she should mention Paul, take up the attitude of being surprised and pained but ready to forgive just this once. I should try to keep off the subject for as long as you can, though. I think you will find that, what with the boredom of her present existence and her fear of you (she regards you with a good deal of wholesome awe, you know), she will be beside you on the altar steps in no time. That's what you really do want, I suppose?'

'Yes, yes,' said Michael, adding uncertainly: 'Poor child, I only hope I shall be able to make her happy. You know, Amabelle, that it is you who will always be the love of my life, don't you?'

'Nonsense, my dear, of course you'll make her happy. You two are cut out for each other, obviously. As for Paul, I'm very fond of him myself, but all the same I feel perfectly certain that she would be wretched with him; he has far too weak a character to marry a girl of her sort. He needs something really hard-boiled. Why, at this very moment he is having an affair with that awful Marcella Bracket, whom he actually dislikes—I've no patience with him sometimes, I must say.'

Michael looked very much relieved. 'Then he's not in love with Philadelphia at all?'

'I tell you the whole thing is nonsense from beginning to end, and it's the greatest mercy that you are about again and can put a stop to it. All the same, I believe that in his queer way he does love Philadelphia, only he hasn't the strength of mind to get rid of the Bracket. Now, Michael dear, you must be off. My last words to you are to be firm and don't forget the diamond bracelet. It ought to work wonders for you.'

Michael followed this advice to the letter. Immediately on leaving Portman Square, he went to Cartier, where he bought a large and beautiful emerald ring and a diamond bracelet of magnificent proportions. With these in his pocket he caught the 4·45 from Paddington, arriving at Compton Bobbin just in time to dress for dinner.

He was met by his Aunt Gloria with the news that Philadelphia had gone to bed with a headache.

'In that case,' he said, 'I think I will go up and see her for a moment,' and before Lady Bobbin, gratified but somewhat scandalized at such haste, had time to utter a half-hearted protest, he had run up the stairs and was knocking at Philadelphia's bedroom door.

It would be idle to pretend that Philadelphia was not pleased to see him. The boredom and depression of the last few weeks had been such that she was ready to welcome with delight any new face, anybody from the outer world. With the greatest reluctance she had forced herself to avoid him by pretending to be ill, feeling in some obscure way that loyalty to Paul demanded this gesture, and when Michael came up to see her immediately on his arrival she was more touched and pleased than she cared to admit.

He sat on the edge of her bed and talked of this and that, cheerfully and without embarrassment, looking most attractively pale and thin from his recent illness. Presently, having made no mention whatever of an engagement, he said: 'Now I must have my bath, or I shall be late for Aunt Gloria, and you ought to go to sleep if you're not very well, so I will say good night. But first of all put out your hand and shut your eyes, darling.' Philadelphia did so, and he snapped the diamond bracelet on to her wrist.

The diamond is a stone possessed for the female mind, however unsophisticated, of curious psychological attributes. Philadelphia looked at the sparkling flowers on her wrist and forgot that she had been about to announce her betrothal to another. She flung her arms around Michael's neck in an access of childlike pleasure and cried: 'Oh, the lovely bracelet. Thank you, thank you, darling Michael. You are sweet to me.'

Amabelle's love potion had done its work for the moment. Its effect, however, wore off sadly during the night, and the next morning, very early, at about six o'clock, Philadelphia woke up tormented with agonies of self-reproach.

'Paul, my darling, darling Paul,' she wept into her pillow. 'I won't lose you; they shan't bribe me like this. I will never give you up, never, as long as I live.' She flung the offending bracelet, which gleamed beneath her bedside lamp, into the farthest corner of the room, sobbing bitterly. After a while she pulled herself together and began to consider her position. The idea had come to her that if she should stay any longer at Compton Bobbin now that Michael had arrived, she would inevitably find herself engaged to him. She knew that she was too weak to offer, alone and unsupported, any real resistance; and she dreaded beyond words the idea of those frightful scenes with her mother which would certainly ensue if she did. If she was ever to escape, now and now only, was the time. It would be her last opportunity. She must go, at once, to Paul.

Having taken this decision she began very quickly to dress. Better leave the house before anybody was about. She slipped downstairs, feeling like an escaping criminal, took the key of the garage from the hall table, climbed out of the school-room window into the cold, dark morning air, and by seven o'clock was well on the road to London in her little car. She would be in time to have breakfast with Paul before he left for his office. Poor darling, how he must hate working in such a place; it was wonderful to think of him doing it for her sake. Everything would be all right when she was with him, and she would be safe again. The idea of seeing him so soon filled her with nervous excitement.

Shortly after nine o'clock she drove up to the house in Ebury Street where Paul had rooms. Her heart beat in great thumps as she rang the front door bell. For an eternity there was no answer; at last, however, the door was opened by an elderly woman who held in one hand a bucket of soapy water. She looked at Philadelphia with hostility and said, in reply to her question. 'Mr. Fotheringay has not been called yet.' Philadelphia hesitated. She felt cold and dazed after her long drive.

'I must see him, though,' she said at last. 'It is very important. I am his sister. Please will you show me the way to his room?'

The woman shrugged her shoulders. 'Mr. Fotheringay is on the first floor, but he gave orders that he was not to be called. You must please yourself,' she said, and falling to her knees she began scrubbing the linoleum on the floor.

Philadelphia went upstairs timidly. She knocked several times on the first door that she came to, and finally, receiving no answer, she turned the handle and walked in. The room was evidently a sitting-room, and at first sight seemed to be empty, although the electric light was burning. Suddenly, however, it was empty no more, for she realized with a start that Paul himself lay on the sofa, fully dressed.

In certain emergencies the human brain neglects to register such subsidiary emotions as that of surprise. To Philadelphia, overstrung, hysterical, and worn out by her long and fasting drive, it seemed quite natural that Paul should be lying on his sofa instead of in his bed, that he should still be wearing evening dress at nine o'clock in the morning, and that although he was fast asleep the electric light should be turned on, shining full in his face. A person of more experience might have been prepared for what followed; Philadelphia only felt an overpowering relief that she had found him again. Everything must be all right now, it seemed.

'Paul,' she said, leaning over him. 'Darling. Wake up.'

No answer. No movement. No sound in the room but that of his thick, heavy and regular breathing. She touched him rather shyly on the arm. 'Please wake up, Paul.' She shook him gently. She shook him really hard. 'Paul, don't be so unkind to me. You must wake up. I've come so far to see you. Please, please, my darling.'

At last he half-opened his eyes, looked at her as though from a great distance, and said in a thick voice: 'For God's sake, leave me alone. I told them not to call me,' after which he turned over deliberately and once more lay motionless.

'Paul, you must speak to me,' she cried, shaking now with angry sobs, and losing all self-control she began to hit him on the chest until he opened his eyes again. This time he seemed to recognize her. He took one of her hands in his and said with a great effort, 'Go away, darling, I'm drunk.' After that neither tears nor protestations could move him.

Philadelphia went slowly down the stairs. That was the end. She must get back to Michael, who would never treat her so. She felt sick and faint now, and was blinded by her tears. The woman who had let her in was scrubbing the front door steps. Philadelphia passed her quickly, aware of curious looks, got into her car and drove down the street until she thought she must be out of sight. Then, oblivious of passers-by, she stopped and cried until she could cry no more. After that she began to think of what she should do next. In spite of her unhappiness she realized that to drive home at once in her present condition would be impossible; she must have something to eat first, and a rest. Whom did she know in London? Her Aunt Loudie was in Switzerland, Sally was almost certainly still on the Riviera. Amabelle—she would be kind. She started up the engine of the car and, after getting

353

lost several times, for she did not know her way about London, she found herself at last outside Amabelle's house. She rang the front door bell; there was no answer. She rang again, and presently a red-faced footman appeared still struggling into his coat.

'Can I see Mrs. Fortescue, please?'

'Mrs. Fortescue has not been called yet.'

Philadelphia was trying to decide what she should say next when she found that the door had been rudely shut in her face. Such terrible things had happened to her already that this incident, which on any ordinary occasion would have caused her unspeakable mortification, seemed quite unimportant. She even sat in her car this time without bothering to move on while she considered what her next step should be. Sally was her last remaining hope, if she was back from the Riviera all would be well. She drove to Fitzroy Square. 'Please, God, let her be there please, please.' This time the door was opened immediately by a fat and smiling charlady.

'Yes, Mrs. Monteath came back last night. Will you come this way, please.'

'Thank you, God, thank you, thank you.'

She took Philadelphia up to the first floor flat, opened the door of it with a special key and precipitated her into a large, light bedroom, where Sally and Walter Monteath were sitting up in bed eating their breakfast.

'A young lady to see you, ma'am.'

'Philadelphia darling!' cried Sally in a loud and cheerful voice.

Philadelphia opened her mouth to say something and then fell to the floor in a dead faint.

When she recovered consciousness she was lying in the bed herself, and Sally was sponging her face with cold water while the charwoman looked on. Walter was nowhere to be seen.

'There, darling,' said Sally, 'you lie quite still and don't worry about anything.'

'I'm so sorry,' said Philadelphia, 'to be such a bother.'

'Don't be silly. Are you feeling all right now?'

'Yes, perfect. I expect I'm rather hungry really, that's why I fainted.'

'Poor sweet. Mrs. Crumpit will make you some breakfast at once. You didn't motor all the way up this morning, did you?'

'Yes, I did.'

'Good gracious. Walter thought you had by the look of the car.'

Philadelphia felt warm, happy and contented. She was in no hurry to tell her story, and Sally did not ask any more questions, but went off to help Mrs. Crumpit in the kitchen. Presently she came back with a most delicious breakfast. While Philadelphia was eating this the telephone bell rang in the next room and Walter's voice could be heard answering it.

'Hullo—yes? Oh, hullo, Amabelle—my dear, she's in our bed, quite all right—she appeared about half-an-hour ago and fainted away. Gave us an awful fright, but she's eating breakfast now. What? I don't know. I've no idea. Oh, very well, we'll keep her for the present then. Right you are, Amabelle. Good-bye.'

'You seem to have caused a perfect uproar,' he said, coming into the bedroom. 'Apparently Michael had been telephoning to Amabelle from Compton Bobbin half out of his mind, and she tried to get on to Paul, but there was no answer; and then by a stroke of luck it occurred to her that we might know something about you. Michael is on his way to London now. I must go and have my bath. See you later.'

'Do tell me all about it,' said Sally as he shut the door. 'I'm eaten with curiosity.'

'Well, you see, Michael arrived at home last night and gave me a diamond bracelet.'

'Darling, how gorgeous.'

'And I simply hadn't the courage to tell him about Paul. I couldn't face the scene with mother; you don't know how terrifying she can be. But I thought that if I went to Paul straight away everything would be all right. I thought it was my only chance. So I got up very early this morning—'

'You must have.'

'And drove up here and went straight to Paul's house, and when I got there,' she said, her voice shaking, 'he was lying on the sofa looking too awful, and he wouldn't speak to me or even bother to open his eyes.'

'Blind, I suppose,' said Sally with the wisdom of experience.

'Yes, he was. At last when I had shaken him for ages all he said was, "Go away—I'm drunk." Sally, I never knew people got drunk in the morning?'

'I expect he had a jolly old hangover,' said Sally. 'What did you do then?'

'As soon as I realized what was the matter I went to Amabelle's, because I thought you were still abroad, but she hadn't been called and the footman was rude to me, so I came here on the chance that I might find you.'

'You've been crying, haven't you?'

'Well, of course. It's so terrible to think that all this time I've been in love with a drunkard.'

'Paul's not a drunkard, my dear; that's absurd. All men get blind sometimes, but they don't expect their girl friends to call at nine in the morning as a rule.'

'Anyway, it's all over between us now. I couldn't bear to see him again after that.'

'Couldn't you?'

'Never. It was too horrible. He could never have done such a thing if he had really loved me. Michael couldn't behave like that; he does love me, I know, and I shall be frightfully happy with him now.'

'I never doubted that you would be happy with Michael,' said Sally in a dry voice. 'For one thing, you weren't at any time properly in love with Paul. He was the first person who had ever made love to you and you fell for him; but that doesn't count.'

'Oh, Sally, you don't understand. I adored him right up to this morning more than anybody in the world. You couldn't go on being in love with somebody after a thing like that had happened, could you?'

'But of course you could. That sort of thing doesn't make a

356

scrap of difference if you really love somebody. When I think of all the times I've put Walter to bed absolutely paralytic with drink! You weren't a bit in love with Paul, my sweet, and you've realized it, that's all. And I think it's a mercy you have, myself, because you are entirely unsuited to each other in every way. You would both have been miserably unhappy. Now, you'll be able to marry that divine Michael and have a really enviable life. Don't cry, darling, but have some more coffee and then I'll lend you some rouge. You mustn't be looking pale for Michael when he comes.'

Two days later Paul read in *The Times* that a marriage had been arranged and would shortly take place between the Marquis of Lewes and Philadelphia, only daughter of Lady Bobbin and the late Sir Hudson Bobbin, of Compton Bobbin, Gloucestershire.

With a sigh, whether of sadness or relief will never be known, he settled down to write the first chapter of his *Life and Works of Lady Maria Bobbin*.

PIGEON PIE

To
PHYLLIS BLAKE, MARGARET CANDLER
and, of course, to the
WONDERFUL OLD SONGSTER
of Kew Green himself

I DEDICATE THIS BOOK

I hope that anybody who is kind enough to read it in a second edition will remember that it was written before Christmas 1939. Published on 6th May 1940 it was an early and unimportant casualty of the real war which was then beginning.

NANCY MITFORD
Paris, 1951

1

Sophia Garfield had a clear mental picture of what the outbreak of war was going to be like. There would be a loud bang, succeeded by inky darkness and a cold wind. Stumbling over heaps of rubble and dead bodies, Sophia would search with industry, but without hope, for her husband, her lover and her dog. It was in her mind like the End of the World or the Last Days of Pompeii, and for more than two years now she had been steeling herself to bear with fortitude the hardships, both mental and physical, which must accompany this cataclysm.

However, nothing in life happens as we expect, and the outbreak of the great war against Hitlerism certainly did not happen according to anybody's schedule except possibly Hitler's own. In fact, Sophia was driving in her Rolls-Royce through one of those grey and nondescript towns on the border between England and Scotland when, looking out of the window, she saw a man selling newspapers; the poster which he wore as an apron had scrawled upon it in pencil the words WAR BEGUN. As this was on the 31st of August, 1939, the war which had begun was the invasion of Poland by Germany; the real war, indeed, did begin more pompously, if not more in accordance with preconceived ideas, some four days later. There was no loud bang, but Mr. Chamberlain said on the wireless what a bitter blow it had been for him, and then did his best to relieve the tension by letting off air-raid sirens. It sounded very nice and dramatic, though a few citizens, having supposed that their last hour was at hand, were slightly annoyed by this curious practical joke.

Sophia's war began in that border town. She felt rather shivery when she saw the poster, and said to Rawlings, her chauffeur, 'Did you see?' and Rawlings said, 'Yes, m'lady, I did.' Then they passed by a hideous late-Victorian church, and the whole population of the town seemed to be occupied in propping it up with sandbags. Sophia, who had never seen a sandbag before, began to cry, partly from terror and partly because it rather touched her to see anybody taking so much trouble over a church so ugly that it might have been specially made for bombs. Further along the road in a small, grey village, a band of children, with labels round their necks and bundles in their arms, were standing by a motor-bus. Most of them were howling. Rawlings volunteered the remark that he had never expected to see refugees in England, that Hitler was a red swine, and he would like to get his hands on him. At a garage where they stopped for petrol the man said that we could never have held up our heads if we hadn't finished it now.

When they got to Carlisle, Sophia decided that she must go by train to London. She had been on the road already for ten hours, and was miserably stiff, but having arranged to help with the evacuation of mothers and children, she was due at a school in the Commercial Road at eight o'clock the following morning. Accordingly, she told Rawlings to stay the night at Carlisle, and she herself boarded the London train. There were no sleepers, the train was full of drunken soldiers, and it was blacked out. Some journeys remain in the memory as a greater nightmare even than bad illness; this was to be one of them. Sophia was lucky to secure a seat, as people were standing in the corridors; she did so, however, sharing the carriage with a Scotch officer, his very young wife, a nasty middle-aged lady and several sleeping men. The nasty lady and the officer's wife both had puppies with them, which surprised Sophia. She had wrenched herself away from her own Milly that morning, unwilling to have an extra object of search among the rubble and corpses. Soon total darkness descended, and fellow-passengers became mere shadowy forms and voices assuming ghost-like proportions.

The officer's wife went to the lavatory, and the little officer said confidentially to Sophia, 'We were only married on Saturday, and she's verra upset,' which made Sophia cry again. She supposed she was going to spend the war in rivers of tears, being an easy crier. The nasty lady now said that it seemed foolish to go to war for Poland, but nobody bothered to take up the point.

'You mark my words,' she said, 'this will mean a shilling on the income tax.'

Whether or not it be true that drowning persons are treated to a cinematograph show of their past lives, it is certainly a fact that during fiendish journeys undertaken with no cheerful object in view most people's thoughts are inclined to take on that drowning aspect either with regard to past or future events. Sophia, achingly tired, but unable to go to sleep, began to re-enact in her mind scenes from her past life.

The only child of a widowed peer, who could write his name, Maida Vale, but little else, she had seen London for the first time at the age of eighteen. An aunt had then taken her out in the world. She fell under the influence of Maurice Baring's novels, her ideal hero was a suave, perhaps slightly bald, enormously cultivated diplomat. Gentlemen of this description did not abound at the balls she went to, and the callow youths of twenty who did, were a source of disillusionment to her. She was not shy and she had high spirits, but she was never a romper and therefore never attained much popularity with the very young. At the end of her first London season, she went to a large house-party for Goodwood, and here one of her fellow-guests was Luke Garfield. He had just left the diplomatic service to go into the City. His very pompous, cultivated manner, excellent clothes, knowledge of foreign affairs and slight baldness gave him prestige in the eyes of Sophia, and he became her hero. On the other hand, Luke saw at once that her charm and unusual looks would be invaluable to him in his career, and in so far as he was capable of such a warm-blooded emotion, he fell in love with the girl. He proposed to her the following November, after she had poured out tea for him in her aunt's drawing-room. His pin-stripe trousers and perfect restraint seemed to her quite ideal, the whole scene could have come out of 'Cat's Cradles', and was crowned for her by Luke's suggestion that their honeymoon should be spent in Rome where he had recently been *en poste*.

How soon she began to realize that he was a pompous prig she could not remember. He was a sight-seeing bore, and took her the Roman rounds with a dutiful assiduity, and without ever allowing her to sit on a stone and use her eyes. Her jokes annoyed and never amused him; when she said that all the sights in Rome were called after London cinemas, he complained that she was insular, facetious and babyish. She was insular, really; she loved England and never thought abroad was worth the trouble it took getting there. Luke spoke Italian in such a dreadfully affected way that it embarrassed her to hear him.

It was on her honeymoon in Rome that she first met Rudolph Jocelyn. He made no great impression on her, being the antithesis of what she then so much admired. He was not bald, suave, or in any sense of the word a diplomat. On the contrary, he had a shock of tow-coloured hair, spoke indistinctly, dressed badly, and was always in a great hurry. Luke disapproved of him; he said that Jocelyn's journalistic activities were continually getting the Embassy in trouble with the Italians. Besides, he kept low company and looked disreputable, and the fact that he spoke Italian like a native, and two dialects as well, failed to endear him to Luke. Some months later Sophia heard that he had mobilized the Italian army in a moment of lightheartedness; his newspaper splashed the martial news, and Rudolph Jocelyn was obliged to abandon journalism as a career.

Sophia had a happy character and was amused by life; if she was slightly disillusioned she was by no means unhappy in her marriage. Luke was as cold as a fish and a great bore; soon however she began to regard him as a great joke, and as she liked jokes she became quite fond of him when, which happened soon, she fell out of love with him. Also she saw very little of him. He left the house before she was properly awake in the morning, returning only in time to dress for dinner, then they dined out. Every Saturday to Monday they stayed with friends in the country. Sophia often spent weeks at a time with her father, in Worcestershire or Scotland. Luke seemed to be getting very rich. About twice a week he obliged her to entertain or be entertained by insufferably boring business people, generally Americans. He explained that this must be regarded as her work so she acquiesced meekly, but unfortunately she was not very good at her work, as Luke never hesitated to tell her. He said that she treated the wives of these millionaires as if they were cottage women and she a visiting duchess. He said they were unused to being treated with condescension by the wives of much poorer men, who hoped to do business with their husbands. Sophia could not understand all this; she thought she was being wonderful to them, but they seemed to her a strange species.

'I simply don't see the point of getting up at six all the time you are young and working eighteen hours a day in order to be a millionaire, and then when you are a millionaire still getting up at six and working eighteen hours a day, like Mr. Holst. And poor Mrs. Holst, who has got up at six all these years, so that now she can't sleep in the morning, only has the mingiest little diamond clip you ever saw. What does it all mean?'

Luke said something about big business and not tying up your capital. Mr. Holst was the head of the firm of which Luke's was the London office, and the Holst visits to England were a nightmare for Sophia. She was obliged to see a great deal of Mrs. Holst on these occasions and to listen by the hour to her accounts of their early struggles as well as to immense lectures on business ethics.

'Lady Sophia,' Mrs. Holst would say, fingering her tiny diamond clip, 'I hope that you and Sir Luke fully realize that Mr. Holst has entrusted his good name—for the good of the business, Lady Sophia, is the good name of Mr. Holst, and in fact Mr. Holst has often said to me that Mr. Holst's business is Mr. Holst—well, as I was saying, this good name is entrusted into Sir Luke's keeping and into your keeping, Lady Sophia. I always say a business man's wife should be Caesar's wife. As I have told you, Lady Sophia, Mr. Holst worked for twenty hours a day for thirty years to build up his business. Often and often I have heard him say "My home is my office and my office is my home" and that, Lady Sophia, is the profound truth. Now, as I was saying . . .' and so it went on.

Sophia, who was never able to get it out of her head that the City was a large room in which a lot of men sat all day doing sums, and who was of course quite unable to distinguish between stock-brokers, bill-brokers, bankers and jobbers, found these lectures almost as incomprehensible as the fact that Mrs. Holst should take so much interest in her husband's profession when it had only produced, for her, such a wretched little diamond clip. Sophia loved jewels, she had fortunately inherited very beautiful ones of her own from her mother, and Luke, who was not at all mean, often added to them when he had brought off a deal.

The train stopped. The Scotch officer, his wife, the nasty lady and their puppies all got out. It was one o'clock in the morning. The carriage then filled up, from the corridor which was packed, with very young private soldiers. They were very drunk, singing over and over again a dirty little song about which bits of Adolph they were going to bring back with them. They all ended by passing out, two with their heads in Sophia's lap. She was too tired to remove them, and so they lay snoring hot breath on to her for the rest of the journey.

Her thoughts continued. After some years of marriage Luke had joined the Boston Brotherhood, one of those new religions which are wafted to us every six months or so across the Atlantic. At first she had suspected that he found it very profitable in the way of deals with older Brothers; presently however he became earnest. He inaugurated week-end parties in their London house, which meant a hundred people to every meal, great jolly queues waiting outside the lavatories, public confessions in the drawing-room, and quiet times in the housemaid's cupboard. Sophia had not been very ladylike about all this, and in fact had played a double game in order to get the full benefit of it. She allowed people to come clean all over her, and even came clean herself in a perfectly shameless way, combing the pages of Freud for new

368

sins with which to fascinate the Brotherhood. So, of course, they loved her. It was just at this time that everything in Sophia's life began to seem far more amusing because of Rudolph Jocelyn whom she had fallen in love with. He came to all the week-end parties, tea parties, fork luncheons and other celebrations of the newest Christianity, and Luke disliked him as much as ever but endured him in a cheery Brotherly way, regarding him no doubt as a kind of penance, sent to chasten, as well as a brand to be snatched from the burning. Brothers, like Roman Catholics, get a bonus for souls.

Sophia and Rudolph loved each other very much. This does not mean that it had ever occurred to them to alter the present situation, which seemed exactly to suit all parties: Rudolph was unable to visualize himself as a married man, and Sophia feared that divorce, re-marriage and subsequent poverty would not bring out the best in her character. As for Luke, he took up with a Boston Brotherly soulmate called Florence, and was perfectly contented with matters as they stood. Florence, he realized, would not show to the same advantage as Sophia when he was entertaining prospective clients; Sophia might not be ideally tactful with their wives, but she did radiate an atmosphere of security and of the inevitability of upper-class status quo. Florence, however saintly, did not. Besides that, Luke was hardly the kind of man to favour divorce. Middle-aged, rather fat and very rich, he would look ridiculous, he knew, if his wife ran away with a poor, handsome and shabby young man. Let it be whispered too that Luke and Sophia, after so many years, were really rather attached to each other.

As she sat in the train reviewing her past life, Sophia felt absolutely certain that it was now over and done with. It lay behind her, while she, with every revolution of the wheels, was being carried towards that loud bang, those ruins, corpses and absence of loved ones. She had been taken very much unawares by the war, staying with her father in a remote part of Scotland where telephone and radio were unknown, and where the newspapers were often three days late. Now in the blacked-out train crowded with soldiers, she was already enveloped by it. The skies of London were probably dark by now with enemy planes, but apprehension was of so little use that she concentrated upon the happiness of her past life. The future must look after her in its own way. She became drowsy, and her mind filled with images. The first meet she ever went to, early in the morning with her father's agent. She often remembered this, and it had become a composite picture of all the cub-hunting she had ever done, the autumn woods and the smell of bonfires, dead leaves and hot horses. Riding home from the last meet of a season, late in the afternoon of a spring day, there would be primroses and violets under the hedges, far far away the sound of a horn, and later an owl. The world is not a bad place, it is a pity to have to die. But, of course, it is only a good place for a very few people. Think of Dachau, think of China, and Czechoslovakia and Spain. Think of the distressed areas. We must die now, and there must be a new world. Sophia went to sleep and only woke up at Euston. She went to the station hotel, had a bath, and arrived at the Commercial Road at exactly eight o'clock. Of the day which followed she had afterwards but little recollection. The women from London were wonderful, their hostesses in the country extremely disagreeable. It was a sad business.

When it was over Sophia went to bed and slept for thirteen hours.

2

She got up in time for luncheon. There had been no loud bang, the house was not in ruins, and when she rang her bell Greta, her German maid, appeared.

'Oh Greta, I thought you would have gone.'

'Gone, Frau Gräfin?'

Arguments and persuasion from Sophia failed to prevent Greta from calling her this.

'Back to Germany.'

'Oh no, Frau Gräfin; Sir Luke says there will be no war. Our good Führer will not make war on England.'

Sophia was rather bored. She had never liked Greta and had not expected to find her still there. She asked whether Sir Luke was in, and was told yes, and that he had ordered luncheon for four. It was a very hot day, and she put on a silk dress which, owing to the cold summer, she had hitherto been unable to wear.

Rudolph was in the drawing-room making a cocktail.

'I say, have you seen Florence? God has guided her to dye her hair.'

'No—what colour—where is she?'

'Orange. Downstairs,' he said, pulling Sophia towards him with the hand which did not hold the cocktail shaker, and kissing her. 'How are you?'

'Very pleased to see you, my darling. It seemed a long time.'

Florence appeared, followed by Luke. Her hair, which had been brown, was indeed a rich marmalade, and she was rather smartly dressed in printed crepe-de-chine, though the dress did not look much when seen near Sophia's.

'Have a drink,' said Rudolph, pouring them out. Florence gave him a tortured, jolly smile, and said that drinking gave her extraordinarily little pleasure nowadays. Luke, who hated being offered drinks in his own house, refused more shortly. 'Lunch is ready,' he said.

They went downstairs.

'Has the war begun?' asked Sophia, wondering who could have ordered soup for luncheon, and seeing in this the God-guided hand of Florence. She guessed that Florence was staying in the house.

'No,' said Rudolph. 'I don't know what we're waiting for.'

'My information is,' said Luke, at which Rudolph gave a great wink, because Luke so often used those words and his information was so often not quite correct, 'my information is that Our Premier (his voice here took on a reverent note) is going to be able to save the peace again. At a cost, naturally. We shall have to sacrifice Poland, of course, but I hear that the Poles are in a very bad way, rotten with Communism, you know, and they will be lucky to have Herr Hitler to put things right there. Then we may have to give him some colony or other, and of course a big loan.'

'What about the Russian pact?' said Rudolph.

'Means nothing—absolutely nothing. Herr Hitler will never allow the Bolsheviks into Europe. No, I don't feel any alarm. We have no quarrel with Germany that Our Premier and Herr Hitler together cannot settle peacefully.'

Sophia said shortly, 'Well, if they do, and there isn't a revolution here as the result, I shall leave this country for ever and live somewhere else, that's all. But I won't believe it.'

Then, remembering from past experience that such conversations were not only useless but also led to ill-feeling, she changed the subject. She had never been so near parting from Luke as at the time of Munich, when, in his eyes, Our Premier had moved upon the same exalted sphere as Brother Bones, founder of the Boston Brotherhood, and almost you might say, God. His information then had been that the Czechs were in a very bad way, rotten with Communism, and would be lucky to have Herr Hitler to put things right. It also led him to believe that universal disarmament would follow the

Munich agreement, and that the Sudetenland was positively Hitler's last territorial demand in Europe. Carlyle has said that identity of sentiment but difference of opinion are the known elements of pleasant dialogue. The dialogue in many English homes at that time was very far from pleasant.

'Then a silly old welfare-worker came up to a woman with eight coal-black children and said, "You haven't got a yellow label, so you can't be pregnant," and the woman said, "Can't I? Won't the dad be pleased to hear that now?" And when we got to the village green the parson was waiting to meet us, and he looked at the pregnant ladies and said, very sadly, "To think that *one man* is responsible for all this." It's absolutely true.'

Rudolph watched her with admiration. He enjoyed Sophia's talent for embroidering on her own experiences, and the way she rushed from hyperbole to hyperbole, ending upon a wild climax of improbability with the words 'It's absolutely true.' According to Sophia, she could hardly move outside her house without encountering the sort of adventure that only befalls the ordinary person once in a lifetime. Her narrative always had a basis of truth, and this was an added fascination for Rudolph who amused himself by trying to separate fact from fiction.

'Darling Sophia,' he said, as she came to the end of a real tour de force about her father, whom she had left, she said, blackening the pebbles of his drive which he considered would be particularly visible from the air, 'I know what your job will be in the war—taking German spies out to luncheon and telling them what you believe to be the truth. When you look them in the eye and say "I promise it's absolutely true", they'll think it's gospel because it'll be so obvious that you do yourself. The authorities will simply tell you the real truth, and you'll do the rest for them.'

'Oh, Rudolph, what a glamorous idea!'

She took Florence upstairs. Florence wriggled a good deal which she always did if she felt embarrassed, and in spite of her conscious superiority in the moral sphere she often felt embarrassed with Sophia. Presently she said in a loud, frank voice, 'I hope it's all right, Sophia. I'm staying here.'

'Oh, good. I hope you're comfortable. If you want any ironing done, just tell Greta.'

Florence said she required extraordinarily little maiding but this did not for a moment deceive Sophia, who had been told by Greta, in a burst of confidence, that Fraulein Turnbull gave more trouble than three of the Frau Gräfin.

Florence now drew a deep breath, always with her the prelude to an outburst of Christianity, and said that the times were very grave and that it made her feel sad to see people pay so little attention to their souls as Sophia and Rudolph.

'We don't think our rotten little souls so important as all that.'

'Ah but you see it isn't only your souls. Each person has a quantity of other souls converging upon his—that's what makes this life such a frightfully jolly adventure. In your case, Sophia, with your looks and position, you could influence directly and indirectly hundreds—yes, hundreds of people. Think how exciting that would be.'

Sophia saw that she was in for a sermon, and resigned herself. She knew from sad experience that to answer back merely encouraged the Brotherhood to fresh efforts.

'You know, dear, Luke feels it very much. It hurts him when you talk as you did at lunch, flippantly and with exaggeration. I wish you could realize how much happier it makes one to be perfectly truthful, even in little ways. Truth is a thing that adds so greatly to the value of human relationships.'

'Some,' said Sophia carelessly. 'Now it adds to the value of my relationship with Rudolph to tell more and funnier lies. He likes it.'

'I wonder if that sort of relationship is of much value. Personally the only people I care to be very intimate with are the ones you feel would make a good third if God asked you out to dinner.'

Sophia wished that Florence would not talk about the Almighty as if his real name was Godfrey, and God was just Florence's nickname for him.

'Oh, God would get on with Rudolph,' she said.

Florence smiled her bright, crucified smile, and said that she was sure there was good material in Rudolph if one knew where to look for it. Then she wriggled about and said, very loudly, 'Oh, Sophia, how much happier it would be for you, and for those about you, if you would give your sins to God. I feel there would be, oh! such a gay atmosphere in this house if you could learn to do just that.'

'Only one sin, Florence, such a harmless one. I don't steal, I honour my father, I don't covet, and I don't commit murder.'

'Perhaps flippancy is the worst sin of all.'

'I'm not flippant but I'm not religious and I never will be, not if I live to be a hundred. It's a matter of temperament, you know.'

This was a false step. Florence now embarked on a rigmarole of bogus philosophy which no power short of an explosion could have stopped. Poor Sophia lay back and let it flow, which it did until the men came into the drawing-room, when Florence gave Luke a flash of her white and even teeth which all too clearly said 'I have failed again.'

'I'm just going up for a little quiet time,' she said. 'I'll be ready in half an hour.' She and Luke played golf on Saturday afternoons.

'I'm just going down for a little quiet time and I'll be ready in about half an hour,' said Rudolph, picking up the *Tatler*. When he got back, he said, 'Come along, Sophia, I'm taking you to the local A.R.P. office to get a job.'

'There won't be any war,' said Luke comfortably, as he settled down to his *Times*.

Sophia and Rudolph strolled out into the sunshine.

'Let's go to Kew,' said Sophia.

'Yes, we will when you have got your job.'

'Oh darling, oh dear, do I have to have a job?'

'Yes, you do, or I shall be through with you. You know that I think it's perfectly shameful the way you haven't done any training the last few months. Now you must get on with it quickly. There is only one justification for people like you in a community, and that is that they should pull their weight in a

375

war. The men must fight and the women must be nurses.'

'Darling, I couldn't be a nurse. Florence has a first aid book and I looked inside and saw a picture of a knee. I nearly fainted. I can't bear knees, I've got a thing about them. I don't like ill people, either, and then I'm not so very strong, I should cockle. Tell you what—could I be a précis writer at the Foreign Office?'

'There haven't been précis writers at the Foreign Office since Lord Palmerston. Anyway, you couldn't work in a Government Department, you're far too mooney. If you can't bear knees and don't like ill people, you can scrub floors and wash up for those that can and do. Now here we are, go along and fix yourself up.'

Sophia found herself in a large empty house, empty, that is, of furniture, but full of would-be workers. She had to wait in a queue before being interviewed by a lady at a desk. The young man in front of her announced that he was a Czech, and not afraid of bombs. The lady said nor are British women afraid of bombs, which Sophia thought was going too far. She gave the young man an address to go to, and turned briskly to Sophia.

'Yes?' she said.

Sophia felt the shades of the prison-house closing in on her. She explained that she would do full-time voluntary work, but that she had no qualifications. For one wild moment of optimism she thought that the lady was going to turn her down. After looking through some papers, she said, however, 'Could you do office work in a First Aid Post?'

'I could try,' said Sophia doubtfully.

'Then take this note to Sister Wordsworth at St. Anne's Hospital First Aid Post. Thank you. Good day.'

Rudolph was in earnest conversation with a German Jew when she came out. On hearing that she was fixed up he said that she might have a holiday before beginning her job. 'You can go to St. Anne's to-morrow,' he said. 'I'm taking you down to Kew now.'

They sat on a bench at the end of the ilex avenue and stared at Sion House across the river. Sophia asked Rudolph what he planned to do, now that the war had begun.

'I hope for a commission, of course,' he said; 'failing that I shall enlist.'

'Somebody who knows all those languages could get a job at home—I mean not a fighting job. Perhaps it is your duty to do that,' she said hopefully.

'Can't help my duty: I'm going to fight Germans in this war—not Nazis, mind you, Germans. I mean huns.'

Sophia agreed with him really. The huns must be fought.

'How strange everything seems now that the war is here,' she said. 'I suppose it is unreal because we have been expecting it for so long now, and have known that it must be got over before we can go on with our lives. Like in the night when you want to go to the loo and it is miles away down a freezing cold passage and yet you know you have to go down that passage before you can be happy and sleep again. We are starting down it. Oh darling, I wish it was over and we were back in bed. What shall I do when you've gone?'

'Don't you anticipate,' said Rudolph severely; 'you never have, so don't begin now. You are the only person I know who lives entirely in the present, it is one of the attractive things about you.'

'If you are killed,' said Sophia, paying no attention.

'You are one of those lucky women with two strings to their bow. If I am killed, there is always old Luke.'

'Yes, but the point is I shall have such an awful grudge against Luke, don't you see? I do so fearfully think the war is the result of people like him, always rushing off abroad and pretending to those wretched foreigners that England will stand for anything. Cracking them up over here, too; Herr Hitler this, and Herr von Ribbentrop that, and bulwarks against Bolshevism and so on. Of course, the old fellow thought he was making good feeling, and probably he never even realized that the chief reason he loved the Germans was because they buttered him up so much. All those free rides in motors and aeroplanes.'

'You can't blame him,' said Rudolph, 'he never cut any ice

over here, but as soon as he set foot in Germany he was treated as a minor royalty or something. Of course it was lovely for him. Why, Berlin has been full of people like that for years. The Germans were told to make a fuss of English people, so of course masses of English people stampeded over there to be made a fuss of. But it never occurred to them that they were doing definite harm to their own country; they just got a kick out of saying "mein Führer" and being taken round in Mercedes-Benzes. All the same they weren't directly responsible for the war. Old Luke is all right, he's a decent old fellow at heart. I feel quite happy leaving you in his hands. I believe he's getting over the Brotherhood, too, you'll see.'

As they strolled across Kew Green to get a taxi, an unearthly yelp announced to them that they had been observed by Sophia's godfather, Sir Ivor King, and sure enough, there he was, the old fellow, waving a curly, butter-coloured wig at them out of his bedroom window. He invited them to come in for a cup of tea.

This faintly farcical old figure was the idol of the British race, and reigned supreme in the hearts of his fellow-countrymen, indeed of music lovers all over the world, as the King of Song. In his heyday, he had been most famous as a singer of those sexy ballads which were adored by our grandparents, and for which most of us have a secret partiality. He was unrivalled, too, in opera. The unique quality of his voice was the fact that it could reach higher and also lower notes than have ever been reached before by any human being, some of which were so high that only bats, others so low that only horses, could hear them. When he was a very young man studying in Germany, his music teacher said to him, 'Herr King, you shall make, with that voice of yours, musical history. I hope I may live to hear you at your zenith.'

The prophecy came true. Ivor King was knighted at an early age, he made a large fortune, gained an unassailable position and the nickname by which he was always known, 'The King of Song', largely on the strength of this enormous range of voice. Largely, but not solely. A lovable and very strong personality, a genial quality of good fellowship, and latterly his enormous age, had played their part, and combined with his magnificent notes to make him not only one of the best known but also one of the best loved men of several successive generations. Among particular achievements he was the only man ever to sing the name part in the opera *Norma*, the script of which had been re-written especially for him, and re-named *Norman*.

The King of Song had toured the world, and particularly the Empire, dozens of times and these tours were indeed like royal progress. In very remote parts of Africa the natives often mistook him for Queen Victoria's husband, and it was universally admitted that he had done more towards welding the Empire in the cultural sphere than any other individual. Quite bald, although with a marvellous selection of wigs, and finally quite toothless, he still maintained a gallant fight against old age, although some two years previously he had succumbed to the extent of giving a final farewell concert at the Albert Hall. He had then retired to a charming house on Kew Green, which he named Vocal Lodge, and devoted himself to botany; in the pursuit of this science, however, he was more keen than lucky.

'She wore a wreath of roses the day that first we met,' he chanted, cutting a seed cake. It was what the most vulgar of the many generations which had passed over his head would call his signature tune, and he sang it in a piercing soprano.

Sophia poured out tea, and asked after his Lesbian irises.

'They were not what they seemed,' he said, 'wretched things. I brought the roots all the way from Lesbos, as you know, and when they came up, what were they? Mere pansies. Too mortifying. And now I'm the air-raid warden for Kew Gardens, in a tin hat—and it will be years before I visit Greece again. It may be for years, and it may·hay be for ever. As you will note, the war has found me in excellent voice. I am singing at the Chiswick Town Hall to-night to our local decontamination squads. Such dear boys and girls. And let me darkly hint at a more exalted engagement in the not-too-

379

too-far-off future. I was trying to decide, when I saw you on the Green, whether I should go to my interview with some Important Personages as a blond or a brunette. I think I favour the butter-coloured curls,' he said, taking off his wig and revealing beneath a head of egg-like baldness.

Sophia and Rudolph were quite used to this, for the King's wigs were as much off as on, and there was never any kind of pretence about them being his own luxuriant hair.

'Yes, I have always liked that one,' said Sophia, 'it softens your features. What important personages?'

'Ah,' said the old singer, 'I can keep a secret. What are you up to, Rudolph? I haven't seen you since the Munich crisis. I may tell you that, having heard that you were doing the Italian broadcast from the B.B.C., I switched on the wireless to listen. Well, I said to Magdalen Beech, poor Rudolph sounds very ill—then we discovered that it was the dear late Pope, and not Rudolph at all.'

Sir Ivor was a fervent Roman Catholic. For a short time, many years ago, he had been married to a woman so pious and so lavish with Sir Ivor's money that she had posthumously been made a Papal Duchess and was accorded the unique honour of being buried in the Vatican gardens. Lady Beech was her sister.

'Now you can tell me something,' said Sophia, glancing at the Sargent portrait, in brown velvet and lace, of Duchess King which hung over the chimneypiece. 'I had a letter from Lady Beech saying what a pity, as we must all so soon be dead, that we shouldn't all be going on to the same place afterwards. What really happens to us heretics, darling old gentleman?'

'Darling pretty young lady, you pop straight on to a gridiron and there you baste to eternity.'

'Baste?' said Sophia.

'Baste. Whenever I have time, perhaps say once in a million years, I will bring you a drop of water on the end of my finger. Apart from this, your pleasures will be few and simple.'

'What I'm wondering is,' said Rudolph, 'how much you

and Lady Beech will enjoy such purely Catholic society for so uninterrupted a spell?'

At dinner that night, Luke's information was that a huge scheme of appeasement, world-wide in its implications, was even now being worked out. He said the wretched Socialists were not making things easy for Our Premier, but that he was too big a man and the scheme too big a scheme to be thwarted by pinpricks in Parliament. Parliament and the Press might have to be got rid of for a time whilst Our Premier and Herr Hitler rearranged the world. In any case, there would be no war. The next morning poor Luke was so wretched that Sophia felt quite sorry for him. He really seemed astounded that Herr Hitler should be prepared to risk all those wonderful swimming-pools in a major war.

When the Prime Minister's Speech and hoax air-raid warning were over, Sophia went round to report at the First Aid Post. Here, in a large garage under St. Anne's Hospital, cold, damp and dirty, pretty Sister Wordsworth was bringing order out of confusion. She really seemed pleased to engage Sophia, in spite of her lack of qualifications, and told her that she could come every day from one to seven. The work was simple. Sophia was to sit behind a partition of sacking, labelled Office, to answer the telephone, count the washing and do various odd jobs. In the case of raids, Sister Wordsworth assured her that while she might have to see knee joints, she would have no intimate contact with them.

Henceforth Sophia's life was sharply divided in two parts, her life behind the gasproof flap of the First Aid Post and her own usual unhampered life outside. Sometimes she rather enjoyed her sacking life, sometimes she felt that she could hardly endure it. The cold stuffy atmosphere got on her nerves, she was unaccustomed to sitting still for hours on end, and what work there was to do, such as counting washing, she did not do very well. On the other hand, she liked all the people in the Post, and habit once having gripped her, as it does so soon in life, she became quite resigned and regarded the whole thing completely as a matter of course.

3

Rather soon after the war had been declared, it became obvious that nobody intended it to begin. The belligerent countries were behaving like children in a round game, picking up sides, and until the sides had been picked up the game could not start.

England picked up France, Germany picked up Italy. England beckoned to Poland, Germany answered with Russia. Then Italy's Nanny said she had fallen down and grazed her knee, running, and mustn't play. England picked up Turkey, Germany picked up Spain, but Spain's Nanny said she had internal troubles, and must sit this one out. England looked towards the Oslo group, but they had never played before, except little Belgium, who had hated it, and the others felt shy. America, of course, was too much of a baby for such a grown-up game, but she was just longing to see it played. And still it would not begin.

The party looked like being a flop, and everybody was becoming very much bored, especially the Americans who are so fond of blood and entrails. They were longing for the show, and with savage taunts, like boys at a bull-baiting from behind safe bars, they urged that it should begin at once. The pit-side seats for which they had paid so heavily in printer's ink were turning out to be a grave disappointment; they sat in them, chewing gum, stamping their feet and shouting in unison, 'This war is phoney.'

Week after week went by. People made jokes about how there was the Boer War, and then the Great War, and then the Great Bore War. They said Hitler's secret weapon was boredom. Sophia hoped it was. She had long cherished a conviction that Hitler's secret weapon was an aerial torpedo addressed to Lady Sophia Garfield, 98 Granby Gate, S.W., and she very much preferred boredom.

Sophia had two friends in the Cabinet. They were called Fred and Ned, and as a matter of fact while Fred was in the Cabinet, Ned had not yet quite reached that sixth form of politicians and was only in the Government, but Sophia could not distinguish between little details like that, and to her they were 'My friends in the Cabinet'. She often dined with the two of them and found these evenings very enjoyable because, although they both had young and pretty wives, it seems that the wives of Cabinet Ministers race, so to speak, under different rules from ordinary women, and never expect to see their husbands except in bed if they share one. So Sophia had Fred and Ned to herself on these occasions. As she liked both male and female company, but did not much like it mixed, this arrangement suited her nicely.

They took her to dine at the Carlton, and talked a great deal about the political prospects of their various acquaintances, and it was talk which Sophia was very much accustomed to, because it had begun years ago, when she was a young married woman taking Fred and Ned out to tea at the Cockpit; only then it had been a question of Pop and coloured waistcoats, and the Headmaster in those days had delivered his harangues in Chapel instead of on the floor of the House. She told them all about her Post, and Ned wrote things down in a notebook, and promised that A.R.P. should be reconstructed on the exact lines suggested by Sophia. She knew from experience how much that meant. Then Fred asked her if Luke was in the Tower yet, and this annoyed her because, while it was one thing to say to Rudolph in the privacy of Kew Gardens that Luke was an awful old fascist, it was quite another to have Fred, that ardent upholder of Munich, being facetious about him; so she turned on poor Fred with great vigour, and gave him a brisk résumé of the achievements of the National Government. She very nearly made him cry, and was just coming nicely into her stride over the National Liberals, of whom Fred was one, when Ned came loyally to his rescue saying 'Ah, but you haven't heard of Fred's wonderful scheme, all his own idea, for fixing Dr. Goebbels.' And he proceeded to outline the scheme.

It appeared that Fred's idea, his own unaided brainwave, was to invite Sir Ivor King, the King of Song, to conduct a world-wide campaign of songful propaganda.

'Harness his personality, as it were,' Fred explained, warming to his subject, 'to our cause. He's the only chap who could bring it off, and it would be wicked not to use him—why, he is one of our great natural advantages, you might say, like—well coal, or being an island. They've got nobody to touch him over there. Now my idea is that he should give out a special news bulletin every day, strongly flavoured with propaganda, of course, followed by a programme of song. See the point? People will switch on to hear him sing (for the first time for two years, you know), and then they won't be able to help getting an earful of propaganda. We'll have him singing with the troops, singing with the air force, singing with the navy, jolly, popular stuff which the listeners all over the world can join in. You know how people like roaring out songs when they know the words. Besides, the man in the street has a great respect for old Ivor, great.'

According to Fred, he and the man in the street were as one, which was strange, considering that, except for the High Street, Windsor and The Turl, he had hardly ever been in a street.

'When you say listeners all over the world can join in, you mean English listeners?' said Sophia. She wanted to get the thing straight.

'By no means,' said Fred, eagerly, 'because, you see, the strength of this scheme is that it will be world-wide. I confess that, to begin with, I forgot that it's not everybody who can speak English. Then of course I remembered that there are Chinks and Japs and Fuzzy Wuzzies and Ice Creamers and Dagos, and so on. Ah! but we can overcome that difficulty. Is there any reason why he shouldn't learn to make those extraordinary sounds which they think of as music? Of course not. No. The old chappie is full of brains and enterprise—take

384

on anything we ask him to, you bet.' And Fred began to give what he thought an excellent imitation of un-English music nasal sounds of a painful quality. A county family who were dining at the next table told each other that this could not be the Minister for Propaganda, after all. Ned beat two forks together as an accompaniment, and they assured each other that neither was that the Member (so promising, such a career before him) for East Wessex.

'The old King is coming to my office to-morrow. I am seeing him myself,' Fred continued, when this horrid cacophony came to an end.

'He will be wearing his curly, butter-coloured wig,' said Sophia.

'We must see that he has a black one made. Don't want any Aryan nonsense in my scheme—I always think Propaganda is awfully un-English, anyway, but what I say, if you have it at all, for the Lord's sake have it good. And, by the way, Sophie, this is all most fearfully hush-hush, you know. Leakage and all that—not a word to Luke or anybody. The element of surprise is vital to the scheme.'

'I see, the old gentleman is your answer to Hitler's secret weapon.'

'I wouldn't go quite so far as that, but I can tell you we are expecting some pretty fruity results. I mean it's a world-wide scheme you see, not just a pettifogging little affair confined to England. And by the way,' he got out a notebook. 'I must remember to tell the police they had better keep an eye on the chap. Think what a coup for the Huns if he got bumped off or anything; I should never get over it.'

Sophia rang up her enemy. Olga Gogothsky (née Baby Bagg) had been her enemy since they were both aged ten. It was an intimate enmity which gave Sophia more pleasure than most friendships; she made sacrifices upon its altar and fanned the flames with assiduity.

'Hullo, my darling Sophie,' Olga purred, in the foreign accent which she had cultivated since just before her marriage and which was in striking contrast with the Eton and Oxford tones (often blurred by drink but always unmistakable) of Prince Gogothsky. 'Yes, I have been back a fortnight; such a journey, darling. And where did you go for the summer? Just quietly with dear Lord Maida Vale? Delicious. Me? Oh, poor little me, I had a very banal time with Pauline Mallory you know, the poetess, in her villa at Antibes. Crowds and crowds of people, parties, nothing else. You can imagine how that palled on me, dearest. Happily my beloved old Ambassador was there. He has her little villa, in the garden, and there he writes his memories. He is sweet enough to say that I inspire him in his work; he read it to me— so interesting, and written, how can I express it, with such art. The old days at the Montenegrin Court—so picturesque. You can imagine. Then Baroness von Bülop was a great friend of his, and he told me some fascinating things about her and her beautiful aunt which were rather too *intime* for cold, cold print. Well, what else—oh yes, Torchon was painting my portrait—he sees me as a Turkish slave girl which is very interesting because when Fromenti cast my horoscope he said that is what I used to be in one of my former lives. (In the Sultan's harem, I was his favourite wife.) Besides all this, I managed to get in a little writing, so you see my time was not quite wasted after all.'

Olga's writing was an interesting phenomenon, rather like the Emperor's new clothes. She let it be known that she was a poetess, and whenever, which was often, her photograph appeared in the illustrated press, the caption underneath would announce that very soon a slender volume might be expected from her pen. Sometimes even the subject-matter would be touched upon: 'Princess Serge Gogothsky, who is at present engaged upon a series of bird studies in verse.'

'This beautiful visitor to our shores is a lady of great talent. The long epic poem on Savonarola from her pen will soon be ready for publication,' and so on.

Once, for several weeks on end, Olga sat alone every evening at a special table at the Café Royal and wrote feverishly upon sheets of foolscap which she tore up, with an expression of agony on her face, just before closing time. Her work always seemed to be in progress rather than in print.

Sophia asked what she was doing as war work.

'Dearest, I must tell you that it's a secret. However, when you hear that I have an appointment under the Government, that I have to undertake great responsibilities, and that I may often be called out in the middle of the night without any idea of where I am to go, you may guess the kind of thing it is. More I cannot say.'

'Sounds to me like a certified midwife,' said Sophia crossly. It was really too much if old Baby Bagg was going to assume the rôle of beautiful female spy, while she herself had drearily admitted to working in a First Aid Post, all boredom and no glamour. Olga lied with such accomplishment that there were some people who believed in her tarradiddles, and Sophia had often been told what a talent for verse, what a delightful touch the Princess had.

'No darling—what a charming joke, by the way, I must remember to tell my dear Chief. No, not a midwife. Though I'm sure it must be far far more exhausting, my Chief is a regular slave driver.'

'Oh, you have a Chief?'

'I only wish I could tell you Who it is. But there must be no leakage. What a wonderful man to work with—what magnetism, what finesse and what a brain! I must allow I am fortunate to be with him, and then the work is fascinating, vital. What if it does half kill me? There, I mustn't talk about myself. Tell me, what are you doing in this cruel war?'

Sophia said that she too had an important job under the Government.

'Really, my darling, have you? A First Aid Post, or something like that, I suppose?'

'Ah well, that's only what I tell people, actually of course it is an excellent blind for my real work. I wonder you don't adopt this idea, say you are working in a canteen, for instance. I'll forget what you've just told me if you like, and spread it round about the canteen!'

'Delicate little me!' cried Olga, 'in a canteen! But darling, who would ever believe such an unlikely thing—they would at once suspect goodness knows what. Well, dearest, I see the Chief waiting for me in his great car with the flag and priority notices, I shall feel quite important as we whirl away to Whitehall. I must fly, darling. Good-bye. I will visit you very soon in your little First Aid Post. Good-bye.'

Sophia then telephoned to her friend, Mary Pencill.

'Now, Mary, listen. You've got to come and work in my First Aid Post,' she said. 'It's perfect heaven. You can't think what heaven Sister Wordsworth is.'

'No, thank you, Sophie. I don't intend to work for this war in any way. I don't approve of it, you see.' Mary belonged to the extreme Left.

'Gracious, just like Luke. He doesn't approve of it either, nor does Florence. You are in awful company. So why are you in this awful company?'

'I can't help it if Luke happens to be right for once. It's sure to be for the wrong reasons if he is. All I know is that everything decent and worth supporting has been thrown away—Spain, Czechoslovakia, and now we're supposed to be fighting for the Poles, frightful people who knout their peasants. Actually, of course, it's simply the British Empire and our own skins as usual.'

'I'm fond of my skin,' said Sophia, 'and personally I think the British Empire is worth fighting for.'

'You can't expect me to think so. Why, look at our Government. Your friends Fred and Ned, for instance, are just as bad as Hitler, exactly the same thing. What is the use of fighting Hitler when there are people like Ned and Fred here? We should do some cleaning up at home first.'

'Anyway, it's Hitler and Stalin now, don't forget the wedding bells.'

Mary had gone P.O.U.M, so she grudgingly conceded this point. 'Ned and Fred are practically the same people as Hitler and Stalin,' she said.

'I never heard anything so silly. Poor Fred and Ned. Well, I mean the proof of the pudding is in the eating. Just suppose now that the Ministry of Information had forgotten to tell us we had been beaten, and one day in Harrods we saw a little crowd gathering, and when we went to look it was Hitler and Stalin. Think how we should scream.'

'I expect you would.'

'So would you. Now, my point is, I often see Fred and Ned in Harrods, and I don't scream at all, I just say "Hullo duckie" or something. See the difference?'

'No, Sophia,' said Mary disapprovingly, 'I'm afraid you don't understand the principle.' She loved Sophia but thought her incurably frivolous.

'Another thing,' she said; 'why have you left the Left Book Club?'

'Darling, I only joined to please you.'

'That's no answer.'

'Well, if you want to know it's because the books are left.'

'Sophia!'

'I don't mean because they are Left and I can't get Evelyn Waugh or any of the things I want to read. I mean because they are left lying about the house. Ordinary libraries like Harrods take them away when one has finished with them. I don't want the place cluttered up with books, so I have left. See?'

'Really, your life is bounded by Harrods.'

'Yes, it is rather. I had rather a horrid dream, though, about its being full of parachutists; my life is slightly bounded by them now, to tell you the truth, I think they are terrifying.'

'Nonsense, they would be interned.'

'That's what Luke says. Still the idea of those faces floating past one's bedroom window is rather unpleasant, you must admit.'

'By the way, I saw Rudolph last night coming out of the Empire with that foreign woman.'

'Who?'

'The one who always wears star-spangled yashmaks.'

'Oh, you mean Olga Gogothsky; she's no more foreign than you or me—although she does pretend to have Spanish blood, I believe.'

'Really—Government or Franco?'

'Baby Bagg. You must remember her at dances.' Sophia was only fairly pleased to hear that Olga had been out with Rudolph, who had announced that he was going to play bridge at his club.

'Anyway, she looks too stupid.'

'She has just told me she has got an important job under the Government, I simply must find out what it is.'

'First Aid Post, probably,' said Mary. 'You haven't told me yet what you do in yours?'

'Well, it sounds rather lugubrious but I absolutely love it. I have an indelible pencil, you see, and when people are brought in dying and so on, I write on their foreheads.'

'Good gracious me, what do you write?'

'M for male and F for female, according to which they are, and a number. That's for the Ministry of Pensions. Then, for the doctor, how many doses of morphia and castor oil and so on they have had.'

'What an awful idea. What happens if you get a negro—or a neanderthal type with a very low forehead? You can't always count on having high, smooth, white brows, you know, like Luke's.'

'Try not to be facetious, darling, it's quite serious. Then I put their jewels into dainty little chintz bags made out of Fortmason remnants.'

'When you say you do all this, what exactly do you mean?'

'Well, darling, I should do it if there was a raid. It's rather like private theatricals, you know what I mean. "It'll be all right on the night" kind of idea. The worse the dress rehearsal, the better the show, and so on.'

Mary became very scornful and said it was the stupidest job she had ever heard of. 'Jewels,' she said, 'in chintz bags. Writing M and F. Really, Sophia, I give up.'

Sophia said it was better than doing nothing like Mary, and they rang off, each in a huff.

When Sophia saw Rudolph she said she had heard that he had been seen out with a duck-billed platypus disguised as a

Sultana. (Olga's rather long, turned-up nose was considered to be one of her great attractions.)

'Yes, my little Puss-puss,' he said, 'I did take the alluring Princess to a movie what time you went whoring round with your Cabinet puddings.'

'I thought you told me you were going to play bridge at your club?'

'So I was, until I met Olga.'

'But where did you meet her?'

'At my club.'

'Rudolph, what a story.'

'Well, I did. She came along in a taxi after I had telephoned to her.'

'Oh. What was she like?'

'Cracking bore, as usual. Talked about nothing but herself. I had to hear the whole story of how Serge blighted her life by refusing to allow her self-expression on the films. As though one didn't know that the old boyar would allow her to do anything which brought in the roubles.'

'She was always having tests,' said Sophia.

'And they were lousy. Well, then of course she is having all those books dedicated to her and pictures painted of her, and so on. But she has abandoned these activities for a very important job under the Government. First Aid Post, I guess. Chap in my club, a doctor, gave her her first aid exam. He said. "Now Princess, if you found a man with a badly broken leg and you had no splint or bandage, what would you do?' and she said, "Take my drawers off and tie the leg to my leg." So of course he passed her.'

Sophia saw that she must look out. She knew very well that when a man is thoroughly disloyal about a woman, and at the same time begins to indulge in her company, he nearly always intends to have an affair with that woman. The disloyalty is in itself a danger signal. She would not have supposed that Olga was exactly to Rudolph's taste, but these things do not follow any known rules and you never can tell.

'Beastly fellow,' she said. 'I see you're in love with her.'

'Rather,' said Rudolph. 'I see you're jealous.'

'Rather.' Sophia got up and rang the bell for the cocktail things. 'I say, darling, by the way, you know Florence?'

'Yes, I'm in love with her too, of course?'

'Very likely. Anyhow, you know she lives with us now. Well, I believe she must be nicer than we thought she was, because, whatever do you think? She keeps a pigeon in her bedroom.'

'Does she now? I thought she kept Luke.'

'No, no, darling, I've often told you. Anyway, there it is, she keeps this terribly nice pigeon.'

'Whatever for?'

'I expect it is her friend. I would love to have a sweet pigeon for a friend, but I must say I never would have thought it of Florence, she doesn't strike one as an animal lover. Milly doesn't like her at all.'

'I call it very queer,' said Rudolph. 'Do you think it might have some religious significance?'

'It's a pigeon, not a dove.'

'Florence wouldn't know the difference. That's it, I expect she is keeping it to let loose over Brother Bones's head next time she sees him.'

'Or maybe she saved its life. Mr. Stone, in our Post, you know, has to keep down the London pigeons in peace time, and he says it's awfully difficult because wherever you put your trap some old lady always pops her head out of a window and sets up a screeching about it and calls in the police and so on. However early in the morning, it's always just the same. So the result is that London pigeons are not really kept down very much, as you may note. Perhaps Florence saw this one in a trap (they get up very early in the Brotherhood, you know), and promised not to let it loose again if she might have it. I like her much better for it, actually.'

Florence now came into the room. She told Sophia that Luke had been guided to ask a hundred people to dinner the next day to talk about Moral Rearmament. 'It's to meet this friend of ours, Heatherley Egg,' she said. (Florence always introduced new people into her conversation with the word 'this'. 'This woman I met in the bus', or 'This cousin of my father's'. It was a habit which maddened Sophia.) 'I have arranged the whole thing,' Florence continued; 'gold chairs and food and so on are all ordered. I just looked in here to say how much we hope you will come to it, as I feel sure you will be interested. Heatherley Egg has just arrived from the States and he will tell us what the President said to him about Moral Rearmament. Just the two of them (the three, I should say, because of course, there was a Third present) talked it over for nearly five minutes, and Heth says—well, you must hear it from his own lips tomorrow evening. There will be members of the Brotherhood from all, yes, I am happy to say, all the European countries.'

Sophia and Rudolph hurriedly explained that they had a very long-standing engagement for the following evening. Florence looked a bit crucified and said how strange it must be to live in a perpetual whirl of thoughtless gaiety.

'I call a hundred people to dinner a pretty good whirl, personally.'

Florence said she must go as she had this First Aid lecture.

'It was her book I saw that awful old knee joint in.'

Sophia went to the telephone and dialled a number. 'You know I really admire her for doing the first aid course, I never would have expected it, like the pigeon, and dyeing her hair. It all shows how I underestimated Florence.' She rang up Vocal Lodge and asked Sir Ivor whether she and Rudolph might dine with him the next day. 'There is a Brotherhood orgy here, and we can't take it.'

'Yes, Sophie, my darling, you may, but you must be nice to the Gogothskys who are coming, and not make poor dear Olga cry like you did last time. Promise? All right, eight o'clock then, I have to be at my post by ten.'

'Thank goodness for that,' said Sophia to Rudolph when she had rung off. 'People from every European country, think of it. I mean the whole point of the war is one doesn't have to see foreigners any more. And as for what the President said to Heth—horrors!'

The Russians marched into Poland on the very day of

Florence's party. Luke was stunned by this practical demonstration of Russo-German solidarity.

'Herr Hitler told me himself that his life's work was to lead a crusade against Bolshevism.'

'Then you ought to have smelt a rat at once,' said Sophia unkindly.

'But he was so earnest about it. He said over and over again that Bolshevism was the greatest force for evil the world has ever known.'

'Of course I don't want to say I told you so, darling, but there's never been a pin to put between the Communists and the Nazis. The Communists torture you to death if you're not a worker, and the Nazis torture you to death if you're not a German. If you are they look at your nose first. Aristocrats are inclined to prefer Nazis while Jews prefer Bolshies. An old bourgeois like yourself, Luke, should keep your fingers out of both their pies.'

Luke must have been quite distracted. He did not even protest, as he usually did, when Sophia called him a bourgeois, that the Garfields were an old Saxon family dating back to before the Conquest. Which, as Sophia would very justly observe, did not affect the matter one way or another.

'And let me tell you,' she went on, 'if you continue to believe everything these foreigners in Germany said to you, you are in for some very nasty shocks, old boy. They have told a lot of people a lot of things not strictly speaking true, and most of us are beginning to get wise. The day they said they would never use gas against civilians every First Aid Post in London let down its gas-proof flaps, and we have all stifled ever since.'

Poor Luke passed his hand over his smooth, white forehead and looked sad. Sophia was sorry that she had been so beastly to him, and said, 'Darling, are you excited for your party to-night?'

'I am not a baby to be excited for a party. It will, I hope, be interesting. Mr. Egg appears to have seen the President.'

So Rudolph was right, and Luke was getting bored with the Brotherhood. She wondered whether it was a religion which took a great hold on people, and whether it would leave the poor fellow with an uneasy conscience for the rest of his life.

Brothers and Sisters now began flocking into the house. They all looked very much alike and might easily, had there not been a hundred of them, have been brothers and sisters indeed. The girls were all dressed in simple little tub frocks with a bastard Tyrolean flavour, they wore no hats or stockings, and quite a lot of grimy toes poked their way out of sandals. They were sunburnt, their foreheads were wrinkled, and their hair and lips were very thin. The young men, of whom there were quantities, appeared at first sight to be extremely well dressed, but their suits were too broad at the shoulder, too slim in the hips, and not made of quite the very best stuff—in fact, they would not stand up to close examination. They answered to names like Heth for Heatherley, Ken for Kennerley, and Win for Winthrop, and spoke with Hollywood accents. They were sunburnt, and when you first looked at them, immensely handsome, like the suits. Their eyes and teeth were blue. The cosmopolitan element in this party was not in evidence, and Sophia thought Florence must have meant Americans from every country in Europe, until she heard a gabble of foreign languages. She concluded that the Brotherhood, like Hollywood, places its own stamp on all nationalities, as it certainly confers a particular type of looks, of clothes, and that 'If this is pleasure give me pain' expression which is permanently on all the faces of its adherents. There was not one soul in uniform.

Rudolph, however, when he arrived to take Sophia down to Kew was resplendent in the full rig of the Wessex Guards.

'I kept it secret for a surprise for you,' he said; 'wait till you see my coat, though, lined with scarlet.'

'Well, you do look pretty,' said Sophia approvingly. Before the war, she had often thought of seeing him in uniform for the first time, and had supposed that she would cry. Now she simply felt delighted. Indeed Rudolph, unusually well shaved, looked handsome and soldierly, an example, she felt, to the brothers. War psychology, so incomprehensible during peace time, already had her in its grip.

Florence introduced Mr. Egg to them. 'Heatherley, this is Sophia Garfield, Rudolph, this is Heatherley.' Brotherhood manners were like that. 'Sophia, you must wait a moment while Heth tells us what the President said to him. He's just going to now.' She got up on a chair and clapped her hands. 'Silence everybody, please. Heatherley is going to tell us what the President said about Moral Rearmament.'

Silence fell at once, and all faces were turned towards Heatherley who was scrambling on to the chair.

'Well, folks,' he said impressively, 'I went to see the President.' Pause. 'We were alone together, just the three of us, you understand. The President is a busy man.' Pause. 'Well, he said to me.' An impressive pause, Heatherley looked all round the room, and finally continued, 'He said "I think Moral Rearmament is a very very fine idea." '

There was a prolonged and reverent silence, broken by Florence who said, 'I always think it is so important to hear the exact words when a man like that makes a statement like that. Thank you, Heth; personally I shall treasure this little scene.'

The Gogothskys were already at Vocal Lodge when Sophia and Rudolph arrived. Olga, greatly to Sophia's delight, for she made a mental collection of Olga's clothes, was wearing a snood. A bit of it came round and fastened under her chin like a beard and she looked, as no doubt she felt, very Slav. The Prince, a huge jolly drunken fellow whom everybody liked, was dressed in Air Force blue; he announced that he was on leave from his balloon, Blossom. It was evident that Blossom had made a man of him. Hitherto his life had been spent trailing about after Olga, making, in return for her considerable income, the small and rather unreal (as he was a British subject), but in his wife's eyes, invaluable, contribution of princedom. Now he was bronzed, clean, fairly well shaven, and apparently quite sober. He and Rudolph slapped each other on the back, compared uniforms and were very gay.

'You managed to get away from your chief,' Sophia said to Olga, her eyes feasting on the snood.

'He heard of my sorrow and begged me to take some leave,' said Olga reproachfully.

'Sorrow?' said Rudolph. 'Why, you are looking a bit widowed, come to think of it. What's up?'

'My relations in Poland—'

'Didn't know you had any,' said Sophia sceptically.

'Didn't you, darling? Yes, indeed, my great-great-great-grandmother was a Paczinska, and I fear my poor cousins must have fallen into Bolshevik hands. You know what that meant in Russia—they were given over to their peasantry to do as they liked with.' Olga gave a tremendous shudder.

Sophia said there must be something wrong somewhere. If the Duchess of Devonshire, for instance, was handed over to the peasantry to do as they liked with, they would no doubt put her in the best bedroom and get her a cup of tea. 'If the peasantry are really such demons,' she said, 'whose fault is that, pray?'

'But I saw in the papers that the Bolshies are going in on purpose to protect you White Russians,' said old Ivor, rather puzzled.

Serge Gogothsky had been brought up in England, and had spent most of his life here. He must, therefore, have been well accustomed to the national ignorance on the subject of foreign affairs, but this was too much even for him. He gave a sort of warbling roar, and jumped about the room like an agonized Petrushka explaining the historical and geographical position of White Russia.

'All right, keep your hair on,' said the old singer, taking his off and adjusting a curl. 'Have another drink.'

This panacea for all ills was accepted, and peace reigned once more until Rudolph tactlessly observed that he was not so enthusiastic about Europe being overrun by the murderous Muscovites as Hitler seemed to be. The Prince once more became very much excited, and said that if the Allies had assisted the White Russians at the end of the last war and enabled them to reinstate the Romanoffs, none of this would have happened.

'What nonsense. The Romanoffs were just as likely to get

imperial ideas as Uncle Joe any day of the week. You Asiatics should be kept out of Europe, that's what it is.'

'Keep your hairs on, dears, and let's have dinner,' said Sir Ivor, who only enjoyed joking conversations of an esoteric kind.

During dinner Sophia noticed that Olga was drooping her eyelids a good deal at Rudolph who seemed not to be disliking it. She cast about for means of retaliation (upon Rudolph, Olga she could always deal with very easily) but saw none to hand. The old gentleman would hardly bring conviction as a stalking horse, and the trouble with Serge was that the smallest encouragement too often led to rape. A tremendous dip of the offending eyelids stung Sophia into action and she turned to Olga with a sweet smile and asked how Savonarola was getting along. She always reserved this question for very special occasions.

'Dearest, there is a war on, you know. Sometimes, however, I do manage to do a little scribbling, busy as I am my poetry simply forces its way on to paper. Last night, during a lull, I read some of my sonnets to the Chief. He says they remind him of Elizabeth Browning's Sonnets to the Portuguese.'

'From,' said Rudolph. 'Who is your Chief?'

Olga gave a great swoop of the eyelids, and said that her job, which was very important, and her Chief, who was very very famous, had to be kept very very secret.

'Bet Haw-Haw knows them,' said Rudolph. 'I suppose you are one of those pin-money lovelies I am always reading about, eh? Come clean now, aren't you?'

'By the way, dears, I have a new job,' said Ivor.

Sophia wrestled with temptation. She longed to take Olga down a peg by being in the know; the old gentleman was just going to tell them himself, so where would be the harm? On the other hand, Fred had begged her to be careful. She decided to wait and see what Ivor said. Meanwhile the conversation flowed on.

Rudolph said, 'I suppose you are a wonderful old spy in a wonderful new wig. I suppose that's what Olga is really, a beautiful female spy, worming her way into the hearts of careless young officers like Serge and me.' Olga, who liked to be taken very seriously, was not pleased. She drooped her eyelids at the Empire *dessus de table* instead of at Rudolph, and Sophia relaxed once more.

'Talking of jobs, you should see Sophia's Post,' went on Rudolph, who entirely against her orders, was always popping in and out of it. 'Serge, old boy, here's a tip for you—the first thing that strikes the eye is a notice, written out in wobbling capitals by our Sophia, which says, "Never give a drink to a patient marked H." See the form, you old mujik, the great thing is never by any chance let yourself be marked H. Farther on, however, you come to notices with arrows attached, also written by our little friend, and therefore extremely unprofessional in appearance, saying, "Males remove underclothing here", "Females remove underclothing here", and these lead, quite logically, to the midwifery department. I had no idea the Borough Councils were such realists.'

'It's called the Labour Ward,' said Sophia; 'don't listen to him, he had no business to come prying round my Post.'

'The Labour Ward has to be seen to be believed,' said Rudolph; 'it's a kind of dog kennel, and the only furnishings are a cradle and a pair of woolly boots. If I were a lady I should bag not having a baby there, I must say, raid or no raid.'

'Poor Sister Wordsworth can't get anybody to take charge of it, did I tell you?' said Sophia, falling happily into talking shop. 'You see, it's awfully dull just sitting and looking at the cradle all day, they prefer the treatment room.'

'But the real thrill is the Hospital Museum,' went on Rudolph. 'It's next door to the Labour Ward—very suitable really, as exhibit A is a bottle containing pre-natal Siamese twins. You should come along one day, Serge, and take a load of the ulcerated stomachs. I promise nobody shall mark you H, and there's a pub up the street.'

'You've none of you taken any interest in my new job,' said the King of Song peevishly.

'Darling Ivor, how beastly of us. Come clean, then. What is it?'

'I'm to go down to Torquay with our evacuated orchids.'

399

4

Sophia sat by her telephone at the Post, and tried not to long for an air raid. On the one or two occasions when she had lifted up the receiver and had heard, instead of the Medical Officer of Health wishing to speak to Sister Wordsworth, 'This is the Southern Report Centre. Air raid warning Yellow,' she had experienced such an unhealthy glow of excitement that she felt she might easily become a raid addict, or take to raids in the same way that people do to drugs, and for much the same reason. Her life outside the Post had ceased to be much fun, for Rudolph, after looking almost too pretty in his uniform for about a week, was now paying the penalty attached to such prettiness in a training camp on the East Coast.

Inside the Post she made up things to keep her occupied, as people do who lie for weeks in bed not particularly ill. She looked a great deal at her watch, knitted, read Macaulay's *History of England*, wrote quantities of unnecessary letters for the first time since she was a girl, and chatted to Sister Wordsworth. Finally, as a last resort, there was the wireless. Sophia hated the wireless. It seemed to her to be a definite and living force for evil in the land. When she turned it on, she thought of the women all over England in lonely houses with their husbands gone to the war, sick with anxiety for the future. She saw them putting their children to bed, their hearts broken by the loneliness of the evening hours, and then, for company, turning on the wireless. What is the inspiration which flows to them from this, the fountainhead, as it must seem to them, of the Empire? London, with all its resources of genius, talent, wit, how does London help them through these difficult times? How are they made to feel that England is not only worth dying for but being poor for, being lonely and unhappy for? With great music, stirring words and sound common sense? With the glorious literature, nobly spoken, of our ancestors? Not at all. With facetiousness and jazz.

Chatting to Sister Wordsworth was her favourite occupation. This young and pretty creature turned out to be a remarkable person in many ways. Before the war, she had been a health visitor, and Sophia, who knew but little of such matters, discovered that this was a profession which required the combination of a really impressive training with such virtues as tact, knowledge of human nature, sense of humour, and a complete lack of pretentiousness. Sister Wordsworth's charming, rather hearty manner was that of a schoolgirl, deceptively young, but she was a nurse, certified midwife, and trained psychologist, and furthermore, had an extensive knowledge of the law. Week after week she kept close upon a hundred idle people in that Post contented, on good terms with each other, and in so far as she could invent things for them to do, busy. Of course, there were troubles and difficulties. A German Jew had come to the Post as a voluntary worker; after two days the nurses had sent a deputation to Sister Wordsworth saying that they could not work in the same building as a Prussian spy, and she was obliged to send him to the next Post in the district where it was to be hoped that a more tolerant spirit prevailed. Sophia had been greatly tickled by this, and had wished that a few Prussians could have had a look at their prototype. She asked why he was supposed to be a spy. It seemed that he had spent half an hour reading the notices which were displayed everywhere in the Post, and which pertained to such things as the horrid fate of patients marked H, hot-water-bottles to be filled at certain specified hours, the quantity of sterilized instruments to be kept handy, and so on. Sophia, who had written most of them out herself, could not believe that the High Command in Berlin would find its path greatly smoothed by such information. Still, as Fred had remarked when she told him about it, 'You can't be too careful, and after all, we are at war with the Germans.' Fred had a wonderful way of hitting nails on the head.

Today it was a Sunday, and all was very quiet in the Post. Sister Wordsworth was out, the wireless programme absolutely impossible, and the workmen who generally made life hideous with their bangings were able, unlike the personnel of the Post, to take Sundays off. Sophia did her knitting. She was a bad, slow knitter, and the sleeves of anything she made were always too short. She listened dreamily to a conversation which was going on beyond the sacking partition. Three of the nurses were discussing a certain foreign Royal Family with an inaccuracy astonishing as to every detail. It all sounded rather cosy and delicious, and Sophia would have liked to join in. One of the penalties, however, attached to immunity from knee-joints was that she was incarcerated in the office. The people in the treatment room had lovely gossips, but the day would come when they would have knees as well; in order to avoid the knees, she was obliged to forgo the gossips.

'ST. ANNE'S HOSPITAL FIRST AID POST

'Darling, darling, darling, darling,

'I say, Florence's bird is house-trained, I saw her letting it out of the window like a dog last thing at night. I only saw this because I happened to be in that loo which isn't blacked out, with the light off, of course, and I heard a great flapping and Florence's window opening, so I was guided to look out. As there is a moon, I saw it quite clearly streaking off to do its business with a most determined look on its face. I waited for ages, but it didn't come back. What d'you suppose it does, peck on the window, or coo or what? Well, I should love to have a terribly nice, pretty faithful house-trained pigeon, what with missing Milly and so on, and I said so this morning to Florence, but she gave me a simply horrid look, so perhaps she thought I was laughing at her or something which indeed I wasn't. Really I am getting quite attached to Florence, and it's nice for Luke having her around, with me here such a lot, gives him something else to think about besides the Income Tax. Poor old thing, he looks fearfully tucked up about that, and of course it must be hell paying all those seven and sixes for a war you don't believe in much. Besides, he feels quite torn in two between his heroes, Our Premier and Herr Hitler, now they don't tread the same path any longer.

'Darling, how is camp life, and do you miss me? Florence quite misses you, you know, perhaps she is in love with you. She keeps on coming into my room to ask what your address is, and what battalion you have joined, and how long you will be training, and who your commanding officer is and all sorts of things. I expect you'll get a balaclava for Christmas; she is knitting one for some lucky fellow, but I think he must be one of those African pigmies with a top knot by the shape of it.

'Oh dear, I do love you, love from your darling

'SOPHIA.

'PS. Olga is really putting on a most peculiar act. She lunched alone at the Ritz yesterday in a black wig, a battle bowler and her sables, and pretended not to know any of her friends. Half-way through lunch a page-boy (she had bribed him no doubt) brought her a note, and she gave a sort of shriek, put a veil over the whole thing, battle bowler and all, and scrammed. So now of course everyone knows for certain she is a beautiful female spy. Poor old Serge has been dismissed from his Blossom because he passed out and so did it; I here they looked too indecent lying side by side in the Park.'

As Sophia finished her letter Sister Wordsworth came in.

'Oh, Lady Sophia,' she said, 'I forgot to tell you that a friend of yours came to see me yesterday morning. She is joining the Post to-morrow for the night shift, full time. It is lucky as we are so very short-handed on that shift.'

'A friend of mine—what's she called?'

'Miss—I have it written down here, wait a minute—oh, yes, Miss Turnbull.'

'Gracious,' said Sophia, 'you surprise me. I never would have thought it of Florence. She hasn't said a word about it to me. Can I go now?'

'Yes, do. I shall be here the whole evening.'

Sophia found herself, for the first time since the beginning of the war, dining alone with Luke. It struck her that he wanted to have an intimate conversation with her, but did not quite know how to begin. Sophia would have been willing to help him; she was feeling quite soft towards Luke these days, he looked so ill and unhappy, but intimate conversations, except very occasionally with Rudolph, were not much in her line.

Luke began by saying that he was going back to the Foreign Office.

'How about your business?'

'There isn't any,' he said shortly, 'and I must tell you, my dear Sophia, that you and I are going to be very much poorer.'

'So I supposed. Well, you must decide what we ought to do. We could move into the garage at the back of the house very easily, and I could manage with a daily maid, or none at all. I should probably have to work shorter hours at the Post in that case.'

Luke, who was always put out by Sophia's apparent indifference to the advantages his money had brought her, shook his head impatiently. 'We shall be forced to make various radical economies by the very fact of there being a war. I shall not travel as I used to, we shall not entertain, there will be no question of any shooting or fishing, and you I presume will not be wanting much in the way of new clothes. There is absolutely no need to reduce our standard of living any further for the present. Besides, I should think it very wrong to send away any servants.'

'Except Greta,' said Sophia. 'I wish to goodness we could get rid of her. I simply hate having a German about the place, and so do the others. Mrs. Round keeps on saying to me, "Not to be able to talk world politics in one's own servants' hall is very upsetting for all of us." I'm sure it must be. And yet I haven't the heart to put her in the street, poor thing. It's all my own fault, I never liked her but I was too lazy to give her notice, you know how it is.'

'Better keep her on for a time, now she is here.'

'Oh yes, I know. We must really.'

They ate on in a polite and not very comfortable silence.

Luke said presently, 'Sophia, I hope you don't object to Florence staying on here.'

'Of course not.'

'She is very poor, you know. I don't know what would become of her unless we could help her.'

Sophia's eyebrows went up. She thought that the Brotherhood must really be improving Luke's character. Hitherto he had despised, disliked and mistrusted people for no better reason than that they were poor.

''Well then, of course we must help her,' she said warmly. 'I wonder—perhaps she would think it awful cheek if I offered to give her my silver-fox coat. I never wear it now, and I know they are not fashionable, but it is extremely warm.'

'That is very good of you, my dear Sophia, and I am sure if you were guided to share it with her she would be only too happy to accept.'

Sophia stifled the temptation to say that she would arrange for it to come clean at Sketchley's first.

'I'm very glad Florence is here to keep you company when I'm at the Post,' she said; 'actually she has joined the Post too now, did you know, but our shifts only overlap by about an hour. It's really very good of her; she is going to do a twelve hour night shift, simply horrible I should think.'

'Florence is, of course, one of the people who believed, as I did, that Herr Hitler and Our Premier between them could make a very wonderful thing of world relationships. Like me, she is bitterly disillusioned by Herr Hitler's treacherous (yes it is the only word) treacherous behaviour to Our Premier. But like me, she feels that this cruel war is not the proper solution, it can only cause a deterioration in world affairs and will settle nothing. People who think as we do are ploughing a lone furrow just now, you know, Sophia.'

'What I can't see is why you think that the behaviour of the Germans has been any worse, or different, during the past few months from what it always is. Anybody who can read print knows what they are like, cruel and treacherous, they have always been the same since the days of the Roman Empire. I can't see why we have to wait for Government Blue Books and White Papers to tell us all this—oh well,' she said, 'what's the good of talking about it now? I really do feel awfully sorry for you, Luke, as you have so many friends over there and thought everything was going to be rosy.'

'Don't misunderstand me,' said Luke, earnestly, 'I consider that Herr Hitler has treated Our Premier most outrageously. At the same time, I feel that if the British people had gone all out for moral rearmament and real appeasement, things need never have reached this pass.'

'The British people indeed, that's a good one, I must say. However, it's now quite obvious to any thinking man that our lot in life is to fight the huns about once in every twenty years. I'm beginning to consider having a baby; we shall need all we can muster to cope with the 1942 class in 1960, who, if there is anything in heredity, will be the most awful brutes.'

Luke, who belonged to the 'We have no quarrel with the German people' school of thought, looked wistful, and presently went off to his smoking-room.

Rudolph wrote:

'It is exactly like one's private here. One of the masters gave us bayonet drill this morning—this is how it goes:

' "The first thing we 'ave got to consider is wot are the parts of a soldier? First you 'ave the 'ead. Now, the 'ead of a soldier is covered with a tin 'at, so it ain't of no good to go sloshing it with a bay'net becos all yer gits is a rattle. Wot ave we next—the throat, and the throat is a very different proposition. Two inches of bay'net there, and yer gits the wind-pipe and the jugular. Very good. Next we comes to wot yer might call the united dairies. A soldier's dairies are well covered with ammunition pouches and for this reason should be left alone, and also becos a very little lower down yer gits the belly. Now it only requires three inches of bayonet in the belly, twist it well, and out they comes, liver and lights and all. Etc. (I spare you the rest of the anatomical analysis.) Now, when pursuing a retreating enemy, you should always make a jab for 'is kidneys becos it will then go in like butter and come out like butter. When the —— is wounded, you should kneel on 'is chest and bash his face with the butt end, thus keeping the bay'net ready in case you want it to jab at some other —— with. You've got to 'ate the ——s or yer won't git nowhere with them." (Tremendous pantomine.) If it wasn't so heavenly, I might easily have felt sick.

'How are you? If you ask me, I think Florence is more of a beautiful female spy than Olga; I call all this bird-life extremely

406

suspicious. I shall be having some leave soon and intend to conduct a rigid investigation in Flossie's bedroom. Meanwhile you be on the look-out for suspicious behaviour—cameras, for instance, people lurking on stairs, false bottoms to trunks and all the other paraphernalia.

'I don't get along without you very well.

'Love and xxxx Rudolph.'

5

The newspapers suddenly awoke from the wartime hibernation and were able to splash their pages with a story which all their readers could enjoy. The idol of the British people, the envy of all civilized nations, the hero of a thousand programmes, The Grand Old Gentleman of Vocal Lodge, in short none other than the famous King of Song, Sir Ivor King himself, had been found brutally done to death in the Pagoda at Kew Gardens. Here was a tale to arouse interest in the bosoms of all but the most hardened cynics, and indeed the poor old man's compatriots, as they chewed their bacon and eggs the following morning, were convulsed with rather delicious shudders. The naked corpse, they learnt, surmounted by that beloved old bald head, had been mutilated and battered with instruments ranging from the bluntness of a croquet mallet to the sharpness of a butcher's knife. This treatment had rendered the face unrecognizable, and only the cranium had been left untouched. His clothes had been removed and there was no trace of them, but his favourite wig, dishevelled and bloodstained, was found, late in the evening, by two little children innocently playing on Kew Green. Those lucky ones among the breakfasting citizens who subscribed to the *Daily Runner* began their day with

WIGLESS HEAD ON KEW PAGODA, HEADLESS WIG
ON GREEN

Later, when they issued forth into the streets it was to find that the placards of the evening papers had entirely abandoned 'U-Boat Believed Sunk', 'Nazi Planes Believed Down', 'Hitler's Demands', 'Stalin's Demands', and the reactions of the U.S.A., and were devoting themselves to

408

what soon became known as the Wig Outrage. 'Wig on Green Sensation, Latest.' 'Pagoda Corpse—Foul Play?' 'Wig Mystery, Police Baffled.'

When the inquest was held, the police were obliged to issue an appeal to the great crowds that were expected, begging them to stay at home in view of the target which they would represent to enemy bombers. In spite of this warning, the Wig Inquest was all too well attended, and the Wig Coroner had a few words to say about this generation's love of the horrible. Indeed, Chiswick High Road had the aspect of Epsom Heath at Derby Day's most scintillating moment.

It would be difficult to do better, for an account of the Wig Inquest than to switch over, as they say on the wireless, to the columns of the *Evening Runner*:

INQUEST ON WIG MURDER
VALET'S STATEMENT
ONLY CURLED LAST WEEK
WAS MURDERED MAN THE KING OF SONG?

'The "colonel's lady and Judy O'Grady" fought for places at the inquest to-day on the body, which was found last Friday in Kew Pagoda, and which is presumed to be that of Sir Ivor King, "the King of Song". The body was so extensively mutilated that a formal identification was impossible, although Mr. Larch, Sir Ivor's valet, swore that he would recognize that particular cranium anywhere as belonging to the "King".

'HIS MASTER'S VOICE

'Giving evidence, Mr. Larch, who showed signs of great emotion, said that Sir Ivor had left Vocal Lodge to go to London at two o'clock on Friday afternoon. He had seemed rather nervous and said that he had to keep a very important appointment in town, but that he would be back in time to change for a local sing-song he had promised to attend after tea. His master's voice, said Mr. Larch, had been in great demand with A.R.P. organizations, and Mr. Larch thought that what with so much singing, and the evacuations in the Orchid House, Sir Ivor had been looking strained and tired of late. By tea-time he had not returned. Mr. Larch did not feel unduly worried. "Sir Ivor had the temperament of an artiste, and was both unpunctual and vague, sometimes spending whole nights in the Turkish bath without informing his staff that he intended to sleep out."

'His Favourite Wig

' "When the children brought in the wig," went on Mr. Larch, "I thought it was eerie, as it was his favourite wig; we only had it curled last week, and he would never have thrown it away. Besides, I knew he had no spare with him. I immediately notified the police." Here Mr. Larch broke down and had to be assisted out of the court.

'Mr. Smith, taxi-driver, said that the old person first of all told him to go to the Ritz, but stopped him at Turnham Green and was driven back to the gates of Kew Gardens where he paid the fare, remarking that it was a fine day for a walk. He was singing loudly in a deep tenor all the while, and seemed in excellent spirits.

'A Very High Note

'Mr. Jumont, a gardener at Kew Gardens, said that he was manuring the rhododendrons when he heard the "King" go past on a very high note.

'The Coroner: "Did you see him?"

'Mr. Jumont: "No, sir. But there was no mistaking that old party when he was singing soprano. Besides, this was his favourite song, 'When I am dead, my dearest'." (Music by the Marchioness of Waterford.)

'At these words there was a sensation, and hardly a dry eye in court. Some fashionably dressed ladies were sobbing so loudly that the Coroner threatened to have them evicted unless they could control themselves.

410

'Continuing his evidence, Mr. Jumont said that Sir Ivor seemed to be walking in the direction of the Pagoda, the time being about 3 p.m.

'A Wonderful Thatch

'Mr. Bott, another employee at Kew Gardens, told how he had found the body. Just before closing time he noticed some blood stains and one or two blond curls at the foot of the Pagoda, then saw that the Pagoda door, which is always kept locked, stood ajar. He went in, and a trail of blood on the stairs led him to the very top where the sight which met his eyes was so terrible that he nearly swooned. "More like a butcher's shop it was, and it gave me a nasty turn."

'Coroner: "Did it seem to you at the time that this might be the body of Sir Ivor King?"

'Mr. Bott: "No, sir. For one thing the old gentleman (who, of course, I knew very well by sight) always seemed to have a wonderful thatch, as you might say, for his age, but the only thing I could clearly see about the individual on the Pagoda was that he hadn't a hair to his name."

'Mr. Bott said, in answer to further questioning, that it had never occurred to him Sir Ivor King's hair might have been a wig.

'One or two more witnesses having been examined, the Coroner's jury, without retiring, returned a verdict of murder by person or persons unknown.

'The Coroner said there was an overwhelming presumption that the corpse was that of Sir Ivor King.'

Next day, the *Daily Runner*, in its column of pocket leading articles called BRITAIN EXPECTS, in which what Britain generally Expects is a new Minister for Agriculture, had a short paragraph headed:

'Mourn the King of Song

'A very gallant and loved old figure has gone from our

411

midst. Mourn him. But remember that he now belongs to the past. It is our duty to say that in the circumstances of his death there may be more than meets the eye. One of our Cabinet Ministers may be guilty of negligence. If so, we should like to see a statement made in Parliament.

'*Our* grief must not blind us to *his* fault. For remember that *we* belong to the future.'

There was more than met the eye. Sure enough, the very next day it was learned from reliable sources that the King of Song has been a trump-card in the hand of the Government. He had, in fact, been about to inaugurate, in conjunction with the B.B.C., Ministry of Information, and Foreign Office, the most formidible campaign of Propaganda through the medium of Song that the world has ever seen. The British and French Governments, not only they, but democrats everywhere, had attached great importance to the scheme. They had estimated that it would have a profound effect upon neutral opinion, and indeed might well bring America into the war, on one side or another. Without the King of Song to lead it, this campaign would fall as flat as a pancake, no other living man or woman having the requisite personality or range of voice to conduct it. It must, therefore, necessarily be abandoned. Thus his untimely and gruesome end constituted about as severe a blow to the Allied cause as the loss of a major engagement would have done.

The horrid word Sabotage, the even horrider word Leakage, were now breathed, and poor Fred, who was given no credit for having conceived the idea, was universally execrated for not having delivered it. In the same way that the First Lord of the Admiralty is held responsible for the loss of a capital ship, so the death of Sir Ivor was laid at poor Fred's door. He made a statement in the House that mollified nobody, and Britain Expected every morning that he would resign. Britain did not expect it more than poor Fred expected that he would have to; however, in the end he got off with a nasty half-hour at No. 10. It was now supposed that the King of Song had been liquidated by German spies who had fallen into Kew Gardens in parachutes, and Sophia said 'I told you so' to Luke, and hardly dared look out of her bedroom window any more.

Sophia was really upset by the whole business. She had loved her old godfather, and having always seen a great deal of him she would miss him very much. On the other hand, it cannot be denied that she found a certain element of excitement in her near connection with so ghastly and so famous a murder—especially when, the day after the inquest, Sir Ivor's solicitor rang her up and told her, very confidentially, that Vocal Lodge and everything in it had been left to her. She had also inherited a substantial fortune and a jet tiara.

Sophia now considered herself entitled to assume the gratifying rôle of mourner in chief. She took a day off from the Post, instructed Rawlings to fill up the car with a month's ration of petrol, and drove round to the Brompton Oratory. Here she spent an hour with a high dignitary of the Roman Church arranging for a Requiem Mass to be held at the Oratory. The dignitary was such a charmer, and Sophia was so conscious of looking extremely pretty in her new black hat, that she cast about for ways of prolonging the interview. Finally she handed over a large sum of money so that masses could be sung in perpetuity for the old gentleman's soul; and when she remembered the eternal basting to which he had so recently condemned her, she considered that this was a high-minded and generous deed on her part. The transaction over, she made great efforts to edge the conversation round to her own soul, but the dignitary, unlike Florence, seemed completely uninterested in so personal a subject, and very soon, with tact and charm but great firmness, indicated to her that she might go. Sophia, as she drove away, reflected that whatever you might say about Popery it is, at least, a professional religion, and shows up to great advantage when compared with such mushroom growths as the Boston Brotherhood.

On her way to Vocal Lodge she went to pick up Lady Beech who had consented to accompany her on her sad pilgrimage. She was to meet the solicitor there, see Sir Ivor's servants and make various arrangements connected with her legacy. Lady Beech lived in Kensington Square. She was evidently determined to take the fullest advantage of Sophia's petrol ration, for, when the car drew up at her front door, she was already standing on the steps beside an enormous object of no particular shape done up in sacking.

'Very late,' she said. 'Most unlike you. I know, darling, that you won't mind taking this little bed to Heal's on our way.'

This rather delayed matters. It became evident, during the course of the drive, that Lady Beech very much wished that Vocal Lodge had been left to her instead of to Sophia.

'Oh, darling, what a pity,' said Sophia; 'silly old gentleman not to think of it. Of course I'm going to give it to the Nation, don't you think that's right, really? To be kept exactly as it is, a Shrine of Song, and I am giving some of the money he left to keep it up. He left nearly a quarter of a million, you know, so I am going to build an Ivor King Home of Rest for aged singers, and an Ivor King Concert Hall as well. Don't you think he'd be pleased?'

'Very wonderful of you, my dear,' said Lady Beech gloomily. 'Tell me, now, had it occurred to you what a very much more interesting gift to the Nation Vocal Lodge would be if somebody lived in it—I mean somebody rather cultivated, with rather exquisite taste? She could preserve the spirit of the place, don't you see? Like those châteaux on the Loire which have their original families living in them.'

Sophia said she had just the very person in mind, an old governess of her own, who was extremely cultivated and had perfectly exquisite taste. Lady Beech sighed deeply.

When they arrived at Vocal Lodge, Sophia was closeted for some time, first with the solicitor and then with Sir Ivor's servants, whom she begged to stay on there for the rest of their lives if it suited them. Larch took her upstairs and showed her all Sir Ivor's wigs laid out on his bed, rather as it might have been a pilgrimage to view the body. He was evidently, like Sophia, divided between genuine sorrow and a feeling of self-importance.

414

'The Press, m'lady,' he said with relish, 'awful they've been. Nosing round everywhere and taking photos. And the lies they tell, I don't know if you saw, m'lady, they said cook had been with Sir Ivor ten years. It's not a day more than seven.'

'I know,' said Sophia. 'I can't go outside the house for them. Why, look at all the cars which have followed us down here.' And indeed there had been a perfect fleet, greatly incommoded, Sophia was glad to think, by the roundabout and, to them, surely rather baffling journey via Heal's.

Lady Beech meanwhile had not been idle. It was quite uncanny what a lot of Sir Ivor's furniture, books, knick-knacks and even cooking utensils had been lent to him by Lady Beech. The house was really nothing but a loan collection. She had, with great forethought, provided herself with two packets of labels, stick-on and tie-on, and by the time Sophia had finished her business, these appeared like a sort of snow-storm, scattered through all the rooms.

'Darling, I have just labelled a few little things of my own which dear Ivor had borrowed from me from time to time,' she said, putting a sticky one firmly on to the giant radiogram as she spoke.

'Very sensible, darling.' Sophia secured the jet tiara, an object which she had coveted from childhood. 'Good-bye, then, Larch,' she said. 'Keep the wigs, won't you, and we'll send them to the Ivor King Home of Rest. The aged singers are sure to need them, and I feel it's just what *he* would have liked.' Larch evidently thought that this idea was full of good feeling, and held open the door of the car with an approving look.

They motored back to London in silence, Sophia loved Lady Beech and would have done almost anything for her, but she knew that it would be useless to present Vocal Lodge to the Nation if Lady Beech was always to be there, sighing at whatever visitors might venture in.

'St. Anne's Hospital First Aid Post

'Darling Rudolph darling,

415

'Well, the Memorial Service, I mean Requiem Mass. Did you see the photograph of Luke and me with the glamorous Mgr? I thought it was quite pretty. The object behind us in silver foxes was Florence in my ex-ones. You never saw anything like the crowds outside the Oratory, and inside there were people all over the statues. When we arrived at the front pew reserved for us, who do you think was in it dressed as what? Of course Olga as a Fr. widow. You should have seen the looks darling Lady Beech gave her. She would keep singing just like one doesn't in Papist churches, and Serge was crying out loud into a huge black-edged handkerchief, fancy at eleven in the morning, but I believe it's really because of his Blossom they say he can't stop.

'As we all came down the aisle Olga threw back her veil, and, supported by Fred, gave plucky little smiles to right and left. I forgot to say poor Fred turned up late, looking too guilty and hoping nobody would recognize him, and of course Hamish insisted on bringing him all the way up to our pew where there wasn't room, and after fearful whisperings Luke had to give up his place to the Minister. Then on the way out Olga felt faint so that she could cling to him as you will note if you see the *Tatler*.

'The whole of the stage world was there, of course, as well as all of us. Just think how old Ivor would have enjoyed it. What waste we couldn't have had it while he was alive, can't you see him choosing which wig he would wear? But you know, funny as it was in many ways I couldn't help feeling awfully sad, especially when we got outside again and saw those huge silent mournful crowds. There's no doubt the dear old creature was a sort of figurehead, and I suppose there can hardly be a soul in England who hasn't heard that—let's face it—slightly cracking voice. I thought *The Times* put it very nicely when it said that the more that golden voice was tinged with silver, the more we loved it. I hope those fiends of parachutists killed him quickly before he knew anything about it—they think so at Scotland Yard because of no cry being heard and no sign of a struggle.

'As soon as Fred had shaken off Olga she came floating up to us in her veil and began hinting that she knew more than she cared to reveal about Ivor's death. I'm afraid I was rather rude to her but really I'm getting tired of Olga in the rôle of beautiful female spy—it's becoming a bore. I've just sent her a telegram saying "Proceed John o' Groats and await further instructions. F.69." Hope she proceeds, that's all. Darling, what a heavenly idea that

Floss might be a B.F.S.—so teasing for Olga if she were. Now get some leave soon and we'll proceed to her bedroom and investigate.

'Love my darling from your darling

'SOPHIA.

'PS. Did I tell you Luke is proceeding to America on a very secret mission for the F.O.? Fancy choosing that old Fascist. I must get him some Horlick's malted tablets for the 100 hours in an open boat which will almost certainly be his fate—I keep advising him to go rowing on the Serpentine to get his hand in. So here I shall be, left all alone with Florrie and her gang, isn't it terrifying for me? Should you say Heatherley and Winthrop are ones too?'

6

Sophia was now designated by the newspapers as 'Wig Heiress'. The reporters pursued her from the pillars of her own front door to the Post, where Sister Wordsworth finally routed them with a hypodermic needle, in an effort to find out how she intended to dispose of her legacy. As she refused to make any statement, they invented every kind of thing. Ninety-eight Granby Gate was for sale, and Sir Luke and Lady Sophia Garfield would take up their residence at Vocal Lodge. They were only going to use it as a summer residence. They were going to pull it down and build a block of flats. (The Georgian Group, wrapped in dreams of Federal Union, stirred in its sleep on hearing this, and groaned.) They were shutting it up to avoid the rates. They were digging for victory among the Lesbian Irises. Only the truth was not told.

Luke, who really hated publicity, even when it took the form of a beautiful studio portrait of Sophia in *Vogue*, because, he said, it did him harm in the City, became very restive, and speeded up his arrangements for leaving England. Sophia spent a busy day shopping for him. Her heart smote her for not having been much nicer to him, as it did periodically, so she tried to atone in Harrod's man's shop, and he left England fully equipped as a U-boat victim. Florence saw him off at his front door and presented him with the balaclava helmet but Sophia, who accompanied him to the station, threw it out of the taxi window explaining that there was a proper machine-made one in his valise. She kissed him good-bye on the platform to the accompaniment of magnesium flares which, rather to her disappointment (because although she always looked like an elderly negress in them, she liked to see photographs of herself in the papers), were prevented by the Ministry of Information from bearing any fruit. Luke's mission was a very secret one. As a final parting present she gave him a pocket Shakespeare to read, she explained, on the desert island where his open boat would probably deposit him.

'And if you hear a loud bang in the night,' she added, as the train drew out of the station, 'don't turn over and go to sleep again.'

'Luke hates jokes and hates the war,' she said to Mary Pencill who was also on the platform, seeing off one of Trotsky's lieutenants, 'so isn't he lucky to be going to America where they have neither?'

Mary carried Sophia off to her flat when the train had gone, and they had a long and amicable talk during which they managed to avoid the subject of politics. Sophia, who was considered absolutely red by those supporters of Munich, apologists for Mussolini and lovers of Franco, Fred and Ned, was apt to feel the truest of blue Tories when in the presence of Mary whose attitude of suspicion and obstruction always annoyed her.

'Still writing on foreheads?' Mary inquired when they were settled down in front of her gas stove.

'It's all very well for you to laugh, just wait until you've got a crushed tongue and slight oozing haemorrhage like one of the patients we had in yesterday—you'll be only too glad to have me writing on your forehead.'

'How d'you mean, yesterday? Was there an air raid—I never noticed a thing.'

'Darling, you are so dense. Practice of course. The telephone bell rings, and I answer it and it says "Southern Control speaking. Practice air raid warning Red, expect casualties." Then, some time later, a lot of unhappy-looking people are brought in out of the street in return for threepence and a cup of tea. They are labelled with a description of their injuries, then we treat them, at least the nurses do, and I write on their foreheads and take them up to the canteen for their cup of tea.'

'With their foreheads still written on?'

'Well, they get threepence, don't they? First of all, we used

419

to practise on each other, but then Mr. Stone very sensibly pointed out what a shambles it would be if there were a real raid and real casualties were brought in and found all the personnel tied up in Thomas's splints, and so on. Think of it! So they work on this other scheme now; it seems much more professional too.'

'Well, all I can say is, if there's a raid I hope I shall be allowed to die quietly where I am.'

'Don't be defeatist, darling,' said Sophia.

The next day Sophia, looking, she thought, really very pretty and wearing another new black hat, went off to the Horse Guards Parade where, in the presence of a large crowd, of the microphone and of cinematographers, she handed over to Fred, who accepted it on behalf of the Nation, a cardboard model of Vocal Lodge, the Shrine of Song.

Fred made a very moving speech. He spoke first, of course, about Sophia's enormously generous action, until she hardly knew where to look. He went on to say that the Shrine of Song would be a fitting memorial to one whose loss was irreparable both to Britain and to the whole world of art; the loss of a beloved citizen and venerated artist.

'And we must remember,' he went on, warming to his work, 'that Death never has the last word. When we think of the King of Song, when we pay our pious pilgrimage to Vocal Lodge, it is not of Death that we must think but of that wonderful old spirit which is still watching over us, merged with the eternal Spirit of Patriotism. The work he would have done, had he lived to do it, will now be left undone. But will it? Those who love him—and they were not confined to this country, mind you, they mourn as we mourn in palaces and cottages the world over—those who loved him know that before he died he had intended literally to devote every breath in his body to an Ideal. He knew that if our cause is lost there will be no Song left in the world, no Music, no Art, no Joy. Lovers of music everywhere, yes and inside Germany too, will remember that the greatest singer of our time, had he not died so prematurely, was going to give his all in the

420

struggle for Freedom. Many an Austrian, many a Czech, many a Pole, and even many a German will think of this as he plays over the well-loved gramophone records, fearful of the creeping feet behind his windows, yet determined once more to enjoy, come what may, that Golden Voice. The cause of such a man, they will think, as they listen to those immortal trills, to that historic bass and of such an artist, must be indeed the Cause of Right. Who can tell but that the King of Song will not finally accomplish more in death than he, or any other mortal man, could ever accomplish in life.

'Oh Death! Where is thy sting? Oh Grave! Where is thy victory?'

This speech, which was extremely well received, put Fred back on his feet again with everybody except that irascible fellow who indicates daily to Britain what she should Expect.

'We learn,' he wrote the following day, 'that Vocal Lodge has been presented to the Nation to be kept as a Shrine of Song. How do we learn this news, of Empirewide interest? Through the columns of a free Press? No! A Minister of the Crown withholds it from the public in order to announce it himself in a speech. Praise Lady Sophia Garfield, who gives. The clumsy mismanagement of the whole affair is not her fault. Examine the record of this Minister. It is far from good. We should like to see him offer his resignation forthwith and we should like to see his resignation accepted.'

However, all the other newspapers as well as Fred's colleagues thought that it was first-class stuff and that he had more or less atoned for so carelessly mislaying the King. He was extremely grateful to Sophia who had given him the opportunity for turning Sir Ivor's death to such good account. He and Ned took her out to dinner, fed her with oysters and pink champagne, and stayed up very late indeed.

Sophia, when at last she got home, was surprised and bored, as well as rather startled, to find Greta in her bedroom. She never allowed anybody to wait up for her. Greta seemed very much upset about something, her face was swollen with tears and it was several moments before she could speak.

421

'Oh Frau Gräfin, don't let them send me back to Germany—they will, I know it, and then in a camp they will put me and I shall die. Oh, protect me, Frau Gräfin.'

'But Greta, don't be so absurd. How can anybody send you back to Germany? We are at war with the Germans, so how could you get there? You might have to be interned here in England if you didn't pass the tribunal, you know, but I will come with you and speak to the Magistrate and I'm sure it will be quite all right. Now go to bed and don't worry any more.'

Greta seemed far from being reassured. She shivered like a nervous horse and went on moaning about the horrors of German concentration camps and how she would certainly be sent to one, unless an even worse fate was in store for her.

'You've been reading the White Paper,' said Sophia impatiently. 'And it should make you realize how very, very lucky you are to be in England.'

'Oh, please protect me,' was all Greta replied to this felicitous piece of propaganda. 'They are coming for me; it may be to-night. Oh please, Frau Gräfin, may I sleep in your bathroom to-night?'

'Certainly not. Why, you have got Mrs. Round in the very next room, and Rawlings next door to that. Much safer than being in my bathroom, and besides, I want to have a bath. Now, Greta, pull yourself together and go to bed. You have been upset by poor Sir Ivor's death, and so have we all. We must just try to forget about it, you see. Good night, Greta.'

Greta clutched Sophia's arm, and speaking very fast she said, 'If I tell you something about Sir Ivor, may I sleep in your bathroom? He is——' Her voice died away in a sort of moan, her eyes fixed upon the doorway. Sophia looked round and saw Florence standing there.

'Well, that's all now, Greta. Good night,' Sophia said. Greta slunk out past Florence, who did not give her a glance but told Sophia that she had come in search of an aspirin.

'I had to go off duty, my head ached so badly.'

'Oh, what bad luck. Would a Cachet Fèvre do as well? I've just been having such a scene with Greta; she has got it into her head that somebody is going to take her back to

Germany, silly fool. I wish to goodness somebody would, I'd give anything to get rid of her.'

Florence said it was always a mistake to have foreign servants, thanked her for the Cachet Fèvre, and went upstairs. Sophia had rather been expecting that now Luke had gone perhaps Florence would be moving too, but she showed no signs of such an intention. However, the house was large, and they very rarely met, besides, she did not exactly dislike Florence; it was more that they had so little in common.

'St. Anne's Hospital First Aid Post

'My own darling Rudolph,
    'Florence has joined the Post, did I tell you, and it really is rather a joke. All those terribly nice cosy ladies who have such fun with the Dowager Queen of Ruritania and whether she had Jewish blood, and whether the Crown Princess will ever have a baby and so on, are simply withered up by Flo who says she finds extraordinarily little pleasure in gossiping nowadays. They had rather fun for a time, coming clean and sharing and being guided and so on, but they never really got into it. The last straw was that Miss Edwards said she simply couldn't tell fortunes any more when Florence was there because of the atmosphere, and Miss Edwards' fortunes were the nicest thing in the Post, we all had ours done every day. Anyhow, it seems that last night the nurses went to Sister Wordsworth in a body and said that although of course Florence is very, very charming and they all liked her very, very much, they really couldn't stick her in the Treatment Room another moment. Sister Wordsworth is wonderful, she never turned a hair. She sent for Florence at once and asked her if, as a great favour, she would consent to take charge of the Maternity Ward, which is that little dog kennel, you know, by the Museum, with a cradle and a pair of woolly boots. As it happens, Florence is very keen on obstetrics and she was delighted. So all is honey again and the Dowager Queen of Ruritania and Miss Edwards reign supreme. Sister Wordsworth says that the head A.R.P. lady in these parts is a pillar of the Brotherhood, and sent Florence with such a tremendous recommendation that she can never be sacked however much of a bore she is.
    'Heatherley and Winthrop have also joined as stretcher-bearers, in fact the Brotherhood seems to be doing pretty well, just like I

never thought it would. I wonder if Heth isn't a bit in love with Florence, there was a form which looked awfully like his on the half-landing when I got back late from the 400 a day or two ago. I was too terrified to look again, so I ran to my room and locked myself in. Probably it was my imagination.

'Love my darling, when are you going to have some leave,

'SOPHIA.'

The telephone bell rang and Sophia answered it. 'Southern Control speaking. Practice RED, expect casualties.' This meant that 'casualties' would be arriving from the street. She ran up to the canteen to warn Sister Wordsworth, who was having tea.

'Thank you, Lady Sophia. Now would you go and ring up the doctor?' said Sister Wordsworth. 'If you hurry, you will catch him at his home address. He said he would like to come to the next practice we have here.'

Sophia ran downstairs again. On her way back to the office she nearly collided with Heth and Winthrop who were carrying a stretcher.

'Casualties already!' she said, and as she was going on she noticed that the 'casualty' under the rugs on the stretcher was her own maid, Greta. For a moment she felt surprised, and then she thought that Florence must have asked Greta to do it; probably they were short of casualties. Greta was far too superior to be bribed by threepence and a cup of tea. She had a sort of bandage over her mouth, and had evidently been treated for 'crushed tongue', a very favourite accident at St. Anne's. She seemed to have something in her eye, or at any rate it was winking and rolling in a very horrible way.

Sophia, as she went to the telephone, giggled to herself. 'Typical of them,' she thought, 'to treat the wretched woman for crushed tongue when really she is half blinded by grit in the eye. Let's hope they'll take it out and give her a cup of tea soon.' As the practice got into full swing Sophia became very busy and forgot the incident. She never saw Greta again.

7

The sensation which was caused by the supposed murder of Sir Ivor King, the King of Song, at a time so extremely inconvenient to the British Government, had scarcely subsided when the old singer turned up, wig and all, in Germany. It happened on the very day that Vocal Lodge was opened to the public, a ceremony which, at the request of the A.R.P., was unadvertised, and which therefore consisted of Sophia, in a simple little black frock, dispensing cocktails to Fred, in his pin stripes, and a few other friends. The house was rather bare of furniture, owing to Lady Beech. Hardly had Fred arrived when he was called to the telephone; white to the lips he announced that he had had news which compelled him to leave for the office at once.

The German Press and Radio were jubilant. The old gentleman, it seemed, was visiting that music-loving country with the express purpose of opening there a world-wide anti-British campaign of Propaganda allied to Song. This campaign, it was considered, would have a profound effect on neutral opinion, and indeed might well bring America into the war, on one side or another. He was received like a king in Germany, the Führer sending his own personal car and bodyguard to meet him at the airport, and he celebrated his first evening in Berlin by singing 'Deutschland über Alles' on the radio in a higher and then a lower key than it had ever been sung before.

Lord Haw-haw succeeded him at the microphone, and in his inimitable accents announced that the Lieder König was too tired to sing any more that evening but that listeners should prepare for his first full programme of Song-Propaganda in two days' time at 6.30 p.m. on the thirty-one meter band.

'You must all be most anxious to hear,' continued Lord

Haw-haw, '*how* the Lieder König come to our Fatherland. (He himself will be telling you *why* he came.) Your English police, it seems, never realized that the body found on the Pagoda at Kew Gardens was, in fact, the body of a wigless pig. Had they not jumped so quickly to conclusions, had they not assumed, as, of course, they were intended to assume, that these bleeding lumps of meat did not constitute the mangled body of the Lieder König, they would not, I expect, have been in such a hurry to bury them. There must be many housewives, whose husbands are at present behind the lines in France, flirting with the pretty French demoiselles, and to whom your Minister of War, Mr. Horribleisha, has not yet paid their pathetically small allowances, who would have been only too glad to dispose of these lumps of pig. For bacon is extremely scarce in England now, and is indeed never seen outside the refrigerators of the wealthy.

'Again I ask, where is the *Ark Royal*?

'Here are the stations Hamburg, Bremen and D x B, operating on the thirty-one metre band. Thank you for your attention. Our next news in English will be broadcast from Reichsender Hamburg and station Bremen at 11.15 Greenwich mean time.'

For a day or two the English newspapers assured their readers that the loyal old 'King' was really reposing in his Catholic grave, and that the Germans must be making use of gramophone records, made before the war had begun, in order to perpetrate a gigantic hoax. Alas! The 'King' only had to give his first full-length broadcast for this theory to collapse. Nobody but himself could say 'Hullo dears! Keep your hairs on' in quite that debonair tone of voice.

'I have come to Germany,' he went on, 'with the express intention of lending my services to the Fatherland, and this I do partly because I feel a debt of gratitude to this great country, this home of music where many years ago my voice was trained, but chiefly because of my love of Slavery. I have long been a member of the English Slavery Party, an underground movement of whose very existence most of you are unaware but which is daily increasing in importance. It is

426

my intention to give bulletins of news and words of
encouragement to that Party, sandwiched between full
programmes of joyous song in which I hope you will all join.

> *'Land of dope you're gory*
> *And very much too free,*
> *The workers all abhor thee,*
> *And long for slavery.'*

After bellowing out a good deal more of this kind of drivel,
the 'King' told a long story about an English worker who,
having been free to marry a Jewess (a thing which, of course,
could never happen in Germany), had been cheated out of
one and sixpence by his brother-in-law.

'Now here is a word of advice to my brothers of the Slavery
Party. Burn your confidential papers and anything that could
incriminate you at once. Those of you who have secret stores
of castor oil, handcuffs and whips waiting for the great dawn
of Slavery, bury them or hide them somewhere safe. For Eden
was seen entering the Home Office at 5.46 Greenwich mean
time this afternoon, and presently the Black-and-Tans are to
conduct a great round-up in the homes of the suspects. For
the benefit of my non-British listeners, let me explain that the
Black-and-Tans are Eden's dreaded police, so called because
those of them that are not negroes are Mayfair play-boys, the
dregs of the French Riviera. They are a brutal band of
assassins, and those who fall foul of them vanish without any
trace.'

Now the sinister thing about all this was that Mr. Eden
really had entered the Home Office at 5.46 on the afternoon
in question. How could they have known it in Berlin at 6.30?
The Ministry of Information decided to suppress so disquieting
a fact for the present.

By the next morning, of course, every single window of the
newly constituted Shrine of Song had been broken. Lady
Beech having removed all her own furniture, books, knick-
knacks and kitchen utensils in three large vans, there was
fortunately nothing much to damage, except the 'King's'
tatty striped wallpapers. Larch and his fellow-domestics gave

427

notice at once, and fled from the Shrine of Shame as soon as they could.

Poor Sophia felt that she had been made a fool of, and wished the beastly old fellow dead a thousand times. She communicated this sentiment to the many reporters by whom she was once more surrounded, but unfortunately, once crystallized into hard print, it did not redound entirely to her credit considering that she was the 'King's' heiress. The dignitary of the Roman Catholic Church, too, was very much displeased at having been bamboozled into allowing a Requiem Mass to be sung for the soul of a pig. Indeed Roman Catholics all over the world were aghast at the 'King's' treachery, the more so as they had always hitherto felt great pride that one so distinguished should be a co-religionist, had regarded his enormous fame as being a feather in the cap of Holy Mother Church herself, and had never forgotten the pious deeds of his late wife, the posthumous Duchess King. At last Papist feeling became so strong on the subject that the Pope, bowing before the breeze, removed the body of the posthumous Duchess from its distinguished resting-place in the Vatican gardens, and had it re-interred in the Via della Propaganda. When a German note was presented to him on the subject, he gave it as an excuse that the younger cardinals were obliged to learn bicycling on account of the petrol shortage, and were continually falling over her grave. Equally furious and disillusioned were music lovers and fans of the 'King' in the whole civilized world. His gramophone records and his effigy were burnt in market towns all over England, his wigs were burnt on Kew Green, whilst in London his songs were burnt by the public hangman.

But the person who really caught the full blast of the storm was poor Fred. He hurried round to No. 10, and did not spend anything like half-an-hour there, but only just so long as it took him to write a letter beginning 'My dear Prime Minister' and to hand over his Cabinet key. He was succeeded at the Ministry by Ned, to Ned's delight hardly veiled. The *Daily Runner* unkindly printed extracts from the 'Oh! Death! where is thy sting' speech, and crowed over

428

Fred's resignation, but was not the least bit pleased over Ned's appointment, and suggested that it was a case of out of the frying-pan into the fire.

Fred and Sophia dined together very sadly at the Hyde Park Hotel. Ned would not risk being seen in such discredited company and kept away, and probably he was wise because, as they went into dinner, they were ambushed and subjected to withering fire by about ten press photographers. Fred could no longer afford oysters or pink champagne, so they had smoked salmon and claret instead.

He was intensely gloomy altogether. 'My career is over,' he said.

Sophia told him, 'Nonsense, think of Lord Palmerston,' but there was not much conviction in her voice.

The next day she heard that he had taken over Serge's Blossom.

'St. Anne's Hospital First Aid Post

'Oh, darling Rudolph, who ever would have thought it of the old horror?

'I must say there is one comfort to be got out of the whole business and that is the broadcasts. Aren't they heaven? I can't keep away from them, and Sister Wordsworth has had to alter all the shifts here so that nobody shall be on the road during them. I can't ever go out in the evening because of the 10.45 one—the 6.30 I get here before I leave.

'Poor Fred sometimes sneaks round, when he can get away from his Blossom, and we listen together after dinner. His wife simply can't stand it, and I don't blame her when you think of the thousands a year it is costing them. Certainly it comes hardest on Fred, but I look a pretty good fool too what with the Requiem Mass, Shrine of Song, and so on.

'It was fortunate about Olga being a plucky Fr. widow you must say, and being photographed with Fred, otherwise how she would have crowed. I hear she was just about to proceed to John o' Groats when she guessed it was me and now she's furious so I must think up some more things to do to her. Perhaps you could think as you're in love with her—do.

'What else can I tell you? Oh yes, Greta has left, isn't it lucky? She

429

came round here to lend a hand with a practice and hasn't been back since and apparently her luggage has all gone so I suppose she just walked out on me. I'm very pleased, I really hated having a German in the house especially as she used to be so keen on all the Nazi leaders, she gave me the creeps you know. So now Mrs. Round can talk world-politics in her own servants' hall again.

'Here everything is just the same. Florence, Heatherley and Winthrop hardly ever leave the Maternity ward at all nowadays. I can't imagine how they squash into that tiny room. They seem to be for ever fetching food from the Canteen. I believe Brothers eat twice what ordinary people do. Anyhow they don't hurt anyone by being there, and Miss Edwards is back on the top of her form again telling the most heavenly fortunes, and isn't it funny she says she can see the same thing in all our hands, like before a railway accident and it is SOMETHING QUEER UNDER YOUR FEET. Thank goodness not over your head because then I should have known it was parachutists and died of fright. She thinks perhaps this place is built over a plague spot, but Mr. Stone says it must be the Main Drain and I suppose there are some pretty queer things in that all right.

'I must fly home now because the old wretch is going to sing Camp Songs (concentration camp, I suppose) at 8 for an extra treat.

'Love and xxx from
'Sophia.

'PS. There is a water pipe which makes a noise exactly like those crickets on the islands at Cannes. Much as I hate abroad, you can hardly count Cannes and it was a heavenly summer, do you remember, when Robin lent the Clever Girl for the Sea Funeral of a Fr. solicitor from Nice and the coffin bobbed away and came up on the bathing beach at Monte Carlo. I wish it was now. Darling.'

Henceforward the doings of the Lieder König were a kind of serial story, which appeared day by day on the front pages of the newspapers, quite elbowing out the suave U-boat commanders, the joy of French poilus at seeing once more the kilt, and the alternate rumours that there would, or would not, be bacon rationing, which had so far provided such a feast of boredom at the beginning of each day. He soon became the only topic of conversation whenever two or more Englishmen met together, while the sale of wireless sets in London were reported to have gone up 50 per cent, and a hundred people of the name of King applied to change it by deed poll. His programmes were a continual treat, especially for collectors of musical curiosities, as, for instance, when he sang the first act from *La Bohème*, 'Tes petites mains sont gelées,' etc., twice through with Frau Goering, each taking alternately the male and female parts. It was after this that he suddenly gave an account of the Prime Minister walking in St. James's Park that very morning, with a list of all the birds he saw and exactly what they were doing; and although the birds, owing to the autumnal season, were behaving with absolute propriety, and therefore nobody need feel embarrassed on that score, the mere fact of such accurate knowledge having reached Berlin so quickly was disquieting to the authorities. On another occasion he sang through an entire act of *Pelléas and Mélisande*, taking all the parts himself; as a tour de force this was pronounced unique and even the *Times* music critic was obliged to admit that the Lieder König had never, within living memory, been in better voice. A touching incident occurred some days later when Herr Schmidt, the Lieder König's music teacher, who had prophesied all those years ago in Düsseldorf that Herr King's voice would make musical history, was brought to the microphone. He was now 108 and claimed to be the oldest living music teacher. His broadcast, it is true, was not very satisfactory and sounded rather like someone blowing bubbles, but the Lieder König paid a charming tribute to the old fellow. He said that as all his success in life had been due to the careful training which he had received from Herr Schmidt, a German, he was so happy that he had the opportunity of helping the Fatherland in its time of difficulty. He and his teacher were then decorated by Herr von Ribbentrop, speaking excellent English, with the Order of the Siegfried Line, 3rd class.

Always at the end of his concerts the Lieder König announced succulent pieces of good cheer for the English Slavery Party. Soon, according to his information, vast concentration camps would spring into being all over England, to be filled with Churchill, Eden and other Marxist—here he corrected himself—Liberals, Jews and plutocrats.

Soon the benevolent rule of National Socialism would stretch across the seas to every corner of the British and French Empires, harnessing all their citizens to the tyrant's yoke, and removing the last vestiges of personal freedom. Soon all nations of the world would be savouring the inestimable advantages of Slavery.

'Here are the Reichsender Bremen, stations Hamburg and D x B operating on the thirty-one metre band. This is the end of the Lieder König's talk in English.'

8

Sophia was dressing to go out to dinner with Fred, Ned and Lady Beech. She took a good deal of trouble always with her appearance, but especially when she was going to be seen in the company of Lady Beech, whose clothes were the most exquisite in London and whom it was not possible in that respect to outshine. Sophia had not attempted to replace Greta and was beginning to realize what an excellent maid that boring German had been; on this occasion she could not find anything she wanted, nor was Elsie, the housemaid, very much help to her.

Sophia was a very punctual character, with the result that she often found herself waiting for people, and indeed must have spent several weeks of her life, in all, waiting for Rudolph. On this occasion Fred and she arrived simultaneously and first, in spite of the many setbacks in her bedroom. He ordered her a drink and muttered in her ear that Ned was behaving as if he had been in the Cabinet all his life. It seemed anyhow that he felt himself firmly enough in the saddle after three Cabinet meetings to be able once more to consort with those victims of circumstances, Fred and Sophia. But of course Fred in the uniform pertaining to his Blossom was hardly at all reminiscent of Fred in the pinstripe trousers of his disgrace; he looked already brown and healthy and seemed to have grown quite an inch.

Lady Beech appeared next, wonderful in sage green and black with ostrich feathers and a huge emerald laurel leaf. Sophia felt at once extremely dowdy.

'You are lucky,' she said, 'the way you always have such heavenly things. I do wish I were you.'

'Child!' said Lady Beech, deprecatingly.

Very late the Minister himself galloped up to them

complaining loudly that he had been kept at No. 10. As his own house happened to be No. 10 Rufford Gate, there was a pleasing ambiguity about this excuse. They went in to dinner.

Fred and Ned were very partial to Lady Beech. She was the only link they had with culture, and Fred and Ned were by no means so insensible to things of the mind as they appeared to be. At school and at Oxford they had been clever boys with literary gifts and a passion for the humanities; it was only their too early excursion into politics which had reduced their intellectual capacity once more to that of the private school. The poor fellows still felt within them a vague yearning towards a higher plane of life, and loved to hear Lady Beech discourse, in polished accents how sadly unfamiliar, of Oscar, Aubrey, Jimmy, Algernon, Henry, Max, Willie, Osbert and the rest. They could talk to her, too, of those of their contemporaries whose lives had taken a more intellectual turn than their own, for Lady Beech is as much beloved by the present as she was by a past generation of artists and writers. Another thing which endeared her to them was the fact that she, unlike anybody else, called them Sir Frederick and Lord Edward and, instead of telling them her opinion of The Situation, flatteringly deferred to theirs. It made them feel positively grown up. She liked them, too; they were such pretty, polite young men, and she particularly liked oysters and pink champagne. When, on this occasion, they suggested that a little white wine would be suitable because of the income tax, and the fact that poor Fred had so little income left to tax, she sighed very dreadfully indeed and they good naturedly reverted to pre-war rations for that evening. The dinner having been ordered to her entire satisfaction, Lady Beech turned to Ned with her usual opening gambit of, 'Tell me, Lord Edward.' This was really rather horrid of her as, hitherto, it had always been, 'Tell me, Sir Frederick.'

'Tell me what you think will happen?'

Ned opened his napkin and said cheerfully, 'Oh gracious, I don't know. Nothing much, I don't expect.'

'Ah! You mean there will be no allied offensive for the moment?'

434

'Hullo, there's Bob! Well, now, Lady Beech, you won't quote me, will you? I never said that, you know. But between ourselves, quite between, well I rather expect we shall all go bumbling along as we are doing until we have won the war—or lost it, of course.'

'Should you say there was quite a good possibility of that?'

'Of what?'

'Of our losing the war?'

'Oh quite a good chance, oh Lord yes. Mind you, of course, we're bound to win really, in the end we always do. All I say is it may be a long business, the way we're settling down about it. Well, Fred, so how's the balloon these days, eh?'

'Up and down, you know. It's rather like playing a salmon, getting her down. I enjoy it. Frankly I enjoy it more than—oh well, it's a healthy outdoor life.'

'Should you say,' asked Lady Beech, 'that the balloons are of much use?'

'I'm told none whatever,' said Ned in his loud jolly voice.

'Ah!' she looked searchingly at Fred who was quite nettled.

'That's entirely a matter of opinion,' he said crossly. 'I should think myself they are a jolly sight more use than—oh well. Anyway, it's a healthy outdoor life for the lads who do it, which is more than you can say for—well, some other kinds of lives.'

'Do you think you can keep off the parachutists?' said Sophia. 'They are the only thing I mind. Give me bombs, gas, anything you like. It's the idea of those sinister grey-clad figures, with no backs to their heads, slowly floating past one's bedroom window like snowflakes that gives me the creeps.'

'They would not be grey-clad,' Ned assured her. 'If they come at all, which is very unlikely (not that the balloons would stop them) they will be dressed as Guards' officers.'

'Lean out of your window and break their legs with a poker as they go by,' suggested Fred.

Lady Beech now broke the ice by saying, 'I was listening to my poor old brother-in-law on the wireless before I came out.'

Everybody had, of course, been dying to begin on this topic

435

but none of the others had liked to, Sophia because of poor Fred, poor Fred because he knew that Lady Beech was the 'King's' sister-in-law, and Ned because, although the least sensitive person in the world, he did feel it was perhaps hardly for him to do so, having made such good capital out of Sir Ivor's defection.

Lady Beech went on. 'He was giving a concert of Mozart, and I must tell you that it was perfectly exquisite. Schumann herself could not have given such an ideal rendering of *Voi che sapete*—I never heard such notes, never.'

'Yes, the old beast can sing,' Fred muttered gloomily.

'I wonder what he feels like,' said Sophia. 'I mean, when he thinks of all of us he must be rather sad. He did so love jokes, too, and I don't suppose he gets many of them, or at any rate people to share them with.'

'It is so strange,' said Lady Beech, 'oh, it is so strange! As you know, I was very intimate indeed with him, and I should have said that he had a particularly strong love of his country, and of his own people. He was so attached to you, darling, and to all his friends—I think I may add, to me.' She sighed. The disposition of Vocal Lodge, although it had proved to be premature, still rankled a little with her. 'Well, there it is. I shall never understand it, never, it seems to me that it can't be true, and yet—— Tell me, Lord Edward, is it possible that he is doing this with some motive that we know nothing about?'

'I couldn't say. I suppose the old buffer gets well paid, what?'

'Oh, you don't know Ivor if you think that would have anything to do with it. He never cared the least bit for money. He had far too much of it for his needs. Why should he want more?'

'I put it down to a morbid love of publicity,' said Fred. He could not speak without bitterness of the wrecker of his career.

'But he would have had publicity under your scheme, Sir Frederick, and with it love and praise instead of hatred and contempt.'

436

'Depends which way you look at it. I expect he gets love and praise in Germany all right.'

'I can't believe that that is much comfort to him. He never cared for Germany as far as I knew; he certainly never sang there. I should have said he cared for nothing, these last years, but his garden. He was even neglecting his voice in order to be able to work longer hours among his cabbages. I reproached him for it.'

'Perhaps they promised him a whole mass of Lesbian Irises.'

'Perhaps they caught him and tortured him until he said he would sing for them.'

'Ah, now that I think is very probably the explanation,' said Lady Beech with mournful satisfaction. 'And curiously enough, just the one that had occurred to me. Terrible, terrible. What should you say they do to him, Lord Edward?'

'Oh, really, I don't know much about these things. Thumbscrew, I suppose, then there was the rack, the boot and the *peine forte et dur*, but I always think a nightlight under the sole of the foot would be as good as anything.'

'Do stop,' said Sophia, putting her fingers in her ears. She could never bear to hear of tortures.

'Actually I wonder if he would do it with such gusto if he had the thumbscrew hanging over him, so to speak. I mean he does get the stuff off his chest as if he really enjoyed it—eh?'

'You forget,' said Lady Beech, 'that Ivor was nothing if not an artist. Once he began to sing he would be certain to do it well, whatever the circumstances. That he could not help.'

'Oh, poor old gentleman,' said Sophia, 'it would really have been better for him to have died on Kew Pagoda all along.'

'Very, very much better,' said Lady Beech. 'Now, tell me, Lord Edward (I am changing the subject to one hardly less painful) supposing, I say *supposing* anybody had a very small sum of money to invest, what would you yourself advise doing with it? I don't mean speaking as a Member of the Cabinet; I just want your honest advice.'

'Personally,' said Ned, brightening up, 'I should put it on a horse. I mean, a sum like that, the sort of sum you describe is hardly worth saving, is it? Why not go a glorious bust on Sullivan in the 3.30 to-morrow?'

'You wouldn't say that if you knew how unlucky I am, would he, child?' she said to Sophia; 'but what I really wanted to know about is these defence loans, to buy or not to buy? I thought you could advise me.'

Ned gave a guilty jump and said the defence loans were just the very thing for her. 'I bought a certificate for my little nipper to-day,' he said, 'but the little blighter wanted it in hard cash. Couldn't blame the kid either—I mean, of course, at that age. In fifteen years he'll be glad—if he's not dead. Well,' he looked importantly at his watch, 'I must be getting back to No. 10.'

'Child,' said Lady Beech, 'have you got Rawlings with you? No? Then perhaps Lord Edward will escort me to a bus.'

Fred and Sophia decided to make a night of it. They went to several very gay restaurants and then to a night club. Here, many hours after they left the Carlton, Fred talked about his Ideals. It seemed that, at night, as he watched his Blossom careering about among the stars, Ideals had come to Fred, and he had resolved, should he ever again achieve Cabinet rank, that he would be guided by them.

'I used to go on, you know, from day to day, doing things just as they came without any purpose in my life. But now it will be different.'

Sophia had heard this kind of talk before; it sounded horribly as though the Brotherhood was claiming another victim. Apparently however, this time it was Federal Union, and Fred expounded its theories to her at great length.

'So what d'you think of it?' he said when he had finished.

'Well, darling, I didn't quite take it in. I feel rather deliciously muzzy to tell you the truth, you know the feeling, like that heavenly anaesthetic they give you nowadays.'

'Oh.' Fred was disappointed.

'Tell me again, darling, and I'll listen more carefully.'

He told her.

438

'Well, if it means the whole world is going to be ruled by the English, I'm all for it.'

'Oh no, it's not like that at all; I must have explained it badly.'

He began again, taking enormous trouble.

Presently someone Sophia knew came up to their table. Sophia was feeling extremely vague. She introduced Fred as Sir Frederick Union. After this he took her home.

9

The Lieder König had just finished one of his Pets' Programmes. These were a terrible thorn in the side of the authorities, who considered that all the other pieces in his repertoire were exceedingly harmless, although the news which was thrown in at the end always included some item proving that the German Secret Service arrangements for transmitting facts to Berlin had ours beat by about twelve hours, and this certainly did tease the M.I. rather. But the Pets' Programmes were a definite menace. Playing upon the well-known English love of animals the wily Hun provided this enormous treat for the pets of the United Kingdom.

'Bring your Bow-wow, your Puss-puss, your Dickie-bird, your Moo-cow, your Gee-gee, your Mousie and your three little fishes to the radio. Or, take the radio out to the stables if your pets cannot be brought indoors. For those raising hens on the battery system these concerts should prove profitable indeed—few hens can resist laying an egg after hearing the Lieder König. The real object of these programmes is not, however, a mercenary one, the object is to bring joy to the hearts of dumb creatures, too many of whom spend a joyless life without song. There is no need for your pets to belong to this category any more: bring them all to the radio and see what pleasure you will give them. The Lieder König himself, who can sing so high that bats can hear him, and so low that buffaloes can, is here expressly to minister to your dumb ones, and bring them strength through joy.'

The old gentleman then came to the radio and gave first a little talk about the muddle of animal A.R.P. in London. Few dogs and no cats, he said, carried gas masks, and gas-proof cages for birds and mice were the exception rather than the rule. The animal first-aid posts were scandalously few and ill equipped. The evacuation scheme had not been a success, and many mothers of dogs had fetched their little ones home rather than unselfishly bear the parting for their sakes. 'I dedicate this concert to the animal evacuees in strange homes,' he said, 'may they think of England and stay away from London until this stupid war is over. Here in Germany you hardly ever see a pet; all the dogs are at the West Wall, and the rest are nobly playing their part, somewhere.' He then delivered a series of shrieks and groans which certainly did have an uncanny effect upon any animals who happened to listen in. Dogs and cats joined in the choruses, horses danced upon their hind legs, and dickie birds went nearly mad with joy. Mice crept out of their holes to listen, while in the country the radio on these occasions proved such a magnet to frogs and snails and slugs that many people thankfully used it as a trap for small garden pests. The authorities at the Zoo had gramophone records made to cheer up their charges during the black-out, and Ming, the panda, would soon eat no food until one of them was played to her.

The results of all this can readily be imagined. On the day after one of these concerts Members of Parliament would be inundated by a perfect flood of letters from sentimental constituents demanding instant cessation of hostilities against our fellow animal-lovers, the Germans. In fact, the Pets' Programme did more for the enemy cause over here than all the broadcasts by Lord Haw-haw, all the ravings of the Slavery Party's organ, *The New Bondsman*, and all the mutterings of Bloomsbury's yellow front put together.

'If the pets all over the world,' concluded the Lieder König, 'were to rise up as one pet and demand peace, peace we should have.'

'Here are the Reichsender Bremen, stations Hamburg and D x B operating on the 31 metre band. The Lieder König wishes to thank all pets for listening. The next Pets' Concert will be on Tuesday next at 9.45.'

Sophia and Fred, who had dined with her, had been listening, for the benefit of those returned evacuees, Milly and

Abbie. Sophia had sent for Milly, against her better judgement, because she did not get along without her very well, and also for protection from the parachutists. She was a French bulldog, as clever as she was beautiful, and Abbie was her daughter. Abbie's blood was mixed, Milly having thrown herself away upon a marmalade Don Juan, one spring morning in Westminster Abbey, but she was very sweet and the apple of Fred's eye. When the Pets' Programme was over, they took their leave, Sophia going a little way up the Square with them in order to give Milly a run after her emotional experience. When they got back, Milly galloped upstairs and burrowed her way under Sophia's quilt until she came to where the hot-water bottle was, when she flopped at once into a snoring sleep.

Sophia followed more slowly. She had a pain which had not been improved by her excursion into the cold. When she reached her bathroom she looked for the Cachets Fèvre, but presently remembered that she had given the box to Florence, and went up the next flight of stairs to Florence's bedroom. She knocked on the door without much expecting any reply: when there was none, she went in.

She had not seen the room since Florence had occupied it, and was quite shocked to see how much it had been subdued. Pretty and frilly as it was, like any room done up by Sophia, Florence had done something intangible to it by her mere presence, and it was looking frightful. The dressing-table, exquisite with muslin, lace, roses, and blue bows, like a ball dress in a dream, and which was designed to carry an array of gold-backed brushes, bottles, pots of cream and flagons of scent, was bare except for one small black brush and a comb which must have originally been meant for a horse's mane. The Aubusson carpet had its pattern of lutes and arrows, with more roses and blue bows, completely obscured by two cheap-looking suitcases. A pair of stays and a gas-mask case had been thrown across the alluring bed cover, puckered with pink velvet and blue chiffon. Sophia, who herself wore a ribbon suspender-belt, looked in horrified fascination at the stays. 'No wonder Florence is such a queer shape,' she

442

thought, picking them up, 'she will never be a glamour girl in stays like that, and how does she get into them?' She held them against her own body but could not make out which bit went where; they were like medieval armour. As she put them back on the bed she saw that the gas-mask carrier contained a Leica camera instead of a gas-mask, and she thought it was simply horrible of Florence never to have taken a photograph of Millie with it. The pigeon, in its cage, was dumped on a beautiful satinwood table, signed by Sheraton; considering how much Florence was supposed to love it, she might have provided it with a larger cage. The poor thing was shuffling up and down miserably. Sophia stroked its feathers with one finger through the wire netting, and remembered a beautiful Chippendale bird-cage for sale in the Brompton Road. She might give it to Florence for Christmas, but Florence seemed so very indifferent to pretty objects. Perhaps, she thought, the bird wants to go out. She opened the cage, took it in her hands, stroked it for a while, and put it out of the window, just too late, evidently, for it made a mess on her skirt.

When she had shut the window and wiped her skirt, Sophia felt an impulse to tidy up: it was really too annoying of Elsie, the housemaid, to leave the room in such a mess. She put away the stays and gasmask case, and then took hold of a hatbox, intending to take it upstairs to the boxroom, but although, as she did so, the top opened, revealing that it was quite empty inside, it was so heavy that she could hardly lift it, so she gave up the idea. Really, her pain was quite bad and she must find the cachets. She opened a few drawers, but they were all full of papers. Then she remembered that there were some shelves in the built-in cupboard so she opened that.

In the part of the cupboard which was meant for dresses stood Heatherley Egg.

Sophia's scream sounded like a train going through a tunnel. Then she became very angry indeed.

'Stupid,' she said, 'to frighten me like that. Anyway, what's the point of waiting in Florence's cupboard—she's on duty, doesn't come off till six.'

Heatherley slid out into the room and gripped her arm. 'Listen,' he said, 'we have got to get this straight.'

'Oh, don't let's bother,' said Sophia, who had lost interest now that she had recovered from her fright. 'God knows I'm not a prude, and Florence's private life has nothing to do with me. Live in her cupboard if you like to; I don't care.'

'See here, Sophia, you can't get away with that. Now, sit down; we have to talk this over.'

'You haven't seen some Cachets Fèvre anywhere, have you? I lent her a box and, of course, she didn't bring them back; people never do, do they? It doesn't matter to speak of, I must go to bed. Well, good night, Heatherley. What about breakfast? Do you like it in your own cupboard, or downstairs?'

She went towards the door.

'Oh, no you don't!' said Heatherley, in quite a menacing sort of voice, very different from his usual transatlantic whine. 'You can't fool me that way, Sophia. Very clever, and I should have been quite taken in, but I happened to watch you through the keyhole. Those bags have false bottoms, haven't they, the gas-mask contains a camera, doesn't it, and there are code signals sewn into the stuffing of those stays. Eh?'

'Are there, how simply fascinating! Is that why they are so bumpy? Do go on!'

'Quite an actress, aren't you, and I might easily have believed you if you hadn't sent off the pigeon with a phoney message.'

'The dear thing asked to go out.'

'Yes, knowing how stupid you are, Sophia, I might have believed that everything had passed over your head, but you can't laugh off that pigeon. So come clean now; you've known the whole works since Greta disappeared, haven't you?'

'What works? Darling Heth, do tell me; it does sound such heaven.'

'As you know so much already, I guess I better had, too, tell you everything. Florence, of course, as you are no doubt aware, is a secret agent, working under a pseudonym, and with a false American passport. Her real name is Edda

Eiweiss and she is the head of the German espionage in this country.'

'You don't say so! Good for Florence,' said Sophia. 'I never thought she would have had the brains.'

'Gee, Florence is probably the cleverest, most astute and most daring secret agent alive to-day.'

'Do go on. What are you? Florence's bottle-washer?'

'Why no, not at all. I am engaged in counter-espionage on behalf of the Allied Governments, but Florence, of course, believes that I am one of her gang. Now, what I want to know is, are you employed by anybody, or are you on your own?'

'But neither,' said Sophia, opening her eyes very wide.

'Sophia, I want an answer to my question, please. I have laid my cards on the table; let's have a look at yours.'

'Oh, on my own, of course,' said Sophia. As Heatherley seemed to be crediting her with these Machiavellian tactics it would be a pity to undeceive him.

'I thought so. Now, Sophia, I need your help. A woman's wits are just what I lack, so listen carefully to me. I have found out a great deal, but not all, about the German system of espionage. By November 10th, I shall have all the facts that will enable the Government to round up the entire corps of spies at present operating in this country. On that day we can catch the gang, Florence and her associates, but not before. Will you come in on this with me, Sophia?' He clutched her shoulders and stared with his light blue eyes into her face. 'Before you answer, let me tell you that it is difficult and dangerous work. You risk death, and worse, if you undertake it, but the reward, to a patriotic soul, is great.'

'Rather, of course I will.' Sophia was delighted. She, and not Olga, was now up to the neck in a real-life spy story.

'Understand, you must take all your orders from me. One false step might render useless my work of months.'

'Yes, yes.'

'And not act on your own initiative at all?'

'No, no.'

'Sophia, you are a brave woman and a great little patriot. Shake.' They shook.

'Can I ask you a question?'

'Go right ahead.'

'Well, what happened to Greta in the end?'

'What did she say to you?' asked Heatherley, with a searching look.

'I don't understand.'

'What did she say when you saw her in the Post on that stretcher?'

'Well, but she couldn't speak. She had a sort of bandage on her tongue, you see.'

'Sophia,' Heatherley's voice again took on that horrid rasping tone, 'you promised to be perfectly frank with me. Come clean now, what was she doing with her eyes?'

'Oh, her eyes. Yes, she must have had a great grit in one of them, I should imagine. She was blinking like mad; I had quite forgotten.'

'She was winking out a message to you in Morse Code. What was that message, Sophia? No double crossing——'

'My dear Heatherley, however should I know?'

'You don't know Morse Code?'

Sophia saw that she might just as well have admitted to an Ambassador of the old school that she knew no French. She decided that as she did long to be a counterspy with Heatherley and that as she could quite quickly learn the Morse Code (she knew that stupid looking Girl Guides managed to do so) there would be no harm in practising a slight deception.

'Semaphore perfect,' she said airily. 'But I must confess my Morse needs brushing up. And anyhow, if you remember, I was running to the telephone when I passed you in that dark passage and had no time at all to see what Greta was winking about. She was such a bore, anyway, I never could stick her. So what happened to her after that?'

Heathley pursed his lips. 'I'm afraid, my dear Sophia, that it was not very pleasant,' he said. 'You must remember that my job is counter-espionage, that I have to suppress my own personal feelings rigidly, and that very very often I am obliged to do things which are obnoxious to me.'

446

'Like in Somerset Maugham's books?'

'Just like—I am glad you appreciate my point. Well, it seems that Florence wasn't feeling any too sure about Greta, who was, of course, one of her corps, and was particularly anxious that Greta should not come up before the Alien's tribunal as she would probably have made mistakes and given them all away, Florence and the rest of them. Also her papers were not foolproof. So, at Florence's bidding, of course, Winthrop and I carried her on the stretcher, just as you saw her, gagged and bound, and put her into the main drain which flows, as you may not know, under the First Aid Post.'

Sophia screamed again. Heatherley went on, 'Yes, my dear Sophia, counter-espionage is a dangerous, disagreeable profession. I should like you to remember this and be most careful, always, how you act. It is absolutely necessary for you to trust me and do exactly what I say on every occasion. We are in this together now, remember, you and I.'

Sophia did not so much care about being in anything with Heatherley, and hoped that all this would not lead to being in bed with him; she seemed to remember that such things were part of the ordinary day's work of beautiful female spies. On the other hand, she felt that she would, if necessary, endure even worse than death in order to be mixed up in this thrilling real life spy drama. The horrible end of poor Greta served to show that here was the genuine article. Fancy. The main drain. Sophia shuddered. No wonder Miss Edwards saw something queer going on under her feet.

'Now, Sophia, I hope you realize,' Heatherley said, 'that whatever happens you are not to tell a living soul about all this. You and I are watched day and night by unseen eyes. These are evil things that we are fighting—yes, evil, and very clever. The telephone, to this house and to the Post, is tapped by Florence's men; our letters are read and our movements followed. We may have got away with this conversation simply by daring to hold it here, in the heart of the enemy country; on the other hand, we may not. As you leave this room, masked men may seize upon us and carry us, on stretchers, to the fate which befel you know who. Of course, if you were to go to anybody in authority with this tale, the gang would know it, and would disperse like a mist before the sun—at the best my work of months would be destroyed, at the worst you and I would suffer the supreme penalty. I may tell you that the War Office and Scotland Yard are watching over us in their own way, and I have secret means of communicating with them. By the 10th November, as I told you before, I shall have all the evidence I need, and then the whole lot can be rounded up. Meanwhile, you and I, Sophia, must be a team. Now you should go back to your room; this conversation has already lasted too long. I shan't be able to speak to you like this again until all is over, so REMEMBER.'

Heatherley squeezed back into his cupboard, and Sophia, highly elated and with her pain quite forgotten, skipped off and slid down the banisters to her own landing. They had evidently got away with that conversation all right, as no masked men pounced out on her and she was soon in bed, kicking Milly off the warm patch which she wanted for her own feet.

10

When Sophia awoke the next day, she had the same feeling with which, as a child, she had greeted Christmas morning, or the day of the Pantomime. A feeling of happy anticipation. At first, and this also was like when she was little, she could not even remember what it was all about; she simply knew that something particularly lively was going to happen.

Elsie, the housemaid, called her and put a breakfast tray in front of her on which there were coffee, toast and butter, and a nice brown boiled egg, besides a heap of letters and *The Times*. Sophia had woken up enough to remember that she was now a glamorous female spy; she put on a swansdown jacket, sat up properly, and admonished Milly for refusing to go downstairs.

'Drag her,' she said to Elsie. Elsie dragged, and they left the room with a slow, shuffling movement, accompanied by the bedside rug.

The letters looked dull; Sophia began on her egg, and was attacking it with vigour when she saw that something was written on it in pencil. Not hard-boiled, she hoped. Not at all. the writing was extremely faint, but she could make out the word AGONY followed by 22.

Sophia was now in agony, for this must be, of course, a code. She knew that spies and counter-spies had the most peculiar ways of communicating with each other, winking in Morse and so on; writing on eggs would be everyday work for them. She abandoned the delicious egg, done so nicely to a turn, and rolled her eyes round the pink ceiling with blue clouds of her bedroom while she tried the word AGONY backwards and forwards and upside down. She made anagrams of the letters. She looked at the egg in her looking-glass bed-post, but all in vain. She would have to get hold of the Chief at once, but how was she to do that? Impossible to send Elsie upstairs with instructions to see if Mr. Egg was still in Miss Turnbull's cupboard, if so, Lady Sophia's compliments and would he step downstairs. In any case he was unlikely to have remained in the cupboard all night, and Florence's bed, a narrow single one, would not harbour any but impassioned lovers with the smallest degree of comfort. This, she somehow felt, Florence and Heatherley were not.

Elsie now returned with Milly, who once more dived under the eiderdown, and, with a piercing snore, resumed her slumbers.

'Did she do anything?'

'Yes, m'lady.'

'Good girl. Would you be very kind,' said Sophia, 'and go and ask Miss Turnbull if she would give me Mr. Egg's telephone number. Say I'm short of a man for to-night.'

Florence, who had only come off duty at six, was displeased at being woken up. She was understood by Elsie to say that Mr. Egg had gone to Lympne for the day, and had her ladyship remembered that there was to be a Brotherhood meeting at 98 that evening.

Sophia saw that she had been rather dense. Of course she might have realized that if Heth had been available to see her there would have been no need for him to write on her egg. Then she saw light.

'He, Egg, is in agony, because he is unable 2 see me before 2 night.' Sophia turned to her breakfast with a happy appreciation both of its quality and of her own brilliance.

She picked up *The Times* and read about the Pets' Programme. It seemed to have fallen very flat with the musical critic. 'Not with Milly though.' Then, without looking at the war news, which she guessed would be dull, she turned to the front page and read, as she always did, the agony column. She usually found one or two advertisements that made her feel happy, and to-day there was a particularly enjoyable one. 'Poor old gentleman suffering from malignant disease would like to correspond with pretty young lady. Box 22 *The Times*.'

When Sophia had finished laughing she became quite wistful. She always called Sir Ivor the poor old gentleman, and he called her the pretty young lady. If only he were not being a dreadful old traitor in Berlin, she would have cut the advertisement out and sent it to him. 'I never should have expected to miss him as much as I do, but the fact is there are certain jokes which I can only share with him. Funny thing too,' she thought, 'suffering from malignant disease, just what he is. National Socialism.' She cut out the advertisement and put it in her jewel case, deciding that if she ever had the opportunity to do so, through neutrals, she would send it to Sir Ivor in the hopes of making him feel small. Her blood boiled as she thought again of his treachery and of the programme of Camp songs, which was exactly similar to one he had given before the Chief Scout some months previously, and which had included that prime and perennial favourite:

> *'There was a bee i ee i ee,*
> *Sat on a wall y all y all y all y all,*
> *It gave a buzz y wuz y wuz y wuz y wuz,*
> *And that was all y all y all y all y all.'*

Sir Ivor and Dr. Goebbels between them had altered the words of this classic to:

> *'The British E i ee i ee,*
> *Sat on a wall y all y all y all y all,*
> *Like Humpty Dumpt y ump ty ump ty ump ty ump,*
> *It had a fall y all y all y all y all.'*

So queer it seemed, and so horrible, that somebody who had had the best that England can give should turn against her like that. Sir Ivor had received recognition of every kind, both public and private, from all parts of the British Empire, of his great gifts. Had he been one of those geniuses who wither in attics, it would have been much more understandable. Sophia got out of bed, and while her bath was running in she did a few exercises in order to get fit for the dangers and exactions of counter-espionage.

On the way to St. Anne's, Sophia bought a Manual of

Morse Code which she fully intended to learn that day. When she arrived however she found, greatly to her disgust, that, as it was Thursday, there was a great heap of clean washing to be counted.

She supposed that she must have a brain rather like that of a mother bird who, so the naturalists tell us, cannot count beyond three; counting the washing was her greatest trial. There would be between twenty and thirty overalls to be checked and put away in the nurses' pigeonholes in the 'dressing-room' which was a sacking partition labelled, rather crudely, Female. Now Sophia, with an effort of concentration, could stagger up to twelve or thirteen; having got so far the telephone bell would ring, somebody would come and ask her a question, or her own mind would stray in some new direction. Then she would begin all over again.

It generally took her about half an hour before she could make the numbers tally twice, and even then it was far from certain that they were correct. On this occasion she made them alternately twenty-five and twenty-eight, so she assumed the more optimistic estimate to be the right one, and stowed them away in their pigeonholes. She was longing to tell Sister Wordsworth about Greta and the main drain, but of course that would never do. She did ask Mr. Stone whether the drain really flowed underneath the First Aid Post and could she see it, to which he replied that it did, and that she could, but in his opinion she would not enjoy such an experience.

'Rats,' he said. Sophia thought of Greta and shuddered. 'As a matter of fact,' he went on, 'some fellows are going down there this evening to have a look round. I expect you could go with them if you like.'

Sophia asked what time, and when she was told at half-past ten, she declined the offer. It would require a bigger bribe than the main drain to get her back to St. Anne's when her work there was finished.

She spent the rest of the day learning Morse Code, partly because she wished to be a well equipped counter-spy and partly (and this spurred her to enormous industry) so that she could wink at Olga in it the next time they met. There was a photograph of Olga in that week's *Tatler* wearing a black velvet crinoline with a pearl cross, and toying with a guitar, beneath which was written the words, 'This Society beauty does not require a uniform for her important war work.'

Sophia, thinking of this, redoubled her efforts of dot and dash. But she found it far from easy, even more difficult than counting overalls, though the reward of course was greater. She sat, winking madly into her hand looking-glass, until she was off duty, by which time she knew the letters A, B and C perfectly, and E and F when she thought very hard. The opportunity for showing off her new accomplishment came that evening. She had gone on duty at the Post earlier than usual, as Sister Wordsworth wanted to go out; leaving it correspondingly early, she was on her way home when she remembered that her house would be full of Brothers. So she looked in at the Ritz. Here the first person she saw was Rudolph, and sitting beside him was a heaving mass of sables which could only conceal the beautiful Slavonic person of La Gogothska herself, in the uniform, so to speak, of her important war-work.

'Hullo, my darling,' said Rudolph, fetching a chair for her. 'You're off very early. I'm dining with you tonight, though you may not know it. Elsie said I could, and she's telling your cook.'

'Good,' said Sophia, without listening much. Her eyes were fixed upon Olga and she was working away with concentration.

'What are you making those faces at me for?' said Olga crossly.

'Dear me,' said Sophia, 'how disappointing. It was just a bet I had with Fred. I betted him sixpence that you were in the secret service, he was so positive you couldn't be, and I said I could prove it. Well, I have proved it, and I have lost sixpence, that's all.'

'What do you mean?'

'Well, darling, I was just telling you, in Morse Code, to proceed to the ladies' cloakroom, and are you proceeding? No. Have you made any excuse for not doing so? No.

453

Therefore, as you evidently don't know Morse Code which is a sine qua non for any secret agent, you can't be that beautiful female spy we all hoped you were.' Actually, of course, Sophia had only been winking out, and with great trouble at that, A, B and C.

Olga said, 'Nonsense. Morse Code is never used in this war; it's completely out of date. Why, what would be the use of it?' and she gave a theatrically scornful droop of the eyelids.

'Well, as a matter of fact, dear, it would be a very great deal of use indeed under certain circumstances. Supposing one happened to be gagged, for an example, it would be possible to wink out messages to the bystanders which, if they understood Morse, would save one's life.'

'Gagged,' said Olga, shrugging her shoulders. 'Gagged indeed. Bystanders! Darling, you have been reading Valentine Williams, I suppose. Let me tell you that in real life the secret service is very different from what the outside public, like you, imagine it to be. Gagged! No, really, I must tell the Chief that.'

'Do,' said Sophia. 'He'll roar, I should think. Naturally, I don't know much about these things. Well, then, what shall I do with the sixpence?'

'I'll tell you when the war is over. Are you working very hard in your little First Aid Post? Poor Olga is overwhelmed with work. Figure to yourselves, last night I was up till six—even the Chief with his iron constitution was half dead. I had to keep on making cups of black coffee for him, and even so he fell asleep twice. Of course, the responsibility is very wearing, especially for the Chief—if things went wrong, it doesn't bear thinking of, what would happen. My knowledge of Russian, however, is standing us in good stead.'

Olga had learnt Russian when she was courting Serge, to but little avail so far as he was concerned, as he did not know a word of it. However, as she had taken the name of Olga, broken her English accent, and in other ways identified herself with the great country of Serge's forbears, she rather liked to be able to sing an occasional folk-song from the Steppes in its original tongue. She felt that it put the finishing touches to her part of temperamental Slav.

454

'I wonder they don't send you to Russia. I hear they find it very difficult to get reliable information.'

'Darling, it would be certain death.'

'Oh, yes, I forgot. You would be handed over to the grandchildren of Serge's grandfather's peasantry, wouldn't you? Very unpleasant. But couldn't you go disguised as a member of the proletariat in no silk stockings and drab clothes? I could give you lots of hints. You share a room with about seven other people and their bulldogs if they have any, and you have no pleasures of any kind. I really think, speaking Russian as you do, that you ought to volunteer.'

'Far, far too dangerous. The Chief would never let me. I may of course have to go abroad later—to Egypt, Turkestan or Wazuristan perhaps, but Russia is entirely out of the question.'

'I call it very cowardly of you,' said Sophia, 'your country should come first. Well, good-bye, I must be going,' and she winked out rather innacurately A, B and C. 'I'm sure the Chief would raise your screw if you knew a bit of Morse,' she said, and got up to go, followed by Rudolph who quite shamelessly left Olga to pay for the drinks.

'Think how rich she must be with all that spying,' he said happily, and kissed Sophia a great deal in the taxi. 'Darling, heavenly to see you. I've got a fortnight's leave.'

'What were you doing with Baby Bagg?'

'Just met her in the Ritz.'

'After you had telephoned to tell her to go there, I suppose.'

'Well, darling, in point of fact, I do feel rather intrigued about Olga's job. I have a sort of feeling that there may be more in that little woman than meets the eye, and I must say she's remarkably secretive. Now if you were a beautiful female spy, my own precious poppet, we should all know all about it in two days. For one thing of course, you would never be able to resist telling funny stories about your Chief. But Olga is as close as an oyster. I must have another go at her before my leave comes to an end.'

Sophia was very much nettled by the unfairness of all this.

Had she told a single funny story about her Chief? Had she not been a counter-spy for a whole day without hinting a word of it to anybody? Of course, she had been about to take Rudolph into her confidence; now nothing would induce her to do so. She would pay him out for being so horrid to her. Because he must be broken of this new predilection for Olga; it was becoming a bore.

'Yes, do,' she said; 'have another go at her. Have it now, won't you—much more convenient for me actually because I want to dine with Heatherley.'

'Heatherley? You don't mean Egg? You don't mean that fearful red-headed brute who told us what the President said? Darling Sophia—besides, you're dining with me, you said you would. I haven't seen you for weeks.'

'Darling, I'm terribly sorry, but I haven't seen Heth all day and there are masses of things I want to talk over with him.'

Rudolph said no more. He stopped the cab, got out into the street, told the man to go on to Granby Gate, hailed another cab going in the opposite direction, jumped into it and disappeared.

Sophia minded rather. She had been pleased to see Rudolph, and excited at the idea of spending an evening with him, more pleased and more excited even than she generally was when she had been separated from him for some time, but he must be taught a lesson. It was quite bad enough for him not to say that he was coming on leave, and to let her find him sitting at the Ritz with Olga. But to have him comparing her in a denigrating manner with that pseudo-Muscovite was altogether intolerable. Women are divided into two categories: those who can deal with the man they are in love with, and those who cannot. Sophia was one of those who can.

When she arrived at her house she found a merry meeting of the Brotherhood was in full and joyous progress. Brothers and Sisters were overflowing from all the reception rooms, and the downstairs lavatory was in constant use. A large photograph of Brother Bones was propped up on the drawing-room piano with a bunch of lilies in front of it, for it was the Brother's birthday. Sophia hurried into the lift, and going to the top floor she got the key of her bedroom from Elsie, who had instructions always to lock it on these occasions against the quiet-timers. Sophia had a very hot bath and changed her clothes. Then she went to look for Heth. It was rather a long search, ending in the coal-hole where he was in earnest converse with one of the thin-haired young ladies. Being members of the Brotherhood they were, of course, not at all abashed at being found in such curious circumstances; they merely showed their gums.

Sophia beckoned to Heatherley and whispered in his ear, 'There will be dinner for two in my small sitting-room in about half-an-hour. I hope you will join me there.'

Heatherley accepted at once. There was always, at these meetings, a large brotherly buffet-meal in the dining-room for which the food was always ordered by Florence, was cold, of the fork variety, non-alcoholic, and very dull. Sophia had an exquisite cook and a pretty taste in food herself, and Luke's wine was not to be sniffed at.

Exactly at the appointed time Heatherley tried the door of the small sitting-room. It was locked. Sophia knew all about the Brothers by now. They would come into her room, and brightly assuring her that she did not disturb them, begin an all-in wrestling match with their souls. She had told Florence that meetings could only take place at 98 Granby Gate, on condition that the Brothers were neither to use the lift nor be guided to force open any doors which they might find locked.

Heatherley announced himself, upon which Sophia let him in. Dinner was waiting on a hot plate, and they helped themselves. Sophia thought he looked like Uriah Heap, and wished she had a more attractive counterspy to work with, somebody say, like the ruthless young German in *The Thirty-Nine Steps*; it was impossible to take much pleasure in the company of Heth. How fortunate she loved her work for its own sake (and that of Olga).

With an alluring smile she gave him some soup.

'What was agony 22 for?' she said.

'I don't know what you're talking about.'

457

'The word, or letters, or code, or whatever it was you wrote on my egg, of course. I took ages trying to decode it, and I wondered if I had the right solution.'

'On your egg?' Heatherley put down his soup-spoon and looked completely blank.

'Yes, yes. Think. Of course it must have been you. This morning I had a boiled egg for breakfast, and written on the shell, in pencil, it had agony 22.'

'Sophia, now, why would I write on your egg when I could so easily call you, come round and see you, or leave a note for you here?'

Why indeed? Sophia felt that she had been a fool.

'Well, you said that we must be so careful, that our letters would be opened, and our telephone tapped——'

'If your telephone can be tapped, so could your egg be. No, Sophia, we need to be very, very careful, but there's no sense in writing on eggs, no sense at all, when we can meet all we want to both at the Post and in this house.'

'Anyway, what is our next move? I want to start work,' said Sophia, to change the painful subject.

'I was just coming to that.' Heatherley paused and seemed to consider her. 'How are your nerves?' he said. 'Pretty good? Fine. I have a very delicate job that I wish to entrust to you, delicate, and it may be dangerous. Are you game?'

'Oh, yes, Heatherley, I think so.'

'O.K. Well, presently, when you have quite finished your dinner, I want you to go back to the Post.'

Sophia was not pleased. She had spent eight hours in the Post that day, and had left, as she always did, with a feeling of immense thankfulness and relief. The idea of going back there after dinner did not appeal to her at all.

Heatherley went on, 'You are to make a list of all the nurses there on night duty. Then I want a copy of every word that is written on the notice-board. When you have done that, go to the Regal Cinema and pin an envelope containing the copy to the second stall in the third row on the left-hand side of the centre gangway. You can give me the list of nurses to-morrow; that is less important. One last word of instruction—

on no account take a taxi, that might be fatal. You will be safe enough if you walk it.'

'Well, really,' said Sophia, 'that is far sillier than writing on eggs. Why can't whoever is going to the third stall in the second row walk into the Post and see for himself what is written on the notice-board?'

'Sophia.' Heatherley gave a fish-like look which for a moment, and until she remembered it was only old Heth, quite struck a chill into her heart. 'Are you, or are you not going to help me in clearing out a nest of dangerous spies? Let me tell you that Florence communicates with the rest of her gang by means of that notice-board. My friend cannot go to the Post himself, it would be as much as his life is worth to venture near it. If I were seen to be in communication with him, I too would have short shrift, but it is of vital importance that he should know what is on the board to-night. I can't get away from this Brotherhood meeting without arousing Florence's suspicions, but I thought I had seen a way of fixing things. I thought you would go for me.'

'Oh, all right, Heth, I will. I only meant it sounded rather silly, but I see now that it has to be done. Have some apple flan.'

11

Now although Sophia supposed herself to be such a keen and enthusiastic spy, she had not really the temperament best suited to the work. It was not in her nature, for instance, to relish being sent out on a cold and foggy evening, after she had had her bath and changed her clothes, in order to do an apparently pointless job for somebody who could quite well do it for himself. Obviously if Heatherley could be closeted for ages in the coal-hole, if he could dine for more than an hour behind a locked door, he could easily escape from the house without Florence or anybody else noticing that he had gone, and do his own dreary work. So she determined that somehow or another she would wriggle out of going, but of course without annoying her Chief as she had not the least intention of being excluded from the delights of counter-espionage, and this might well happen should she be caught out disobeying orders. Sophia was very good at not doing things she disliked, and soon her plans were laid. She remembered that, exasperated by her long and unequal struggle with the overalls, she had herself, that very evening, written out a notice to the effect that those nurses who wanted to have their overalls sorted when they came back from the wash, should write their names clearly both on the overalls themselves and on their pigeon-holes so that Sophia should know where to put them. When she had pinned this to the board, there had been no other notice there, and she had been particularly pleased, thinking that more attention would be paid to it on this account. Now a notice written out by Sophia would not, in the nature of things, contain Florence's secret instructions to her corps of spies. Sophia therefore decided that she would explain to Heatherley that there had been nothing on the notice-board; impossible to make a copy of nothing, so she had done no more about it. That disposed of the notice-board. As for the list of nurses on night duty, she could find that out from Sister Wordsworth's ledger in the morning. And in order to make perfectly certain of not seeing Heatherley before she arrived at the Post she decided to go immediately after breakfast to Phyllis Earle and have her hair done.

As soon as she had reached these comfortable decisions, and with the prospect now of a delicious evening with *Caroline of England* in her warm bed, she became extremely nice, indeed almost flirtatious to Heatherley during the rest of their meal together. When it was over, and Heth had enjoyed brandy and a huge cigar (unlike Florence he did not despise his creature comforts at all), she went upstairs most cheerfully, put on her fur coat with its pretty, scarlet-lined hood, and then was shepherded by a quite unusually genial Heth, through a few Brothers who had finished eating, to the front door.

'I'm afraid it's rather foggy,' he said, peering out with his pale eyes into a solid curtain of fog.

'All the better. I am less likely to be followed,' said Sophia.

'And cold.'

'Ssh. Think of our cause, dear Heatherley.'

'You understand that on no account must you take a taxi,' he reminded her. A more competent spy, she thought, would have seen the impossibility of walking more than two steps in her high-heeled velvet sandals. Anyhow, what did the man think she was, for heaven's sake, a marathon walker?

'No taxi, no indeed.' She stepped gaily into the fog.

'Sophia, you're wonderful.'

'No! No! Good-bye! Good-bye!'

Heatherley shut the front door. Sophia waited a moment and then she went down the area steps, let herself in at the back door and took off her shoes. The servants were in the servants' hall with the wireless blazing away, the back-stairs were pitch dark, and Sophia, using her torch, crept up them and hoped that she would not fall over Heatherley and his girl friend, quiet-timing. They could hardly have got there yet,

461

she thought. On the first floor a door led from the back-stairs into the ballroom, a room which was used about twice a year for parties, and otherwise kept shut up, with dust sheets. She was rather surprised to notice, through the cracks of the door, that the lights were on. Wonderful how the quiet-timers seep into everything. She crept to the door and looked through the keyhole. What she saw turned her to stone.

In a group near the door stood Florence, Heatherley, Winthrop, a microphone, and Sir Ivor King, the Lieder König.

'I reckon,' Heatherley was saying, 'that she will be gone an hour at the very least, in this fog. Five minutes to the Post, ten minutes to copy out the notices, three-quarters of an hour to the Regal and back. And this is a very conservative estimate, I may add, for the fog is thick outside, and I have not allowed for her stopping to talk to anybody at the Post. So you see there is no danger, and we have ample time for everything. If the servants should happen to hear us, they will think we have switched on the radio and old Ivor is coming over the air better than usual. But they will surely be listening to him themselves downstairs.'

Florence was looking cross. 'I still think it was perfectly stupid of you to tell her anything at all.'

'Say, we've talked all this over before, haven't we? She was wise to everything already, and it was a choice between making her think she was in on the racket, or taking her for a ride. If we had adopted the latter course, the police would have been rubbering round this house and the First Aid Post, and we should have been in a regular spot. Another thing, how would I have got her away this evening if she hadn't been told the works, or some of them—as it is she's just eating out of my hand, will do anything I order her to.'

'Yes, there's something in that,' said Florence grudgingly.

'I tell you,' Heth continued, 'I shall be glad when this business is over and we can do a bunk. I'm not so wild about the inspection of the drain to-night; it may mean they are on to something, or it may be just a routine affair. Either way, I don't like it.'

'In one minute it will be a quarter of,' said Winthrop. He took up a position in front of the microphone, gazing at his wrist-watch. The others fell silent.

'Germany calling, Germany calling,' Winthrop said, with a very slight German accent and in an entirely different voice from his usual one. 'Here is the Lieder König who is going to give you one of his inimitable programmes of Song Propaganda, so popular with lovers of song and also with lovers of propaganda the world over. The Lieder König.'

Sir Ivor stepped smartly to the microphone. Sophia saw that, out of deference no doubt to the taste of his employers, he was wearing an Aryan wig of metallic brilliance; each curl was like a little golden spring. He raised his voice in song, 'Kathleen Mavourneen the Grey Dawn is breaking,' then he gave a short news bulletin, during the course of which he exactly described that evening's Low cartoon, and also reminded his listeners that Sir Kingsley Wood was due to visit three aerodromes in Yorkshire the following day.

Then Winthrop spoke. 'The Lieder König thinks you would like to know certain facts which have come our way recently. In your great, free, British Empire, in the colony of Kenya, to be exact, there are two honest, thrifty, industrious German farmers, Herr Bad and Herr Wangel. These worthy men have been dragged away from their homes, for no better reason than that they were German-born, and put into the local prison. The prison is a wretched hut, the beds in it are unbearably hard, and the central heating hardly works at all. The prisoners are only allowed baths twice a week. But the worst scandal is the food which is offered to these Germans. Let me read out the bill of fare, considered by your Government as being sufficient for two grown men.

'Breakfast. A liquid supposed to be coffee, some milk substitute, two lumps of beet sugar, pseudo-eggs and a loaf of brackish bread.

'Luncheon. A so-called veal and ham pie, things which look like potatoes and beans, crab-apple pudding, cheese which is full of mites.

'Tea. Tea (a nerve tonic indispensable to the decadent English, but which we Germans despise).

'Dinner. A thin soup, fish, which is well known in these parts to cause leprosy. The leg of some sheep which had had to be killed, turnips and beetroot such as one feeds to cattle.

'There was no tin of biscuits by their beds in case they woke up hungry in the night.

'When you hear that things like this can happen in your great, vaunted, rich Empire perhaps you will demand that your statesmen, who can allow two honest and unoffending farmers to be so treated, should stop worrying over the scum of Polish cities in luxurious concentration camps, and should be a little bit more concerned about the beam in their own eye, for a change.

'Ask Mr. Churchill, where is the *Ark Royal*?

'Here is the Lieder König again.'

'Well,' said Sir Ivor, 'I hope you have all been as much shocked as I have by the brutal ill-treatment of Herr Bad and Herr Wangel. And now I am going to sing an old favourite, "Under the Deodar".'

He did so, and wound up his programme with 'Fearful the Death of the Diver Must Be, walking alone, walking alone, walking alone in the Dehehehe-he-he-pths of the Sea,' a song of which both he and his admirers were extremely fond, as, at the word 'depths', his voice plumbed hitherto uncharted ones, and any seals or hippos who might happen to be around would roar in an agony of appreciation. 'Good night, dears,' said the old König, 'keep your hairs on. By the way, where *is* the *Ark Royal*?'

'This ends,' said Winthrop, resuming his place at the microphone, 'our programme of Song-Propaganda in English, arranged and sung by the Lieder König.

'Here are the Reichsender Bremen, stations Hamburg and D x B, operating on the thirty-one metre band. I have a special announcement for my English listeners. There will be a Pets' Programme to-morrow from station D x B at 9.30 Greenwich mean time.'

'Now we must scram,' said Heatherley, 'we can always

464

wait in the Maternity Ward if the drain inspection is not finished.'

They all, including the old gentleman, began to struggle into anti-gas clothing. Sophia waited no longer. She flew upstairs to her bedroom and locked herself in, dumbfounded by what she had seen.

Her mind was in a whirl. If Heatherley, who pretended to be an American counter-spy, was really a German spy, perhaps the 'King of Song' was pretending to be a German spy, but was really an English counter-spy? Was he in the pay of the gang, or merely hoaxing them; was he perhaps longing, but unable, to get a message through to the outside world or was he only too anxious that his shameful secret should be kept? Was he neither spy nor counter-spy, but just a poor old gentleman who got a taste of the thumbscrew twice a day? She wondered, irrelevantly, whether he had seen in the newspapers the paeans of praise followed by the dirges of disillusionment which had so prominent a place in them. Suddenly she remembered that advertisement in *The Times*: 'Poor old gentleman suffering from malignant disease would like to correspond with pretty young lady.' Perhaps he did want to correspond with the pretty young lady, perhaps in fact, it was he who had written on her egg 'Agony (column, box) 22', and who had sent in the advertisement. But if he could do all this, surely he could equally well write to her, to Rudolph or even to poor Fred directly.

Sophia felt that life had become very complicated all of a sudden. She wished she were more versed in the intricacies of spying, and she very much wished that she could remember more about what had happened in the limited number of spy stories which she had read at various times (generally, of course, on journeys, and how often does one remember anything read on journeys?) At what stage, for instance, does the beautiful heroine abandon her lone trail and call in the heavy hand, large boots and vacant faces of The Yard? She rather thought not until the whole plot had been brilliantly unmasked, except for a few unimportant details, by the glamorous amateur spy herself. This was a point of view

465

which appealed to Sophia, who had to consider Rudolph and Olga as well as King and Country. She went to sleep, having decided on a policy of watchful waiting.

The next day, when Sophia arrived at her First Aid Post, she found an atmosphere of subdued but horrified excitement. She immediately concluded that something untoward had happened at the Theatre; the nurses were always retailing awful atrocities they had witnessed there, and by Theatre they did not at all mean, as anybody else would have, the play; the 'He' of these entertainments was not Tom Walls, but the Surgeon, the 'She' not Hermione Baddeley but the Patient; in short, 'the Theatre' was not the Gaiety but St. Anne's Hospital Operating Theatre. The dramas enacted there alternated, as at the Grand Guignol in Paris, between gruesome tragedy and roaring farce. Sophia supposed that a dead man must have come to life; the reverse which too often happened, could never have caused such a stir.

Nurses were standing about in little groups, whispering, their eyes as round as marbles. Even Sister Wordsworth and Mr. Stone, whom Sophia found in the office, were looking quite concerned.

'Don't tell Lady Sophia, she wouldn't like it,' said kind Sister Wordsworth, remembering about the knees.

'What?' said Sophia. 'But of course you must tell me. I am so curious, I have the most curious nature in the world. If you don't tell me, I shan't get a wink of sleep, or give you one minute's peace until you have. So please, dear Sister Wordsworth.'

Of course they were dying to tell her really. It seemed that, during the drain inspection of the previous night, something too horrible had been found down there, brought up, carried through the Post (dripping, my dear, the smell), and taken to the Hospital mortuary. Sophia began to guess what this object might be, and sure enough, it was the body of a young woman, bound and gagged, and with its face completely gnawed away by rats. Greta.

'But how on earth could it have got there?' she asked, in a shaking voice.

'Why, poor Sophia looks as white as a sheet. I told you we shouldn't tell her. Sit down here, my dear, and have a cup of tea.'

'They say it must have been washed down from much higher up. Nothing to do with this place at all.'

'I should hope not indeed,' said Sophia. 'We should never get another outside patient for practices if they thought they were going to be popped down the main drain when we had finished with them.'

'Outside patient—what an idea. Whatever made you think of that? Well, here's your tea, drink it up, and you'll feel better. We all think it was so clever of Miss Edwards, the way she saw something queer under our feet. I'm longing to have my fortune done again, now that there isn't any more.'

Sophia, however, was beginning to think that there was something very queer indeed, no less a thing than the headquarters of Florence's gang and the hide-out of Sir Ivor King himself; otherwise, why did they hold their broadcast in her ballroom on the night of the drain-inspection? Why did they all work so assiduously at the Post? She had seen a plan of the hospital and knew that underneath the garage there were vast cellars and tunnels, as well as the main drain, no doubt admirably suited to Florence's purpose. A more convenient place, in fact, it would be hard to imagine, a place where people wander in and out at all hours, often bandaged and on stretchers, or disguised in the sinister uniform of the decontamination squad. Could anything be more ideal? Then if, for any reason, the Post became temporarily unsuitable for their purpose, as it had done the previous evening during the drain inspection, they could repair, with their old ally (or victim) to Granby Gate, and under the guise of Brothers could hold their meetings and conduct their broadcasts there. Florence might not be a glamour girl, but she seemed to be a most efficient spy. Sophia hoped that this would all be a lesson to Luke, and that he would, in future, investigate the antecedents of his soulmates before introducing them into the home.

467

12

Luke wrote an extremely entertaining letter from America. The change of scene had evidently done him good; he appeared to be in high spirits, and to have cast off the gloom in which he had been enveloped before leaving England.

He said that, having always heard from Mary Pencill that America was the one truly democratic country in the world, quite free from class distinction of any kind, it had seemed to him rather odd that the talk should run almost entirely on such subjects as how charming the late Lady Fort William used to be. 'Another topic which is nearly always introduced, sooner or later, is what do the English think of America? When I reply that, although most Englishmen have heard of America, not one in ten actually believes in it, they seem almost incredulous.' He also said that they were quite indignant at what seemed to them to be the boring progress of the war, and that on the whole, he thought, they hoped that Germany would win. They hoped this, of course, in the kind of irresponsible, guilty way a child hopes the house will catch fire. 'They have a juvenile point of view and in particular an extreme love of sensation.' He had nearly finished his work, he said, and would soon be home. Had had an interesting time, but was looking forward to being back in England again; he would be flying home by clipper. No mention of Florence, Herr Hitler, or the Brotherhood, and in fact Luke's journey to the New World would seem to have readjusted his perspective as regards the Old.

The news that her husband's return was imminent put an altered complexion on things for Sophia, who realized that she must hurry up with her unmasking activities. Luke was already much disliked owing to his well-known sympathies of the last few years, and it would be extremely awkward for him if a nest of spies were to be found lodged in his house while he himself was there. If, on the other hand, they were tracked down and handed over to justice, by means of the great brilliance and deep cunning of his wife while he was engaged in work of national importance abroad, it would be quite a different affair, and could reflect only to his credit.

Sophia decided that she must immediately find out where the King of Song was hiding, or being hidden, and get into communication with that treacherous and venal (or, alternatively, loyal and disinterested) old body. She felt that even if the former adjectives proved to be correct, he would not have lost all his affection for his godchild; she could not somehow imagine him handing her over to Heatherley, the drain and thumbscrew. If really on the side of England all along, he would be only too glad to be assisted from the clutches of his captors. She hoped he would not prove to be drugged, like Van der Lubbe, but supposed that he would hardly be in such good voice if so. The more she thought of it, the more she felt certain that he must be underneath the First Aid Post, and that one clue to his whereabouts lay in the snacks which Florence and Heatherley carried from the canteen in such quantities. Their appetites had become quite a joke with the nurses. The maternity ward was too small to hide a mouse, but next door to that was the hospital museum, a huge, half dark vault, of a most sinister shape and size. The manhole which led to the main drain was in Mr. Stone's little office, so they would not be able to use that; investigation, she felt, should be made in the museum.

She also decided that it was no longer possible for her to blaze a lone trail through the jungle of spies and counter-spies that her life had now become. After all, she had a lot of valuable counter-espionage work to her credit; the brilliant piece of feminine intuition which had prevented her from leaving the house on Heatherley's bogus errand, as many a lesser woman might have done, having led to the sensational discoveries that the King of Song was still in this country, that Heatherley Egg, far from being a counter-spy, was a counter-counter-spy, and that Winthrop, if not Heatherley himself, was a German. In *The Thirty-Nine Steps*, even Scudder, who, like her, preferred to work on his own, had finally bequeathed his little black notebook to an accomplice; Sophia had no black notebook: all the more necessary that she should have an accomplice. At any moment she might be drained, and then nobody would ever know that she had been a beautiful female spy all along. It was a dreadful prospect.

The choice of an accomplice lay between Fred and Rudolph, and while Rudolph probably had more initiative and more spare time at present, she really favoured Fred on account of his being so much more under her thumb. There was quite good reason, knowing what she did of Fred's character, to hope that in his eyes she would be the Chief; Fred was used to Chiefs, and in fact had never yet been without one during the whole of his life. Rudolph, as she very well knew, would order her about or ignore her, just as it suited him; besides, it would give her the most intense pleasure, as well as serving him right for flirting with Olga, to leave Rudolph out of all this until she could point to the fruits of her activities in the shape of at least three prisoners in the Tower. Having therefore, quite decided upon Fred, to the point of lifting the receiver of her telephone to ring him up, she suddenly remembered the main drain and the possible fate of inept counter-spies. Fred had a young and lovely wife who seemed to be devoted to the idea of him; he also had two fat babies. Rudolph had nothing but a perfectly horrible sister who had often been very rude to Sophia. She rang up Rudolph.

Rudolph was by now bored to death with Olga and her long stories about a job and a Chief that too palpably did not exist. On the other hand, she having been the cause of his break with Sophia, he had felt himself obliged to haunt her company. When he realized that he was being summoned back into the fold he made no secret of his delight.

'Serge came round this morning to horse-whip me,' he said; 'wasn't it fascinating? It seems that he bought a horse-whip at Fortnum's on Olga's account, and he turned up here with it very early, about nine. He hadn't been to bed at all (there's a new place called The Nuthouse, we'll go to-night). The porter telephoned up to my room and said, "There's a gentleman in sporting kit, wants to see you most particular," so I had him sent up with my breakfast, and in comes old Voroshilov, furling and unfurling a great whip; I felt quite giddy. So I ordered some drinks and he sat on my bed and told me that Olga bumps up his allowance every time he horse-whips anybody for making a pass at her, because she read somewhere that this was the form in Imperial Russia. Then he told me all about his Blossom. He simply loved his Blossom, apparently he never loved any other creature so much in his life. He says it was grossly unfair, the way they dismissed him; he only passed out because she passed out first and he couldn't think of anything else to do, with her lying there so flat and dead looking, and the idea of her being in the charge of poor Fred makes him quite sick. I should think he feels quite sick, quite often actually, because he is busy drinking himself to death—he was, anyway, of course, so it doesn't make all that difference. Still, it's rather dreadful to see the poor old tartar so sad and low; he used to be such a jolly old drunk, but he was crying like anything; he has only just gone. When do I see you, shall I come round now or meet you at the Post?'

'No, neither. I don't want to be seen seeing you, you see.'

'Why ever not?'

'Well, I can't explain for the present.'

'Good heavens, Sophia, is Luke cutting up rough?'

'Luke's not back yet, and you know quite well he never cuts up rough. I will meet you at the Ritz in half an hour.'

'You'll be seen seeing me there all right. However,' said Rudolph quickly, not wishing her, as in her present eccentric mood she easily might, to change her mind, 'meet you there, darling; good-bye.'

Sophia smiled to herself. That evening spent with Heatherley instead of with Rudolph had been wonderfully productive of results, one way and another.

When she arrived at the Ritz, Rudolph was already there reading an early edition of an evening paper. He stood up to greet her, hardly raising his eyes from the paper. Sophia sat down beside him, then, remembering what she was, she bobbed up again in order to see that nobody was lurking behind her chair and that there was no microphone underneath it.

'Walking round your chair for luck?' said Rudolph, still reading.

'Put that paper down, darling. I've got a very great deal to tell you.'

'Go ahead.'

'Stop reading, then.'

'I can read and listen to you quite well.'

'Probably you can. But I can't talk to you while you're reading. Darling, really you are rude. You might have been married to me for years.'

'To all intents and purposes I have.'

'That's very rude, too. Thank heavens I have Luke to fall back on.'

'Poor old Luke. You always talk about him as if he were a lie-low.'

'So he is, and it's a jolly nice thing to be. The more I see of you, the more I like Luke, as somebody said about dogs. Rudolph now, please don't let's quarrel. Put that paper down and talk to me.'

Rudolph did so with bad grace. They were both by now thoroughly out of temper with each other.

'Well, what is it?'

'Darling, now listen. You know about me being beautiful?'

'You're all right.'

'No, Rudolph, please say I'm beautiful; it's part of the thing.'

'I suppose you're going to tell me you're a beautiful female spy?'

'In a way, I was.'

'Yes, I'm quite sure you were. And that you have a Chief, but you don't feel happy about his loyalty, so you're really working on your own, and the War Office and Scotland Yard haven't got an inkling of what you're up to because you're blazing a lone trail, but soon there will be sensational revelations, and you will be a national heroine. Oh God! women are bores in wars.' Rudolph returned to his paper.

Sophia left the Ritz in a great temper, and went straight to her Post where she had lunch alone at the canteen. It was much too late now to ring up Fred; he would be with his Blossom; she would have to make investigations on her own after all.

13

Sophia had wondered why the canteen was so empty, and when she got downstairs she found the reason was that the Post was in the throes of a major practice. This event had been canvassed with great excitement for the past few days, and nothing but Sophia's preoccupation with other matters could have put it out of her mind. As soon as she arrived, she was engulfed in it. Not only did the Southern Control hiss into her ear 'Practice red, expect casualties', not only did casualties covered with 'wounds' of the most lugubrious description appear in shoals—these things had often happened before and been regarded as part of everyday work—to-day was made memorable by the fact that a real (not practice) Admiral was scheduled to escort a real (not practice) Royal Princess round the Post to see it at work.

Sophia immediately saw that if she was ever going to conduct investigations, this would be the time. Heatherley and Winthrop were on continual stretcher duty and would not be able to leave the Treatment Room for a moment, except to carry 'cases' upstairs to the Hospital. Only Florence was unemployed; this must be remedied. Sophia went into the Treatment Room in search of Sister Wordsworth. It was a hive of industry; dressings and splints were laid out in quantities, and the instruments were all getting a double dose of sterilization, as though the royal eye were fitted with a microscopic lens which would enable it to note, with disapproval, fast gathering clouds of streptococci. Sister Wordsworth stood surveying the scene.

Sophia said, 'Can I speak to you a moment?' and suggested that if everything was supposed to be in progress exactly as though there had been a real raid, surely Florence ought to be sent to a practice pregnancy. Sister Wordsworth saw the force

474

of this argument, and taking hold of the next woman 'patient' who appeared, she bundled her into the Labour Ward.

'Sixty-five if she's a day,' she said in a loud cheerful aside. 'I should think it will be a very difficult delivery. Have the forceps handy, Sister Turnbull, and plenty of hot water.' Florence looked very peevish indeed, and prepared to do as she was told with a bad grace.

At this moment the real Princess appeared, and jokes were forgotten.

As soon as H.R.H. had seen her office, and gone through into the Treatment Room, Sophia summoned up all her courage and left her chair by the telephone. If it rang while she was gone, Sister Wordsworth would never forgive her; this would have to be risked, among other things. She ran down a back passage to the hospital museum. The door was locked but she had Sister Wordsworth's master-key, with which she opened it. Florence was standing in the Labour Ward, the door of which was at right angles to that of the Museum; she appeared to be leaning over her aged victim, and her back was turned on Sophia who slipped into the Museum carefully, shutting the door behind her. Then, shaking with terror, she switched on her electric torch and crept down the main avenue between the glass cases. She passed the pre-natal Siamese twins, fearful little withered white figures, unnaturally human and with horrible expressions of malignity on their faces. She passed the diseased hearts and decayed livers, and reached the case of brains with tumours on them. Then her heart stood still. On the floor beneath the brains, shining in the light of her torch like a golden wire, was a springy butter-coloured curl which could only have come from one source. The horrified curiosity felt by Robinson Crusoe when he saw the footstep of Man Friday, the ecstasy, and joy of Mme. Curie when at last she had a piece of radium, were now experienced with other and more complex sensations by Sophia. For a minute or two she almost choked with excitement; then, recovering herself, she followed in the direction in which (so far as a curl can be said to point) it pointed. Under the large intestines another one winked out a welcome, under the ulcerated stomachs was a third. The passage ended with a case of bladders against the wall, and under this was a curl. Very gingerly Sophia pushed the case. It moved. She put down her torch and lifted the case away from the wall. Behind it there was a door. As she opened this door she knew that she must be the bravest woman in the world. As a child, if she had been extremely frightened of something, she used to remind herself that she was descended from Charles II, and this had sustained her. She now invoked this talisman, to but little avail. The Merry Monarch had lived too long ago, and blankets the adult Sophia knew to have more than one side. In any case, even if his blood did flow in her veins, she thought, the worst terrors he had faced were Roundheads and death on the block, or, later in life, highwaymen who would have been easily charmed by a guinea and a royal joke. A hospital museum with its grisly exhibits, the darkness, the main drain, possible rats and creeping spies, were a test of nerves which might well break down the resistance of a man far braver than Charles II had ever shown himself to be.

She was now faced by a long flight of stone stairs leading, she supposed, to some fearful dungeons. She went down them, and then down a short passage at the end of which was another door which she opened. Sitting in quite a cheerful little room with an electric fire was the old gentleman himself.

'Darling,' he cried, 'what has happened—are they all caught? How did you get here? Where are the police?'

'Ssh,' said Sophia, her knees turning to jelly. 'I am all alone. I came down from the Post.'

'But my darling child, this is terrible, so terribly dangerous. You must go back at once. But just listen carefully to me. They—(do you know who I mean, Florence and the others?)'

Sophia nodded. 'Yes, I know about them being spies; go on.'

'They have got some scheme on foot which I must find out. They are putting it into execution next Friday, in three day's time. It is something devilish; I have half guessed what, but I

476

must know for certain. Apart from that, I know everything about the German spies in this country. Now I want you to tell the police where I am and all about Florence and Co., so that they can be watched. But I also want them to wait before rounding up the gang until six o'clock on Friday evening. It, whatever it is, will happen at ten o'clock that night, so if I don't know all by six, I probably never shall. Anyhow, I don't dare leave it until later. Now quickly go back. If they find you here they will put us both in the main drain, and all my work will have been wasted. Go, go. Be careful now. Good-bye till we meet again, my dearest. Good-bye.'

Something in the old King's manner terrified Sophia. He looked at her, she thought, as if he never expected to see her again in life; he spoke with the abruptness and irritation of a badly frightened man. She turned and fled back, up the stairs to the museum; here, with shaking hands, she put back the case of bladders as she had found it against the door. Then she crept through the medical curiosities and out again into the Post. The door of the Labour Ward was shut this time and the coast seemed clear. She ran as fast as she could to the office, collapsed into her chair and felt extremely faint; she held her head between her knees for a few moments until the giddiness had passed off. She longed for brandy, which she knew to be unobtainable.

The Royal inspection was still in progress; indeed, although it seemed to her like several days, Sophia had only been away from the office for ten minutes, and very fortunately the telephone bell had not rung once during this time. It did so now, 'Southern Control speaking, practice white.' Sophia decided that she was not temperamentally suited to the profession, which she had so gaily chosen, of secret agent; she was not nearly brave enough. Her teeth were still chattering, her hand was trembling so much that she could hardly lift the telephone receiver. She would blaze her lone trail no longer, that evening the whole affair was going to be placed before Scotland Yard, and her responsibility would be at an end. This comforting resolution greatly strengthened her nerves; a large, red-faced policeman would be more stimulating than brandy and she would insist on having one to watch over her until Friday. She wondered if she could persuade him to sleep in her bathroom, and thought that nothing could give her so much happiness.

Sister Wordsworth now made a cheerful reappearance, having just seen the Princess out to her car. She said that everything had gone off perfectly. Sister Turnbull's patient, it seemed, had come through her dangerous and unusual experience as easily as if she had been twenty instead of sixty (twin boys, Neville and Nevile, after the Blue Book), and was now with all the other patients enjoying a nice cup of tea in the canteen. The Princess had been charming and had amazed everybody, royal persons always being assumed to be half-witted, deaf and dumb until they have given practical proof to the contrary, by asking quite intelligent questions. The Admiral had winked at several of the nurses, and had been bluff, honest-to-God, hearty and all other things that are expected of seafaring men. In the short, everybody had been pleased and put into a satisfied frame of mind and the Post rang with the rather loud chatter which is induced by great relief from strain. Sophia, joining with the others, almost forgot her nightmare experiences in the museum.

When the time came for her to go home, however, she felt that she really could not face the terrors of the black-out and walk, as she generally did. She was feeling frightened again, and the idea of masked men waiting to boo out at her from behind sandbags was too unnerving. So she telephoned for a taxi. As she got into it, she wondered whether she really ought to go straight to Scotland Yard before going home. After some hesitation she decided that she felt too tired and dirty. Dinner and especially a bath were necessary before she could undertake such an expedition; besides, it was quite possible that she might even persuade some fatherly inspector to go and see her, in comfort, at Granby Gate, which would be much nicer.

She took a whisky and soda to her bedroom, undressed slowly before the fire, and wrapped herself in her dressing-gown; then she sat for a time sipping the whisky. She felt very much restored, and presently went to turn on her bath. Sitting on the edge of it was Heatherley.

Sophia huddled into her dressing-gown, paralysed with terror. She had a remote feeling of thankfulness that she had put on the dressing-gown; as her bathroom led out of her bedroom and had no other entrance she very often did not. Heatherley had an extremely disagreeable, not to say alarming expression on his face, and she was far too much unnerved to reproach him for being in her bathroom, or indeed to say anything.

He stood up and barked at her, and any doubts left in her mind as to his being a German were removed.

'You were seen this afternoon, coming out of the Hospital Museum. What were you doing there?'

Sophia felt like a rabbit with a snake. 'Oh, nothing much,' she said. 'I always think those Siamese twins are rather little duckies, don't you?'

She saw that this had teased Heatherley and it occurred to her that he did not know about her finding the King of Song. She rather supposed that if he had even guessed at such a thing, she would by now be going for a swim down the drain. 'Pull yourself together, you're descended from Charles II, aren't you?' Sophia was enough of a snob to feel that this equivocal connexion put her on a superior footing to Heatherley whether he was American or German, neither country having, as far as she could remember, existed in Charles II's day. 'Now do you agree,' she babbled on, playing for time, 'that Charles II was far the most fascinating of all our Kings?'

'I'm afraid I have not come here to discuss Charles II. I have come to inform you upon two subjects. First, you should know that I am not, as you supposed, a counter-spy.'

'Hun or Yank?' asked Sophia. A spasm of intense rage crossed Heatherley's face. She was beginning positively to enjoy the interview.

'I am the head of the German espionage system in this country. My name is Otto von Eiweiss. Florence is Truda von Eiweiss, my wife. Heil Hitler.'

479

'Your wife!' said Sophia, 'goodness me, all this time I've been thinking you fancied her!'

'Secondly,' went on Heth, taking no notice of her but trembling with anger, 'Truda and I think you know too much. We think you have been prying into affairs which do not concern you. We also think that you might soon begin to prattle of these affairs to your friends, who, although they all belong to that decadent class which we National Socialists most despise, might in their turn (purely by accident, of course, they are too soft and stupid to have any purpose in life) harm us with their talk. So, in order to make certain that none of this shall happen, we have taken your bulldog, Millicent, into protective custody, as we have noticed that in your unnatural English way you seem to love her more than anything else. In three days' time, if you behave exactly as we tell you, she will be back once more under your eiderdown, but otherwise——'

'Quilt,' Sophia corrected him mechanically. She despised the word eiderdown. Then, suddenly, realizing what he meant, 'My bulldog, Millicent—— Milly? You fearful brute,' and she forgot all about Charles II and what fun it was to tease Heth, and went for him tooth and nail.

Heatherley warded off her bites and scratches with humiliating ease, and twisting one of her arms in schoolboy fashion, he continued, 'Now, be quite quiet, and listen to me.'

'Ow, this hurts; let me go.'

'Are you going to be quiet? Good. Now I shall continue our little chat. The bulldog, Millicent, as I was just remarking, is in protective custody.'

'Where?'

'I shall not divulge.'

'Has she had her dinner at six?'

'If her dinner-time is punctually at six she most probably has. She was removed from your house at six-thirty precisely.'

'Oh! Where is she, please?'

'It is no concern of yours where she is.'

'You brutish hun, of course it is a concern of mine. In this weather. She will catch cold, she will get bronchitis. These

480

dogs have frightfully weak chests. Savage—kaffir—fuzzy-wuzzy—you——'

'To call me all these things will not advance the cause of Millicent, very far from it. She is now in my power, and you had better be nice to me.' Heatherley leant towards her with a horrible leer.

'I shall tell Florence about you coming into my bathroom when I have nearly nothing on,' she said. This shot appeared to have gone home. Heatherley looked quite disconcerted.

'The bulldog,' he said, after a pause, 'will be returned to you in perfect condition so long as you have been obedient to us and stuck not only to the letter but also to the spirit of our instructions. Otherwise, I regret to inform you that not only will she be vivisected for several hours and then put, as Greta was put, still alive, into the main drain, but that, long before you can act, you also will have ceased to live.'

'Devil. I must say I shouldn't care to be you, after you are dead. Would you like to hear what will happen to you? Well, you'll lie on a gridiron to eternity and baste—do you hear me, BASTE.'

'Instead of abusing me, and threatening me with the out-worn superstitions of a decadent religion, it will be better for you to listen to what I have to say.

'For the next three days and nights either Florence, or Gustav, whom you know as Winthrop, or I myself will be watching you like lynxes; you will never be out of the sight of one or other. Florence will take night duty and sleep in your room. Gustav and I will take turns by day. If you make the smallest sign to anybody, or convey any message to the outside world, we shall know it, and within half an hour the bulldog Millicent will be wishing she had never been born.'

'How do you mean Florence will sleep in my room? There's only one bed.'

'It is a very large one. You can take the choice between sharing it with Florence and having another bed made up in your room.'

'Ugh!' Sophia shuddered. Then she rang the bell, and feeling uncommonly foolish, went into her bedroom, where she told Elsie that she had been suffering from nightmares, and that Miss Turnbull had very kindly consented to sleep in her room.

'Oh, and Elsie, tell Mrs. Round that I have taken Milly to the vet, to be wormed, will you? She'll be about three days.'

'Yes, m'lady. We were all wondering where Milly had got to.'

When Elsie had gone, Heatherley came out of the bathroom and said, 'One last word. I warn you that you had better act in good faith. It will not avail you to do such things as, for instance, write notes in invisible ink on match-boxes, for we shall act on the very smallest suspicion. Your telephone here is cut; please do not have it mended. It will be the safest from your point of view, and that of your bulldog, if you were to see nobody at all except the personnel at the Post. Of them, I may tell you that ninety per cent are members of my corps, and will assist in keeping you under observation. Miss Wordsworth received last night in an omnibus a *piqure* that will incapacitate her for a week at least.'

'I see, you are white slavers as well as everything else.'

'Mr. Stone, as you are aware, has gone away on holiday. You will sit alone in the office, and either Gustav or myself will often sit there with you. When you think you are quite alone, one of us will be watching you through a rent in the hessian.'

Sophia lay awake all night. Florence did not, it is true, snore so loudly or so incessantly as Milly, nor was her face so near to Sophia's as Milly's generally became during the course of a night. What she did was to give an occasional rather sinister little 'honk' which was far more disturbing. But in any case Sophia would probably have lost her sleep. There seemed to be no way out of the quandary in which she found herself, look at it how she would. Even supposing that she was anxious to sacrifice Milly to the common good, which she was not, very, it seemed to her that she would only have time to give one hysterical shout before she was herself overpowered, gagged, and put down the drain, or, if in the street, liquidated in some other way. Then her secret, like Scudder's, would die

482

with her, for it was too late now to begin keeping a black notebook. The prospect was discouraging.

She turned about miserably racking her brains until she was called, when the sight of Florence sitting up in bed, and disposing of an enormous breakfast, quite put her off her own. For a moment she forgot her troubles in the fascination of seeing how Florence fixed herself into the stays, but with so many so much weightier affairs on her mind, Sophia hardly got the best advantage from this experience. For one thing she was tortured by wondering who would give Milly her morning run and whether she would do all she should. If she was being kept, like the old gentleman, underneath the Post, there was unlikely to be such a thing as a bit of grass for her, unless some kind of subterranean weed grew beside the main drain. Then there was the question of food.

She had sent Florence to Coventry. Florence, she considered, having lived with her all these months and accepted her fur cape, only to repay by kidnapping Milly, had proved herself to be outside the pale, what Lord Haw-haw calls 'not public school'. Sophia would not and could not speak to her, so she would have to discuss Milly's diet-sheet with Heatherley, and meanwhile she decided that she would take a dinner for her in a parcel when she went to the Post.

She and Florence spent a dismal morning together in Harrods, where, whenever Sophia saw somebody she knew, Florence threatened her with the barrel of a gun which she kept in her bag; after this they went off, still in silence and rather early, to the Post. Sophia was clutching a damp parcel of minced meat which she deposited in the Labour Ward when they arrived, and hoped for the best. She thought it was a gesture rather like that made by primitive Greek peasants who are supposed to put out, in some sacred spot, little offerings of food for the god Pan.

Heatherley's predictions were correct. Sister Wordsworth was off duty, ill. Mr. Stone was away on a week's holiday, and Sophia sat alone in the office. Heatherley and Winthrop took it in turns to watch over her, and the first thing she saw when she came in was a dreadful, unwinking, pale blue eye pressed against a tear in the sacking. There was nothing to be done, nothing whatever. She felt quite sick, and the hours dragged away slowly. Even Macaulay's *History of England* held no more charms for her, the landing of the Prince of Orange among the rude fisher-folk of Torquay with a background of ghostly future villas was a painted scene which could not have much interest for one who sat on such a powder-barrel as she did. The question uppermost in her mind now was 'What is going to happen on Friday?' but the more she thought, the less she could form an opinion. Perhaps it was only that on that day Florence and her corps of spies were leaving the country; she felt, however, that it was something far more sinister. The assasination of some public man, for instance; although it was difficult to think of any public man whose assassination would not greatly advance the Allied cause, and the same objection, multiplied by about twelve hundred, would, of course, apply to blowing up the Houses of Parliament. In Sophia's opinion, this would no longer even be an æsthetic disaster, since they had been subjected to the modish barbarism of pickling.

That evening Fred dined with her, a long-standing engagement. She was told that she could choose which of her three chaperons should attend her on this occasion, and chose Heatherley. He was the one she hated the most, because she was quite certain it was he who had thought of abducting Milly, and she hoped to be able to tease him by talking about Germany with Fred and at him. Unfortunately this did not work out very well. A Fred racked with ideals, and in the grip of Federal Union, was quite a different cup of tea from the old, happy-go-lucky Fred who used to join with her in blasting abroad, its food, its manners, its languages, its scenery, and the horrible time one had getting there.

'I can't see eye to eye with you, my dear Sophia,' he said pompously,when she thought she had worked him up to better things. 'I think of all foreigners, even Germans, in quite a different light now. To me they are our brothers in Union. Whatever happens, don't you see, we must finish the war with a great glow of love in our hearts—the punishment we are giving them should be quite in the spirit of "this hurts me more than it does you".'

Heatherley gave a loathsome snigger.

'I beg your pardon? Of course, Mr. Egg, as you come from the United States of America, you can tell us all about Federal Union from experience, I am sure you must think highly of it?'

'It works very badly over there, and would be quite useless in Europe. In Europe you have one Power so far in advance of all the rest that ethical sense as well as common sense would put the other countries in complete submission to its dictates.'

'Yes, that's what I always say,' said Sophia, 'but, of course, it will be an awful bore having to rule over those fiendish foreigners, and I rather doubt if we can be bothered. Perhaps we could make the French do it for us.'

Heatherley smiled in a superior way. He seemed far too comfortable to please Sophia and she greatly feared that his plans, whatever they were, must be maturing satisfactorily for him. She made no attempt to communicate in any way with Fred, knowing that, quite alone and uninterrupted, it would have taken her a good hour to explain the whole matter to him. Fred liked to get to the bottom of things, to ask a hundred questions and to write a great deal in his notebook; his particular temperament rendered such devices as tapping on his leg in Morse Code (even had Sophia been sufficiently expert to do so) much worse than useless. She very wisely left the whole thing alone.

The evening was not a great success. Fred asked where Milly was, and when told about the vet, reminded Sophia that she and Abbie had been wormed together less than two months before. He went on to tell her what a strain it was on a dog's inside, asking what evidence she had of Milly's worms, until poor Sophia could have screamed. Then they listened to the King of Song, but he was not really much in form. At the end of his programme, however, there was a drop of comfort for Sophia when he sang, very distinctly, 'Milly is my darling, my darling, my darling, Milly is my darling, the young bow wow dear,' after which she heard, or thought she heard, a rumbling snore. If Milly was with the old gentleman that would be nice for both of them, and especially, of course, for the old gentleman. At last Fred took his leave, after which Heatherley escorted Sophia, who was by now very sleepy in spite of all her cares, to join Florence in her bedroom.

This was the end of the first day.

14

The next morning Sophia, having enjoyed from sheer exhaustion, an excellent night's rest, awoke feeling more resolute. She had often heard that the Germans are the stupidest people in the world; when she remembered this and also the fact that, until she had found out that they were spies, she had always looked upon Florence, Heatherley and Winthrop as being the greatest bores she knew, it seemed to her that it should be possible to outwit Truda, Otto and Gustav, even if they were three to one against her. She stayed in bed until it was time to go to St. Anne's, thinking very hard.

Clearly the first thing to be done was to write out a concise report of her situation, and this she must keep handy in case she had an opportunity, unobserved, of giving it to some reliable person. Hatred of Heatherley, even more than fear, lent her courage and cunning, and when she had been at the Post a little while, she put down her handkerchief over a stump of pencil on the table. Presently she picked up both handkerchief and pencil and went off to the lavatory, the only place where she could be out of sight of the unholy trinity, one of whose members followed her to its very door. Here she wrote, very quickly, on her handkerchief, 'Spies. Milly and Ivor King imprisoned below Post. Tell police but act carefully. I am watched. No joke.' She had to waste valuable space and time in saying 'no joke' because she knew that if this missive should happen to reach any of her friends they would be sure to think it was one and act accordingly. The trouble now was to think of somebody to give it to, as, although she felt certain that Heatherley was bluffing when he said that nearly all the nurses were his fellow-spies, she did not know any of them well enough, now that Sister Wordsworth was away, to be positive beyond doubt of their integrity. She thought that if, by the next day, nothing else had turned up, she would, as a last resort, give the handkerchief to one of them; meanwhile she hoped for luck.

The sister in charge of the Treatment Room brought a Mrs. Twitchett into the office. She was one of those fat women whose greatly overpowdered faces look like plasticine, and whose bosoms, if pricked, would surely subside with a loud bang and a gust of air. The sister introduced her to Sophia, saying that she had already been taken on at the local A.R.P. headquarters as a part time worker for St. Anne's; Sophia's business was to note down all particulars on the card index.

'Emma Twitchett,' she wrote, '144 The Boltons. Qualifications, First Aid, Home Nursing and Gas Certificates. Next of kin, Bishop of the Antarctic. Religion, The Countess of Huntingdon's Connexion.'

Here Sophia looked up sharply and saw, what in her preoccupation had not hitherto dawned on her, that Emma Twitchett was none other than Rudolph. For the first moment of crazy relief she thought that he must know everything and have come to rescue her, Milly and Sir Ivor. Then she realised that this could not be the case. He was merely bored and lonely without her, and was hoping that he would get back into favour by means of an elaborate joke. It was absolutely important to prevent him from giving himself away in the office, while under the impression that they were alone. As soon as she had scribbled down Mrs. Twitchett's particulars, she hurried him out of the Post.

Although it could not be said that Sophia had hitherto proved herself to be a very clever or successful counter-spy, she now made up for all her former mistakes by perfectly sensible behaviour. The luck, of which she had been so hopeful, had come her way at last and she did not allow it to slip through her fingers. She conducted Mrs. Twitchett, as she always did new people, round the Post, chatting most amicably. She was careful to omit nothing, neither the rest room upstairs, the canteen, the ladies' cloakroom nor the room with the nurses' lockers. She hoped that Rudolph would notice, and remember afterwards, how Winthrop, without giving himself the trouble to dissimulate his movements, was following them closely during this perambulation. Sophia was only too thankful that it was Winthrop who, she estimated, was about half as intelligent as Heatherley. At last she took Mrs. Twitchett to the exit and showed her out, saying 'Very well then, that will be splendid; to-morrow at twelve. Oh yes, of course,' she said rather hesitatingly and shyly, 'Yes, naturally, Mrs. Twitchett, I'll lend you mine.' She took out her handkerchief and offered it to Rudolph with a smile. 'No, of course, bring it back any time. I have another in my bag; it's quite all right. Good, then, see you to-morrow; that will be very nice. So glad you are coming; we are rather short-handed, you know.'

She went back without even glancing at Winthrop who was hovering about inside the Post, and who followed her to the office. Then she sat for a while at her table trembling very much and expecting that any moment she would be summoned to the drain, but as time went on and nothing had happened, she took up her knitting. If she had a certain feeling of relief that, at any rate, she had been able to take a step towards communication with the outside world, she was also tortured with doubts as to whether Rudolph would ever see what was written on the handkerchief and whether, if he did, he would not merely say that women were bores in wars. Olga had certainly queered the pitch for her rivals in the world of espionage as far as Rudolph was concerned. Also, if he did have the luck to read and the sense to follow her directions, would he be in time? He must hurry; she felt sure that after to-morrow any action which might be taken would be too late to save Milly and the old gentleman, certainly too late to catch Florence. To-morrow was what the posters call zero hour. The rest of that day dragged by even more horribly slowly than the preceding one, and there was no sign from Rudolph. She could not help half expecting that he would have got some kind of a message through to her; when seven o'clock arrived and there was nothing, she was bitterly disappointed. Heatherley conducted her home in a taxi, dined with her and never let her out of his sight until Florence was ready to take charge of her. Sophia did not sleep a single wink; she lay strenuously willing Rudolph to read her handkerchief.

On the morning of the third and last day, Sophia would have been ready to construe anything which seemed at all mysterious into a code message from Rudolph. But nothing of the sort came her way. She eagerly scanned her egg for a sign of calligraphy, however faint; it was innocent, however, of any mark. The agony column of *The Times* was equally unproductive nor had Milly contributed to the dog advertisements; there was not even a mention of French bulldogs. Her morning post consisted of nothing more hopeful than *Harrod's Food News*. In fact, it became obvious to Sophia that Rudolph had never read her SOS at all, or if he had that he did not believe in it. Two large tears trickled down her cheeks. She decided that if nothing had materialized to show that Rudolph was helping by four o'clock, she would abandon Milly and the old gentleman to death and worse in the main drain, and dash out of the Post on the chance of finding a policeman before she too was liquidated.

Having made up her mind to some definite action, she felt happier. She jumped out of bed, dressed in a great hurry and led poor Florence, who suffered a good deal from fallen arches, round and round Kensington Gardens for two hours at least.

When Sophia arrived at the Post, accompanied by a limping Florence, the first person she saw was Mrs. Twitchett. Her doubts were dispersed in a moment and great was her relief. Rudolph must certainly be working on her side; it would be unnatural for anybody to go to the trouble of dressing up like that, twice, for a joke. Mrs. Twitchett was busily employed in the Labour Ward, but found time, when Sophia came down from her luncheon in the canteen, to go round to the office and give back the borrowed handkerchief. Sophia put it away in her bag without even looking at it.

'So kind of you,' said Mrs. Twitchett. 'I have had it washed and ironed for you, of course. And now you must forgive me if I run back to the Labour Ward. I am in the middle of a most fascinating argument with Sister Turnbull about umbilical cords. Thank you again, very much, for the handkerchief.'

Rudolph's disguise was perfect, and Sophia did not feel at all nervous that Florence would see through it; he had, in his time, brought off much more difficult hoaxes, and she herself had not seen who it was yesterday until he began to make a joke of the card index.

Presently Sophia gave a loud sniff, rummaged about in her bag and pulled out the handkerchief. Rudolph really did seem to have had it washed and ironed, unless it was a new one. Slowly she spread it out, gave it a little shake and blew her nose on it. The letters 'O.K.' were printed in one corner, so that was all right. She began to do her knitting. An almost unnatural calm seemed to have descended on the Post. Several people, as well as Sister Wordsworth, were on the sick list, and the personnel were so depleted that it was not even possible to hold the usual practice in the Treatment Room. The wireless, joy of joys, was out of order. One nurse came in and asked Sophia for a clean overall in which to go to the theatre, and Sophia felt guilty because she had known that this girl's own overall was lost in the wash and she ought to have sent a postcard about it to the laundry. As she got a clean one out of the general store, she assured the girl that she had done so and was eagerly awaiting the reply. It seemed that to-day was to be a gala at the theatre, with two cerebral tumours and a mastoid. This nurse had been looking forward to it all the week. Sophia helped her with her cap, and she dashed away to her treat, singing happily.

Sophia felt very restless, and wandered into the Treatment Room where, done out of the ordinary practice, the nurses, in an excess of zeal, were giving each other bed pans. Further on, in the Labour Ward, Sister Turnbull and Mrs. Twitchett sat on the floor counting over the contents of the poison cupboard. Mrs. Twitchett was enlarging on the most horrid aspects of childbirth. Then Sophia went back to the office, and

491

hour upon hour went by with absolutely nothing happening until she thought she would scream.

Suddenly, just before it was time for her to go off duty, all the lights went out. This was always happening at the Post; nevertheless Sophia found herself under the table before she had time consciously to control her actions. A moment later she heard Winthrop push his way through the sacking curtain and he began to flash a powerful torch round the office, evidently looking for her. In one more minute he must see her. Sophia experienced a spasm of sick terror, like a child playing a too realistic game of hide and seek, and then, almost before she had time to remember that this was no game at all, two more torches appeared in the doorway, and, by the light of Winthrop's which was now flashed on to them, she could see Mrs. Twitchett, accompanied by the reassuring form of a tin-hatted policeman. For a few moments the office resembled the scene of a gangster play in which it is impossible to discover what is happening; however, when the shooting and scuffling was over, she saw Winthrop being led away with gyves upon his wrists, and this gave her great confidence.

'Sophia, where are you?' shouted Rudolph.

Sophia crawled out from under her table feeling unheroic, but relieved.

'Good girl,' he said. 'You all right?'

He took her hand, and together they ran through the Post, which seemed to be quite full of men with torches, shouting and running, towards the museum. This was also full of policemen. They went past the Siamese twins, past the brains and came to where the case of bladders lay in pieces on the floor; beyond it the door stood open. Framed in the doorway, with the light behind him making an aura of his golden hair, stood the old gentleman with Milly in his arms.

'We've got Winthrop all right,' said Rudolph, 'what about your two?'

Sophia was busy kissing Milly, who showed enthusiasm at the sight of her owner.

'She looks a little bit all eyes,' she said; 'otherwise quite well. Oh, Milly, I do love you.'

492

'Florence and Heatherley have scuttled themselves in the main drain,' said Sir Ivor, 'and I could do with a whisky and soda, old dears.'

15

Rudolph had only just been in time. He confessed that when he first read Sophia's message on the handkerchief he had felt excessively bored. Every woman in London seemed to have some secret service activity on hand. Then he remembered that Sophia's manner had been rather queer, and that, although she must have known who Mrs. Twitchett was, she had not given him so much as a wink, even when they were outside the Post. She was looking white and strained and anxious, and the circumstance of her having the handkerchief ready to give him was peculiar. Finally there was something about the way she had worded her message that made him think this was, after all, no silly joke, but an affair which called for some investigation.

Accordingly, when he had divested himself of his Twitchett personality and was once more respectable in uniform, he hurried round to Scotland Yard with the handkerchief which he showed, rather deprecatingly, to Inspector McFarlane. The Inspector, however, so far from laughing at him, was exceedingly interested. He told Rudolph that for a long time now the authorities had suspected that the old 'King' was broadcasting in this country; that furthermore, Scotland Yard was on the track of three dangerous spies, the leaders of a large and well organized gang who were known to be in London and who so far could not be located. Quite a lot had been discovered about their activities, but nobody had any idea who they might be or where to find them. Rudolph told him about Florence, of how he had jokingly suggested that she was really a spy, and of the pigeon in her bedroom, and the Inspector, who was quite interested to hear all this, said that the Boston Brotherhood, or any such cranky society, and an American accent would provide an admirable smoke-screen for clever spies. He also said that the gang he was looking for certainly used pigeons, two of which had been shot down over the Channel quite recently.

The long and the short of it was that the Inspector told his two best men that they must somehow penetrate into the cellars of St. Anne's. He advised Rudolph on no account to make any attempt at communicating with Sophia until they knew more, as her life might easily be endangered if he did.

'By the way,' he said, glancing once again at the handkerchief, 'who is Milly?'

'Milly,' said Rudolph angrily, for this made him look a fool, 'since you ask me, is a blasted bitch.'

'A friend of Lady Sophia's?'

'You misunderstand me, Inspector. No, her French bulldog. She is potty about the wretched animal, and certainly if anyone wanted to get Sophia into his power an infallible way would be by kidnapping Milly.'

'I see. So my men must look out (unless the whole thing is a joke) for Sir Ivor King and a French bulldog. If it should prove to be a joke, you must in no way distress yourself, Mr. Jocelyn. In war-time we are bound to explore every avenue, whether it is likely to be productive of results, or not. Every day we follow up false clues, and think ourselves lucky if something turns out to be genuine once in a hundred times. I am very grateful to you for coming round, and will let you know of course if there are any developments.'

Rudolph went to the Ritz from Scotland Yard, and here he saw Olga, who was telling quite a little crowd of people that she was hot-foot on the track of a gang of dangerous spies, and soon hoped to be able, singlehanded, to deliver them over to justice. Mary Pencill was also there, assuring her admirers that Russia's interest in Finland was only that of a big brother, not, she said, that she held any brief for the present ruler of Russia, who had shown his true colours the day he had accepted the overtures of Hitler.

In the middle of the night, Inspector McFarlane sent for Rudolph to go and see him. He had some news. One of his men had actually seen the King of Song in his subterranean cubby-hole; not only that, he had managed to hold a short whispered conversation with him. Sir Ivor told him that the gang had now entirely dispersed with the exception of Florence, Heatherley and Winthrop. Florence was planning to leave for Germany, taking Sir Ivor with her, the following day at 8 p.m. An hour later, a time fuse, which was already in one of the cellars, would go off, setting in motion an elaborate network of machinery connected with the whole drainage system of London. Every drain would be blown up, carrying with it, of course, hundreds of buildings and streets; the confusion and loss of life would be prodigious, the more so as none of the bombs would explode simultaneously, and people hurrying to safety from one part of the town to another would find themselves in the middle of fresh explosions. London would lie a total wreck, and prove an easy prey for the fleet upon fleet of aeroplanes which would now pour over it, dropping armed parachutists. Taking advantage of the city's disorganization, and led by Heatherley and Winthrop, they would soon be in possession of it. London would be destroyed and in enemy hands, the war as good as lost.

'So, you see,' remarked the Inspector, 'it was just as well that you did not treat Lady Sophia's message as a joke. Oh, and by the way, Sir Ivor has the dog with him. He says her snoring gets on his nerves.'

'I'm not surprised. What anybody wants to have a dog like that for——!'

The Inspector told Rudolph that he had better become Mrs. Twitchett again and go to the Post. Like this he would be able to keep an eye on Florence and also to reassure Sophia, whose nerves, if nothing were done to relieve her anxiety, might give way, greatly to the detriment of the Inspector's plans. He wanted to leave the gang undisturbed until nearly the last minute, as it was important that no message should get though to Berlin which would prevent the now eagerly awaited arrival of the parachutists. The War Office was seething with arrangements for their reception.

Everything went off beautifully except that the fusing of the lights, a pure accident, had enabled Florence and

Heatherley to dive into the main drain before they could be arrested. It had happened just as the Inspector's men were pouring into the Post through the ordinary entrance and also by means of the drain, and had momentarily caused some confusion.

'We should have preferred to catch them alive,' said the Inspector, 'but there it is.'

Sophia was rather pleased; the idea of Florence as Mata Hari in her silver foxes was repugnant to her, and besides, it would have been embarrassing for Luke. Far better like this.

Presently the air was filled with Dracula-like forms descending slowly through the black-out. These young fellows, the cream of the German army, met with a very queer reception. Squads of air-raid wardens, stretcher-bearers, boy scouts, shop assistants and black-coated workers awaited them with yards and yards of twine, and when they were still a few feet from the earth, tied their dangling legs together. Trussed up like turkeys for the Christmas market, they were bundled into military lorries and hurried away to several large Adam houses which had been commandeered for the purpose. Soon all the newspapers had photographs of them smoking their pipes before a cheery log fire, with a picture of their Führer gazing down from the chimneypiece. Sir Ivor King went several times to sing German folk songs with them, a gesture that was much appreciated by the great British public who regarded them with a sort of patronizing affection, rather as if they were members of an Australian cricket team which had come over here and competed, unsuccessfully, for the Ashes.

16

Sophia was not acclaimed as a national heroine. The worthy burghers of London, who should have been grateful to her, were quite displeased to learn that, although their total destruction had in fact been prevented, this had been done in such an off-hand way, and with so small a margin of time to spare. Sophia was criticized, and very rightly so, for not having called in Scotland Yard the instant she had first seen Florence letting a pigeon out of her bedroom window. Had the full story of her incompetence emerged, had the facts about Milly seen the light of day, it is probable that the windows of 98 Granby Gate would have shared the fate of those at Vocal Lodge, which were now being mended, in gratitude and remorse, at the expense of all the residents of Kew Green. Actually, Sophia was damned with faint praise in the daily press, and slightly clapped when she appeared on the News Reels.

In any case, the King of Song had now soared to such an exalted position in the hearts of his fellow-countrymen that there would hardly have been room for anybody else. Wherever he showed his face in public, even in the Turkish bath, he was snatched up and carried shoulder high; the taxi he had modestly hired to take him from the Ritz, where he had spent the night after being rescued, to Vocal Lodge, was harnessed with laurel ropes to a team of A.T.S., who dragged him there through dense, hysterical crowds. The journey took two and a half hours. He arrived at Vocal Lodge simultaneously with Lady Beech's three van-loads of furniture which she was most thoughtfully re-lending him. Larch, overcome with shame at the recollection of his own Peter-like behaviour, was sobbing on the doorstep; the glaziers were still at work on the windows, and in fact, the whole place was so disorganized that Sir Ivor got back into the taxi, very much hoping that it would be allowed to return under its own steam. The taxi man, however, glad of the opportunity to save petrol, signalled to the local decontamination squad who seized the ropes and dragged it back to the Ritz. This journey, owing to the fact that the decontamination squad was in full gas-proof clothing and service masks, took three and a half hours, and one of them died of heart failure in the bar soon after the arrival.

All the secrets of the German espionage system were now as an open book to the astute old singer, who had had the opportunity of looking through many secret documents during the course of his captivity and had committed everything of importance to memory. Not for nothing had he the reputation of being able to learn a whole opera between tea and dinner. Codes, maps of air bases, army plans, naval dispositions, all were now in the hands of the M.I.; while the arrangements for the occupation of England, perfect to every detail, were issued in a White Paper, much to the delight of the general public.

It was universally admitted that Sir Ivor had played his cards brillantly. When Winthrop, alias Gustav, had approached him, shortly before the outbreak of war, with the offer of a huge sum if he would lend his services to Germany, he had seen at once that here was a wonderful opportunity to help his country. He had accepted, partly, as he told Winthrop, because he needed the money, and partly because he was a firm believer in slavery. Then, very cleverly, he had resisted the temptation to communicate with Scotland Yard before disappearing; had he done so, the Eiweisses, through certain highly-placed officials now languishing in the Tower, would inevitably have found out, and the 'murder' of the old gentleman would have been one indeed.

The Eiweisses, close friends of Hitler, had been preparing their position since the Munich *putsch* of 1923, and as Heatherley Egg and Florence Turnbull were quite well-known citizens of the United States, and the most trusted lieutenants of Brother Bones. They were known to be bores, on both sides of the Atlantic; more sinister attributes had never been suspected, least of all by the worthy Brother himself. In the end they seemed to have been undone by a sort of childish naïveté. Sir Ivor could always dispel, as soon as they arose, any doubts of his *bona fides* by talking to them of his old music teacher at Düsseldorf, of the German Christmas which he loved so much, of the duel he had fought as a student, and his memories of the old beer cellar. He aroused a nostalgia in their souls for the fatherland, and thus he lulled any suspicions which they might otherwise have had. Picture the delight with which his fellow-citizens now learnt of this duplicity. The old music teacher (long since dead, the broadcast, like the duet with Frau Goering, had been a hoax) was really a Polish Jew, the 'King' detested beer, he had never spent a Christmas in Germany, and the scar on his temple, which, so he had told the von Eiweisses, was the result of a duel, had really been acquired in a bicycling accident many years ago when he had toured the Isle of Wight with the posthumous Duchess and Lady Beech, in bloomers.

As for Rudolph, while everybody admitted the value of his work, nobody could forbear to smile; the public took him to their hearts as a sort of Charley's Aunt, and he soon figured in many a music-hall joke. His colonel sent for him and drew his attention to the rule that officers should not appear in mufti during war-time.

Sophia gave a dinner party in honour of the King of Song and of Luke's safe return from America. It was a large party. The guests included Lady Beech, Fred and Ned and their wives, Mary Pencill, Sister Wordsworth, the Gogothskas, Rudolph, a girl called Ruth whom Luke had met on the clipper and who was now staying in Florence's room at 98 Granby Gate, and, of course, the King of Song himself in the very wig which had been found by the innocent gambollers of Kew Green, and which he had borrowed for the evening from the Scotland Yard museum of horrors.

Olga arrived late enough to be certain of being last, but not so late that dinner would have been started without her.

500

Years of practice enabled her to hit off the right moment. She was in the uniform of her important war work, and wore a small tiara which she had bought back from the American who had bought it from Serge's father. It bore historic associations, having belonged, so she alleged, to Catherine the Great, one of whose lovers one of Serge's ancestors, of course, had been. Sophia had once caused very bad feeling by asking whether the diamonds were yellow with age or whether Catherine the Great had been disappointed in Serge's ancestor. Olga now made herself the centre of attention by the announcement that she was leaving almost at once for Kurdistan, on a very important mission.

'To-morrow,' she said, 'I go down to Suffolk to say adieu to Moushka; early next week I leave.'

Moushka was old Mrs. Bagg. In Olga's pre-Russian days she had been known as Mummie, which had been all right for the mother of Baby Bagg. Princess Olga Gogothsky required a Moushka. Serge, on the other hand, always called his parents Pa and Ma; but then he pronounced his own name, as did all his friends, like the stuff of which schoolgirls' skirts are made. Olga gave it a very different sound—'Sairgay'.

'I suppose, now that Sophia has caught all the spies in London, there is nothing much left for you to do here,' said Rudolph, loyally.

'Spies!' The Princess gave a scornful twist to her lips as though spies were enormously beneath her attention, now-adays. 'No, I have important business to do there, for my Chief, with the Kahns.'

Nobody asked who the Kahns were.

Serge was in the seventh heaven. It seemed that, by dint of enlisting under an assumed name and as a private, he had managed to get back to his Blossom. Determined not to lose his love a second time, he was now on the water-waggon, but even this experiment had not dampened his spirits, and he appeared to be the happiest living Russian.

Fred and Ned had once more reversed positions. Ned had proved to be even more of a failure at the Ministry than Britain had expected he would, and there had been, the day before Sophia's dinner, a Cabinet purge during which Ned was sent off to try his luck in another place. As we do not yet live under a totalitarian régime, this other place, was, of course, that English equivalent of the grave, the House of Lords. Meanwhile, Fred, reinstated in both popular and Ministerial esteem by the triumphant return of Sir Ivor King, was back at his old job. This change was, luckily, to the satisfaction of both parties. Ned's wife had for some time been making his nights hideous with her complaints and assertions that at her age (she was nearly thirty) it was quite unheard of not to be a peeress and made her look ridiculous, while Fred had never taken to Blossom with Serge's ardour and had really been hankering after that Cabinet key all the time.

Fred and Sir Ivor were soon discussing the campaign of Song Propaganda which was to be launched the following week.

'We must especially concentrate, of course, on bigger and better Pets' Programmes than ever before,' said the Minister.

'You're joking!'

'What? Indeed I am not.'

'Of course the Pets' Programmes were simply put in to tease the Germans,' said Sir Ivor, 'and I also hoped they would show people here that the whole thing was bogus.'

'Then you very much under-estimated our English love for dumb animals,' Fred replied pompously. 'Let me tell you that the Pets' Programmes were the only ones the Government were really worried about—why, every man, woman and dog in the whole country listened to those wretched programmes. You should have seen, for instance, how much Abbie and Milly enjoyed them. They never missed one. Why, entirely owing to you, there is now a Pets' League of Peace and Slavery, with literally thousands of members. The Pets wear awful little badges and pay half-a-crown. They had a mammoth meeting last week in the Dell at Hyde Park.'

'We'll soon alter that,' said the old gentleman. 'I will start a Society for Patriotic Pets and make them pay five bob.'

'Please will you two come in to dinner.'

Sophia sat between the King of Song and Luke, because, as

she explained, she had not yet had a word with Luke since his return. 'We shall have to have the Clipper,' she said in an undertone to her godfather, who quite understood. They had it. After a bit they were able to leave Luke and Ruth having it together, with Lady Beech, who, like the Athenians, loved new things, lending an occasional ear. The pink sunrise, the pink sunset, the next sunrise and the food.

Sophia asked Sir Ivor about Agony 22, but he was quite as much in the dark about the great egg mystery as Heatherley had been.

'Come now, pretty young lady,' he said. 'How could I get at your egg?'

'I know, but in spy stories people seem to manage these things.'

Ned here chimed in with the news that many eggs nowadays have things written on them.

'I expect there is a farm called Agony, and that egg was laid in 1922,' he said.

'But why should there be a farm called Agony?'

'You never can tell; farms are called some very queer things. When I was Under-Secretary for Agriculture——'

'By the way, Sophie, you must be feeling a bit easier on the subject of parachutists, eh?' asked Fred. Anything to stop Ned from telling about when he was Under-Secretary for Agriculture.

'Well, yes, but there's such an awful new horror; I think of nothing else. I read in some paper that the Germans are employing midget spies, so small that they can hide in a drawer, and the result is I simply daren't look for a hanky nowadays.'

'Don't worry; we've caught nearly all of them. The Government are issuing an appeal to-morrow for old dolls' houses to keep them in.'

Lady Beech, having heard the Clipper out to the last throb of its engines, now collected a few eyes, for she liked general conversation, leant across the table, and said to her brother-in-law, 'Tell me, Ivor, dear, what sort of a life did you have under the First Aid Post?'

'Oh yes,' said all the others, 'do tell us how it was.'

'Spiffing,' said the old Edwardian. 'They fitted up a Turkish bath for me, and I spent hours of every day in that. Then one member of the gang (I expect you would remember him, Sophie, a stretcher-bearer called Wolf) used to be a hairdresser on one of those liners, and he brushed my—er—scalp in quite a special way, to induce baby growth. And by jingo he induced it!' And sure enough Sir Ivor snatched off his wig and proudly exhibited some horrible little bits of white fluff. 'After all these years,' he said. 'I was stone bald at thirty, you know; the man must be a genius. He is now in the Tower and I am making an application at the Home Office to be allowed to visit him once a week, for treatment. It is all I ask in return for my, not inconsiderable, services.'

'Tell me, Ivor, did you not feel most fearfully anxious when the weeks passed and you had no communication with the outside world?'

'Rather not. I know how stupid Germans are, you see—felt certain they would give themselves away sooner or later, and sure enough they did and everything was O.K. just as I always guessed it would be.'

'Bit touch and go?' said Luke.

'Keep your hair on,' said the old Singer. 'A miss is as good as a mile, ain't it?'